W9-CBV-884

SUSAN KRINARD

never expected to become a writer. She "fell into it" by accident when a friend suggested she try writing a novel, and that novel sold to a major publisher two years later. She now considers herself incredibly fortunate in finding a career so perfectly suited to her love of words and storytelling.

Susan incorporates fantasy into her romance novels and has made a unique place for herself in the romance genre. She's won several awards and has been a finalist in the Romance Writers of America RITA® Awards competition. She has published eleven books and four novellas. Her most popular stories are those featuring her "romantic werewolves," but she's also written tales of time travel, distant worlds, ghosts and the ancient fairy folk.

TANITH LEE

began writing at age nine, and since then, she's published over seventy stories in novels and short-story collections. In the 1970s and early eighties, four of her radio plays were broadcast by the BBC, and she wrote two episodes of the BBC TV cult series *Blake's Seven.* Her work has been translated into over fifteen languages, and she has twice won the World Fantasy Award for short fiction.

Tanith Lee lives with her husband, writer John Kaiine, in England, where they share their home with one black-and-white and one Siamese cat. Check out her Web site at www.tanithlee.com.

EVELYN VAUGHN,

aka Yvonne Jocks, is a firm believer in the magic of stories. Her own have included six Silhouette romances, five historical romances and ten fantasy stories in various anthologies. She currently teaches community-college English in Texas, where she lives with a seventeen-year-old cat named Simone, a cocker spaniel named Kermit and too many imaginary friends to easily count. Check her out at www.evelynvaughn.homestead.com.

SUSAN KRINARD
TANITH LEE   EVELYN VAUGHN

WHEN
DARKNESS
FALLS

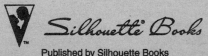

Published by Silhouette Books
America's Publisher of Contemporary Romance

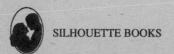 SILHOUETTE BOOKS

WHEN DARKNESS FALLS

Copyright © 2003 by Harlequin Books S.A.

ISBN 0-373-21822-2

The publisher acknowledges the copyright holders of the individual works as follows:

KISS OF THE WOLF
Copyright © 2003 by Susan Krinard

SHADOW KISSING
Copyright © 2003 by Tanith Lee

THE DEVIL SHE KNEW
Copyright © 2003 by Yvonne A. Jocks

This edition published by arrangement with Harlequin Books S.A.

® and TM are trademarks of Harlequin Books S.A., used under license. Trademarks indicated with ® are registered in the United States Patent and Trademark Office, the Canadian Trade Marks Office and in other countries.

Visit Silhouette at www.eHarlequin.com

Printed in U.S.A.

CONTENTS

KISS OF THE WOLF

Susan Krinard

To the "Prickly Chicks," cheerleaders extraordinaire.

Chapter 1

What a way to come home.

Dana St. Cyr stood at the sloping shoulder of a narrow road edged by cattails and a stand of bald cypress trees, tapping the toe of her shoe on the gravel as smoke poured out from under the hood of her rented Lexus. In every direction, as far as the eye could see, lay mile upon mile of swamp, with not a gas station in sight.

The sun beat down on Dana's head and shoulders, plastering jacket and blouse to damp skin. How could it still be so hot in mid-September? Why in the world had she decided to leave her cell phone in California? If she had to walk all the rest of the way to Grand Marais...

Big Marsh. That was a good name for a town in the backwaters of southern Louisiana, even if this was more swamp than marsh. Dana blew out her breath and glanced down at her Prada mules. *Practical,* she thought in mild self-disgust. *Where did I ever get the idea that anything other than sneakers would be practical in a place like this?*

But she hadn't worn sneakers since the age of sixteen, when she'd decided who and what she was going to be. All that certainty had vanished a few months ago, when suddenly it wasn't enough to have a thriving career as one of San Francisco's top plastic surgeons, blessed with an elegant penthouse overlooking the Bay and several closets full of Paris couture. The perfect life she'd built had grown inexplicably flat and lonely.

And that was why she was standing here on the road in the soggy heat of a Louisiana afternoon. She still remembered Uncle Charles's stories of the bayou. "If you ever get in trouble," he'd said, "go home to Beaucoeur Parish. You'll always find a welcome there, with your own people."

People she'd never met. People who actually liked living in a place like this.

She sighed and pushed damp hair out of her face. The road was still deserted. Birds sang in the cypress trees and tangled thickets of impenetrable scrub. A few white, fluffy clouds scudded across the sky.

Dana pulled off one shoe and flexed her toes. The last thing she intended to do was stand here and wait to be rescued. A few blisters weren't going to kill her. The worst part would be arriving in Grand Marais with a psychological disadvantage, the stranger from California who got herself broken down in the middle of nowhere.

It's not as if you care what they think. You don't have any expectations, remember? This was a crazy idea, anyway, and if not for Uncle Charles...

The cattails by the side of the road rustled with the motion of some hidden shape. Dana lost her balance and leaned against the Lexus, the small hairs rising on the back of her neck. Did they have bears in Louisiana?

You're being ridiculous. It's probably a deer, or maybe an opossum.

But it was not a deer, and definitely not an opossum. Dana blinked, and a tall, very human form emerged from the undergrowth.

The man moved a little way toward her and paused, regarding her silently. Dana assessed him with a keen eye developed over years of sculpting faces, inching her way toward the car door and the can of pepper spray in the glove compartment.

Her first impression was of height, broad shoulders and a shock of red-brown hair. But it was the face beneath that hair that made her forget about the pepper spray. Even if the swamp sheltered escaped criminals or crazed hermits, surely none of them could be quite so strikingly attractive.

Mid-thirties, she calculated. Nonsmoker, not a shred of excess weight, high cheekbones, firm chin with a dimple she couldn't improve on. A mouth with lips just full enough to be sensual without sacrificing masculinity. Strong, straight nose. Eyes just a little deep set, a shifting turquoise under dark, straight brows.

The rest of the body matched the face, beautifully proportioned, narrow through hips and waist under a clean white T-shirt, thighs muscular in blue jeans painted with mud to midcalf. Dana couldn't see his feet behind the tall grass, but his hands, thumbs hooked in his pockets, looked as graceful as a concern pianist's.

The Greeks had made statues like this, but nature seldom duplicated their talents. Not without help. If genes like his were common, she would be out of a job. And then maybe she would have time for a love life....

The man took a step toward her, breaking the spell. Dana flung open the car door and dived across the seat. *Idiot. Who knows better than you how little a face has to do with the soul inside?*

"Are you in need of assistance, ma'am?"

Dana's fingers slid off the button of the glove compartment. She peered out the passenger window, where the face gazed back at her, lips curved up at the ends as if he knew exactly what she'd been thinking.

She flushed, slid back into the driver's seat and folded her hands in her lap. The doors were unlocked. He could get in if he wanted, but she would be damned if she let him think she was afraid, especially when he was circling his finger in an unmistakable request that she roll down the window.

Calmly cursing herself, she punched the window button. Hot air flooded the car, and with it the subtle scent of male: cotton, soap, perspiration and a whiff of motor oil. The man leaned down and rested his elbow on the door.

"You're not from around here, are you?" he asked.

His voice was a low drawl, tinged by an agreeable accent that reminded her of Uncle Charles. She searched his eyes for any clue as to his intentions, but found only blue-green sparkling with mischievous light over depths she couldn't begin to plumb.

"A very astute observation," she said coolly. "You don't by chance know how to repair my car?"

"It's possible," he said, his gaze wandering to the open neck of her blouse. "Where are you headed?"

"Grand Marais." *If it's any of your business.* "Do you live in this area?"

He rested his dimpled chin on his knuckles. "You're still a good five miles from town, if you don't count the shacks and fishermen's camps along the levee. You have family in Grand Marais?''

"Lucky guess." Better that he know she wasn't alone and without resources, just in case—though her skittishness was beginning to seem very foolish. "Augustine Daigle is my great-aunt. Do you know her?"

"I've met her." He cocked his head and studied her with sharper interest. "You're a Daigle?"

Dana wondered if this kind of inquisitiveness was specific to Louisiana. "St. Cyr, actually. Aunt Augustine is my mother's aunt. My parents left this area in their twenties. This is the first time I've been here."

Now, what had possessed her to babble on so? Something about his lazy, half-lidded eyes invited her to confide in him, a total stranger, in a way she wouldn't confide in her closest friends back home. She tried to reassemble her guard, but the stranger's demeanor had radically altered in the short time she'd been talking. He had drawn back from the window, and his eyes had lost all of their friendliness.

"You look like a woman who enjoys fine things," he said, all the melody gone from his voice. "Grand Marais is a simple place, with simple people. I don't think you'll like it there. If I were you, I'd go back where I came from."

Dana realized her mouth was hanging open and closed it with a snap. "I beg your pardon. I won't trouble you any further, but if you have a cell phone I can borrow…"

"I'll tell them you're here." His mouth set in a straight, grim line. "Take my advice. Don't stay in Beaucoeur Parish."

Chapter 2

His last words were drowned out by the roar of a car approaching at high speed from the east. He looked toward the road, and Dana caught a flicker of something breathtakingly dangerous in his face before he turned away.

"Wait!" she called after him. "You haven't told me your name—"

But he was gone. Just like that, vanished, without even a swaying branch to mark his passage. The noise of the car—a very new, very expensive BMW convertible—had become deafening, and Dana winced as it pulled up beside the Lexus.

This seemed to be her day to find astonishingly handsome men in the swamp, she thought absurdly. A flash of white teeth in a tanned face, tousled blond hair and the insouciant air of great wealth dazzled her sight like heat rising from hot pavement. The driver stopped his engine and leaned over the seat.

"Well, hello there," he said. "I'll hazard a guess that you didn't park here just to take in the—" He hesitated, peering at her over the top of his sunglasses. Blue eyes crinkled in consternation and darted away, searching the thicket where the first stranger had disappeared. Just as Dana was about to speak, he removed his sunglasses and turned his blinding attention on her again.

"Forgive my bad manners, miss. I trust that I may be of assistance?"

Dana felt her spine relax. She didn't know this man any better than the other one, but he was something she understood: rich, confident, and sure of his place in the world. She'd had several boyfriends exactly like him. The difference lay in the accent; Mr. BMW's voice had the graceful cadence of a quintessential Southern gentleman.

"I hope so," she said, offering her hand. "I'm Dana St. Cyr, on my way to Grand Marais. I'm afraid the rental company has quite a bit to answer for."

"So I see." He took her hand in a firm grip, making no concession to her gender. "Chad Lacoste. St. Cyr, of the Baton Rouge St. Cyrs?"

"My father was from New Orleans."

"And you're from the West Coast."

"I suppose my accent gives me away."

He grinned. "Believe me, I knew you weren't from around here the moment I saw you."

She guessed he meant it as a compliment. "I flew in from San Francisco two nights ago. Apparently I wasn't very well equipped for this expedition."

"You've been crossing the Atchafalaya Basin—nothing but camps and oil rigs for miles. It's lucky I decided to go for a drive this afternoon." He shook his head. "I'd hate to see you hitching a ride in one of those beat-up trucks the locals use."

"You're not local, Mr. Lacoste?"

"Chad, please. We don't stand on formality here in the bayou."

So she had observed. "Chad. I take it that you don't live in this area?"

"Not in Grand Marais, but outside of town on a piece of land drier than most, in a plantation house built by my great-great-grandfather. Quite a pile, really. I usually spend a few months each year at Bonneterre. The rest of the year it's New Orleans, New York, London. In fact, I haven't been back to the parish for several years." He smiled at her with open appreciation. "It looks as if my stay won't be as tedious as I'd feared."

Before she could think of an appropriate response, he jumped out of the convertible and gallantly opened the passenger door. "If my lady will step into my carriage?"

She grabbed her purse and the suitcase in the back of the Lexus and scooted into the convertible's leather seat, instinctively smoothing her trousers and doing up the top buttons of her blouse. Chad Lacoste hopped in beside her and gunned the engine. The moment she was buckled in, he stepped on the gas pedal and sent the BMW hurtling down the road.

Dana braced herself, struggling to concentrate on the rather monotonous scenery. She felt Chad's eyes on her and wished he would watch the road instead.

"Enough about me," he said abruptly. "What brings you to Beaucoeur Parish, Miss St. Cyr?"

"Doctor," she said, clearing her throat. "But please do call me Dana."

"Doctor. How interesting." He shifted gears and accelerated. She expected him to ask more questions, but he seemed to be waiting for her to speak. She decided to change the subject.

"Chad...did you happen to see the man I was speaking to just as you arrived?"

His face clouded, and she was reminded of the instant when her first would-be rescuer had changed so completely from lazy-eyed rogue to ominous stranger.

"Remy Arceneaux," Chad said, biting off the words. "You don't want to have anything to do with him, Dana."

"Oh? Does he have a bad reputation?"

"Worse." His jaw set, and she was considering pressing for details when the first recognizable structures appeared by the road.

Many of the buildings were little more than shacks or cottages, but as they crossed a bridge and entered the town proper, Dana noted that there seemed to be a single main street along which most of the businesses were located. Among them she recognized a brick church with a cemetery, a small market and hardware store, some kind of dance or game hall, and a tiny bank.

"Welcome to Grand Marais," Chad said, his voice heavy with sarcasm. "If you can find anything 'grand' about it." He raced down the center of town at seventy miles an hour, past desultory pedestrians, barking dogs and the tiny police station. Dana guessed that there wasn't much more to Grand Marais than she could see—the side streets didn't seem very long, and the tallest building was only two stories high.

She spotted a two-pump gas station next to an ancient hotel and tapped Chad's arm. "You can let me

off there,'' she said. ''They must have a tow truck
somewhere in town.''

''You didn't tell me where you're staying.''

''With my great-aunt Augustine Daigle.''

Chad slammed on the brakes. Fortunately, no one
was behind him. ''Daigle?''

''My grandmother's sister. I know she lives on the
edge of town....''

She could have sworn that Chad's tan face turned a
shade more pale as he swerved into the gas station lot.
He set the brake, left the engine idling and vaulted over
the closed door as if some private demon nipped at his
heels.

''I'll be right back,'' he said. Without further explanation, he strode into the booth-sized convenience store
attached to the station.

Dana sighed and pinched the bridge of her nose. She
could get out here, of course, and find whatever passed
for a taxi in a small bayou town like this. But it seemed
rude to leave after accepting a ride from Lacoste, however reckless his driving. It couldn't be that far to
Great-Aunt Augustine's.

''Sally?''

She turned at the unfamiliar voice. A middle-aged
man, the station attendant by the look of his stained
overalls and the rag in his hands, was staring at her in
obvious confusion.

''I'm afraid not,'' she said. ''My name is Dana St.
Cyr.''

''St. Cyr?'' He twisted the rag into a tortured spiral.
''But you look...you look just like her—except for the
hair. And the clothes.'' He spoke the last part of the
sentence as if to himself, but the uneasy expression on
his face remained. ''You knew Sally?''

"Sally who?"

Chad emerged from the convenience store before the attendant could answer. He glanced at the older man with a frown.

"No gas today," he said brusquely. He paused at the side of the convertible and tapped a cigarette out of a new pack of Marlboros. "Smoke?" he asked Dana.

She shook her head and looked for the attendant. He was gone. "Do I look like anyone you've met?" she asked Chad.

He lit the cigarette with a gold lighter and took a drag. "Why? Has that man been bothering you?"

For reasons she couldn't fathom, she had no desire to discuss the attendant's peculiar reaction with Lacoste. "Nothing," she murmured, reaching for the door handle. "I'd like to thank you for driving me into town. I'll just go see about that tow truck—"

"Forget it." He dropped into his seat and released the brake. "It's already taken care of. And anyway, this is door-to-door service."

While Dana glanced behind to see if the local police had noticed such an easy source of revenue, Chad shot out of the gas station, past several more commercial buildings and into a residential area at the north end of town. He took a sharp left at a tilted stop sign and followed a curved lane past small frame houses, some in disrepair and others neatly kept, with modest flower gardens and whitewashed verandas.

He pulled up in front of one such house, an attractive cottage that smelled of fresh paint. In one motion he snatched up Dana's suitcase from the back seat and opened her door.

"The residence of Augustine Daigle," he said, sweeping his hand with a flourish.

After seeing the rest of Grand Marais, Dana wasn't surprised at the small size of her great-aunt's house. In fact, it seemed rather cozy.

And when did you ever have any use for cozy? She stepped out of the convertible and gently pried her suitcase from Chad's fingers.

"I don't know how to thank you," she said, and hesitated. Well, why not? If his worst habits were smoking and speeding, he shouldn't be too hard to manage. "Perhaps I can take you to dinner once I'm settled in."

"Are you asking me on a date?" he said, grinning around his cigarette.

"Let's just say that I don't know too many people in Grand Marais, and I may need a native guide."

Chad laughed and slid behind the wheel. "That's one thing you can bet on, Doc," he said. "We'll be seeing each other again. Very soon."

The rumble of his engine obscured every other sound, so it was several moments before Dana realized that the cottage door had opened. An elderly woman stood on the porch, arrayed in a bright floral housedress and Birkenstock sandals. Her white hair was neatly arranged in a bun, and her face was youthful in spite of a multitude of wrinkles. This was a woman who'd never visited a plastic surgeon.

The woman took a single hesitant step forward. "Sal—" She stopped, blinked several times and slowly held out her hands. "You must be Dana. How wonderful to see you at last."

"Aunt Augustine." Dana set down the suitcase and

took her great-aunt's hands. "I know I wrote that I wouldn't be coming until next week...."

"Hush. You should have come much sooner, *chère*." Augustine pulled Dana into a hug. She smelled of potpourri, oranges and fresh bread. The intimate contact should have been uncomfortable, but it was not. Dana felt strangely moved, as if she had indeed come home.

"We have so much to talk about," Augustine said, releasing her. "So much. But I have a question before we go in and have something cool to drink. Was that Chad Lacoste who just drove off?"

So Aunt Augustine knew Chad. If his family was as wealthy as he'd implied, that was no surprise. Such affluence would be noticed in a place like this.

"Yes," Dana said. "We just met. He drove me into town.... My rental car broke down in the swamp. He said he'd arrange to have a tow truck pick it up."

"I see." Augustine's brown eyes grew distant, and then she shook herself like a robin in a birdbath. She took Dana's hand and led her into the house. "I have your room all made up. It's small, but I hope you'll find it comfortable."

"I'm sure I will." Though the words were rote courtesies, Dana found that she meant them. The whole cottage smelled very much like her great-aunt, and the wooden floor was carpeted with handwoven rag rugs. A piano stood in one corner. Antique furniture graced the small living room. The window air conditioner labored to cool the house, but its modest effects were considerably more pleasant than the damp heat outside.

When Dana stepped into the guest bedroom, she was enchanted. The brass bed was piled high with plump quilts and decorative pillows, lace doilies were draped over the dresser and bedside tables, and a carved wooden rocker stood in one corner.

"Here you are," Augustine said. "The bathroom is just down the hall. If there's anything you need that I've forgotten, tell me. I was about to heat up some gumbo for supper."

Dana set her suitcase on the floor beside the bed and glanced longingly at the quilts. "Thank you, Aunt Augustine."

"Call me Gussie. No one has called me Augustine since Jules passed." She caught the direction of Dana's gaze. "You take a nap, now, and I'll come get you when supper's ready."

Once Gussie had bustled away to the kitchen, Dana kicked off her mules and collapsed onto the bed. It creaked and settled under her with a contented sigh that matched her own.

It felt marvelous to close her eyes, and for a moment she thought she might actually fall asleep. But a certain persistent image danced behind her eyelids: a tall male form, friendly and hostile by turns, whose turquoise gaze locked on hers as if to convey a silent message of warning.

Of what? Who is Remy Arceneaux, and why did Chad advise me to stay away from him?

She sat up, raking her hands through her hair. The smell of onions and spices wafted through the house, reminding her how hungry she was after a very skimpy breakfast of beignets in New Orleans. Too restless to sit still, she slid off the bed and prowled about the room, touching this object and that, until she came to the dresser and the lovingly framed photo displayed there.

Her first thought was that she was looking **at** a portrait of herself. She picked up the photo and studied it more carefully. The woman in the picture, arm in arm with Gussie, was alike enough to be Dana's twin in height, figure, coloring, even in features, but the small details made the difference clear.

The woman in the photo was tanned from forehead to ankles—the kind of tan one got from strong sunshine and not a tanning salon. She wore very little makeup, and her blond hair was drawn back in a careless ponytail, not sculpted into a neat bob like Dana's. She wore an open-necked, sleeveless plaid shirt, a pair of shorts with numerous overstuffed pockets and scuffed hiking boots. The last time Dana had dressed like that had been for a grade school field trip.

Dana had no lost twins that she knew of; she'd been an only child. But the gas attendant had mistaken her for someone else. And Gussie had given her such an odd look when they'd first met...

"Her name was Sally."

Gussie stood in the doorway, hands tucked into the pockets of her apron. She looked from the picture to Dana's face, and in her eyes were answers to the questions Dana had yet to ask.

"You two are alike as two mudbugs in a ditch," Gussie said. "That's why I was surprised when I saw you. I couldn't tell from that small picture you sent.... I couldn't have imagined."

Dana set the picture down. "Someone in town mistook me for her," she said. "Who is she?"

"Your cousin—my granddaughter." Gussie sighed and sat down in the rocker, her wide hips just fitting between the curved arms. "You do look like her, but I can see you must be very different."

"Does she live in this area?"

"Sally...disappeared five years ago."

Chapter 3

A chill lodged on the back of Dana's neck. "Disappeared?"

Gussie closed her eyes. "She was so full of life, from the time she was a little girl. She drew everyone to her, like a light. In school, the boys were all in love with her. More than one wanted her for his wife. But she chose to leave Grand Marais. She went to the city, to study at the university." Gussie smiled. "She wrote me sometimes. She worked very hard, and when she was done, she had a degree in the study of birds— 'ornithology,' she called it."

"I didn't know," Dana murmured. "I'm so sorry."

Gussie seemed not to hear. "When her *maman* was dying…a little more than five years ago…she came home to be with us. She heard about a special bird in our swamps, very rare, and she stayed on to look for it. One day she went into the swamp and never came out again."

The idea of being lost in those swamps was terrible enough, but to imagine dying there... Dana touched the grinning face in the photo with a fingertip. It seemed unbearably cruel that one so young and happy should have met such a fate.

"They looked for her," Gussie went on. "They searched the 'chafalaya for days. They never found a sign of her. There were rumors—" she laughed "—there are always rumors. But Sally wasn't the kind to get herself lost in the swamp or anywhere else. We all knew she wasn't coming back."

With rare impulsiveness, Dana knelt and took her hands. After so many years of examining faces from every angle, she knew what lay behind her great-aunt's impassive expression. Grief—hidden, unhealed, devastating.

"I am sorry," Dana repeated softly. "I wish I had known her."

Gussie patted her hand. "I'm sure she would have felt the same. This is the room I kept for her when she visited. She would want you to be comfortable here." She sniffed. "The gumbo needs stirring." She got to her feet and hurried out of the room, leaving Dana to contemplate her story.

So much for the placid appearance of Grand Marais. Even small towns could hide a multitude of sins. Was one of them murder? How had Sally died, and why?

Dana wasn't prepared to intrude on Gussie's grief just to satisfy her curiosity. Yet she couldn't help but feel, however irrationally, that she and Sally shared something more than a face.

I could have gone anywhere to "find myself" and put my life back on course—New York, Hawaii, Europe. Is there a reason I felt drawn to come here, where so many of my mother's family lived and died?

She knew the notion was foolish, that she should put morbid thoughts of poor Sally's disappearance from her mind. But even when she was full of gumbo and had enjoyed an hour of pleasant, untroubled conversation with Gussie, her mind bounced back and forth between two people, man and woman, each vanished in the endless swamp: Sally Daigle and Remy Arceneaux.

Sleep was out of the question. Sally's eyes watched her from the photo, as if trying to convey a message from the other side. After a fruitless hour of staring up at the ceiling, Dana climbed out of bed and went to the phone Gussie kept in the kitchen. She thumbed through the phone book in the faint hope that the person she wanted had a listed number.

There it was: Lacoste, Reuben. Chad's father, no doubt, unless he had other relatives in the area. Dana was prepared to take that chance. She punched out the number and waited tensely as the phone rang.

A sleepy female voice answered with a formal "Lacoste residence." Dana introduced herself and asked for Chad.

"I'll see if Mr. Lacoste is available, Dr. St. Cyr," the woman said, and put Dana on hold. Only a minute passed before a familiar accented voice came on the line.

"Dana?" Chad said. "I didn't expect the pleasure of hearing your voice again so soon."

"I'm sorry to be calling so late. I hope I didn't disturb you?"

"Not at all. I'm at your service, day or night." He just managed to avoid innuendo in his tone, but Dana could not mistake his interest.

"I know I owe you a dinner, but I have another favor to ask of you."

"Fire away."

"I'd like to go into the swamp, and I thought perhaps you might be able to recommend a guide."

"Go into the swamp? That's not one of the amusements I'd expect a woman like you to enjoy."

In that, he was correct, or would be at any other time. "I have a very specific reason. I've learned that my cousin, Sally Daigle, disappeared in that area a few years ago, and I'd like to see where…" Now she was sounding ridiculous. How could she explain this strange, unaccountable feeling she had to learn more of Sally's fate?

"Sally?" Chad repeated. "No one knows where she was lost."

At least he wasn't surprised; of course, he'd reacted when she'd given Aunt Augustine's last name. He might have known Sally. He, too, might have grieved her passing.

"I know it sounds a little odd, but I'd really like to see what she saw before she…before she disappeared. Call it a whim, if you like. I do realize that I'll need an experienced guide—"

"You've got one. It so happens that I grew up in this area, and I know the swamp as well as anyone except the old-timers who live on the bayou. I'll take you myself."

"I wouldn't want to inconvenience you—"

"No inconvenience. I knew Sally. She'd have been grateful that you took an interest in her."

"Perhaps you can tell me more about her."

Papers rustled. "I'm free tomorrow, if you want to go so soon. Maybe you'd like to rest a few days, get used to the climate."

"If it's convenient for you, I'd like to go tomorrow."

"That's fine. Tell you what—I'll pick you up tomorrow morning, around six o'clock. It's a good idea to get started early. The ground is fairly dry this time of year, but there's still a lot of mud—wear jeans and sneakers and a long-sleeved shirt. Mosquito repellant, too. I'll take care of the rest.''

"I appreciate this, Chad."

"Think nothing of it. Oh, before I forget—the mechanic is working on your Lexus. It should be fixed in a day or two."

"That's terrific, thanks." Dana rested her hand on her chest, amazed at the rapid beat of her heart. It wasn't Chad she was thinking of. "I owe you two dinners now."

Chad chuckled. "We'll see. Six o'clock tomorrow morning, then."

Only after she'd thanked him again and hung up did Dana wonder why he'd been so willing to guide her himself, and on such short notice. He wasn't the type to like getting muddied up. It was natural to assume he wanted more from her than a couple of dinners out, but Dana had no intention of leading him on. She would have to be up-front with him on that score, sooner or later.

Tomorrow's worries would take care of themselves. At the moment she had to figure out what she could wear into a swamp. Jeans and sneakers were not among the clothing she'd packed. Perhaps Gussie had something she could borrow until she had time to buy whatever the local stores had to offer.

Whatever the inconvenience, she wasn't going to let such small matters as the "proper" clothing for swamp-walking get in her way. By this time tomorrow night, she hoped to have rid herself of this peculiar obsession with her identical cousin.

If only she could say the same of Remy Arceneaux.

* * *

The woman swore with surprising vehemence, pulling her leg out of the sucking mud and shaking it as fastidiously as a cat. Remy didn't laugh. He'd been tailing her ever since Chad Lacoste got them lost and left her with the boat while he went in search of "help," and there was nothing humorous in watching this particular female flounder around in the area where Sally had died.

She was Sally's double. Remy had seen it immediately when he'd met her at the roadside, but he hadn't realized who she was until she mentioned the name Daigle.

Sally Daigle had been like fire, impulsive and warm. This one was just the opposite. Her hair was a paler blond than Sally's, and her face, even smudged and streaked, held both reserve and strength of purpose in its delicate, symmetrical contours. Remy had witnessed that strength more than once today when Lacoste had proved his utter incompetence at playing swamp guide.

Fortitude and patience weren't her only assets. Outlandish as Ms. St. Cyr was, in a tentlike cotton shirt, belted jeans several sizes too big and tight sneakers black with mud, she had an unmistakable elegance in her bearing. Her beauty was not like Sally's, sculpted in wind and rain and sun. It had been honed and refined by city living, ambition and money.

Once, Remy had lived in the city. He'd nursed aspirations appropriate to a fast-rising young stockbroker who'd ridden out the hard times with almost miraculous skill. He'd walked through the French Quarter with women like this one on his arm.

No, not quite like Ms. St. Cyr. She reminded him of the creeks they had in the north: chilly, clear, likely to freeze your hand off if you made the mistake of dipping it in.

But he couldn't quite call her cold. Oh, no...he'd seen something in her eyes yesterday that told him she might not be what she first appeared. Those eyes were the color of brandy, the kind that could make a man drunk with a single sip. If it didn't poison him first.

Maybe that was why he was attracted to her in spite of everything.

Put it back in your pants, Arceneaux. The last thing he needed was a personal interest in a woman who looked like Sally Daigle. Every one of his instincts scraped that it was no coincidence to find Sally's cousin poking around in this part of the swamp the day after she arrived in Grand Marais.

She came with Lacoste. That's no coincidence, either.

That was the reason, the only reason, why he'd followed her and why he was about to do something stupid. *What in hell will Tris do when he sees her? Do you really want to put him through that again?*

Remy plowed the damp earth with the toe of his boot, alarming a copperhead, which dove under a mat of last year's leaves. *Can you just let her go without making her understand?*

How could he make her, an outsider, understand, when even the locals regarded the Arceneaux brothers with the deepest suspicion and crossed themselves when they saw Remy or Tris in town?

With a whispered oath, Remy walked up to the bank where she was struggling with the grounded boat. Even that arrogant son of a bitch Lacoste should have known better than to bring a motorboat out where the water was so low. Too much to hope that he would blunder into old *Mauvais-Oeil*'s territory and get himself eaten by the nastiest gator in this part of the swamp, Evil-Eye.

Ms. St. Cyr looked up as Remy approached, freezing still as a doe caught in headlights. She remembered him, all right. Maybe she'd even had time to hear the rumors.

Remy smiled. "Hello," he said with a mocking salute. "Seems like every time we meet, you're in some kind of scrape."

The woman placed dirty hands on her hips. "Do you have another warning for me, Mr. Arceneaux?"

So she'd learned his name. *Lacoste, of course.* "I think it's a little too late for that now, *chère,*" he said. "What fool told you that you could bring a boat out here in September?"

She didn't deign to answer but left the boat where it was and battled her way up the bank to dry ground. She rested her back against a cypress stump and folded her arms.

"You, I suppose, know everything there is to know about this swamp?"

"I know that only the main channels are deep enough for a boat this time of year. I'm amazed you got this far." Casually he walked down to the craft and heaved it onto the bank. "What's done is done. You'd better come with me and get cleaned up."

"I'm waiting for my friend. He should return any minute."

Remy laughed. "I don't think so. It's after five, and he'll be lucky if he gets to the main road by nightfall." He made a show of looking around at the sluggish water, the thickets of swamp privet and the still-green cypress leaves overhead. "You like snakes and gators, Ms. St. Cyr?"

"About as much as I like strangers who appear and disappear with rude and cryptic comments."

He lifted a brow. "I still think I'm better company than what you'll find if you spend the night here. Especially since the mosquitoes are about to start hunting."

She glanced at the brown water winding among the water hyacinth and alligator weed, undoubtedly weighing her chances of walking out of the swamp alone. But Remy was certain of one thing; *she* was no fool, no matter how proud she was. She knew she wasn't equipped for this. Was she cursing Chad Lacoste under that mask of perfect composure?

"Can you lead me out of the swamp?" she asked. "I can pay for your services."

"Ah, *chère,* I'll just bet you can." He looked her up and down to see if he could get a rise out of her. Her eyes sparked into a genuine glare.

"Will one hundred dollars be enough?"

"I'd say yes, if it wasn't so close to sunset. Wouldn't do it for any amount after dark."

"Then what do you suggest, Mr. Arceneaux?"

"Guess you'll have to come to my place." He grinned at the way she stiffened up like a possum encountering a fox. "Don't worry, *chère.* Whatever the movies tell you, we ignorant swamp folk don't jump on anything that moves."

Chapter 4

Ms. St. Cyr considered his answer, trying to decide whether or not to take offense. "I'm not concerned about that, Mr. Arceneaux—"

"You might as well call me Remy."

"—*Mr. Arceneaux*, but I can't help but wonder at your offer of hospitality after your behavior yesterday."

If she wanted an explanation now, she wasn't going to get it. Maybe he could find a way to warn her, and maybe he couldn't, but he planned to be the one asking questions.

"If I was rude, I apologize," he said. "I can offer you supper, a clean bed, privacy, and a ride back to town in the morning. You'll be safe as a baby gator in its mother's jaws."

She frowned. "I still don't understand—"

"You don't know much about people around here,

chère, even if you're kin to the Daigles. It'll take an hour on foot to get to my place. You coming?''

She hugged herself and gnawed on her lower lip, a habit very much at odds with her confident demeanor. It made her seem more vulnerable, somehow, especially when she started slapping at her neck as the mosquitoes' advance guard began its evening onslaught.

Ms. St. Cyr caught him watching. ''I used repellant,'' she protested, trying without success to keep her hands at her sides.

''Mosquitoes just like some people better than others,'' he said. ''Once they get a fix on you, ain't no repellant gonna do the job.''

''So I—'' whack ''—see. Well, Mr. Arceneaux, it seems that your kind offer is my only salvation.''

''*Allons.* It's Remy. No one's called me Mr. Arceneaux in—'' Oh, about six years, since the days when he'd had an office on the tenth floor, with his own secretary and Herman Miller furniture. ''In a long time.''

''Remy,'' she said, a mere breath, as if she could hold back from that small intimacy by turning his name into a sigh.

''*Bon.''* He held out his hand. ''Shall we go?''

At least she tried not to be obvious about it when she sidestepped his hand and strode ahead of him just to prove that she wasn't afraid. He caught up and pulled her out of the path of a particularly nasty mud hole. She flinched a little at his touch, but it wasn't fear that lit her eyes when they met his.

Hé bien, but the woman had fine eyes. And she wasn't nearly as good at hiding her feelings as she thought she was. Remy winced at the sudden tightness of his jeans. Even something as relatively harmless as sheer, uncomplicated mutual lust was a very bad idea.

He took several steps away from her and set out across the highest ground. "Why did you come into the swamp today, Ms. St. Cyr?"

"It's *Dr.* St. Cyr."

Ah, a touch of frost to quench the fire he'd seen in her a minute ago. "Doctor?" he said. A perverse little devil of mischief made him stop short. He held up his thumb to display the tiny cut he'd received while pulling the motorboat onto the bank. It would be gone in half an hour, but she didn't know that.

"You think you can fix this for me, Doc?"

She just barely kept herself from crashing into him. "I'm not...that kind of doctor."

"You mean there's a kind of doctor who doesn't know how to mend a cut?"

For the first time, he was treated to the sight of her blush. It started at the neckline of her shirt and crept up to stain the marble contours of her face in a delicate and very tasteful shade of pink.

"I'm a plastic surgeon," she said. Primly, as if she were somehow ashamed. Her pleasant fragrance, underlain by the scents of soap, deodorant and some mercifully subtle perfume, took on a tinge of unease.

A plastic surgeon. That explained the sense of wealth, the confidence, the air of superiority. He was willing to bet she was at the top of her field, though she couldn't be more than thirty.

At the moment, though, she wasn't confident. He realized that he wanted her comfortable with him, even though he wasn't likely to see much of her after tomorrow morning. At least he hoped he wouldn't. Or did he?

He struck a melodramatic pose. "Tell me, Doc—do you think I could benefit from your special talents?"

She gave him a look of utter contempt. "If you've ever looked in a mirror, you know damned well you wouldn't."

"Ouch." He grinned sheepishly. "I guess you only operate on ladies with double chins and middle-aged men with beer guts?"

"Do you mind if we change the subject?"

"Don't you like what you do, Doc?"

"Dana," she said gruffly. "My name is Dana."

It suited her. Strong and feminine at the same time. "Dana. You think I'm a pretty conceited *cochon,* don't you?"

"Conceited, yes. I don't know about the other, since I don't speak French."

She was willing to admit ignorance, which was quite a bit for a woman like her. He knew. Maman had always said he had something to prove every day of his life.

"I can see we'll have to have a few lessons tonight," he said as he began to walk again. "*Cochon.* Pig."

"I wouldn't go that far," she said, coming up beside him. "Tell me some other words."

"The name for your friend with the buzz is *maringouin.* Just over there, under the black willows, are a couple of white-tailed deer—*chevreuils.* You don't see them too much in south Louisiana these days. Just about now the rabbit—*lapin*—is looking for his dinner, and the owl—*hibou*—is getting ready to hunt him. The woodpecker, *piquebois,* is turning in for the night. And soon you'll hear the bullfrogs—*ouaouarons*—begin their evening chorus."

Dana's lips moved, repeating the words. "You speak like someone who loves this place."

Remy was quiet for a time, debating how to answer. As a boy, he had loved the swamp and the endless adventures he and Tris found there. But his restlessness had pulled him away, to the university and a career in the city. In the six years since his return, he had learned all over again how to value such simple thing as peaceful nights, family loyalty and running free where men seldom intruded.

But love? The very word was one he'd put from his mind long ago.

"I grew up in this parish," he said at last, guiding her through a button bush thicket. "Cajuns—*Acadiens*—start learning about the swamp almost the day they're born."

"Is your family here, as well?"

"Scattered throughout south Louisiana. I don't see them much. What about yours? Where did you grow up?"

"San Francisco—the Bay Area." Something in her tone told him that she was no more ready to talk of her past than he was. "I was an only child."

That must have been difficult. For all his problems with his family and his status as the Arceneaux "black sheep," he'd never felt alone as a boy. Acadians tended toward large and close-knit clans, his even more so than most.

He was the one who had left *them*.

By unspoken agreement, he and Dana fell silent, concentrating on the nearly invisible trail winding among the broom sage and chokeberry shrubs. They skirted the edge of Matou Lake, dotted with the knobby projections of cypress knees, and Remy could smell the scents of sun-warmed metal, tomato vines and sea-soned cypresswood that meant home.

It was time to warn Tris.

He stopped Dana with a light touch on her arm. "Wait here," he said. "There's something I have to check."

Dana glanced up at the darkening sky but didn't pro-test. Remy jogged into a willow grove, out of her sight, and ran another quarter mile so that there was no chance she would find him if she went looking.

In the fading twilight, he took a deep breath, lifted his head and howled.

He knew Tris would hear him. He'd been very clear before he left; if he gave the warning, it would mean he wanted Tris well away from the houseboat until he signaled that it was safe to return. Tris wouldn't find it a hardship to spend the night in the swamp, but Remy hoped his younger brother's curiosity didn't get the better of him.

Once the message was given and answered, Remy ran back the way he'd come. Dana stood where he had left her, arms wrapped around her chest as she searched the darkness. She released her breath when she saw him.

"Where did you go?" she demanded.

"You miss me that much, *chère?*"

"Did you hear something...unusual a few minutes ago?"

Remy put on a puzzled expression and shrugged. "You mean the howl? Probably some hound chasing a coon."

"It didn't sound like a dog to me. Are there any wolves in Louisiana?"

"Not anymore." She was sharp, this one. "They were killed off years ago. Let's go."

He waited until he was sure she followed, and then he led her across the remaining half mile to the banks of the bayou, where the houseboat rested on low water. The sun had gone down behind moss-draped cypress and tupelo, but the lamps shining from the deck made a beacon for weary travelers.

You'd better be gone, Tris, Remy thought. He pointed toward the lights. "Home. I can almost smell the fish sizzlin'."

Dana stopped and stared. "A houseboat?"

"Don't worry. I put it together myself."

She threw him a dubious look and paused at the ramp to examine the steel-riveted hull of the old barge, the small cabin with cypress roof on top, and the large pots of tomato and pepper plants on the open deck.

"It's perfectly safe," he said, grabbing her hand. "I don't know about you, but I'm hungry as a wolf."

To his surprise, she let him pull her up the ramp. The boat hardly rocked under their footsteps; she seemed to take comfort in its solidity. There was no sign or scent of Tris.

Remy seated Dana at the small table in the kitchen next to the propane stove and started a pot of coffee. While he worked, Dana gazed about the room with barely concealed curiosity.

"Do you live here alone?" she asked.

He grinned at her over his shoulder. "What do you think?"

"Without seeing the rest of the house, I'd guess you do."

"Why is that?" He poured the freshly brewed coffee

into a mug with The State Of Louisiana printed on it and set it in front of her.

"It's utilitarian. Spartan. Women can live that way, but they usually don't prefer to."

He pulled an exaggerated frown. "Ah, *chère*—now you know my sad story. None of the ladies will have me."

"You mean your charm isn't enough?"

He sat down across from her and gazed into her eyes. "You think I'm charming as well as arrogant?"

She let the steaming coffee consume all her attention. "Thanks for the coffee. It tastes wonderful."

With a chuckle, he got to his feet and set about preparing the bass for supper, refusing her offer of help. "Any Cajun who can't cook fish is a sad specimen. And anyway, I'll bet you don't cook."

"I—" Her voice took on that stiff, guarded tone once more. "I usually don't have time."

"And me, I have all the time in the world."

"You never told me what you do for a living."

"A little of this, a little of that. I know the best water holes for the fishermen, and I keep the tourists out of trouble."

"Like me?"

"Is that what you are, Dana—a tourist?"

She turned her mug around and around in her hands. "I told you, I have family here."

"So you did." He slipped the bass strips into the pan. "But you never did tell me why you came into the swamp today."

Her silence lasted long enough for him to slice the onions and bell peppers. Finally she said, "I came here to find the place where Sally Daigle died."

Chapter 5

Dana had seen many faces undergo major alterations, often under her own skilled hands. But the way Remy Arceneaux's expression changed was beyond anything in her experience.

One moment he was affable, flirtatious and, yes, charming. The next he was regarding her as if she were a deadly enemy. He had looked this way when they'd met on the side of the road, but his behavior since then had put that disconcerting moment from her mind.

No more. His eyes had become cold. "I told you," he said softly, "that you shouldn't come here."

"Actually, you said I shouldn't stay in Beaucoeur Parish."

"And I meant it." Abruptly he turned back to his fish, banging the utensils in a way that set her nerves on edge.

What had she said? Something about Sally Daigle, or her death, had set him off. And Chad Lacoste had warned her about him. Was there some connection between the warning and Remy's reaction to the name of a dead woman? The name spoken by the cousin who looked just like her.

She had a thousand questions, but Remy's demeanor seemed to wrap a muffling veil about both of them. She picked at the fish he set before her, knowing she ought to find it delicious but unable to enjoy it. Soon thereafter, Remy disappeared down the short connecting hall and returned with a terse comment about showing her to her room.

Dana would have liked nothing better than to walk right out the door and leave Remy to his brooding. But she was dead tired, grimy, and desperate for a little peace and quiet. Remy showed her the small bathroom, complete with sink, shower and a toilet occupied by an outboard motor. She turned down his offer to restore the facility to its original function and accepted a flashlight and directions to the outhouse set several yards back from the bayou. She didn't relish the thought of using it after dark, but at least she would have a full harvest moon for company.

A few sentences later, Remy left her to herself. She heard him moving around for a few minutes, and then the houseboat settled into an eerie silence. The small window was no impediment to the myriad sounds of a bayou night: the singing frogs Remy had mentioned, hoarse bellowing she guessed might be the voice of an alligator, and…once more…that eerie howling.

She sat down on the bed, a narrow affair clearly not intended for two. Remy's, she supposed. The room was as bare bones as the kitchen, with little in the way of decoration except for an old fishing pole hung on the wall and a colorful but amateurish oil painting in an incongruously ornate frame.

Dana got up to study the painting, wondering if it might be some early work of Remy's. It depicted the swamp, and though the technique was inexpert, there was obvious love behind the depiction of the brown water, green trees and blotches of color indicating wild-flowers. But the scrawled signature at the bottom spelled out another name: Tristan.

A relative, perhaps. At least he cared about someone enough to hang that person's work on the wall of his bedroom.

After a quick peep into the hall, Dana washed up, made a hasty trip to the outhouse—it wasn't nearly as awful as she feared—and gratefully returned to the boat and the relative safety of her borrowed bedroom.

She found an oversize red T-shirt, printed with the image of an alligator in a baseball cap, lying across the bed. She fingered it, trying to decide whether or not she should wear something that plainly belonged to Remy. In the end she pulled it on, preferring it to nudity in a strange bed and with a strange man in very close proximity.

Once under the covers, her soiled clothing draped over the room's single wooden chair, she made a token effort at sleep. She was hardly surprised when it refused to come. The sheets and T-shirt, though freshly laundered, held a faint masculine scent she couldn't ignore. The night noises seemed to grow louder and louder; if Remy was still awake, he gave no indication of it.

Remy. He was the reason for her insomnia—he and his grin, his compelling eyes and his changeable moods. *Face it,* she told the ceiling, *you're attracted to him.*

Most women would be. The difference was that she knew better. There was about as much likelihood of a romantic relationship between her and Remy Arceneaux as there was between a cottontail and a cottonmouth.

That painted a pretty picture. Dana sighed and pushed aside the blankets. It was still hot, and now that the sun had set the mosquitoes might not be quite so bad. A little walk on the deck...

Her bare foot brushed something dry, sleek and definitely moving. She gave a brief, strangled shriek and bolted across the room. The object of her terror flicked its tongue at her.

"Dana?"

The door swung open and Remy stepped in, his gaze darting back and forth in alarm. Then he saw the snake, and the tension went out of his shoulders. In a darting motion almost too swift for Dana to follow, he snatched the reptile just behind its darting head.

"Is this what you were screaming about?" he asked.

Dana flushed. "Didn't you say this boat was safe?"

"It's just a li'l ol' milk snake." He lifted the creature's head to eye level as if he were including it in the conversation. "Now, if it was a water moccasin, you might have something to worry about."

"And that's supposed to reassure me?"

"Guess you don't see too many snakes in San Francisco."

Dana eased behind the bed. The room seemed about ten times smaller with Remy in it. "Not too many bellowing alligators, either, or howling wolves."

"I told you..." Remy trailed off as if he'd forgotten

what he was about to say, his gaze falling slowly from her face to the T-shirt, which extended to Dana's upper thighs. She had completely forgotten what she was wearing—or not wearing.

Dana had blushed more in the past couple of hours than she'd done in nearly thirty years. She made no effort to cover herself. Remy might consider that a victory.

"Don't you think you should put the poor snake outside?" she suggested.

He looked down at his hand in surprise. *"Oui,"* he said. "It's scared half to death." With pointed haste, he turned on his heel and left the room.

Unfortunately, the door didn't lock. Dana dove back under the sheets and pulled them up to her chin. A little while later she heard footsteps on the deck outside, then a longer period of silence. She imagined serpents of every description crawling all around the room. What had Remy said about water moccasins?

Coward. You're on edge about everything tonight. All you have to do is—

A face appeared at the window, a pale blur in moonlight. Dana shot up, clutching the sheets to her chest.

The face was not Remy's. That was all she was sure of. The hair was darker than his, and the eyes stared at her, unblinking, like those of a madman.

Dana was no hapless heroine of some derivative teen horror movie. She tore her gaze away from the window long enough to search for a makeshift weapon. When she looked back, the face was gone.

She sat very still, listening for movement, any sound beyond the pounding of her heart. Surely it hadn't been her imagination, that face. After the incident with the snake, she was less than enthusiastic about running to

Remy. It might be midnight or 2:00 a.m., or even later, but dawn still seemed very far away.

She had almost begun to doze off from sheer exhaustion when the howling came again: uncanny, drawn-out, and filled with such mournful pleading that Dana felt her throat close in sympathy. On impulse, she got up and struggled into her mud-caked jeans and sneakers. She crept onto the deck, keeping close to the wall.

The howling had stopped, but her investigation was not in vain. The light of a single lantern caught the gleam of red-brown hair—Remy, walking down the ramp so noiselessly that he might as well have been floating.

It was not instinct that drove Dana to follow. Instinct might be considered a survival mechanism, and this was pure stupidity. She dashed into her room, grabbed the flashlight and ran after Remy, hoping she hadn't already lost him.

The moon was still full, though it had moved lower in the sky, and so bright that she didn't need the flashlight. Remy was almost out of sight. She stalked him as quietly as she could, expecting him to turn and see her at any moment.

But he had other things on his mind. All of a sudden he began to jog along the narrow path, and Dana had to use all her concentration to keep up.

Remy vanished behind a line of cypress trees. When she reached the other side, she didn't know whether to feel relief or horror.

A man lay sprawled on the boggy ground, and Remy knelt beside him, talking in a soft voice. He didn't seem to notice as she drew closer. Within a few steps she could see that the man on the ground was not simply taking a rest. He was, unaccountably, quite naked. His lower leg was caught in what could only be an animal trap of some kind, and Remy was in the process of prying the jaws of the trap apart with his hands.

The man gave a barely audible whimper. Dana cast away her doubts and knelt at Remy's side. He looked up, his expression conveying chagrin, fear and relief, all at the same time. She saw immediately that the man in the trap was the one she'd seen at her window.

He was young—younger than Remy—but the vulnerability she recognized in his face was not merely that of youth, or even of pain. He gazed directly into her eyes while Remy worked, just as he'd stared through the window. Her discomfort didn't come from his nudity; she'd seen plenty of nude bodies, in all shapes and sizes. Now, if it were Remy instead...

Get your mind back on the problem at hand. And the problem was not the reason the young man had gotten himself caught in a trap while running around naked, but the injury to his leg. That was something a doctor ought to be able to help.

And how long has it been since you set a bone or stitched up a wound outside of a sterile operating room? Dana moved closer to Remy, her shoulder brushing his, as he snapped the jaws of the trap apart and tossed the ugly contraption several yards away. The young man winced.

"Remy?" he said.

"It's all right, Tris." Remy glanced at Dana, his expression closed and grim. "I need to take him back to the boat."

"He's injured." Dana bent over the young man's leg and examined it by flashlight. "It's a nasty wound.

He may have a fracture. He ought to go to the hospital right a—''

"That won't be necessary." Remy positioned his arms under the young man's back and knees, lifted him gently and set off for the houseboat.

"You're crazy," Dana said, jogging to keep pace. "A doctor should look at his leg."

"You're a doctor."

"A doctor with the right equipment, under sanitary conditions. This is not the Stone Age."

"I know what's best for him."

"You do, do you? Just who is he?"

Remy never broke stride. His eyes glittered in the moonlight. "Tristan is my brother."

Dana St. Cyr was quiet for the remaining distance to the boat, and for that Remy was grateful. She was bound to have questions, and he had to think up answers quickly.

He carried Tris onto the boat, pushed open the door to Tris's bedroom with his foot, and laid his brother down on the bed. Dana was right behind him. If she'd seen this second bedroom before, she would have known he didn't live on the boat alone.

At the moment she was intent on Tris and not on Remy's deception. She arranged the sheets and blankets to cover all of Tris except his leg, and then glanced up at Remy.

"I need you to get me some clean cloth for washing—something that can be torn easily, and boiling water, in two containers," Dana said briskly. "Also soap, and rubbing alcohol if you have it, whiskey if you don't. I may need to make a splint if his leg is broken. I don't see any bone protruding, thank goodness."

Without waiting to see if he would obey, she leaned over Tris and touched his cheek. "How are you doing, Tristan? Can you talk to me?"

Tris gazed at her as if he'd seen a ghost whose haunting he welcomed. "All right," he repeated. "You'll...stay with me?"

"Of course I will. And as soon as you can be moved, we're taking you to the hospital."

Remy strode out of the room. If he didn't do as she asked, she would think him a heartless son of a bitch. But soon enough she would see that her concerns were completely unnecessary.

Then the questions would come. Remy prayed that Tristan wouldn't make things worse.

By the time he returned with the cloth and boiling water, Dana had pulled a chair up beside the bed and was examining Tristan's leg.

"No broken bones," she said. "Your brother is very fortunate." She smiled at Tris, who couldn't take his eyes from her. "I'll have a better idea what's what when we clean this blood away." She let the water cool slightly and scrubbed her hands vigorously in one of the bowls. Only then did she dip a washcloth into the second bowl and begin dabbing at the wounds.

"I don't understand," she murmured. "That trap should have done much more damage." She frowned. "These wounds are superficial. If I didn't know better, I'd say they were already healing." She turned to Remy. "How did you know?"

Remy stared at the wall. "I could see it wasn't bad," he said. "Tris is always getting into some scrape or other."

She shook her head. "It's been quite a while since I've...done this kind of work. But I haven't forgotten that much.'' She patted Tris's shoulder through the blanket. ''Any pain, Tristan? If we go to the doctor, we can make sure you'll be all right.''

There was something very admirable in the way Dana took Tristan's part and watched over him, though their meeting had been unusual, to say the least. She even spoke to Tris as if she understood that he needed gentle handling.

Nothing about Dana St. Cyr was what Remy might have expected. But that didn't change the facts. She had to get out of this swamp, and out of the parish.

''I'll make a bargain with you, Dana'' Remy said. ''If you still think he needs to go to the hospital when we're ready to leave in the morning, I'll take him.''

Dana finished cleaning Tris's leg with the alcohol and bandaged the wound with torn sheets and cotton towels. ''There might be infection. I won't change my mind.''

''I think it's time to let my brother rest.''

''Yes.'' Dana gathered up the remains of her make-shift medical kit and covered Tris's leg. ''I'll be right outside if you need me, Tristan. Call if your leg starts feeling any worse, all right?''

Tris nodded, but it was apparent that he was fighting sleep. Once he was out, he would be out for hours. Remy guided Dana from the room and closed the door.

''Why are you afraid of the hospital, Remy?'' she asked as soon as they were back in the kitchen.

Remy put on the coffeepot. ''I'm not afraid of hospitals or doctors. We just don't need them.''

''We? You and your brother? You've never been sick a day in your life, I suppose?''

''You said you came out here to find out what happened to Sally,'' he said.

"Yes. But what does that have to do with—"

He turned on her, eyes narrowed and fists clenched. "I guess you haven't been in town long enough to hear the rumors. Didn't you know that the Arceneaux brothers are the chief suspects in Sally's disappearance?"

Chapter 6

"What?"

"You heard me." Remy sloshed hot coffee into a mug and gulped it down. "Everyone figures one or both of us had something to do with it. If they had any evidence…" He wiped his mouth with the back of his hand. "I don't want more rumors started because of you."

Dana folded her hands on the table. "*Did* you have something to do with it?"

He laughed. "Why should you believe anything I tell you?"

"I don't know. I can see you've been trying to protect your brother in some way, even from me."

"Tris isn't like other people. He's sensitive, a dreamer. There were problems in school and afterward. He—" Hell, he'd been about to tell her things he'd never told anyone. "They could destroy him."

He waited for more questions, the kind he couldn't

answer. But she held her silence and gazed out the black square of the window. If she was afraid, she didn't show it. She was too damned brave for her own good.

"I've often wondered," she said, "what it would have been like to have someone to care for the way you do for Tristan."

He didn't allow himself to consider the deeper implications of her personal revelation. "You mean you don't think I'm a callous bastard for not taking him to the hospital?"

She met his eyes. "I don't understand you, Remy. Is it my approval you want? I thought you were trying to get rid of me."

For a skilled surgeon, she cut much too close to the bone. "That's right. I don't want you around here. Anyone in town would tell you the same, if Lacoste hasn't already."

"And I could vanish into the swamp as easily as Sally did."

He couldn't bear the calm, almost indifferent way she spoke of it. It made him sick, and at the same time he teetered on the edge of confiding everything to her.

And that would make him more certifiably crazy than Tris had ever been.

"You'd better go lie down if you want to be in shape to go back to town tomorrow," he said.

"But how can I be sure you won't murder me in my bed?"

"You can't. Should I make some more strong coffee?"

She got up from the table and started for the hall. At the corner, she turned back and looked into his eyes.

''What happened to Sally isn't a joke. Not to me. And I mean to find out what happened, one way or another.''

In the morning, almost every sign of Tristan's wound was gone.

Dana looked under the loosened bandages one more time and finally admitted the obvious. Somehow, miraculously, the young man had healed overnight. There were faint, pale lines where the trap had cut into his skin. That was all.

She expected an ''I told you so'' look from Remy, but he was distracted by other concerns. He'd made up a small pack, including sandwiches and drinks and a number of other useful items for their trek back to town, though at least part of the way would be on the bayou. He didn't show her a map. He evidently didn't want her to remember the way to or from his sanctuary.

At her insistence, Tris remained in bed, though he made soulful puppy-dog eyes at her and seemed to want to say something important. Either he was painfully shy, or something was holding him back. After intercepting a stern look Remy intended for his brother, she thought she knew what that something was.

Remy was fiercely protective of his brother. Why? What was he trying to hide? Could there be any truth to his warning about their part in Sally's disappearance?

No matter how hard she tried, she couldn't believe either Remy or Tristan were involved in anything like murder. Even so, half of her conversation last night had been sheer bluster. She should be relieved to escape.

She went along quietly when Remy announced that it was time to go. He helped her into a small aluminum motorboat, cast off from the cypress-wood dock and started up the bayou. Their course followed a mile or two of twisting channels, and some time later Remy jumped out in shallow water and pulled the boat onto relatively dry ground. Then he led her cross-country until they reached an area that looked vaguely familiar from her venture with Chad.

Yesterday, however, she and Chad had been alone. Now the little patch of mud was swarming with men, some in the uniforms of local law enforcement, others in civilian clothing.

Remy stopped in his tracks behind a screen of willows, nostrils flaring. "I have to go," he said. "You'll be safe now."

From you? she wanted to ask. But she spotted Chad among the men and realized there would be no more time for questions. When she turned to say goodbye, Remy was gone. She stepped out into the field.

Chad came rushing toward her. "Dana!" he cried. "Thank God you're all right. You'll never believe what happened—"

"You got lost," she said. "It's okay, Chad. I'm fine. I don't know where your boat is, however."

"Never mind about that." Chad moved as if to embrace her but stopped at the last minute, frowning at the willow thicket. "How did you get back here?"

"I ran into an old fisherman who showed me the way." Now, why had she found it necessary to lie? "Are all these people here for me?"

"I wasn't going to take any chances with your life," Chad said, grabbing her hand. "The swamp can be dangerous for people who don't know it."

Dana refrained from pointing out that Chad obviously didn't know it, either. "As I said, I'm fine now. If you'll introduce me to the man in charge, I'll thank him for his trouble."

"That would be Detective Landry of the Beaucoeur Sheriff's Department. I'll introduce you."

She let Chad pull her away, noting with clinical interest that she felt nothing at his touch. Nothing at all. It wasn't just annoyance with what he'd done yesterday. No, it was something else. *Someone* else.

Remy Arceneaux.

She thanked Detective Landry and the volunteer searchers, apologizing for pulling them out of their beds so early. Landry was quite gracious, but he studied her with an almost uncomfortable intensity.

"You didn't happen to run into the Arceneaux brothers out here, did you, ma'am?" he asked.

It was much easier to lie to Chad than to this man with his knowing eyes, but she couldn't bring herself to admit the truth. "As I told Chad, a fisherman helped me. I never did get his name."

"I see." Landry looked from her to Chad with a frown. "Well, you're okay, and that's all that matters. Unless you need to see a doctor, I'll take you home now."

"That's not necessary—" Chad began.

"I think it's best if the lady comes with me."

"Don't worry," Dana assured Chad. "I'll call you tomorrow."

Chad gazed at her, a world of hurt in his eyes. "You're angry."

"Not at all. I'd just like a good night's sleep." She freed her hand from Chad's grip. "Please don't worry about me."

"I swear I'll make this up to you. We could fly out to New Orleans and get the best meal you've ever tasted."

"Thanks, Chad. I'll think about it."

"Don't think too long." He graced her with his most charming smile. "I insist."

Dana smiled politely and turned to the open door of Landry's car. Chad stopped her.

"Did you find anything...about Sally?"

Dana's heart skipped a beat. "How could I? I didn't know where I was going most of the time."

"Thank God you didn't run into Arceneaux." Landry closed the door, and Chad bent to the window. "Remember what I said about him and his brother. Don't come back here alone, Dana."

Whatever else he'd planned to say was lost in the car's rumble as Landry drove along the well-defined ruts in the mud, leading a caravan of the other searchers. Aunt Gussie was at the door to meet her when Landry pulled up in front of the house.

"Mon Dieu," Gussie said, knotting her apron in her fists. "Thank God you're all right." She searched Dana's eyes and turned to Landry. "Thank you so much, Detective. If anything had happened—"

Landry touched her arm. "It's all right, Madame Daigle. We didn't even have to search. She found her way back on her own."

"Oh, my." Gussie grinned. "You're a mess. Come and have some tea, and we'll get you cleaned up. Detective, you want to come in for a bit? I just made a pecan pie."

"Perhaps another time." Landry glanced at Dana. "You take care, Doctor."

"I will." She shook Landry's hand. "Thanks again."

Gussie waved to the detective and hustled Dana into the house. Soon Dana was soaking in a warm bath, her hair clean and her clothing in Gussie's washing machine.

Afterward she and her aunt enjoyed tea and pecan pie. Dana realized how famished she'd been. And when Gussie offered her a spot of bourbon with lunch, she also realized that the day's events had rattled her much more than she'd suspected.

The drink gave her the courage to bring up the subject that had never left her mind.

"What do you know about the Arceneaux brothers?" she asked Gussie as they sat in the tiny living room.

"You didn't see them in the swamp, did you?"

"I...I've heard about them," she said carefully. "I've heard they have a reputation in town."

"Reputation." Gussie hunched her shoulders and worked furiously at her knitting. "All the Arceneaux in this part of the parish have a 'reputation.' Not that anyone sees much of them. Most of them are hermits, almost never come to town. But they're said to be...strange. Not like other folk. Some even say they're not to be trusted. Dangerous."

Did Gussie know from personal experience? Had she ever suspected Remy or Tristan Arceneaux of being involved in her granddaughter's disappearance? Dana could think of no way to ask.

But Gussie read her mind. "Some say," she said softly, "that those brothers might have been with Sally right before she vanished."

"Do you think they're right?"

"I don't know." Gussie dropped her knitting and closed her eyes. "No one ever found anything. Only talk." She sighed. "When Sally was in school, one of those boys was sweet on her. Chased after her everywhere but never did any harm. Sally was always nice to him. Felt sorry for him. Then Chad Lacoste came along and swept her off her feet.''

''Chad?''

''Didn't I tell you?'' Gussie smiled sadly. ''They were engaged to be married once. But Sally up and went off to college in the city, and Chad went somewhere else. He was here when Sally came back to look for that bird, though. I thought they might get back together again.''

''But they didn't?''

''Maybe they would have, but Sally…that's when she went missing.''

Chad and Sally?

Dana leaned her head back against the armchair, absorbing this new and surprising information.

Chapter 7

Everything Aunt Gussie had said about the Arceneaux seemed to be true.

Dana talked to several people in town, including the man at the gas station who'd mistaken her for Sally. He was the first, though hardly the last, to clam up at the mention of Remy and Tristan Arceneaux.

Others had more to say. The elderly couple who ran the combination hardware and grocery store on the main street were eager to regale her ears with superstitious tales of men who could change into wolves and hunted by moonlight. Grand Marais's sole hairdresser told Dana how all the girls had been after Remy Arceneaux in school, and how their parents had warned them away from him. Not that he'd ever shown interest in any of them; no, he'd always had his sights set on escaping Beaucoeur Parish. And he *had* escaped—for a while. Until Sally vanished and the rumors started.

That was when he and Tristan went to live in the swamp, and the rumors grew.

By the time she had spoken to a dozen townspeople, Dana was used to being stared at as if she were a ghost. She knew that Remy had left behind a career in the city to take care of his brother, though it was still unclear what had happened to make such a radical change necessary.

It all came back to Sally Daigle, and the suspicions that one or both of the Arceneaux brothers were responsible for what had happened to her.

No one, however, had any facts. No evidence of any kind had ever been found, not even Sally's body. She'd been seen talking to one of the brothers a few hours before she disappeared. That, and the way the Arceneaux were viewed in Grand Marais, was enough to settle their guilt in the minds of many.

But that wasn't good enough for Dana. All her life she had relied on her own judgment when there had been no one else to trust. That judgment had told her that she had to get out of San Francisco, away from her staid routine, and search for the one essential element her well-ordered life was missing. If she was ever to trust her instincts again, she had to learn the truth. She owed her cousin, and herself, that much.

Lost in her own troubled thoughts, Dana became aware that someone was shadowing her along Main Street. The damp hair on the back of her neck prickled in alarm. But when she turned her head, all she saw were the usual scattered pedestrians, moving slowly in the midafternoon heat.

She was just about to turn for home when Tristan stepped around the corner of a building. His eyes darted from side to side as he approached her.

"Tristan?" she said. "Are you looking for me?"

His lips parted. "Sally?"

"I'm sorry, Tristan. I'm not Sally. I'm her cousin, Dana. We met yesterday, remember?" She took a step toward him. "How are you feeling?"

"Good," he said, ducking his head. "Remy said you helped me."

So he didn't remember. Perhaps his problems were more severe than she had guessed. "Does Remy know you're here?"

Alarm lit his face, and at first she thought she had frightened him with her question. But the sound of footsteps from behind told her that Tristan was concerned with someone else. She turned quickly.

"Detective Landry," she said. "I was just—"

"I told you to stay out of town," Landry said to Tristan, as if she hadn't spoken. "Go home. *Allez.*"

"Wait a minute," Dana said. "He hasn't done anything wrong."

In the time it took for her to address Landry and turn back to Tristan, the young man was gone.

"I've been keeping an eye on you, Dr. St. Cyr," Landry said. "You've been warned about the Arceneaux brothers. I suggest you pay attention to those warnings."

"Detective, if you know something about Sally, if you can tell me anything at all—"

But Landry was already walking away. Dana clenched her teeth on a shriek of frustration. What was the matter with the people in Grand Marais? Were they all crazy? Was she crazy to get involved with the bizarre doings in this peculiar country?

No, not crazy. Just a little reckless, which she so seldom was. She continued to walk in the direction she'd been headed before Tristan arrived, brooding over Landry's words. She couldn't stop thinking about Tristan. Was he in some new trouble?

Just as she completed the thought, she caught sight of Tristan's dark-haired form moving among the shadows of a side alley. She turned into the alley, hoping he wasn't spooked enough to run away from her as he had from Landry.

But he came out at once, greeting her with a smile that transformed his face to a remarkable and astonishingly masculine beauty. "Miss Dana?"

She breathed out a sigh of relief. "Tristan, how did you get to town? Did you drive?"

"Walked. It's not far."

Somehow she guessed that "not far" to the Arceneaux brothers might be quite a distance by her standards. "All right. I'm going to take you home. Will you come with me?"

He nodded, and she led him to the Lexus she'd left parked at the curb half a block down the street. Faces, staring from the sidewalk or gaping out of storefront windows, turned to follow their progress. Dana thought she was beginning to understand Remy's extreme protectiveness.

It was easy enough to retrace Chad's route into the swamp, first on a paved road, then gravel lanes, and finally onto an overgrown jeep trail that proved a challenge for the Lexus. Dana realized how foolish she'd been to offer Tristan a ride. She had only the vaguest idea of the direction in which Remy's houseboat lay.

"Stop here," Tristan said. "I know the way."

Dana parked the car on a dry patch of ground. "Can I get there and back before sunset?"

"You don't have to come."

"I'd like to, Tristan, if it's all right with you."

He smiled with genuine pleasure and offered his hand. She took it. This time she would pay attention, so that she could retrace her steps the next time she came. She had no doubt that she would.

Tristan was very solicitous of her as he set off through the trees, pausing frequently to make sure she kept up. After a half-hour's walking, they reached a familiar open space.

That was when she saw the wolf. It stood, quite still, in the center of the field, red coated and bigger than any wolf had a right to be. Its face was turned toward her, its triangular ears pricked and alert. It definitely knew she and Tristan were there.

Hadn't Remy said there weren't any wolves in Louisiana? Was this animal a fugitive from some local zoo, or someone's exotic pet? Even she knew that wolves didn't make good pets. She also knew they usually didn't attack humans, but that thought was not particularly comforting.

Tristan showed not the slightest sign of fear or wariness. He started forward, moving confidently toward the animal. Dana caught his arm.

"Tristan! It might be dangerous."

The sound of Tristan's laugh startled her as much as the wolf. "Don't worry, Miss Dana. It's only Remy."

The game was up.

Remy heard Tris's casual statement and knew his choices were very limited. He could remain a wolf and scare Dana away, in which case he might soon be facing a mob of unwanted and hostile visitors; he could vanish into the swamp and hope Dana would continue to believe his brother was crazy; or he could decide to trust her.

"It's all right, Remy," Tristan called, making the decision for him. "You can tell Miss Dana. She'll understand."

A wolf's eyes didn't roll nearly as well as a man's. Remy's curses emerged as a series of growls. Dana continued to grip Tristan's arm, her eyes wide and fascinated, her scent only a little tinged with fear.

Dana St. Cyr was fundamentally levelheaded, intelligent and very, very stubborn. Once she saw what he was about to show her, she would probably believe. For good or ill.

Remy flattened his ears, shook his coat and willed the Change. When it was finished, he found Dana sitting on her rump with her mouth open and her skin very pale. Tristan patted her shoulder.

"I told you," he said. "Remy won't hurt you."

"He's right," Remy agreed, rising from the grass. "All those stories about *loups-garou* who hunt humans are pure hogwash."

Dana gulped. "Loo…gah-roo?"

"Close enough." He was keenly aware that the grass wasn't quite tall enough to cover his anatomy above midthigh. Well, she was a doctor, wasn't she? Embarrassment was the least of her problems. "In English, you'd say 'werewolves.' I've always preferred the French term, myself."

"Oh, my God," she whispered. And then, as he'd predicted, she took firm hold of herself and scrambled to her unsteady feet, leaning on Tristan for support. "This isn't a trick, is it?"

"No." Remy took a step in her direction, and she stiffened. He took another, but she held her ground.

"You...are the wolf?" she demanded.

"Oui."

"You don't even need a full moon?"

Either her dry sense of humor was returning, or she had already begun to accept. "That's only a story," he said. "Just like silver bullets and wolfsbane."

"I see." She glanced at Tristan and ran her tongue over her lips. Remy's eyes were drawn to the motion, and he continued to stare at her mouth with as much fascination as she observed him.

"Is Tristan...?" Her expression cleared. "When we found Tristan caught in the trap, he had just...done what you did. Hadn't he?"

The practical question drew him from his study of her very enticing mouth. "You catch on quickly. I think we'd be more comfortable talking back at the houseboat."

"Is that where you left your clothes?"

He grinned, showing all his teeth. "You sound disappointed, *chère.* I can send Tristan back, and we can stay right here, you and me."

"What if I say that I want to go home?"

"'Fraid not. Not yet. We don't like our little secrets bandied around, you see."

She folded her arms across her chest. "And if I decline to go with you?"

"You have such an elegant way of saying things, *chère.*" He bowed, a foolish gesture in his current state. "Tris and I would be heartbroken if you didn't come for supper tonight."

"Yes," Tris said eagerly. "You've got to come, Miss Dana."

In spite of her poker face, Dana's thoughts were easy to read. "People will start asking questions if I don't come home. My great-aunt will be worried, and several people saw me with Tristan.''

That might, indeed, pose a problem. But Remy wasn't about to let Dana go her own way until she'd heard a more complete explanation of what she'd seen today.

''Nothing will happen to you,'' he said, setting all levity aside. ''You do want to know more, don't you? About what we are?''

''And about Sally?''

''You won't know unless you come.''

She tilted her head to one side, challenging him with a direct stare that should have set his hackles on end. Instead, he felt a strengthening of that attraction he'd felt since their first meeting. She wasn't *loup-garou*, but she might as well have been.

''All right,'' she said. ''I'll come for a few hours. If you promise to put some clothes on.''

''*Je vois.* Then there is some flaw in me you can fix, Doc?''

''I don't have a remedy for your current…difficulty.''

Difficulty, indeed. He was aching with desire, and this particular distress manifested itself in a very public fashion.

''That's too bad, *chère*,'' he said. ''Maybe one will come to mind.''

''When this swamp freezes over.'' She smiled and tapped Tris's shoulder. ''Lead on, Tristan.''

Remy was tempted to run as fast as his legs would carry him on the unlikely chance that he could outdistance his lust. He broke into a trot ahead of Tris and Dana, reaching the boat in time to pull on jeans and a T-shirt before the others arrived. He sat on one of the

oft-mended lawn chairs on the deck and watched Dana
stride up to the ramp.

Maybe it was because she had accepted his true nature so readily, or maybe it was her unruffled courage
in the face of the impossible. She looked far more
beautiful to Remy now than she had at the side of the
road in her pricey couture. Putting on clothing had not
eased his lust in the slightest.

He stood up as she approached and extended his
hand, making a bet with himself. If she walked past
him without stopping, he would resolve to stay away
from her, listen to his common sense and ignore this
inconvenient attraction.

But if she took his hand...if she looked into his
eyes...

She glanced at his hand and then at his face. Slowly
she clasped his fingers in her own.

Remy didn't know whether to howl or curse.

Chapter 8

I'm the captive of a naked wolfman, Dana thought, sitting at the kitchen table across from Remy while Tristan puttered around on deck. *Make that formerly naked.*

Not that Remy's clothed state was much comfort. He could be dressed for a jaunt in the Arctic, and she would still be painfully aware of him and what she had seen.

She could reconstruct everything in perfect detail: Her first view of the wolf; the remarkable change to human, half-hidden in a reddish veil of mist; then Remy himself, standing there, utterly shameless, in all his glorious nakedness.

She'd been thinking about Greek statues the first time she saw him. She just hadn't been imagining in quite enough detail. Certain parts of Remy were more impressive than on any statue she'd ever seen.

And while she was sitting here trying to fight off a

long-unfamiliar sensation of pure sexual attraction, a part of her stood back and asked all the sensible questions her body preferred to disregard. If there really were such things as werewolves, and if Remy was one of them, could she believe his insistence that they weren't what legend and film made them out to be? Could she afford to discount the possibility that Sally might have fallen prey to men who weren't quite human?

"I had my lunch."

She started at Remy's voice. "I beg your pardon?"

"Just wanted to reassure you that I'm not going to eat you...at least, not in the way you're thinking."

A wash of heat gathered at the pit of Dana's stomach. "I thought you said that werewolves don't kill people."

"They don't. Not as a rule." He leaned his chin on his hand and stared at her with unblinking turquoise eyes. Now that she looked at them more closely, she could see that they had a feral quality, slightly tilted above his high cheekbones.

Wolf's eyes.

"Go ahead and ask," he said.

"All right. Are there more of you...how do you spell that word?"

"*L-o-u-p-s-g-a-r-o-u.* Plural. And yes, there are more of us. We generally don't go around announcing our presence."

Maybe they didn't need to. Maybe people sensed the truth without knowing exactly what it was. "Your parents? Family?"

"Most of my immediate family live in this or adjoining parishes. But we aren't the only *loups-garou.*"

"In Louisiana?"

"In this country, even in San Francisco. Probably other countries, as well."

"You're serious."

"I am about this. Like I said, we make sure that not too many people know about us."

That meant that she, Dana St. Cyr, was one of a privileged few. What would happen if she couldn't persuade Remy to trust her? She wanted very badly to trust him.

"You said that you can change whenever you want to?"

"*Oui*. We're born with the Change, the way people are born with their eye color."

Oh, not nearly so simple as that. "You don't consider yourselves human?"

He smiled. "Depends on who you ask."

"Where did you come from?"

"We don't know the answer to either question. Our lineage goes back to Canada, and then to Europe. We know there are others." He flexed his hand on the table. "We heal quickly—you saw that with Tris. We're stronger and faster. We keep some wolf senses even when we walk as men."

"But when you change…can you still think like a man?"

"Ordinarily, yes. We keep our intelligence and all our memories." He frowned and glanced toward the door. "Tris…he's different. He—" Abruptly he rose from the table. "Let's just say that there are always exceptions."

What had he been about to reveal about Tristan? That something wasn't right with his memory?

"There's still one question you haven't asked," he said.

"Only one?" she said with a lame attempt at humor.

"You want to know why all the stories say that we're killers. What happens if we ever lose control of the wolf side of ourselves." He paced back and forth across the floor of the kitchen. "We're like anyone else—we come in all kinds, all beliefs. My family has never liked to deal with ordinary people. They keep to themselves and stay in the parish. Few of them have ever left, even for a short time."

"But you did."

"You've been asking around."

"I like to know whom I'm dealing with."

"So do I." He favored her with a lopsided smile. "Yes, I left the parish. I attended L.S.U. in Baton Rouge, got my degree. Everyone at home thought I was crazy."

"Is that why you and Tristan live out here alone? Why did you come back to Grand Marais?"

His mouth set in a hard line. "I told you I'd answer your questions about *loups-garou*. My personal life is off-limits."

"What about Sally Daigle?"

She knew at once he wasn't going to answer, but she couldn't let it go. Not now. "You told me that you and Tristan were prime suspects in Sally's disappearance. You tried to warn me off several times, but now you're confiding what must be your deepest secret." She breathed in slowly. "I need to know, Remy. Did you have anything to do with it?"

The silence dragged out over several excruciating minutes.

"No."

Dana closed her eyes. *I knew it.* "I just had to be sure. Do you know who—"

"I don't know anything. Drop it, Dana."

He was lying, but there wasn't much chance that she

would get him to open up with direct tactics. Something was still very much out of whack here. Remy knew much more than he was telling.

"Well," she said, "now that you've explained what you're willing to explain, can I go?"

"Just like that?"

"I give you my word that I'll keep your secret. No one will ever hear about *loups-garou* from me."

"I believe you." He sauntered back to the table and pulled his chair closer to hers, the seductive charm returning to his eyes and his smile. "You all done with questions?"

"For the time being."

He reached across the table and stroked the tips of her fingers with his. "You really want to go?"

"I told you that people will be looking for me."

Remy played with her fingers, rubbing them with deliberate, sensuous strokes. "What if I don't want you to?"

The most sensible thing to do would be to withdraw her hand from his, get up and retrace her path to the Lexus. There was still a chance that Remy wouldn't let her go, but that wasn't likely. He'd gone far in trusting her, and she was flattered when she ought to be wary.

Werewolves, for God's sake. Was that why she was so drawn to a man she'd met only two days ago? Was he truly the embodiment of "animal magnetism"? Or was it the very possibility of danger that made her feel as if she were willingly drowning in his turquoise eyes?

"That's right," Remy whispered, turning her hand palm up and tracing its surface with lazy circles. "Just relax, *chère*. No reason to hurry, is there?"

"You don't want...people coming out here again—"

"They won't." He began rubbing her arm just below

the sleeve of the plain cotton shirt she'd bought at the store in town. "You figured out a cure, Doc?"

Dana was beginning to feel as if she'd downed several cocktails in a row, and she never drank. "Cure?"

"For my 'condition.'"

He wasn't talking about the werewolf condition. Oh, no. No man had looked more ready than he had when he'd confronted her after his change. Her mouth went dry. If she were to touch him beneath the table, she had a good idea what she'd find.

The idea excited her. *What's gotten into you?* she asked herself with a last grasp at sanity. Yet the way she felt now was hardly more bizarre than what had led her to cancel all her appointments, pack up and leave San Francisco with no idea of where she was going or what she wanted.

For the first time since her teens she was adrift, uncertain. She was prepared to throw herself headfirst into an abyss that might be filled with flames or icy water or have no bottom at all.

But what she wanted...suddenly that seemed very clear.

"Why are you so sure I have the cure?" she asked.

He lifted her hand and kissed her palm. "Instinct. That's one thing I never question."

Dana shivered. "If I followed my instincts..."

"You don't want to do that, *chère*. Mine'll have to work for both of us." He opened his mouth and drew his tongue along the underside of her arm. "You taste good. Too good to waste."

She tried, and failed, to shake him off. "I'm...I'm not a virgin, you know. I haven't exactly gone to waste."

"But it's been a long time, hasn't it?" He moved

his chair until it bumped against hers. "Too long. And you've never known anyone like me."

"No. I've never—" She felt his lips on her neck and sucked in her breath. "I haven't met too many werewolves."

"Then you've got a real treat in store for you, *chère.*"

"I'm...afraid to ask why."

"Don't worry." His breath feathered the corner of her mouth. "We make love like you do. We're just better at it."

"You are conceited, you know that?"

"I thought we'd established that already." He pulled back a little and grinned, giving true meaning to the word *wolfish.*

"My," she whispered. "What big teeth you have."

"All the better to eat you with, my dear." And he kissed her, cupping the back of her neck in his hand in a firm but gentle hold. Heat surged through her, barely contained, a savage wanting as heedless as that of any creature of the night. She opened her mouth to him, and he laced his fingers in her hair and deepened the kiss as if he intended to devour her.

Dana lost all sense of time. Awareness returned in the form of a noise she couldn't ignore, a sorrowful wailing that made Remy jerk away and leap to his feet in alarm.

Howling. There was no mistaking that cry, which seemed born out of the fragments of a broken heart.

"Damn," Remy swore. "Damn, damn, damn!"

Dana shook away the muffling haze of desire. "What is it? What's happening?"

"It's Tris." He pounded his fist on the table. "He must have seen us."

To her dismay, she realized she'd forgotten all about Remy's younger brother. "But why should that—"

He swung about, brows drawn in a scowl that she sensed was aimed more at himself than at her. "Haven't you figured it out yet? He was in love with Sally Daigle. He's never gotten over her."

Of course. That's what Aunt Gussie told me—one of the Arceneaux boys was in love with her.

And I look like Sally. Tristan called me by her name.

"There's no telling what he might do," Remy said. "I've got to go find him."

"Maybe I'd better come with you."

"Forget it. After…what we've been doing, it's going to be difficult enough for me to get him to come back." Remy headed for the door and stopped, his knuckles white as he gripped the doorjamb. "Can you find your way back?"

"I paid attention when Tristan brought me here," she said. "I still think—"

"Be careful. There's plenty of daylight, but don't stop until you get to your car." He hesitated. "And thanks for bringing Tris back. He shouldn't be going to town. He could have been hurt."

And you think he may be in trouble now. A disturbing thought struck at her heart. *A danger to himself— or to others?*

"You be careful," Dana said.

"I will." He flashed her that ironic grin. "Don't think we're finished, *chère.*"

And with that, he was gone. She imagined him stripping off his clothing, becoming a wolf, racing off in pursuit of his wayward brother.

She, however, was bound to ordinary human shape. Still off balance from the day's events, Dana returned the way she and Tristan had come, ears straining for howls or other indications of Remy's passage. Only the occasional bird's song accompanied her across the field, through the cypress trees and all the way back to the Lexus.

Once behind the wheel, she had time to think. She had to admit that she was a little relieved that her liaison with Remy had ended when it did, even if she regretted the circumstances. She'd come very close to committing herself to a path she wasn't sure she wanted to take.

And what about tomorrow? Would they take up where they'd left off, as Remy had promised?

She found no answers. Aunt Gussie met her at the door with a message that Chad Lacoste had called, several times.

"He seems mighty anxious to meet with you," she said. "Kept asking where you were and when you'd be back." She shook her head. "He was always very nice to Sally. A true gentleman. But I can't help but wonder…"

She didn't complete the thought, but Dana did it for her. *I wonder if it's because I look like his lost love? Maybe that's why he was so ready to help me. But I'm not Sally. And if he's still obsessed with her the way Tristan is, I'll have to make that very clear.*

But not tonight. She'd had enough drama to last her a year, and she had a feeling it wasn't over.

She went to bed early, but it was no use. She worried about Tristan; she worried about Remy, who certainly didn't need her concern. The tossing and turning continued until after midnight. She was listening to Gussie's grandfather clock strike one when someone tapped on the bedroom window.

Chapter 9

Dana's heart jumped into her throat. A pair of strong, brown hands lifted the unlocked window sash. Dana scrambled upright on the bed.

Remy stuck his head through the window, heaved himself up and tumbled into the room, landing easily on his feet like a cat.

"Remy!" Dana exclaimed, collapsing onto the bed. "You scared the hell out of me."

He didn't offer up one of his half apologetic, half challenging grins. "I haven't found Tristan."

With a strange conviction, Dana knew why he had come to her now. He was worried sick about his brother, and he trusted her enough to seek…comfort, was that the word? A man like Remy needing comfort from an ordinary woman?

"It shouldn't be this hard," he said, plopping down into the corner rocking chair. "Tris isn't that subtle, and I'm a good tracker. The best. He can't just have disappeared.''

Dana climbed off the bed, grateful that she was wearing pajamas that gave excellent coverage at such a vulnerable moment. She went to Remy's side, hesitated and finally sat on the floor next to him.

''I'm sorry,'' she said. ''Surely he'll come back?''

He looked down at her, his expression softening. ''I thought he might have come here,'' he said. ''But you haven't seen him?''

''No.'' She wanted to reach out and take his hand, but she folded her fingers in her lap instead. ''What are you afraid of, Remy?''

Instead of taking offense, he sighed and leaned against the back of the rocking chair. ''My brother…you asked why I came back from the city. It was because of Tris. He needed someone to look after him.''

''And there wasn't anyone else?''

''No. Even my family…they were never at ease with him.''

So things weren't so different among these *loups-garou* than they were with humans. ''You gave up something to come back. Something that mattered to you.''

''I had a career—stockbroker with a major firm. It was never as important as my brother.''

How many layers in this man had she yet to uncover? A stockbroker, no less. She had a feeling he'd been good at it, too. And now he was living out in the swamp for his brother's sake.

''When I was young, I used to pretend I had a brother or sister. My relationship with my parents…wasn't the greatest.''

"I'm sorry."

She shrugged. "It gave me the motivation to succeed."

"My only motivation was to get out of this parish. But since I've come back…" He squeezed her hand, but she sensed that his thoughts were far away. "I've learned to appreciate things I missed before. The way butterweed covers the fields with gold in spring. The cypress groves where snowy egrets nest in summer. The thunderstorms crashing around you as if the world is ending. The frogs and the warblers singing, and all the other sounds you can't hear in the city. Even the hurricanes."

"You make it sound very beautiful."

"Not something you'd noticed, I guess. Sometimes it takes a while for outsiders to see it."

"I guess I am an outsider," she said, hiding a twinge of hurt. "I think I always have been, even in San Francisco."

He took her other hand and pulled her to her knees. "Could be this is the place where you'll finally belong."

For a minute Dana was unable to speak. She was dangerously close to tears. This was a new Remy, a man with great empathy and understanding. And she realized she did more than lust after Remy Arceneaux; she liked him. She liked him very much.

"Tris may still come here," she said. "Or he'll just go home when he's tired of running. Give him a little time, Remy. Sometimes you just have to let go."

"I hope you're right." He bent forward, resting his forehead against hers as if they were old and dear friends. The contact was both restful and stimulating, and she felt sensation streak down her spine to end in overwhelming need. The same need she'd felt hours ago in Remy's kitchen.

Remy felt it, too. He was acutely aware of Dana's state of near-undress, the fact that she was naked underneath the thin silk of her pajamas. The cloth, the bed, the very air was infused with the scent of this woman, and her unique fragrance had begun to take on a taste he couldn't have ignored if he tried.

Arousal. Oh, he'd sensed it on her before—a scattering of molecules suspended about her like an invisible net, released by her body entirely without her knowledge. But she couldn't be ignorant of what was happening to her now. She was too observant to miss what was happening to him.

Damn it, he should leave. Now.

He pulled back. "You'd better send me away."

She tilted her face, and loose blond hair fell over her forehead. His fingers itched to bury themselves in that cascade of sunlight. He clenched his fists and surged up from the chair.

"I'm going. Lock the window behind me."

Dana caught his hand. "Do you still want me to be afraid of you, Remy? You're not doing a very good job."

"You're playing with fire, *chère.*"

"Maybe I haven't done enough of that in my life," she said, twining her fingers through his. "I think I might even learn to like this Cajun heat."

He threw her a look of amazement. Was she trying to seduce him? It didn't fit with what he knew of her. The funny thing was, he scarcely knew anything about her, yet he felt as if he'd known her all his life.

She was human, and that meant the feeling he had for her wasn't the *folie d'amour* that sometimes overcame *loups-garou*. A werewolf who found the *âme soeur*, soulmate, in another of his kind was bound to her for life.

His parents had been determined to mate him, according to tradition, with one of his Arceneaux cousins. He'd refused such a fate by running away. Now, it seemed, destiny had played a joke on both him and his family.

Dana gave an uneasy chuckle and released his hand. "Did I shock you? I'm not exactly an expert at...I've been out of the loop so long I don't even know what they call it these days."

Remy hardened his heart. "They still call it sex."

"I...suppose they do."

"Is that what you want from me?" He crouched before her, staring into her eyes. "A little roll in the hay?" He bared his teeth in a grin. "Are you still curious about how werewolves do it, *chère?*"

It wasn't every human who could meet a werewolf's gaze without flinching. "Is there something I ought to know?" she asked. "Is it catching?"

Hé bien, but she was a cool one. He couldn't say the same for himself. "That's one thing you don't have to worry about." He stroked her lower lip with the ball of his thumb. She closed her eyes. "We're not animals. I am a man, and if you don't want me to stay, you'd better say so now."

Her breath hissed out between parted lips. "Stay."

He'd never had a plainer invitation in his life. Hell, he'd had his share of lovers in the city, and a few here at home. None of them had any complaints that he knew of. But every one of those women had known there weren't any strings attached.

Did Dana?

"Has there been anyone for you?" she asked. "Anyone important?"

He drew his fingers down her chin and let them fall to her breast. "You want promises, *chère,*" he said, stroking her nipple through the silk, "you better find yourself another man."

Her clear eyes met his. "I don't want another man. I want you."

He groaned deep in his chest. One last chance. "Devastatingly attractive as I am, I don't carry protection in my pocket. Unless you—"

"I thought of that. I'm prepared." Color washed over her cheekbones. "Unless, of course…you don't want me."

Gone was the confident, self-contained professional who had propositioned him so calmly. Her lip betrayed the slightest hint of a tremble. This beautiful, intelligent woman was afraid of rejection, braced to accept the humiliation of falling flat on her face.

He answered her in the best way he knew how. As they knelt there on the floor, thigh to thigh, he cupped her face in his hands and kissed her.

Dana claimed to have been "out of the loop," but her response was neither hesitant nor in the least virginal. She kissed him as if she'd been storing up about a hundred years' worth of sexual appetite and was ready to use it all on him. He had a feeling this was the Dana St. Cyr very few people ever knew.

Take it easy, Remy. He should be able to keep his head. He could try, anyway.

"Slow down, *chère,*" he whispered, kissing the side of her neck. "I'm not goin' anyplace." Carefully, he undid the top button of her pajama top, and then the next, and the next. Her breasts were firm and round in his hands. She arched against him, pliant as a dancer, and he felt her reach for the snap of his jeans.

He scooped her up into his arms, kissing her nipples one at a time, and carried her to the bed. She slid from beneath him before he could lay her down, and he thought she'd had second thoughts at about the worst possible moment.

But she hadn't. She fumbled for the knob of the drawer in her bedside table and pulled out a package. She looked at it and then at Remy, one brow arched, and suddenly burst into helpless giggles. Remy realized it was the first time he'd heard her outright laugh.

"You think it's funny?" Remy demanded. "See if you're still laughing when I'm through with you." He snatched the package from her hand, set it on the table and began to undo his shirt, lingering provocatively at each button. Dana stifled her snickers behind her hand, but her eyes followed his motions with flattering attention.

Damn, but he was just as nervous as she was. He finished unbuttoning his shirt and peeled out of it with exaggerated rolls of his shoulders, wondering if his skin looked as hot as it felt.

"You like what you see, sugar?" he asked with a suggestive leer. "You want me to come on over there and show you how it's done?"

Her laughter had stopped, but her eyes shone very bright. She flipped back the bedcovers and held out her hand.

All the silly posturing fled his thoughts. This was no joke. He went to stand before her, gazing down at that solemn, lovely face. She undid his zipper with unsteady hands. She caught him as soon as he was free, and her fingers stroked up and down his length while she slid the condom into place.

After that he stopped thinking. He knew from her scent that she was more than ready for him, that she would gladly have taken him inside without any fore-play at all. But he didn't want it that way. Not with her. He tugged off his jeans and stretched out beside her, sliding his hand under the waistband of her paja-mas.

She was naked underneath. She closed her eyes and gave herself up to his caresses.

Her skin was wet silk where he touched her, warm and welcoming. He stroked her with his fingertip, so delicately, seeking the rhythm that would give her the most pleasure. Her hips lifted eagerly. He kept the rhythm going as he kissed her stomach just below the arch of her ribs.

"Remy," she murmured.

"Let me taste you," he said.

She shivered. He pulled the pajamas down over her hips and thighs. They tangled about her ankles, and she kicked them away.

"Jolie blonde," he said with heartfelt admiration. He left a trail of kisses along the slope of her belly and stopped at her honeysuckle curls. Her scent was mad-dening. Her taste was beyond anything he could have imagined.

Dana remembered what it felt like to have sex, but she knew now that she'd never truly made love. The way Remy touched her with his finger and his mouth was not mere expertise. It was profound tenderness that took as much delight in giving as in receiving.

She could have let herself go and come to comple-tion alone, but that was not the way she wanted it between them. With gentle tugs she pulled him up, glorying in the feel of his body rubbing hers.

Thigh to thigh, hands clasping, they kissed. Dana wrapped her legs around Remy's hips. He didn't need further encouragement. He entered her with controlled abandon, stroking deep and then withdrawing in a way designed to give pleasure with every movement.

She lost track of anything but the incredible feel of him inside her, his muscles flexing and releasing, his breath hot on her shoulder. They climbed to the stars in perfect tandem. She clutched his shoulders and arched up, up, urging him over the top with cries and whispers of joy.

Still he held back until he felt her shudder, and then he let himself fall. She took him in with all her heart. Remy whispered endearments, and kissed her neck and face until she remembered to breathe.

If ever a human being felt like howling, she did. Remy nuzzled her neck.

"Again?" he asked.

She chuckled, bursting with bubbles of laughter like warm champagne.

"What is it?" Remy murmured into her hair. "What's so funny?"

She shook her head and kissed the dimple in his chin. It wasn't funny at all. She had just discovered that werewolves really did make love just like humans. But she knew there would never be another man, human or otherwise, for her but Remy Arceneaux.

Chapter 10

The alarm clock showed a little past three in the morning when Remy finally remembered to look. He found it difficult to move, let alone think, with Dana's hair spread across his chest and his lungs filled with the heady scents of their lovemaking.

Her breath grazed his damp skin, and her hand swept up and down his arm in a soothing, hypnotic rhythm. He swallowed hard. He'd forgotten to warn her that *loups-garou* really did have one major advantage over human males: they could keep it up all night long.

But not tonight. Not with Tristan still on the loose and Dana's great-aunt snoring in the next bedroom. And those were the least of his problems.

"Are you okay?" she murmured, kissing his shoulder. "You weren't too disappointed, I hope?"

He propped himself up on his elbow and leaned over her, tracing his finger along the curve of her jawline.

"*Allons, allons.* What kind of talk is that for a smart, sophisticated lady like you?

She gave him a sly, delicious smile. "Let's just say I'm a very quick study. Of course, I'm sure I haven't had as many lovers as you have. It may take me a while to catch up."

"Don't even think about it." He heard the growl in his own voice and stopped. One hour with her and he was already talking like a jealous boyfriend. Talking like one, and feeling the knot tighten in his stomach when he thought of Dana with anyone else. Ever.

"I mean," he said more gently, "that you should never follow my example in anything, *chère.* And you shouldn't take chances."

"Like the one I took with you?"

"Exactly." He swung his legs over the side of the bed and grabbed his jeans. "You listen to me. Stay away from Chad Lacoste. Whatever you do, don't trust him."

She sat up, drawing her knees to her chest under the sheets. "He said almost the same thing about you."

"Yeah. I'll just bet he did." He dressed hastily, hoping he wouldn't turn to see the hurt in her eyes.

"Why mention Chad now?" she asked. "Are you afraid I'll seduce him next?"

He deserved her scorn. He could have controlled himself, and he hadn't. He needed to put space between them again, but not at the cost of losing her trust.

"I mentioned Chad," he said, shrugging into his shirt, "because he's here."

"What?"

"He's right outside your front door."

"How can you know that?"

"I smell him."

"Why would he come at this hour?"

Remy was relieved at the suspicion in her voice. If she was on her guard, that was all he could ask. "Did you know Sally and Chad were an item some years ago?"

"Gussie told me." She pushed aside the sheets, slid off the bed and strode to the dresser against the wall. If she was self-conscious about her nudity, she didn't show it. "She said Chad almost married Sally."

"Did she also tell you how furious Chad was when she refused to get back together with him five years ago? He still thought she belonged to him, but she had other ideas. She had her own life. Chad wouldn't let it go."

Dana turned from the open drawer, a pair of sensible high-cut cotton briefs in one hand. "What are you suggesting?"

He backed toward the window. "I'll be right outside."

"Wait! Remy, you can't—"

But she could hear, as he did, the firm knock on the front door. Clothing rustled as she finished dressing, and then her footsteps hurried from her bedroom and into the hall.

There was an extended pause before the front door swung open, admitting Chad into the house. From his position outside the open window, Remy heard the entire conversation. It was easy enough to imagine what wasn't spoken aloud.

"Chad," Dana said, feigning surprise. "What could be so important at this hour?"

"You didn't call," he said, couching the accusation in good-natured tolerance. "I've been thinking about you, Dana. Every day."

"I've only been here a few days."

"And you've been busy, haven't you?" Chad moved across the creaking floorboards of the living room. "Asking about the Arceneaux brothers. More than asking. You were seen with Tristan in town."

"He didn't do me any harm. I don't believe he's dangerous."

"Dana, Dana. I've tried so hard to make you understand." A faint scrape of wood on wood. "Poor Sally. So beautiful. I'm surprised that your aunt still keeps pictures of her around. I wouldn't think she wanted the painful memories."

"And what about your memories, Chad? You were in love with her."

"It was common knowledge." He put down the picture frame. "Yes, I loved her. I would have done anything for her."

The silence after that lasted so long that Remy almost climbed back through the window. He smelled anxiety, fight-or-flight hormones underlying Dana's scent. But there was no threat from Chad Lacoste. Yet.

"I think you'd better go," Dana said at last.

"I'm afraid you misunderstand me, Dana," Chad said. "I don't want to leave it like this. You and I—"

"At a more appropriate time, perhaps. Good night."

Chad's footsteps clumped toward the door. "Good night, Dana," he said softly. "Sleep well."

The door opened and closed with a solid click. Remy jumped through the window and was waiting when Dana entered the bedroom. She was fully dressed in a blouse and jeans, her face revealing no obvious distress at her encounter with Lacoste. Remy wasn't fooled. He moved close to her, sickened by Lacoste's smell lingering on her skin where he had touched her hand.

"Are you all right?" he asked.

"Fine." She said. "Though I don't understand why he dropped by so late. He didn't seem quite…rational. Though he didn't cause any trouble—unless you count the way he looked at me."

The hair rose on the back of Remy's neck. "And how was that?"

"I'd rather not speculate." Her smile faded. "I took your warning to heart. You were about to say something else about Chad before he arrived."

"It'll have to wait. Tristan's still out there."

"What aren't you telling me, Remy?"

He hated leaving her like this. She had a right to know what he suspected, what he most feared. But the time wasn't right. He still wasn't sure. He might never be.

"Stay here," he said. "Stay in the house until I come for you."

"I'm on your side. And Tristan's. Why can't you believe that?"

The smooth words he might have answered got tangled up in his throat. "I'm sorry, Dana." He slipped out into the night. She didn't call after him.

It had been too much to hope that he would find a solution to the turmoil of his emotions in Dana's bed. But when he caught Chad's scent on the thick night air, he knew there was a different kind of satisfaction to be had. Satisfaction, and another chance at the truth.

Chad had scarcely gone any distance at all. Remy found him and his BMW less than a quarter mile away, parked at the curb of a street lit only by the setting moon and the red embers of his cigarette.

He reeked of more than cigarette smoke. His hand clenched and unclenched on the steering wheel as if he were working up to some difficult and unpleasant decision.

Remy stepped in front of the convertible and leaned against the warm hood. "Hey," he said. "Aren't you on the wrong side of town, Lacoste?"

Chad dropped his cigarette with a curse, waving his burned fingers. He snatched up the smoldering butt before it could burn his expensive upholstery and tossed it over the side of the convertible. For just a moment his eyes reflected the fear Remy had sensed. Then his mouth curved into a contemptuous sneer.

"I might ask the same of you," he said, slumping back in his seat. "What the hell do you think you're doing?"

"Looking out for a certain lady you don't have the sense to leave alone."

"And just what do you want with her, Arceneaux? She's way out of your league."

"Could be." Remy leaned closer, smiling at Lacoste through the windshield. "But she's exactly what you want, isn't she? A perfect replica of Sally Daigle. Only, she's on to you, Lacoste, the same way Sally was at the end. She knows better than to trust you."

"Because you warned her?" Lacoste laughed. "You think she trusts *you?* Oh, I know she's met with you a few times on her quest for the truth about Sally. I'm sure she's heard all the stories by now." He tapped out another cigarette and regarded it thoughtfully. "I hardly think she's the type to let her imagination run wild when the evidence so clearly points in one direction."

"*Vraiment?* Then why did she kick you out of her house, *chèr?*"

Chad flushed to the roots of his sandy hair. "I know

who to blame for that, Arceneaux. And once I've had a few chats with the right people, Dana won't need to be concerned with your lies any longer.''

''Ah, *oui*. You'll have a word with your father's cronies and have me and Tris run out of town.'' Remy licked his thumb and rubbed at a smudge on the buffed silver surface of the BMW. ''But you can't really be rid of me, can you? I know what I saw that day. I know who hated Sally enough to kill her.''

''You know what you saw? Your own brother, with blood on his hands, raving about Sally—your poor, crazy, dangerous brother, rejected by his secret sweetheart.'' Lacoste lit his cigarette. ''You can't be rid of me, either, can you? It eats at you all the time, doesn't it—the possibility that Tristan killed Sally, and that I have enough evidence to put him away if you ever make one accusation against me.''

Remy kept his expression lazily indifferent, though his guts churned with sickness. The bastard was right. The fear was always there—fear for his brother, and fear of what Tristan had never been able to remember.

''Maybe if Dr. St. Cyr hadn't come to town,'' Remy said, ''this might have gone on for years. Stalemate.'' He turned his thumb so that his nail scraped the paint he had been polishing. ''But you made a mistake chasing after her, Lacoste.''

''I don't have to chase anyone. They come to me, sooner or later.'' He studied the tiny new scratch on the hood. ''I feel real sympathy for you, *mon ami*. For the first time in your life, you've been driven to grand acts of chivalry on a lady's behalf. Too bad the effort will be wasted.''

''It won't be wasted if I call your bluff.''

''And watch your brother go through a trial? See him

lose what's left of his sanity in prison?'' He blew a stream of smoke over the windshield. ''You know I can make it happen. The people around here are halfway to convicting him already.''

''You can't accuse anyone if you're gone.''

''Dead, you mean?'' Chad laughed. ''You think you can kill *me* and just walk away?''

Remy growled in his throat. Chad had always counted on his father's influence, confident that Remy would never dare touch him. All his life, Remy had preferred to avoid entanglements, combative as well as romantic. He hadn't competed for anything until he went to the city. He hadn't cared enough.

Even what happened to Sally hadn't driven him to violence. He had too many doubts. They had held him back every time he'd seen Lacoste's smirking face.

But Lacoste had gone one step too far. He had threatened not only Tris, and he'd made it very clear that he wasn't going to leave Dana alone. The sleeping wolf had awakened…the beast that would stop at nothing to protect its chosen mate.

Remy's mind went blank. *Chosen mate.* The idea had slipped into place so quietly that he hadn't noticed it. Even as he tried to scoff it away, it remained lodged as firmly as a snapping turtle in its shell.

Loups-garou usually mated for life. Among the Arceneaux, only a few had married humans. But mating was a serious matter for his people, one of the primal, instinctive drives that could thrust the wolf nature into dominance.

Remy felt it rising in him. For all the legends, *loups-garou* were not natural killers, no more than humans. But their greater strength, speed and senses made them far more efficient at killing if the need arose.

The Change bubbled in Remy's veins. He wanted to wipe that smile from Lacoste's face, hear him beg for mercy the way he imagined Sally Daigle had begged.

He could finish Lacoste, here and now. When he was done, no one would suspect murder. The sheriff's department would wonder what kind of animal could tear a man apart like tissue.

"You're not the only one who can hide a body," he whispered.

Chad lost his nonchalance. He sat up in his seat and swallowed a lungful of smoke.

"You're insane," he choked.

"It isn't insane to make sure that Dana is safe from you the way Sally wasn't."

"And what about making her safe from your brother?"

Remy snapped his arm around the windshield and caught Lacoste by his collar. *"Maudit chien."*

"You'd better find him," Lacoste wheezed. "Unless you—" He gave a rasping chuckle. "Looks like the law is heading right this way. Why don't you tell him about it?"

Cursing his lack of resolve, Remy turned. An unmarked vehicle he recognized as Detective Landry's had just arrived at the cross-street stop sign and was turning toward them, headlights stretching like grasping fingers.

Remy released Lacoste and backed to the rear of the convertible, putting it between him and the approaching vehicle. A part of him felt relief at the escape from bloodshed, but the other part wailed in despair and rage.

You can't let him escape. He must *be the killer. Not Tris. Never Tris. Prove it, once and for all.*

Tires squealed on pavement. Remy felt a shattering impact against his hip, and then he was falling, tumbling head over heels. The convertible roared away as he slammed up against the curb.

I told you, the wolf howled. And then it was silent.

Chapter 11

Remy woke with his aching head pillowed on something soft, the deliriously sweet smell of woman all around him.

"Remy! Remy, can you hear me?"

He opened his eyes. A face swam into focus, framed by loose blond hair. Eyes wide. Mouth pinched with fear.

Dana. His delightful pillow was some portion of her anatomy, and he was in her room at Aunt Gussie's, lying on her bed. He had no idea how he had made his way here. His body was a knot of pain.

"Remy?"

"I'm...all right." Not quite true, but if he was still alive, he would recover eventually. His memory returned in patches: the argument with Chad, the internal debate over life and death, the arrival of Landry's car, and then falling...excruciating pain...darkness.

His senses told him that it was still well before daybreak. No one had observed Chad slam his car into Reverse and strike down a shadowy figure, apparently not even Landry. And why the hell was Landry patrolling in town, where the police had jurisdiction?

He tried to sit up, clutching his middle. Dana pushed him back down again and squirmed out from under him.

"All right, my foot," she said, adjusting the blankets. "I should have taken you to the hospital as soon as you showed up." She shook her head. "I almost did when you wouldn't wake up, but I was afraid of what they might discover if they examined you. You said your kind heal fast, but you were out for so long.... Do you understand me?"

He nodded gingerly. "You were...right not to call outside help."

She muttered something under her breath. "Look at me." He winced as she shone a penlight in his eyes, first one and then the other. "Good. Now focus on my finger as I move it—don't turn your head. Excellent. Just a few more tests to be sure."

"How did I get here?"

She left him for a moment and returned with a glass of water. "You weren't gone more than twenty minutes when I heard a noise at the window. I found you lying on the lawn, bleeding and barely able to talk. I just managed to get you inside without waking Gussie. Here, drink this."

Remy gulped down the water and made a mental examination of his body. Dana had loosened or removed most of his clothing, and he could feel the pull of bandages here and there when he shifted his weight. His back, neck and limbs still functioned, however reluctantly. He touched his forehead, bound with a thick strip of cloth, and his chest. Cracked ribs would repair themselves. The swelling at his temple was going down and would vanish in a few more hours.

Whether Chad had acted by design or impulse, he hadn't put Remy out of commission. What might have killed a human had only damaged him, and not permanently.

Remy's werewolf nature had saved him, and instinct had brought him straight to Dana's arms.

"How long have I been out?" he asked.

"A couple of hours. As I said, if you were a normal man, I wouldn't have taken this risk. People who remain unconscious for an extended period may never wake up, and you were covered in blood. It took me a few minutes to realize that you didn't have any serious injuries other than the concussion, no fractures except in the ribs. The superficial cuts and bruises were already healing." She helped him finish the water and put the glass on the bed table. Remy noticed that her hands were shaking.

He caught one of them and held it. "You did the right thing, Dana."

Gradually her trembling stilled. "I hope to God I never face a situation like that again. How did it happen?"

"Chad. He tried to run me over."

Dana shot up from the bed and paced across the room. "He tried to kill you?"

"He's running scared. He might do anything now."

She turned on him, fierce as a she-wolf. "Don't you think it's about time you told me exactly what's going on? You've been hinting that Chad had something to do with Sally's disappearance, and everything that's happened suggests you're right. Why haven't you gone to the police?''

Remy closed his eyes. Either he was going to have to trust Dana one hundred percent, or the lies would dig a chasm too deep for either of them to cross.

''I haven't gone to the police,'' he said slowly, ''because no matter what the truth is, it will probably destroy my brother.''

Dana sat down in the rocking chair, wondering how many more ''surprises'' she could take in twenty-four hours.

''Destroy Tristan?'' she repeated. ''What are you saying?''

Remy gazed at her with a grimness that came from something far more devastating than mere pain, or even what Chad had tried to do to him. ''You swear to me, Dana St. Cyr—you swear that you'll never speak of what I'm about to tell you.''

''Of course. I—''

''And you swear,'' he said, ''that you won't go to the police, no matter what you hear.''

This was serious indeed. Dana consulted her conscience and then her heart. The two should have been in conflict. They were not. She looked into Remy's eyes and knew there would be a way to make it come out right.

''I give my word,'' she said.

He sank back on the pillows. ''I warned you about Chad with reason. But I can't be sure he murdered Sally. I can't be sure of anything.'' His voice took on the monotone of complete detachment, as if he were telling someone else's story.

''Five years ago,'' he said, ''the day Sally was last

seen in Grand Marais, I was out in the swamp looking for Tris. I'd seen Sally Daigle at the edge of town the day before. She was arguing with Chad—a pretty nasty fight, though Chad was careful to keep it private. I didn't think anything more of it, even when Tris told me he was taking Sally into the swamp to look for some special bird.''

Dana laced her fingers over her stomach as if she could contain the dread gathering inside her. ''Go on.''

''When Tris didn't return at nightfall, I went to look for him. I found him wandering in a daze. He told me Sally was dead.''

''Oh, God.''

Remy's face showed no expression. ''He couldn't tell me anything else, but I found part of his shirt a little distance away. It was soaked in blood. I could smell a storm coming. I took Tris home, and then went looking for Sally.''

''You…didn't find her.''

''I caught another scent—Chad's. He smelled like men do when they're beyond terror. I found him running out of the swamp, half-naked and caked with mud. Sally's scent was on him. I remember thinking that I didn't have to worry any longer, because Chad must have done it.''

Dana squeezed the armrests of the rocking chair. ''You'd been afraid that Tristan had killed Sally.''

''Yes.'' Remy stared at the far wall. ''I confronted Chad. He tried to give me some excuse for being in the swamp, but when he saw I wasn't going for it, he turned cold as ice. He told me that he'd followed Tris and Sally to the swamp, and he'd seen Sally's body. She was dead, all right. And maybe it didn't look good that he was out there in the swamp like that, but it would look even worse for Tristan when everyone knew he'd had an unrequited love for her, that she'd rejected him more than once."

"But she rejected Chad—"

"Yes. He never denied hurting Sally. But he made clear that if I ever implicated him in any way, even said I'd met him in the swamp, he'd make sure my brother was blamed for Sally's death. He had evidence to implicate Tris thoroughly. I believed him. His father used to have the whole parish in his pocket. I knew as well as he did who the police would believe."

The urge to run to Remy and comfort him was so overpowering that Dana had to force herself to remain in the chair. Remy didn't want comfort now. This poison had lingered inside him for five long years.

"After Chad left, I looked for the body. I never found it. By then the rain was coming down hard, and all trace of Sally was gone, washed away. No signs of violence. Nothing. So I went back to Tris. He didn't remember what had happened. When I tried to get him to talk about Sally, he... I was afraid he'd hurt himself."

So much made sense now that hadn't before. Dana thought of Tristan's gentle face, his confusion, his reaction to her when he'd seen her for the first time.

"It wasn't only that you were afraid what Chad would do to Tris if you went to the authorities," she said.

"No." Anguish was naked on Remy's face. "I could never be sure. I wanted to believe Chad was guilty. But Tris—Tris had blood on his clothes."

There wasn't a damned thing Dana could say. The full horror of Remy's dilemma caught her by the throat like a strangler's grip, silencing all hope of foolish, futile words. She got up from the rocker and knelt at Remy's side.

"If Chad killed Sally," he whispered, "I've let a murderer go free to protect my brother. But if Tris had anything to do with it…"

"I don't believe it," she said. "I'll never believe that Tris could kill anyone."

He turned his head to look at her, and the veil over his eyes lifted. "Now you know why I keep him with me on the houseboat. He's my responsibility. Whatever happens to him, whatever he does, will be my doing."

And he truly believed that, Dana realized. He blamed himself not only for failing to expose a murderer, but for being absent while his younger brother's mental state deteriorated into that of a possible killer. Remy's punishment was to abandon his career and his life in the city, and live with this terrible guilt in a place where he and Tristan were regarded with suspicion and even fear.

"You're wrong, Remy," Dana said. "No one can take responsibility for all the actions of another person, not even someone you love."

"And what would you do?" he asked in a whisper. "If I hadn't made you swear, would you turn him in?"

"I don't know what I'd do," she said. "I know what you have to do if you're going to go on living with yourself and make any kind of life for you and Tristan. You need to know the truth, Remy, and deal with it. But you don't have to do it alone."

"Are you saying you'll be with me?"

He tried to conceal his pain with a crooked, self-mocking smile, but it didn't work. Dana's heart clenched at the yearning in his question and her own ardent response to it.

"I may not know Tristan well, but I care for him. I care for you, Remy. I—I'll do anything to help both of you."

"Then I ask one thing—that you stay right here until I find Tris and bring him home."

"You just admitted that Chad tried to kill you. You can't go out in this state."

He grimaced and pushed himself up on his elbows, tensing his lower body to rise. "All I have to do is Change, and the rest of me will heal."

"Can you change now?"

The muscles in his face locked in concentration. He let out a long, slow breath. "Not yet."

"Then you've got two choices—stay here and recuperate until you can change, or take your own personal physician with you."

He shook his head, jaw set, but she could see she'd already won. "If I don't take you with me, you'll probably go after Chad yourself." He shifted his legs toward the edge of the bed. "We'll go back to the houseboat first, in case Tris has returned."

"That makes sense. Hold on, there." She bent to work her arm under Remy's shoulders and helped him sit. No one touching him now would ever believe that he'd been the victim of vehicular assault a few hours ago. She didn't quite believe what had happened in the three days since she'd arrived in Grand Marais.

It wasn't the discovery of werewolves that most amazed her, or even getting mixed up in murder. It was the simple fact that she had, improbably and miraculously, fallen in love. And love gave her the courage to face whatever lay ahead of them.

Checking to make sure that Gussie was still securely in her room—thank God the woman slept like the dead—Dana quickly assembled a small pack of supplies she'd prepared for further excursions into the swamp, including several energy bars and a powerful flashlight. She dashed off a brief note, informing her great-aunt that she'd gone for an early-morning walk and might not be back until afternoon.

On her way to her room she stopped at the piano to touch the photograph of Sally's smiling image.

If you can hear me, Sally—help me find the truth. Help me give the living peace and lay your memory to rest.

Dana felt Sally's spirit beside her as she helped Remy dress in his stained clothes, took him to the Lexus and drove to the dock where he kept his motorboat. By the time they cast off, Remy was moving without apparent discomfort, though she had a feeling he would conceal any lingering pain from her. He'd made himself very vulnerable in her room and now seemed bent on making up for it by remaining as distant as possible.

She'd almost told him she loved him. What if she had? He wasn't ready to hear those words. She didn't know if he ever would be. Even if all they had together was a one-night stand, she was fully committed to her course.

The bayou was dark as pitch, but Remy found his way unerringly to the houseboat. A single light burned on the deck. Remy bounded up the ramp and disappeared into the cabin. Another light came on in the kitchen.

As soon as Dana entered the cabin she knew Tristan wasn't there. Remy's face was stony.

"Tris was here," he said. "Sometime within the past hour. I should still be able to pick up his trail."

"If he came back, shouldn't we wait for him here? He was probably looking for you."

"No. Something's wrong. I can feel it." He leaned heavily on the kitchen table and dropped his head between his shoulders. "You won't be able to keep up with me, Dana."

"You mean that you intend to leave me behind."

"I'm sorry." He began to unbutton his shirt. "I can travel much faster as a wolf, following Tris's scent." He paused and met her gaze. "I want you safe. Stay here. Please."

That stiff but heartfelt request made it very difficult for Dana not to promise. "What choice do I have, other than to return to town?"

His mouth relaxed. "That's my *chère amie.*" He dropped his shirt over the chair and started on his jeans. "If I don't come back in a few hours…"

"Don't worry about me. Concentrate on finding Tristan. Keep safe."

"You ought to know by now how tricky it is to get rid of a werewolf."

"That's what I'm counting on."

He finished undressing, and Dana was aware of a strange self-consciousness between them, as if they hadn't shared a bed and dangerous secrets. She stepped around the table and laid her palms on his chest. Goodbyes were as inappropriate now as the yearning to feel that magnificent body entwined with hers.

She kissed him instead. Remy returned the kiss with banked ferocity, pulling her hard against him, and then let her go. He was out the door before she recovered her balance.

Dana ran out onto the deck just in time to see the wolf bound away into the umber dawn. She sank down against the wall and watched the mist rise, lit from within as if by some spectral fire.

A man came up the path from the swamp, hands tucked in his belt. Dana jumped to her feet. She knew him; Detective Landry, who had the unfortunate tendency to show up when he was least wanted.

"Hello," she called out, as if she had nothing to hide. "Can I help you?"

Landry touched his hat. "Ma'am," he said. "I'd like to speak with Remy Arceneaux."

"I'm sorry. He isn't here at the moment." She went halfway down the ramp and smiled at Landry with as much ingenuousness as she could muster. "Can I take a message?"

Landry shared Remy's disconcerting talent for the unblinking stare. "Do you know where he's gone?"

"I'm afraid not. He left just before dawn."

"I see. You wouldn't happen to know anything about a hit-and-run incident earlier this morning?"

Dana froze. "Was someone hurt?"

He sighed and shifted his weight onto one hip. His hands remained near his belt. "Mrs. Daigle overheard you and Remy discussing coming out to the swamp. The two of you were seen leaving town a couple of hours ago, in your car. I think you know more than you're letting on."

Apparently Gussie wasn't quite the heavy sleeper Dana had believed.

"Is it a crime in Louisiana to go for a drive with someone of the opposite sex?"

"Only if your intent is obstruction of justice." Landry started up the ramp, and Dana retreated to the cabin doorway. "I think it's time that you and I were straight with each other, Doctor. I know Tristan Arceneaux is missing, and Remy's been looking for him. I know someone tried to hurt Remy early this morning. I know he was with you afterward. And I think you know exactly what he is."

Chapter 12

Dana ignored her pounding heart. "Am I under investigation, Detective?"

"Dr. St. Cyr, I'm on your side, as much as I can be. You're Sally's cousin. That's why I've been keeping an eye on you. There are still plenty of folks around here who would jump to conclusions if they knew Remy and Tristan are *loups-garou.*" His brow wrinkled in concern. "Here, maybe you'd better sit down."

A chair would have been welcome, but Dana managed to stay on her feet. "You...know?"

"Yes." His expression was entirely serious. "That's why I've come to talk to Remy. This has gone far enough."

"I don't understand."

"I've assumed you're not stupid, Doctor, and I'd appreciate the same courtesy. If I thought you were in any real danger from Remy, I'd have kept you away from him. I'm guessing that he told you about Sally

and the rumors surrounding Tristan. You met Chad Lacoste, and you know what he tried to do to Remy.
You've been wise not to trust him.''

Dana released her breath. "You suspect Chad in
Sally's disappearance? Why haven't you arrested
him?''

"I can't expect you to understand the complexities
of the situation, but I do expect your cooperation.''

"You warned Tristan away from town, as if he were
a criminal.''

"Until this matter is resolved, it's my duty to protect
him like any other citizen. If Remy's in trouble—''

"It's Chad you should be pursuing, not Remy.''

Landry's gaze hardened. "Did it ever occur to you
that Remy might go after Chad?''

It hadn't. She'd convinced herself that Remy and
Tristan couldn't be involved in Sally's presumed death,
but Remy had every reason to hate Chad.

"He's looking for his brother,'' she said firmly.
"That's all that matters to him right now.''

"I hope you're right, because Chad isn't anywhere
I can find him, and there are just a few too many people
missing for my comfort.''

"All I can tell you is that Remy went into the
swamp. If I knew where, I'd be with him right now.''

"That I can well believe.'' Landry favored her with
a wry smile and glanced down the path. "It will be to
Remy's advantage if I can—'' He stopped, tilted his
head and frowned. "I have a call, Doctor. I strongly
advise you to go home and wait. I'll be in touch.''

Without another word he returned the way he had
come. Dana waited a few minutes and followed him
down the path. She heard the distant growl of a car's

engine and then only the natural sounds of early morning.

She suspected that Detective Landry had been distracted from his pursuit of Remy, which was all to the good. But she faced the same dilemma as before: stuck here like some nineteenth-century soldier's wife waiting for her man to come home.

Waiting around simply wasn't in her nature. She ran back into the cabin, retrieved her pack and took the path away from the houseboat. Of course, there was no sign of Remy's passage; she doubted that even a skilled wildlife tracker could follow him.

Only a little way, she told herself. *It's better than doing nothing.* She knew she could get as far as the place Chad had left her that first day, where Remy had rescued her. Perhaps, if she were very lucky, some other clue might come to her by then.

Half a mile into her trek she stumbled upon a minor miracle. Someone had neatly tied a bit of red cloth to a branch at the point where the path dwindled into several narrow tracks. It might have been some other hiker who'd left the sign, but there weren't many intruders near Arceneaux land. Remy certainly wouldn't have left them for her to follow.

Tristan might. He trusted her, and she was prepared to grasp at even the most fragile hope. She took the indicated track.

It wasn't an easy way. Soon Dana gave up brushing leaves and twigs from her hair and clothing, focusing all attention on finding the next marker. She discovered it draped from the upright, broken branch of a rotting log.

Someone had left these markers, and it wasn't Remy. Tristan had been back to the houseboat; surely he'd left them deliberately. And that meant he wanted to be found.

Dana offered up a prayer and broke into a run.

No one, to Remy's knowledge, had ever compared the speed of a true wolf to that of a *loup-garou*. But Remy ran faster than he ever had in his life, racing into the swamp with ears pricked and nose alert for the trail he must find.

It led him to the edge of a nameless pond where Tristan's bare feet had sunk into the mud. That was where he found the strip of red cloth. Remy paused only to confirm that it belonged to Tristan, and then he leaped across the water and settled into a tireless lope. He remembered the way; he had come this path five years ago, when he had found Tristan whispering words of death.

Sally's death. A murder left unconfirmed because the body had never been found.

The body. Remy redoubled his pace, paws flying over the ground from ridge to slough and over the next rise. He knew, with a certainty deeper than logic, where Tristan had gone, and why.

Tristan knew where to find the body.

Tris didn't kill Sally. He did not. So Remy told himself, over and over again, but the words brought no consolation.

At least Dana is safe.

The rising sun bled pink into the sky above the cypresses, renewing Remy's urgency. Birds clattered from their sleeping places as he passed, and a gator sank under the surface of the black water with an indignant slap of its tail. The scent he pursued grew stronger, and then overwhelming.

Tristan. And he was not alone.

Remy skidded to a halt behind the last intervening thicket at the edge of a thigh-deep slough. On the opposite bank knelt Tristan with Chad Lacoste behind him, one hand resting on Tris's shoulder with brotherly solicitude. At Tristan's feet, beside a waterlogged stump, lay the skeletal remains of a human being.

Wisps of rotted cloth and rope still dripped from the bones, but it wasn't that which caught Remy's attention. Tangled among the cervical vertebrae near the skull was a chain, discolored from its long tenure under the water. Hung from the chain was a silver ring set with a stone that still, after all these years, swallowed the dim light and sparkled like sweet memories.

Maman's ring, given to Tris on his eighteenth birthday, just before she died. He had put it on a necklace and never taken it off...until around the time Sally vanished. He'd said he didn't know how or where he had lost it.

Now Sally's corpse, what remained of it, wore the necklace in silent accusation. Tears ran down Tristan's face, though he made no sound. He lifted his hand as if to reach for the pendant. His fingers trembled.

"What more proof do you need?" Chad asked with nauseating gentleness. "You knew exactly where to find the body. How could you know that, Tristan, unless you were here when Sally died?"

A howl of rage built in Remy's throat, but he swallowed it back. *Wait. Listen.* Chad had tried to kill Remy; he wouldn't hesitate to hurt Tristan as well if he were provoked. It wasn't an accident that he was here. Either he'd followed Tris or come to this place on his own. What happened in the next few minutes might solve all the mysteries and set Tris free.

Or it might condemn him utterly.

"You'll feel so much better when you admit it, Tristan," Chad said. "You loved Sally. So did I. You owe it to her to tell the truth."

Tristan squeezed his eyes shut. "I...don't remember."

"You don't want to remember. I understand. But things will never be right until you clear your conscience." Chad leaned closer, patting Tristan's arm. "It's so simple. All you have to do is turn yourself in. I'll make sure you get a fair hearing. I know a few good doctors who might even be able to get you a lighter sentence. After all, you couldn't have known what you were doing, could you?"

"Please," Tristan whispered.

Remy gathered his haunches for a leap. His muscles screamed with the need to launch himself at Chad, take him by the throat, choke and rend and tear—

"Let me help you," Chad murmured. "You had an argument with Sally. You used your hunting knife to kill her, didn't you? You were afraid someone would find the body, so you wedged Sally under this sunken log and tied her up with rope so the bones wouldn't fall apart or be moved by the current."

Submerged. Remy ground his teeth. That was why he'd never been able to find the body; the scent had been masked by water. A werewolf might think of such a precaution.

"You made yourself forget," Chad went on. "Until today. Then you came here, because in your heart you knew it had to end once and for all. You brought Sally up into the light."

"I...found her."

"And you can't hide it anymore. Everyone in Grand

Marais saw you wearing that ring constantly after graduation. I saw it around Sally's neck the day before she died—you gave it to her. And here it is.''

''Yes,'' Tristan wept. ''Yes.''

With a roar, Remy crashed out of the thicket and spanned the slough in a single jump. Chad's expression went blank, and then he staggered back with a hoarse cry and fell on his rump.

Remy pinned him down, legs straddled over Chad's rigid body. Chad squeaked and closed his eyes against the sight of teeth mere inches from his throat. Through the haze of his anger, Remy realized that Tris hadn't even looked in their direction.

Tris's sanity was a thousand times more important than any dream of vengeance. Remy backed away, warning Chad with a growl, and Changed.

Remy didn't bother to gauge Chad's reaction; simple shock would keep the man quiet for a few minutes, at least. Turning his back on his enemy, Remy crouched beside Tristan and took him by the shoulders.

''Tris, can you hear me? Look at me, *'tit frère.*''

No flicker of recognition came back into Tristan's eyes. He drew his knees up to his chest and began to rock forward and back like a disconsolate child.

''I remember,'' he said. ''I found Sally. I did it.''

''No.'' He pulled Tris against him. ''No, Tris.''

''What more proof do you want?'' Chad rasped. He lay with his back against a cypress trunk, arms braced at his sides, body racked with tremors. ''You—whatever you are—'' He laughed. ''Is that why you're not in a hospital? You're not even human?''

Remy stared at Chad over Tristan's head. ''You'll be lucky to make it to a hospital.''

''You'd rather kill me than face the truth, is that it?

You just heard your brother admit to his crime. Of course, that probably doesn't mean anything to a monster like you." He shook his head. "It makes perfect sense. I'm surprised your brother used a knife instead of his teeth."

"*Liar.* You did this to him. You made him believe it."

"Did I? If you were so sure of his innocence, why did you leave me alone all these years?" His laughter took on the edge of hysteria. "Or is it because you have other secrets to hide?"

Remy was frankly amazed that Chad's reason had been so unaffected by what he'd witnessed. He smelled of fear, and yet he hadn't panicked. That stubborn grip on rationality made him all the more dangerous. There was only one way to silence Lacoste, keep him from destroying Tristan and exposing the Arceneaux heritage.

"Are you going to kill me?" Chad demanded. "Yes, that's right. Tear me apart with your bare hands." He leaned back against the tree trunk and plunged his fingers into the damp earth, laughing until tears ran down his face. "You're a natural-born killer, just like your brother."

"You're wrong, Chad."

Dana stood at the opposite bank, breathing hard, her hair a mat of tangles and her clothes dirty and torn. "Remy's not a murderer," she said. "And neither is Tristan."

Remy's first inclination was to curse Dana's muleheadedness and whatever skill or luck had brought her here. But when he met her gaze across the water, his treacherous heart knotted with relief and gratitude. He let his eyes speak for him.

"Come and join our little party, Dr. St. Cyr," Chad said. "Though I really don't think you're dressed—or is that undressed?—for the occasion."

In a handful of seconds Remy stood over Chad, hands poised to strike. Dana waded through the slough as coolly as a model gliding down a runway.

"You're not sinking to his level, Remy," she said. "I know you too well." She regarded Chad with a look of open loathing. "I presume that *he* knows what you are.... I wish I could have seen his face when he found out. How is Tristan?"

"He doesn't recognize one. He may be in shock."

"And I may have a way of reaching him."

"Dana—"

"Trust me." She gazed down upon Chad like an ancient goddess preparing to pass judgment. "I know you tried to kill Remy last night. Did you come straight here afterward, to make sure the body was still hidden?"

"Dana, Dana," Chad said, clucking sadly. "You know about the Arceneaux brothers, and yet you can make such accusations? I assure you that when I arrived, Tristan had already exhumed the body. What does that suggest to you?"

"You knew exactly where to come. Or was it coincidence that you happened to meet Tris in this very spot, especially considering your tendency to get lost in the swamp?" She sighed with an air of much-tried patience. "I think you knew where Sally was all the time. You loved her, and she rejected you—"

"As you have, *ma chèrie.*" He pointed at Remy. "For *that.*"

Dana touched Remy's arm, and an electric charge of inopportune desire shot through him. "You aren't half

the man—or beast—Remy is,'' she said, ''but you may
be the worst that humanity has to offer.''

"Perhaps you didn't hear Tristan's confession.''

"A forced confession,'' Remy snarled. ''You
twisted his mind, *fils de putain.*''

"If I were you, Chad,'' Dana said, ''I'd start telling
the truth. I'm not sure I can control Remy if he decides
to kill you.''

Chapter 13

Remy almost laughed at her air of aloof nonchalance. It might even have convinced him if he hadn't smelled the anxiety she hid so well. He bared his teeth at Chad and pulled against Dana's restraining hand like an attack dog on a cheap chain.

Chad shrank back against the tree. "You can be a party to my murder, Dana, but everything you care about will die with me."

"That remains to be seen." She turned her back on Chad and knelt before Tristan. "Tristan, look at me."

"He can't help you," Remy said to Dana, gripping her elbow. "He doesn't even hear us. You have to get him out of here. Leave Lacoste to me."

"That's the last thing I can do. Trust me, Remy. Please. What date, day of the week and month did Sally disappear?"

Remy knew that everything hung upon his decision—to let another person hold Tris's welfare in her hands, or take an irrevocable step that would save Tris's life, and perhaps his sanity, at the expense of his soul. And his own soul, as well.

Remy is not a murderer, Dana had said with all the courage and conviction he had come to admire. She believed in him. Now he had to believe in her.

He let out a harsh breath. "It was a Wednesday. September sixteenth."

Dana nodded and grasped Tristan's shoulders, compelling the younger man's undivided attention. "Tristan," she said gently, "this is Sally. Sally Daigle. Today is Wednesday, September sixteenth, and it's time for us to find the truth."

She knew her guess was right when Tristan's blank stare began to change. The fear in his eyes receded, along with the horror of memories he could not face. In their place was a calm pleasure, as if he had just discovered a rare flower growing out of the muck.

"Sally," he said. "I'm glad to see you."

"I know." She took his hands and knelt, drawing him down with her. "Do you remember why we came out to the swamp today?"

"To look for your special bird, the one I've seen in this area. I said I'd guide you to find it."

"That's right. We came out here together. We were alone."

"Yes." He ducked his head shyly. "Do you still have the ring I gave you?"

He must mean the pendant lying among Sally's bones. Dana had noticed it immediately, and the reminder chilled her to the core. "Yes, Tristan. I still have it. You gave it to me here, in the swamp. But something happened, didn't it? Something we didn't intend."

His eyes lost their confidence, but he was not yet frightened. "I didn't want to leave you even for a minute," he said. "But I thought I knew where to find your bird in a place you couldn't reach. I wanted to capture it for you, as a gift."

"So you left me alone. But I wasn't afraid."

"No. You were never afraid. But while I was gone, I heard voices. It sounded like fighting. Someone was with you. I came back." His face lost its color. "No. Sally. No."

"It's all right," Dana said. "Who was with Sally— with me—that day? What did you see?"

"You were lying on the ground," he said in a monotone. "You didn't move. *He* was with you. He had something...something—"

"Who was it, Tris?" Remy broke in, staring at Chad. "Who killed her?"

Tristan shook his head wildly. "He ran away. I tried to help her. Too late." A tear spilled from under his eyelid. "I left her alone. All alone."

"That's how I found him," Remy said, his face rigid with suppressed emotion. "He had Changed, and his memory was affected."

Dana took Tristan's face between her hands. "You're remembering now," she told him. "It's almost over, if you can be brave a little longer. For Sally's sake."

The haze in his eyes cleared, and Dana knew he recognized her for who she was. The vulnerable, childlike lines of his face took on a new definition, a firm maturity—a change just as startling as that of man into wolf.

"For Sally," he whispered. "I forgot so much. But when I met you, it started coming back. I knew where

Sally's body was hidden. I didn't know if I put her here, but when I found the body where I expected it to be, I thought it meant I'd... *Dieu.*"

"Go back to that day five years ago, Tris. Try to remember."

"I couldn't think when I saw her lying there. The man with her—"

"Was it Chad?" Remy demanded.

Tristan wouldn't look at him. "I hid until he came back. I saw him tie Sally to the log and push it under the water. He took the ring—the chain I'd given her—"

"Damn you, Lacoste," Remy said quietly. "I should have killed you."

Tristan gave Chad no chance to reply. "I didn't think," he said. "I Changed and went after him. He was so afraid he dropped the knife—"

Tristan shot to his feet and ran in a tight circle on the bank, like a bloodhound pursuing a scent. He darted to the nearest hollow cypress stump, running his hands over the rough bark. He dashed to a second tree, and a third, searching every nearby stump with frantic purpose.

Out of the corner of her eye Dana saw Chad climbing to his feet. Remy slammed Lacoste against the tree, fell intent in every line of his body.

"Remy," she said. "Don't—"

She forgot her warning as soon as it left her mouth. Tristan had plunged, legs first, into the deep hollow of a cypress stump. From within she could hear the rustling of leaves and the echoing thumps of Tristan's body striking rotted wood. He emerged from the tree with a bundle in his hands and jumped nimbly to the ground.

"I remember," he said. He placed the bundle almost reverently on a patch of dry ground near Dana's feet and knelt beside it.

"Don't touch it!" Remy said, still poised to strike Chad at his slightest motion. "It may be evidence."

"It's all right, Remy." Carefully Tristan began to unwrap the top layers of what appeared to be sturdy nylon, perhaps the remains of a windbreaker. Underneath lay a relatively dry and much cleaner layer of cloth. And within the cloth...

A knife. A hunting knife. Dark blood caked the handle and the dull blade like the stain of sin.

Remy swore. Chad had gone positively grim. Only Tristan seemed at peace.

"I didn't chase him very far," he said. "After I Changed to human again, I found the knife he dropped when he ran away. But I didn't remember what had happened—only that Sally was dead. I was afraid to touch the knife. I found Sally's jacket in the bushes, so I used that and my shirt to wrap the knife and hid it in the stump, under a pile of old leaves." He looked from Dana to Remy and finally at Chad. "I know who killed her."

"Quel génie," Remy said almost reverently. "You preserved the evidence." He turned on Chad with an evil grin. "It's over, you bastard. You're going down."

"You think it'll be that easy? I'll ruin you—and Dana."

Howling like a banshee, Tristan leaped up and flung himself at Chad. The two men tumbled into the slough. Remy shuddered, torn between the desire to protect Tris and the need to be in on the kill. He scrambled down the muddy bank.

"Remy!" Dana's voice seemed very distant, but it

pulled him like an invisible bond. "Chad might be armed!"

Without breaking stride, Remy plunged into the battle. Chad's fragile humanity was no match for a *loup-garou*, even Tris. Already he cringed under Tristan's flailing blows, soaked to the skin and scratched in a dozen places. But Dana was right. If Chad was carrying, he was desperate enough to use lethal force. A bullet to the heart or brain could kill a werewolf as surely as it would a man.

Remy reached for the nearest body and caught Tris by his collar, ready to toss him to the bank. In that second, Chad recovered. Silver metal flashed in his hand. Tristan was directly in his line of fire. There was nothing left of reason in Chad's eyes, nothing to stop him from a second murder. Or a third.

"Don't be a fool, Chad," Dana said from behind Remy. "If you kill anyone now, you'll have to kill all of us. You know it won't work."

Lacoste staggered, his .38 fixed on Tris. "Are you so sure, Doctor?"

Dana took a step closer to the bank. Remy willed her away, to the safety her stubborn heart refused. "Go, Dana," he begged. "Go to the police."

She addressed Lacoste as if she hadn't heard Remy's plea. "You wanted Sally, and she rejected you," Dana said. "It wasn't right. You could have given her so much, and she chose to turn her back on all of it. On you. No one does that to Chad Lacoste."

Chad chuckled under his breath, but the sound was strangled and thin. "You think you can condescend, Dana? Do you think you're better than Sally? Better than me?"

"I think you want me the same way you wanted

Sally. Maybe you thought you could start over. Maybe you were just crazy. But sooner or later, when I rejected you, you would have killed me.''

"You stupid bitch. I could have made it right."

Remy lunged. Lacoste fell on one knee and pointed his gun directly at Dana. Tristan yelled. Swamp mud sucked at Remy's legs like drying cement.

"I haven't got much to lose now, have I?" Chad said conversationally. "You really should have listened to me, Sally. Or is it Dana? I suppose it doesn't matter now, does it?" He began to squeeze the trigger.

"It's *me*," Remy snarled. "I took Dana from you. She always wanted me."

Chad's aim never wavered. "Is it any surprise when a bitch goes after a dog?"

Remy gave in to compulsion and Changed. Chad swung his gun wildly. One bullet cracked out before Remy shattered the bones of Chad's wrist.

Lacoste dropped the gun and fell into the water with a shriek. Remy felt Dana's warm hand slip through the upper layers of his fur as if he were a familiar and beloved pet.

"What do you think, boys?" she asked. "Should we bury him with Sally?"

Her words were so chilling that even Remy shivered, in spite of his own desire to feel his teeth around Lacoste's throat.

Tristan leaned against Remy's other side. "That will make us as bad as he is. Can't we just hurt him a little?"

Chad had had enough. "I won't...I won't tell," he croaked. "I swear."

Dana sighed. "You made a mistake, Chad. You didn't know that we're all around you, we *loups-garou*.

If anyone heard you talking about what you saw here today—anything about wolves at all—you'll wish you could spend your life in prison. It's time for you to tell the truth.''

Chad whimpered. Remy stepped into the water. He had no opportunity to encourage Chad's confession, for the morning breeze brought the unmistakable scent of man—Detective Landry. Tristan was already on his feet, staring across the bayou.

Clothes or no clothes, Remy knew he couldn't be discovered in wolf shape. He backed out of the water, snatched Tristan's pendant in his jaws, and started for cover.

"Hold it," a deep voice said. "All of you. That means you, Remy Arceneaux."

Remy dropped the pendant and froze, as much in surprise as in response to the command. Landry had addressed him. As a wolf.

"Thank God," Chad cried. "Officer, these people—"

"I'd advise you not to say anything else, Lacoste," Landry said. "We're going to do this by the book. And I'm not talking fairy tales." His gaze swept from the skeleton to the knife and at last to Dana. "I admire your gumption, Doctor, but not your sense. As for you—" He studied Remy with a faint frown. "Might as well come on back, Arceneaux. I'm sure you'll have a few interesting stories to tell me."

Chapter 14

Chad hadn't put up much of a fight when Detective Landry took him into custody. He had certainly not hesitated to offer veiled bribes and not-so-veiled threats, reminding Landry that he had friends in the sheriff's department, not to mention the state government. Any fool could see he'd been framed. What the hell was Landry thinking, letting the Arceneaux brothers go free? He would have Landry booted out of his job, and he wasn't going to find employment anywhere else in this part of Louisiana....

Dana, standing nearby with Tristan and Remy, watched Landry assist Chad into the back of his car and lean over for a private discussion with the prisoner. Chad was remarkably quiet when Landry closed the door.

"Remy," Landry said, beckoning.

Remy adjusted the thin blanket over his shoulders and glanced at Dana. In the hectic moments that had followed Chad's capture, she'd managed to summarize her conversation with the detective at the houseboat. Now Remy knew what Landry knew, but he remained on his guard. He went to join the detective, moving stiffly with lowered head and clenched muscles

The conversation was too soft for Dana to hear. She observed Remy's expression as it shifted from wariness to amazement and bemusement. After a few minutes Landry dismissed Remy with a nod and went to make another call on his radio.

"Well?" Dana asked.

"We're related," Remy said. "*Incroyable.* Apparently his father was *loup-garou,* and he's known about Tris and me all along." He shrugged. "I never even guessed he was one of us. Landry wouldn't say much about it, except that he's kept his true nature a secret until now. Something about a promise to his mother."

"A werewolf detective," Dana mused. "Quite a lucky break."

"More than lucky. Landry was one of the detectives on the case when Sally disappeared. He'd heard all the rumors about Tris but never quite believed them. He knew most *loups-garou* aren't killers, and those who are wouldn't commit a crime and stick around afterward. He suspected Lacoste but couldn't pin it on him without something solid. He's pretty sure that the new evidence will clear Tris and implicate Lacoste in Sally's murder."

"Thank God." Dana looked for Tris, who'd kept mostly to himself since Landry's opportune arrival. He seemed lost in his thoughts, but there was nothing in his behavior to suggest that he was anything less than sane.

"Poor Sally," he'd said as he'd walked beside Dana

to the detective's vehicle. "All she wanted was her bird. I wish I could have found it for her."

Dana had squeezed his shoulder. "You still can, Tris, when this is over. I think Sally would have liked that."

He'd nodded and stepped aside, perhaps pondering the events of the past few hours. Remy had watched him with some concern, but he also seemed to sense in his brother a change for the better.

"We'll have to go in for questioning," he said, following Dana's gaze, "but Landry thinks he can spare Tristan the worst of it." He lowered his voice. "Said something about misplacing Tristan's pendant. *Loups-garou* look after their own."

And where do ordinary humans fit in? "I'm glad it's over. Sally will finally have justice, and maybe Tristan can get on with his life." *And both of us with ours.*

She tried to think past the lump in her throat. Her ordeal was over, but the next few days were going to be very hard for Tristan. There was still a chance that Chad would stick to his original threat of attempting to implicate Tris. He would certainly hire the finest lawyers the state had to offer. But the odds, and evidence, were stacked against him now, and Dana had a feeling that it wouldn't take much more to drain him of that psychopathic confidence in his own power. Even if Chad babbled about men who changed into wolves and back again, no one was likely to believe him—or admit to believing him, anyway.

"You were brilliant, you know."

Dana came out of her thoughts and focused on Remy's voice. "Was I?"

"Those sinister hints about werewolf revenge, pretending to be one of us. I wouldn't have thought of that myself—we're usually trying to avoid the 'evil monster' reputation, not encourage it. But you pushed him right over the edge." He grinned. "You haven't been holding out on me, *chère?* Hiding a little *loup-garou* blood you're not talking about?"

She shook her head. "When I came here, I didn't like who I was anymore. I thought I might find a part of myself I was missing, and I did. But it isn't what you think." She smiled dryly to conceal the ache in her heart. "Sorry to disappoint you."

"Disappoint me? You crazy, woman?" In full view of the car's occupants, Remy pulled Dana into his arms. "You scared me half to death back there. Lacoste might have shot you—"

"But he didn't. This was as much my fight as yours. Sally was my cousin. I think I was…brought here to help lay her to rest."

"You've done that, *chère,*" he murmured, running his hands up and down her mud-stained sleeves. "You're a hell of a lot braver than I'll ever be."

"Ah, yes. That's why you tried to keep me out of it and urged Chad to shoot you instead."

"I should never have let him get away with what he did."

"You were trying to protect Tris, your family. And even if you were wrong then, you made it right."

"I hope so. Still, getting you involved…"

"Maybe it's not much comfort, but I've had more fun these past few days than I've had in the past ten years."

"Fun?" Remy's hands tightened on her arms as if he wanted to shake her. "If this is your idea of fun, Dr. St. Cyr, I don't think I'll survive your notion of discomfort!"

She clucked with mock severity. "And here you're the one used to roughing it, while I'm the pampered city girl who arrived in Grand Marais wearing a Prada blouse and pearls. Don't tell me one little adventure has turned you into a wimp?"

"Only where you're concerned."

"Why, *Monsieur* Arceneaux," she said, dipping a slight curtsy, "I hardly know how to answer such overwhelming gallantry."

With a subtle shift of his hands he held her still, compelling her to meet his gaze. "There's only one way, *chère*." He swallowed. "You said you felt you were brought here to set Sally free. Is that the only reason?"

She held her breath. "Should there be another one?"

"Maybe…maybe you were supposed to come here. Not only to save Sally and find your real life, but to… *Enfer!*" He lifted her onto her toes, kissed her passionately and let her go. "Did I mention that Landry's half-human?"

For a moment she wasn't sure she'd heard him correctly. "You mean one of his parents was—"

"What does that tell you?"

"Werewolves and humans…they can—" Where was this unaccustomed modesty coming from? She was a doctor, for pity's sake. How many naked men had she seen in her career? She'd even kissed a few in her private life.

Not one of those men had been Remy Arceneaux.

"Our people wouldn't have survived this long as a race if we kept completely to ourselves," he said. "Whatever the elders say, we couldn't live without humans, no matter how much trouble they cause."

She felt positively dizzy. "I'm sure there are plenty

of women who'd be willing to…contribute to your genetic diversity."

His voice softened to a near whisper. "You don't want children? I can understand—"

Oh, God. "I want—" *I want your children.* "Would they be able to change?"

"It's a dominant trait." He nuzzled her neck. "How 'bout it, *chère?*"

"What are you trying to say, Remy?"

"I'm saying that I can't live without you, Dana St. Cyr. If you think you can put up with me and my swamp."

"Are you asking me to stay with you?"

"I'm asking you to marry me and make a life here, in this parish."

Be sure, Dana. Be completely sure. She clamped down on her irrational joy and faced him squarely. "I thought you wanted a life in the city, excitement, challenge. You can go back to that now that Tristan will be cleared."

"I could. But you see, I've learned how to appreciate the things I couldn't when I was younger. The swamp is a part of me. And you…you've become a part of me, too."

She searched his eyes. "Is that enough? I'm only human. I can't do half the things you can."

"But you can heal, Dana. You have your own gifts. If you can see yourself fixing up simple country folk instead of rich city slickers—" He faltered. "Most people in this parish live from paycheck to paycheck. I'm not sure how much market there'd be for plastic surgery. Maybe you'd rather—"

"I left that life when I came to Louisiana," she said firmly. "I'm not going back. I think I may even have found the courage to take up the kind of practice I gave up a few years out of medical school. Not for money, but for something else.''

"For love.'' Remy took her face between her hands. "You could come to love this place, these people. My people, and the ones like your aunt Gussie. They aren't bad, you know, only ignorant.''

"And perhaps, with a human at your side, you might dispel some of that ignorance.''

"It's a start.'' He rested his forehead against hers. "Not just any human will do, you know. It has to be the one I love. My wife.''

Dana breathed in the words and held on to them until they filled her chest to bursting. "I suppose it's a good thing that I love you. It'll make putting up with your wisecracks a little easier.''

"You love me?'' Remy grabbed her waist and lifted her off her feet. "Say that again.''

"I love you.''

Remy's grin spread and spread until he couldn't contain it any longer. He bent back his head and howled until the birds rose in squawking masses from the trees and Landry jumped out of the car to investigate the ruckus.

"Keep it down, Arceneaux,'' he said gruffly. "You're scaring the prisoner.''

Remy took Dana by the hands and danced her in a circle, ignoring his blanket as it went sailing off into a mud puddle. "Now, ain't that just the damnedest shame,'' he drawled. "Let's give him something else to think about, shall we?''

And he kissed her until the cypress trees spun overhead.

* * * * *

Dear Reader,

I'm very excited to introduce my first work for Harlequin/Silhouette, "Kiss of the Wolf." When editor Leslie Wainger approached me about contributing to a dark fantasy anthology, I jumped at the chance. I've always considered her a leading light in the world of paranormal romance.

I knew immediately what I wanted to write—an idea that had been floating around in my head for years. After doing a number of historical paranormal novels, I was eager to return to a contemporary setting. I'd always been fascinated by southern Louisiana and Acadian culture. And since werewolves and the bayou just seem to go together, it was natural for me to combine the two in a story based on my *loup-garou* series.

Remy Arceneaux is a bit of a rogue and an outsider. He and his brother Tristan have "reputations" in the town of Grand Marais; their names are connected with the mysterious disappearance of a local woman. It takes the arrival of Dana St. Cyr, a sophisticated doctor from San Francisco, to break open the mystery and uncover Remy's secrets. But can their love survive the truth?

I hope that you enjoyed "Kiss of the Wolf" as much as I enjoyed writing it. I love to hear from readers. You can reach me at Sue@Susankrinard.com.

Sincerely,

Susan Krinard

SHADOW KISSING

Tanith Lee

Chapter 1

She saw him that first day, in the old garden. It was a sort of shock. Addie hadn't warned her.

He stood just behind the riot of ivy and overblown roses, with the sun on his face. Vivien's heart lurched. Never, in all her life, had she seen a man so handsome. No, perfect.

For some while she stood there, gazing up at him. And then she spoke aloud. "Well, I shall have to paint you. If you'll allow me to." But of course he would. He was made of stone.

"You are so unworldly, Viv."

"Yes."

Vivien never liked being called by that particular moniker, but Addie nearly always used it. The "unworldliness" Vivien had to accept. Not every artist, every painter, was like that, of course. Some were very practical.

The nonartistic Addie Preece was certainly practical. That Saturday morning when she brought around the keys, she stared dismissively at Vivien's tiny Camden apartment.

"Please take the money for a taxi," said Addie. She slapped down a ten-pound note, which wasn't enough for the cab fare from here to there. "I can't understand why you don't drive. No car, no computer—and you still don't have a mobile phone. You are so unworldly, Viv."

And Vivien had coolly agreed.

She had already agreed to be live-in caretaker of Addie's flat for three weeks, while Addie was in the south of France and Spain.

The flat was the last in a terrace of incredibly gracious London houses, dating from the eighteen hundreds, mostly now turned into apartments to die for. Addie, however, was moving out in the near future. When she had invited Vivien there last week, to suggest she flat-sit, Vivien had glimpsed furniture and belongings already under dust sheets or packed in large sturdy boxes, rather like Addie herself.

"I haven't decided when I'll go. The first offer on the flat was way too low. I'm holding out for several thousand more." She had assured Vivien, "I won't offer to pay you for flat-sitting. But it's quiet here—the other flats are empty, as is the next-door property— another reason someone needs to keep an eye on things. But you could paint, couldn't you? There's a garden—" She had waved at the closed after-dark drapes. "It's private, exclusive to this flat. And otherwise, none of this is a big responsibility, is it? I'll leave you a list of anything you might need to know."

Addie, Vivien thought, was like certain wealthy people—rather mean. She had chosen Vivien because Vivien owed her a favor and wouldn't ask for payment.

So all this was like an interview—similar to the interviews Vivien had had with Addie when Addie put her forward for book-jacket illustrations with three reputable publishers. Interviewer and interviewee. They weren't friends.

I don't have any friends, Vivien thought, except Ellie, who has now moved back to the States. And no lovers.

That Saturday, after Addie had delivered the keys, Vivien had paused by her ornate, dusty mirror and looked at herself pensively. She saw a slim, pale woman of twenty-eight. Her mass of dark hair poured back from her face and over her shoulders, unrestrained, and her large gray eyes met themselves in the glass, almost questioning. Her second name was Gray. People made jokes about gray-eyed Vivien Gray. And *he* had said to her, "Eyes gray as glass…"

Angrily Vivien turned from the mirror and the memory.

No friends, no lovers. The one she had loved ultimately hadn't wanted her, and in the three years since, *she* hadn't wanted anyone else. And he was stuck there, in the bottom of her heart, like bottled darkness.

The taxi was hot and stuffy—the underground would probably have been worse. It was late July, the summer like a hot blue lid clamped down over London. When they reached Coronet Square, the trees in the small public park looked tarnished.

Vivien lugged her bags and folded-up easel round to the arched doorway of the gracious ground-floor flat.

Ten minutes later, throwing open Addie's French

doors to the private garden, Vivien, startled and pleased, went out along a lush green avenue, between rowdy bay trees and tangled lilacs, turned a corner and saw—*him*.

He was a life-size statue. He stood there, six feet tall, and naked but for a little modest drapery at the hips. He had no look of anyone she had ever known— yet his beauty made him seem somehow familiar. Influenced rather by Greek Classical style, but with a hint of Art Nouveau. He was astonishing.

Even his marble was polished by weather rather than stained or chipped—or maybe he had been recently cleaned. At the thought of washing and rubbing this smooth male surface, Vivien felt a strange heat come into her face. How absurd.

His eyes were bleak, yet not truly blank in the way of most statues. His hair was long, thick and chiseled to look like sea waves coiling down his back. His body was faultlessly proportioned—long runner's legs, the torso leanly muscular, shoulders wide, neck a column. It made her think of lions, pumas, hunting dogs of the Renaissance. His face was that of a pagan god.

She studied him some while.

Tomorrow, she would sketch the statue. It was a must.

Only as she was about to turn away did she see that letters had been cut into the plinth where he stood. Vivien drew off the thin veil of ivy, and read, "My heart is turned to stone; I strike it, and it hurts my hand."

She thought she knew the words—Shakespeare, surely—but which play? Ellie would have known right off.

The sun now moved behind tall surrounding buildings. Shadows fell, changing the color of the roses to blood.

The flat was absolutely enormous. She hadn't seen it properly on the previous occasion. A hall, with a spacious cloakroom on one side and a dining room and cupboards on the other, led into a vast, weird and wonderful eight-sided room, with cornices and elaborate plasterwork overhead. It had a narrow window at one end, and more French windows at the other. Further doors led off into a couple of separate halls.

There were, altogether, three bedrooms, plus Addie's study, which was a barren room full of files and *four* computers—all switched off and under plastic tents—two bathrooms in ceramic tiles, and a small conservatory off the kitchen that also opened onto the garden. No plants lived in the conservatory. Addie never bothered with things like that, which was why the garden had run, literally, to seed.

The kitchen had a larder full of closed boxes and crates and depleted wine racks and a main area with white counters sparsely manned by microwave, coffee grinder and so on.

The fridge was the size of a small bus, and contained a bottle of Evian, half a carton of milk—which had gone off—and one slice of white bread, and a lettuce leaf that had obviously escaped and hidden long ago. Vivien needed to go shopping.

When she came back from the expensive local store, it was almost seven. The phone was ringing on and on, its tape clearly already message-full. As Vivien touched the phone, it rang off. Then, as she went back down the hall, it began again.

"Hello?"

"Finally! Is that Adelaide Preece?" It was an impatient female voice.

"No, I'm afraid she isn't here right now."

"Who on earth's that then I'm speaking to?"

Vivien frowned. "May I ask who *you* are?"

"Cinnamon Boyle-Martin." Then, before Vivien could respond, she added rudely, "and you're Ms. Whoever, right. So, my partner and I would like to come round tomorrow as agreed. Okay?"

"Why, exactly?"

"Adds must have told you. My partner and I are interested in some of her stuff."

"She didn't say anything."

"Too bad. She's selling off a few things. I'll bring her letter if I must. Do you have e-mail?"

"No," said Vivien firmly.

"Well, we'll be by about ten-thirty tomorrow morning."

"I'm not—"

"Ciao!" warbled Cinnamon, and was gone.

Had any of this been on Addie's lists of instructions? There was one under the grinder, but that seemed to be a warning not to use Addie's coffee beans. The other list, Vivien, who had not paid it much attention, now checked over. Ah. Scratched in the corner she read, *Antique scavengers—CS and spice name, poss sun.*

Vivien decided to worry about it tomorrow.

As the dark began to gather, she sat by the French windows on a chair released from its dust wrapper. The statue wasn't to be seen from here. She shut her eyes and, not expecting to, fell asleep.

The nearly naked, perfect man stood before her, among the trees. Slowly his head turned towards her—his eyes gleamed, human and alive, full of dark light....

Vivien woke with a start. It was nearly 11:00 p.m.

She switched on a lamp, which glimmered out through the glass and down the path. Presently she undid the doors and went out.

Looking back up at the building, if she had had any doubts, now she could see there were no lights anywhere, nor in the large house that immediately adjoined this one. Empty, as Addie had said. The dividing garden wall, half-hidden in creepers and trees, was ten feet high at least.

Vivien walked back down the path, feeling strange yet foolish.

He stood there now in darkness. Yet faint illumination from the electric false "gas lamps" of the square dappled him through the leaves.

Vivien stared. Who could ever compare with *this?*

Are you falling in love with a statue? Vivien asked herself. Listen, Gray, there are some mistakes even *you* aren't allowed.

Her heart beat fast. That was the artist in her, she thought sternly, excited by the prospect of sketching this wonderful image.

She could imagine telling Ellie, and Ellie hooting with laughter, hurtling her back to sanity once more. But she couldn't very well call Ellie in New York on Addie's phone.

Vivien turned smartly to go back indoors.

Something...

She stopped, looking now intently where her shadow fell away from the dim streetlights. The shadow was faint, too, and broken up by the shade-shapes of leaves—but there beside it stretched another, second shadow, which was male. By some fluke of the garden's contours, the shadows suggested he stood right beside her. His right arm extended slightly, as if…as if he had put his hand on her shoulder, intimately inviting her to stay….

Vivien looked back—it was irresistible. There he stood, above her, not close at all, unmoved and cold with night.

Vivien had set her alarm clock for seven-thirty, as usual. *Un*usually, it hadn't managed to wake her. She opened her eyes just before ten.

She was standing in her robe, hair still damp from the shower and a mug of mint tea in hand, when the door buzzer sounded on the kitchen wall.

Horrified, Vivien remembered what she had thought she wouldn't forget.

"Hello, yes?"

"Yes, this is Cinnamon Boyle-Martin and my partner, Connor Sinclair. Going to let us in?"

Her instinct was to say no. But good manners forced from her a reluctant "All right. Just a minute."

She drained her scalding tea like brandy. Confound it, why was she so nervous? They couldn't be burglars if they knew Addie—could they?

Vivien, vulnerable in her long, belted robe, shook back her hair and undid the front door. And there they stood, against the morning sunlight.

Her first impression was of Cinnamon, as rash and gaudy as expected. The tall man stood just behind her.

As Vivien's eyes adjusted, every element inside her body seemed to turn itself over. She didn't know what she felt—but fear was surely paramount.

For she had seen the man at the door *yesterday*. Clothed and colored in, Connor Sinclair was like Addie's statue in every way but one: *He* was flesh and blood.

Chapter 2

His hair was very thick and long, and black—very black. From the tanned, expressionless mask of his face, two eyes, heavily inked in by brows and lashes, looked down at Vivien. They were the color of hot black coffee—and cold as ice. He wore jeans and a white T-shirt, both of which showed very clearly the exact lines of a strong and muscular body, broad shoulders, narrow hips, long legs. The sleeves of the shirt were rolled up. His muscled forearms were the deep brown color of oak wood and dusted by dark hair. Beautiful hands, Vivien thought stupidly, powerful and calloused, with long fingers whose ends were squared rather than tapering—a working artist's hands. Had she noticed this on the statue—the statue whose living double this man was?

Decidedly, his eyes were as bleak and ungiving.

The Cinnamon woman was gabbling off some stuff about Addie, which Vivien wasn't taking in. Suddenly

the man spoke over her, not loudly but with the perfect
pitch of an actor.

"Shut up, Cinnamon." And then to Vivien, he said
flatly, "I don't know who you are, but either you can
let us in, or I can call the police."

"*What?*" Vivien now stared at him in astonishment.

"Well, you could be a vandal, or a squatter, couldn't
you. Adelaide didn't say anyone was going to be here,
except for herself. I suppose she *isn't* here?"

Vivien tried to pull herself together. "No, she's not.
I'm minding the place while she's away."

"Really? We'll have to take your word for that,
won't we."

From stupefaction, and then purely physical admiration, Vivien felt herself pass into a rapid rage. How
had he so flawlessly wrong-footed her? She should
slam the door in his face and call the cops herself—

Cinnamon thrust a card and a letter into Vivien's
hand. Vivien read the card: Scavengers Ltd. And then
his name: Connor Sinclair. The badly written letter was
from Addie. It agreed to something unreadable on Sun-
day.

"All right," said Vivien. She stepped aside, and
Cinnamon dived past her like some sort of dyed-blond
raccoon.

As *he* moved forward, Vivien found herself shrink-
ing back against one wall, as if to be touched by him
might burn her—or would it be frostbite?

He stalked down the hall. Cinnamon was already in
the octagonal room, turning round and round, hair and
jangly earrings dangling back so she could view the
corniced ceiling.

"Pity we can't scrape *that* off, eh, Conn?"

"Mmm."

Noncommittal, he stood there, dominating the space. If the statue was six feet tall, Connor Sinclair was more like six foot three. A difference, then.

Oh, there were plenty. The statue, for one thing, didn't have these eyes, or these bladed lashes, so dense, long and black. Didn't have any of the colors. The statue was...unclothed.

A tingling flame stirred out of nowhere, suddenly, in Vivien's spine. Her sense of sexual desire was so abrupt, so unwanted, it was almost hurtful.

"I gather she's left crates somewhere?" His musical, infuriating voice.

Vivien gathered herself together again.

"Yes, the kitchen."

"That's what I'm going to look at, then. Also there's something I want to see in the garden. If all that's quite all right with you?"

His sarcasm was like a wasp sting.

"I can't very well stop you," she said.

"No. So I suggest you let me get on."

Vivien realized that, in this labyrinth of a flat, she must show him the way to the kitchen.

It was like taking the manorial lord downstairs. The second hallway became some long ramble in a stately home, and Vivien, the downstairs maid, lowest of the low.

She could feel him at her back—actually *feel* his presence, like great heat...cold...*pressure*.

The kitchen might have been the surface of the moon. She gazed at it dementedly, and surprised herself by saying, apparently as cool as ever, "The crates are in the larder. That's there—"

"Thank you. I can actually see where it is."

Cinnamon came springing in with a clatter of her ghastly jewelry.

"I'll leave you to it," said Vivien, picking up her pot of mint tea. She would offer these creatures nothing. A shame, it might have been fun to poison them....

Back in her bedroom, Vivien threw on clothes, jeans and a loose black shirt, one of three she preferred to work in. She brushed her hair and it sizzled with sparks.

For heaven's sake, she thought. He doesn't matter. They'll be gone in an hour or less.

Someone rapped on her door. It had to be him. It was like the knock of the Spanish Inquisition—besides, no jangle of bangles.

"Yes?"

She stood glaring up at him. He was plainly as indifferent to her annoyance as to her.

"I need to see the garden now."

"Do you."

"The French doors are locked."

"So you just came along to this room?" She thought, *He knew where I was. He must know this flat, I'm sure of it.*

"The sooner you allow me to do my work here, the sooner I'll be out of your hair." As he said this, he glanced at her hair, then glanced, it seemed to her, right into and *through* her eyes. The effect on her was intense, and to dispel it, she had to look and move away.

Back then to the eight-sided room. Cinnamon, crosslegged on the floor, had a box-load of items spread out before her like exotic wares on an Eastern carpet. Vivien had no notion if these things—bowls, little boxes, candelabra—had come from Addie's selected crates or been stolen by the Scavengers from cupboards.

When she had found the key and unlocked the doors, he walked straight past her into the garden.

It was a glorious day, hot already, the shade blue along the path, and the scent of late lilac and rose mingling with the dustier aromas of London. He paused, looking around him.

Vivien thought once more, *He knows this place.*

He headed off along the path and unfalteringly turned the corner at the biggest lilac tree. He was now out of sight. And he was where the statue was.

Cinnamon rattled out and down the path.

Nearly hypnotized, Vivien followed her.

He was standing looking up…at *himself*. His hair, which wasn't tied back, poured down his back in shining black ropes. From this angle, Vivien couldn't see his face. Correction—yes, she *could*. For there it was again, looking back at him from the plinth.

Cinnamon, too, was squinting at the statue. Abruptly she announced, "Y'know, it's a bit like you, Conn."

Vivien recoiled. She didn't know why. As if, ridiculously, the resemblance, so underestimated, had become her property to defend.

Connor Sinclair said, not looking round, "So I've been told. I never see it, myself."

"No, but it *is*—it could *be* you, sort of—"

"I'm not *that* damned effete," he said.

He turned. He looked over Cinnamon's head at Vivien. "The statue's what I'm really after. I expect you guessed that? It's called *Jealousy*."

Vivien swallowed. "Why?"

"You don't know the quote cut in the base? No—" Scornful of her ignorance, he spoke the line in his dark, extraordinary voice: "'My heart is turned to stone; I strike it, and it hurts my hand.' From *Othello*. Perhaps you don't know the play.''

''Of *course* I know the play,'' Vivien replied icily. ''Presumably this comes after his mind has been turned against his wife by Iago—when Othello begins to plan to kill her.''

''Ten out of ten,'' said Connor Sinclair.

Cinnamon yawned. ''I never could stand Shakespeare.''

''No, Cinnamon,'' he said. That was all.

But she must have the hide of a rhinoceros, Vivien thought with reluctant envy, not to have shriveled at his tone.

By half-past twelve, Vivien decided she would have to go back to the main room and ask when they would be leaving. As she had been sorting her painting things in the bedroom, she had thought she heard the front door open and shut, but then had made out again the distant noises of objects being packed up or moved.

When she walked in, only he was there, sitting on the dust-sheeted couch, turning a tiny white figurine round in his hands.

Vivien angrily noted they had made themselves coffee—and from the Colombian beans Vivien had bought herself yesterday as a treat. At least he, the monster, hadn't drunk her milk. The dregs in his mug were black—just like his eyes.

He paid Vivien no attention. She might have been a small spider that had just crawled out on the carpet. Unless he didn't like spiders, in which case he would, of course, step on her.

''Has your partner left?''

"My— Oh, Cinnamon. She isn't my partner, in any sense of the word. But yes, she's gone."

"And are you planning to leave?" Vivien asked, as discourteous as Cinnamon had been. "I have things to do."

"Don't let me stop you."

"You *are* stopping me, Mr. Sinclair. You're in my way. I need to set up in here."

At that he looked up. She found it very difficult to meet and hold his eyes. When she did so, he smiled fastidiously, and then himself looked away. She had obviously failed another test.

"Set up? You have plans to redecorate the room?" He wrapped the figurine in newspaper. "You don't strike me as the painter-decorator type."

"I'm not. I paint pictures. Your intrusion is holding up my work."

"I see. All right. Another ten minutes and I'll be out." Deflated, Vivien turned to go. He said, "However, I'm afraid I'll be back tomorrow. I'll be bringing someone in to look at the statue."

"That garden isn't open to the public, Mr. Sinclair," she said frigidly.

He stood up. "While these debates with you are undoubtedly delightful, Ms.—?"

"Gray—"

"Ms. Gray. They seem to be wasting a lot of our mutual time. The statue is mine, and I'm moving it out. To do that successfully I need someone else to take a look at it first."

"*Yours?* How can it be yours? It's part of the flat garden and it's from the late-nineteenth century—"

"I know that. Listen, Ms. Gray, I suggest you phone

Adelaide Preece. Obviously she forgot to inform you of any of this.''

"I can't phone her—"

He swore. It wasn't the worst Vivien had heard, but coming from him, it was like a cold blow in the stomach.

He had produced a mobile phone. As he hit the buttons, Vivien grasped he was phoning Addie in France.

Feeling like a reprimanded child, and entirely mutinous, Vivien sat down on the nearest chair.

Connor Sinclair spoke to the mobile.

"Adelaide, good morning. Yes, Connor. Were you? Well, never mind, you're awake now. There is a young woman living in your flat. She's—let's see—approximately a hundred and seven pounds, five foot four, has a few yards of brunette hair, and—" he stared in Vivien's face, insulting, frankly terrifying "—eyes like Chaucer's nun, gray as glass.''

Vivien's mouth fell open. She shut it firmly.

He was saying, "You know about her? Oh, good. Would you have a word with her, then? She is quite tenacious about guarding what she considers to be your property, including the statue in the garden. She would make someone a lovely guard dog. A rottweiler, possibly.''

He strolled to Vivien and handed her the phone. He looked amused at her embarrassment and anger. How dare he—all those personal details. To make it worse, he had judged her height exactly, even if he had knocked two pounds off her weight. As for the Chaucer quote…only one other had ever applied that to Vivien. The reference had shaken her.

But Addie's voice, gruff with disturbed post-travel sleep and irritation, pounced into Vivien's ear.

"Didn't you read my note, Viv?"

"Yes, it didn't say—"

"The antique bits I've already sold him. The statue is Connor's own property, like a couple of other things there. For heaven's sake, I bought the flat from him in the first place."

"Oh." Vivien felt herself flush. She didn't really know why. But she certainly had made a fool of herself, or been made a fool *of*.

"Just let him get on with it, okay? Please don't call me again unless it's urgent."

The signal ceased as abruptly as a slap.

Vivien handed the mobile back to Connor Sinclair, her hand seemingly numbed by the feel of his personal electricity all over it.

"I'm sorry. She didn't tell me, so I didn't know."

"Now you do."

He pointed at the new boxes he and Cinnamon had packed. "I'll take those out to the van."

She propped the front door open to make the maneuver easier for him. He carried the boxes out two by two, making nothing of their weight, as he had verbally made nothing of hers. Or, of her.

Why should she apologize to him, anyway? He was a boor and a monster. He could have explained himself, and found the kitchen and keys on his own.

The van was light blue. There was no lettering on it.

He came back along the front path and stopped in front of her. The sun was high now, gilding the black of his hair. She saw for the first time, with sudden surprise, that his chiseled nose was slightly crooked— an imperfection!

"I'll be here about 9:00 a.m. tomorrow, Ms. Gray,

with one other person. Should he and I bring any ID? Perhaps family records...or would our passports do?''

Vivien looked him in the eyes. ''Just bring better manners, Mr. Sinclair.''

He started to laugh. She hadn't expected that. Oh, but it must amuse him so, when anyone was brave enough to answer back.

She left him to it, retreating inside and shutting the door with what she hoped was the right amount of controlled vehemence.

Her blood was boiling. But she couldn't entirely deceive herself—it wasn't only from fury.

Nor was her mood improved when, clearing up the mess of spilled coffee beans, spoiled milk and clogged grinder Cinnamon had left, Vivien found the other half of Addie's note. It was squashed in with Addie's warning about the use of coffee, and it picked up on the other note about CS and Scavengers, adding that a statue was due to be taken from the garden.

Grim though Addie's handwriting was, there could now be absolutely no doubt.

Despite her best efforts, Vivien couldn't come to grips with any work that day.

The octagonal room, to which she had brought her drawing and painting materials, was soon littered with torn-off pages marked in useless lines and curls. She was getting behind on the single commission she had been given this year, which was for a book-jacket. Addie had got her the commission. Another black mark.

Vivien's plan had been to work all morning, take a short lunch break, then allow herself to sketch the garden, and the statue.

She hadn't earned the right to attempt that yet, after

her failure with the commissioned work. The heavens agreed with her, it seemed. As she stood in the kitchen eating a piece of brie and an apple, the skies blackened, and then emptied out a downpour of rain that crashed against the conservatory roof.

The storm didn't clear until dusk was coming down.

She couldn't sleep. Finally she must have dozed, but woke at 2:00 a.m., alert and startled, as if someone had shouted in her ear. She had an idea the phone had been ringing, but now it wasn't.

She had been dreaming. What had the dream involved?

Vivien could remember only that it had somehow been…uncomfortable.

She got up, and went along to the kitchen to make herbal tea.

As she waited there for the kettle to boil, her bare feet on the Italian-tiled floor, the close, still night around her, Vivien caught herself once more thinking about Connor Sinclair.

Every time she did so, sparks of anger filled her. But also just *sparks,* glittering through and through her body, making her even angrier. It was this, she knew, that had stopped her working. And probably this that she had dreamed about.

Vivien, don't fancy a man who has the social skills of a pig crossed with a hunting leopard. The voice in her head was reasonable and sane. *You'll get hurt.*

Oh—she thought back at it—and I've never been hurt before, have I.

Why had Connor Sinclair used that one phrase—the one *he,* back there in her past, had used? *Eyes gray as glass…*

I won't think about him. About *either* of them.

She took her tea back to bed, downed it and dropped herself on the pillows, determined to lose consciousness, despite the ominous creakings of the unknown flat above and around her. She managed to sleep almost at once.

The rain was gone, just a light crystal sparkle here and there on bay leaves and rose petals. In the ghostly lambency of the streetlights the statue stood on his plinth, gazing down at her. His eyes were dark now. *Alive* now.

In awe, but not horror, Vivien watched as he stepped casually off the plinth. He walked towards her, and Vivien, half surprised at herself, backed away.

Surprised because it seemed really quite natural that a stone man had moved, and now approached her.

He walked in a slow, easy prowl. Yet he was, despite the living eyes, still a creature formed from marble.

Raindrops brushed off into Vivien's hair; she felt them on her bare skin. She was naked, then, as the statue—*more* naked than he.

She continued to edge away. And suddenly the glass of the French windows met her back, cold in the warmth of the heavy summer night.

He did not pause. Why would he? She had no escape from him now.

She imagined, astonished, what it would be like, that icy caress of smooth stone hands, sliding over her naked body, gently teasing on her breasts, subtle and sure between her thighs....

But somehow, she was in through the closed doors, *inside* the glass and in the room—though still he came towards her and still she backed away.

His hands were not yet on her, but on the lock of

the doors. Could he undo it? Had she even locked them—did she want this, *desire* it—or was she utterly afraid…?

Vivien woke. She threw herself upright in the bed, gasping—and heard again, in the waking world, the quiet scrape of stone against metal.

''Oh God—''

Vivien sprang from the bed, slamming at the light switch, blinding herself for a moment as the lamps came on.

Her impulse was to race for the French doors and secure them. Then something occurred to her. She couldn't surely have heard such a soft scraping from *here*. No. It must come from much nearer, from down the hall—the conservatory off the kitchen.

Vivien wildly pulled on a T-shirt. She flew along the passage. She jumped into the kitchen, bashing on the overhead light as she passed. She had had to do it all like that. Her true inclination had been to hide under the bed.

Beyond the lighted kitchen, the black glass box of the empty conservatory showed only the faintest wisp of filtered lamplight.

Nothing was out there. Nothing wonderful and terrible scratched at the door.

Where light fell on the paved path between the trees, the rain had already dried. Only shadows lay there.

Vivien checked the door. It was locked, the padlock rusty, bolted, too, on the inside. The glass, Addie had informed her, like that of the French doors and all the windows, was bulletproof.

Vivien went to check every window, and the French doors in the octagonal room. Nothing was out of place, despite the apprehension she felt each time. Only the closeness of night, dully synchronized by far-off London sounds—none of which were like the noise of stone fingers moving on a lock.

She did *not* go to check if the statue was still on the plinth. Instead, she left on every light in the apartment.

At five-thirty, when it was full daylight, Vivien got up again and showered and dressed. She hadn't got any more sleep, and she had that muzzy, cinder-eyed reaction to insomnia she always did. When she went back to the kitchen and looked through into the conservatory, however, her blurry vision showed her something that last night, in the brilliance of the kitchen spotlights, she hadn't seen.

It lay there in the conservatory's far corner. Now unmissable.

A rose. Perfect, she thought, until she touched it. Only the stem, fierce with thorns, stayed intact. The flower's head had already fallen apart—or been shattered—every petal like a drop of blood.

Chapter 3

"Hi. I'm Lewis Blake. You must be Ms. Gray?"

Vivien stared at the tallish, heavily muscular man in her doorway. He wore a tattered black T-shirt, and jeans covered in dust or chalk—both garments seemed to have been expensive but he had cheerfully ruined them without a backward glance. He *looked* cheerful, too, despite his bristly shaven head and the gold ring through his eyebrow.

Not meaning to, like a child watching for Santa Claus—or the bogeyman—Vivien's eyes slid around him.

"Don't be apprehensive yet," said Lewis Blake, grinning in a curiously kind manner. "I'm afraid he *is* coming—but he'll be about five minutes. Monday morning traffic leaves nowhere to park the van."

"You mean Mr. Sinclair?" Vivien thought she sounded arch and silly. "You're here with him about the statue?"

Lewis nodded. "Sure am. But it's fine if you want to wait till he gets here, to verify my status. I can appreciate you don't just want to let any old stranger loose in the flat."

"A shame Mr. Sinclair didn't appreciate that." It was out before she could contain it.

But Lewis Blake looked intently at her. "Sorry about that," he said.

"*You* didn't do it."

"No, well...I don't have much reason to."

"Oh, look," she said, "please come in."

As they walked in through the first hall, Lewis said, "Do I gather he gave you a bit of a rough time? He can be... Well, there are reasons, I suppose."

Vivien ignored this. The monster hadn't even arrived yet, and already they were talking about him, conjuring him up.

Her head ached from lack of sleep. From puzzling over a broken rose that couldn't have been where it was.

"Would you like some coffee?"

"Love it. Ta."

They went along to the kitchen. Vivien poured them a mug each. Lewis enthusiastically spooned brown sugar into his.

"Nice garden out there. I like letting things relax in a garden. I've got a woman like a demon, though, daren't leave her alone five minutes but she's off hauling wildflowers out of the lawn. Butterflies like those. Will she listen? But I'm crazy about her anyway. Need to be. With her family, she's probably nuttier than I am."

Vivien felt an actual pang of envy. For Lewis Blake and his woman with a nutty family. How good that sounded. Some people did manage to have those, and also to meet each other and be happy in a relationship. What was the secret?

She liked him despite her envy. He was *likable*—if only by default.

"Tell me about the statue," Vivien said. She wasn't making conversation; by now she felt she needed to know.

"It's a genuine Nevins. You've never heard of him, probably. A little-known but now somewhat collectible sculptor of the late 1800s. Someone wants this one for a film from the period. That's what we do at Scavengers. We don't pick up antiques to sell. We hire them out to film companies and the theaters. You may have seen bits of our stuff in movies. Ever see *The Lion's Answer?*"

"Yes," said Vivien.

"We practically dressed every set. Statues, fountains, chairs, clocks—the National Theatre had a load of things off us for their last production of *Venice Preserved.*"

"I saw that, too."

Vivien was mildly, pleasantly impressed. Or was that only because Lewis was a nice guy and actually bothering to speak to her like a human being?

"That statue of Connor's, though, that's got a funny history," said Lewis.

"Funny how?"

"Well, more a *rotten* history. Er, I guess it's all right to tell you, you'd find it in any book that listed Nevins. He took up with a married lady, an actress. In fact, she was the wife of the subject of the statue. And—" Lewis broke off.

Vivien saw he had said more than maybe he had

meant to. Why such a dark secret about something over a century old?

She decided to tease him. "The usual tale, then. Infidelity, jealousy, crime and punishment."

She saw he wasn't teased, only on edge.

"While Nevins was sculpting the handsome image of the lady's husband, and making love to the lady, the husband found out. As they do. He was an actor-manager—one of those fantastically successful ones, a bit like Tree, and Martin-Harvey—he had it all in front of him. But he went off his head and shot her—Emily, his wife. And then he shot himself. The quote on the base—Nevins put it there afterwards, before he went and drank himself to death. Nevins, you see, the angry husband never touched. Nevins is supposed to have said he wished Sinclair had done it—punished him, too."

Vivien spoke softly. "You said *Sinclair?*"

"Yup. Forget I'm saying this. I mean, Connor is my boss, he started Scavengers.... But the jealous actor was Patrick Aspen Sinclair, and his wife was Emily Sinclair, famous in her day for her portrayals of Juliet and Ophelia. Some people say the Nevins statue looks like Conn. It does. Conn won't ever see it. But there's a reason for the resemblance. Patrick and Emily died young, he saw to that. But they left children. Patrick Aspen Sinclair was Connor's great-great-grandfather."

Something cold and shadowy had settled in the kitchen.

Into the depths of it the front-door buzzer drilled with the shock of a bullet.

"I'd better go let my boss in," said Lewis. He was his old breezy self again. "Remember, I didn't tell you any of this."

* * *

Vivien's impulse was to vacate the kitchen and find something "urgent she must do elsewhere." There was also, of course, the opposite impulse.

Resist, she thought. Connor Sinclair is the worst kind of man, and he has fallen deeply in dislike of you—which is mutual. Admire his looks if you must. That's all.

A double dose of coffee had cleared her head—perhaps too much. She felt hyped up and a little dizzy.

The other question remained. How had a shattered red rose gotten into the conservatory through a locked and bolted door?

Almost irresistibly, she walked into the conservatory. She stood there looking at the rose. Who could she have asked about *this?* In the day's heat, already the petals and the stalk were withering.

She was standing over the dead rose when Lewis—and Connor—came into the kitchen. She had left flight too late. She must turn now, and confront him.

"I like these tiles, Conn," Lewis was saying—trying, Vivien supposed, to behave as if they were all normal people.

Connor said, "They're all right."

His voice seemed to pull Vivien's eyes towards him, like some kind of science fiction power-beam.

He wore black jeans today and a sky-blue shirt tucked into them. His body, which all his clothes seemed carefully made to describe, filled Vivien with a deep, thrilling, deadly vertigo. She wished she could step out of her body and shake herself.

Somehow, she spoke levelly. "Good morning, Mr. Sinclair."

"Good morning, Ms. Gray." His eyes flicked over

her, and were gone. "Do we have your gracious per-
mission to go into the garden?"

Vivien saw Lewis raise his eyes to heaven.

She refused to be fazed.

"Both doors are unlocked. You know where everything is. I'll leave you to it."

As she left the room, she heard Lewis give a low,
half mocking, half appreciative whistle. "Well, that's
you sorted, Conn."

Connor said nothing.

Reaching the bedroom, Vivien shut her eyes. She
found Connor's face was as clear in her mind as if
some artist, far more clever than she, had painted it on
the inside of her lids. The fiery dark of his eyes, the
straight black bars of his eyebrows, the nose that wasn't
quite straight, the long slim line of his mouth—what
would it be like to kiss that mouth…to taste that
mouth…to—

Vivien growled. *No.* He is *nothing.* And stop skulk-
ing here like some kid with a crush.

She marched out and along to the octagonal room.
She flung open the French doors. She set up her easel
and laid out her sketchpad and brushes. She would not
hide. Life would go on.

She got no further than that.

She saw him suddenly. Connor was striding back up
the path from the garden like the incarnation of a storm.
Straight into the room by the doors she had opened.
His face now was a mask of granite.

"What the *hell* have you been doing?"

Vivien put down the pad.

"What?"

"I said, what have you been doing? No, don't

bother. It is very obvious, *Ms.* Gray, what you've been *trying* to do.''

"I don't know, *Mr.* Sinclair, what you're talking about."

"Don't you?" He glowered at her. She had never, she thought, known before the full meaning of that expression. "Then, you'd better come and see, hadn't you."

"Don't talk to me as if I'm some ignorant child."

"Then, don't act like one."

Lewis appeared behind Connor. "Er, Conn, maybe—"

"Maybe what?" Connor's steely rage was now turned on Lewis, who backed off, holding up placatory hands.

"Er, Ms. Gray, it's like this—"

"*Someone*—" Connor cut through "—and who *ever* could that be? *Someone* has been attempting to remove the statue. Now, perhaps this was a neighbor, clambering over the wall for a merry bit of vandalism. Or maybe it was a little crook called Vivien Gray, who got some mates in to try to lift the statue, now that she knows it might be valuable—"

He stopped in midsentence. Vivien, white as any marble, flared back at him. "I think what you just said could be slanderous. Do you really think, if I were to *do* such a thing, I'd still be hanging around here?"

"Yes. Because you didn't manage the job."

Lewis said, uneasily, "It *has* shifted. But, Conn—"

Vivien ceased to hear either of them. Through the drumming in her ears, the implication of all this—now far beyond any petty accusation—hit home.

The statue had *moved*—

When she darted past both of them and down the

garden, on legs that were made of water, Vivien dimly realized this might well look like proof to him of her guilt. Did it matter? Not if a man formed from marble could move....

She was standing in front of the statue, staring at it, trembling, when Lewis came out to join her.

"Oh boy— Vivien, may I? Vivien, look, I'm really sorry. I mean, there was rain yesterday, and see, the plinth is all over ivy. Things like that can tilt—dry weather, sudden rain—I've said all that to him. But when Connor's in a temper... Nevins cut the figure off the plinth anyway, when he had the lettering cut in," Lewis added. Vivien wished he would be quiet. "Old Patrick's pinned to the base now, and his feet were resculpted—so if the base tilts, well, that could do it—"

Vivien went on staring at the statue, angled there on its plinth, one strong, arched foot—*half off the base*— like that of a man about to step free, step down, walk towards her. As she in turn backs away....

I am packing up and going back to Camden.

Vivien had made her choice. She would call Addie tomorrow, apologize and explain that some fictitious emergency required her to rush elsewhere.

Addie would be miffed. She might make sure Vivien got no further work with Addie's pet publishers. It couldn't be helped.

Vivien hadn't thought she would feel homesick for her closet-size flat. Now she longed to be there.

Of course, she had been foolish about the statue. Once Lewis Blake had shut up and gone, having patted her arm consolingly, she began to see the ordinary truth of what he had said.

Obviously the ground had become waterlogged; the statue had shifted, dislodged one foot. Maybe all this had even happened before. Statues did not, of themselves, move. Or, only in dreams.

Nevertheless, this place was unnerving her, stopping her working. And, too, *he* would be coming back again, for Patrick Aspen Sinclair. Lewis Blake had explained as much, contritely, before he went away. Connor had already gone, it seemed.

Lewis looked very embarrassed. Vivien had tried to be civil. It wasn't Lewis's fault.

Vivien cleaned up in the flat, stripped the bed she had used and put the sheets in the washing machine. She cleaned the bathroom she had used and the kitchen. She didn't want to make more trouble for herself with Addie than was unavoidable.

At about 6:00 p.m., the telephone rang in the hall.

Leave it? It wasn't her problem now.

But the phone kept on. It rang for five minutes, stopped, and immediately began again. Perhaps it *was* Addie?

"Hi, Lewis Blake here. Look, have you got a couple of minutes?"

"No, really, Mr. Blake. Sorry."

"Hang on. Please, Vivien. I've been wrestling with this all afternoon. I didn't know whether to tell you or not. I mean, I *shouldn't*. But then, after the way Connor was with you... Heck, Vivien. I think you've got a right to know why he was such a bastard."

"Just his natural talent, I thought," said Vivien acidly.

"That's not completely fair on him. And yes, he was stinkingly unfair to *you*. I'd better spill the beans."

"I don't want to hear any more of your unpleasant friend's secrets."

"Oh, look—"

"If I thought I could do it, I'd sue him and call you as star witness."

"You're really angry," said Lewis glumly.

"You're *surprised?* Excuse me, I *am* really busy. It was good to meet you, Lewis. Thanks for trying to help. But I'm not interested in his reasons. Goodbye."

As she put the receiver down she heard Lewis say, "Two of a kind."

Who—? She and *Connor?*

That riled her worse.

She hauled the sheets from the machine and beat them into folded submission for the airing cupboard.

Then she took from the cabinet the bottle of Merlot that she had bought herself for the weekend and hadn't opened.

Tearing out the cork, she told herself it was sacrilege to drink this delicious velvety wine as a tranquilizer, but really, right now, nothing else was going to work.

After three or four sips, and one gulp, she put the glass down half-full.

The evening was still brilliant. A drop of westering sunlight somehow evaded the surrounding houses and burned like a ruby in her glass. Red for passion. For a broken rose—and a man mad with jealousy, who shed the blood of his wife, and next his own, and left her lover alive to bear the red, shameful guilt of it.

Now, too late, she asked herself just what Lewis had been going to tell her about Connor Sinclair. Should she have heard him out? The secret of the statue was dire enough. What other event was worse—so bad Lewis had had to "wrestle" with it—all afternoon?

She had found the card of a cab firm under Addie's phone. An odd name, Cwick Cabs. So much for Addie's insistence that she drove herself always.

Vivien had packed her things and was in the first hall waiting for the cab, when the doorbell went. Good, they were early. Vivien opened the front door at once.

And Connor Sinclair was outside, standing there in silence and the last rays of the sun.

Chapter 4

In the rich golden light, his skin, too, seemed made of gold, and with the black hair, the blue of his shirt and the scarlet flowers he carried, he had become almost heraldic. There was a great difference to him. His face was no longer frozen, or angry, but set and grave.

"Before you slam the door in my face," he said, "though you have every right to, may I ask you to allow me to apologize?"

What had she anticipated? Anything but this.

She said nothing. But neither did she slam the door.

"I'm not at my best when I'm freaked out, Vivien Gray, and as you may realize from my behavior, I was very freaked out, both yesterday and today. However, that is no excuse. Please believe me, I don't expect you to forgive me. But I appreciate your allowing me to say I'm sorry for behaving like scum. I brought you these. Maybe you'll just throw them on the floor and tread them into pieces. Why do I think you won't? It's not their faults—the roses—and I suspect you're a very just woman.''

There were two dozen of them, each exactly the scarlet of the roses by the statue. She stared at them. But when he held them out, she took them.

She said, ''There are roses in the garden, Mr. Sinclair.''

''I know. But if you pick any, they don't last. I thought these might brighten up the rooms full of dust sheets and shut boxes, or even that soulless toilet-white Adelaide uses for her kitchen.''

Vivien stood there, holding the roses.

He stood there, looking at her, his eyes searching her face with a slow, waiting stillness.

It was a moment out of time, captured like some glowing seed in the resinous amber of the setting sun.

She said, ''I'll put them in water. Thank you.''

She wanted to be dignified and cold. She couldn't turn either mood on, it seemed, not with this man standing here in front of her, near enough his scent reached her—his warm clean skin and hair, the hint of some masculine cologne, unidentifiable, unique.

Something about him now made Vivien want to cry.

Which was more stupid than anything.

He had behaved, as he said, like scum. A few roses he could obviously well afford, and a glib apology, shouldn't suffice to take away the sting.

But no, the apology hadn't been glib.

Vivien could see something there, lingering behind his eyes, the something that his former discourtesy and knifelike words had cunningly kept concealed.

''Well,'' he said. ''Thanks for accepting the token. I'll leave you in peace.'' He turned and went back towards the road.

Vivien didn't move.

In another instant he had swung round and returned to her. Her heart bolted into breakneck speed.

"Look, I meant to say, I'll send Lewis over with the gang for the statue. Obviously, I'm the last person you'll want to see. Vivien, please believe I am really sorry for the bloody rubbish I said to you."

"You're afraid that I *will* sue."

He smiled, seeming glad she had come back at him with her own touch of wryness.

"Feel free. I won't contest the case. What damages would you settle for?"

Everything was happening too fast. As well as the pain and dark behind his eyes there was now the appearance of this playfulness, an elegant and winning charm—which after a second he shut away again, as if to play like that now was to insult her further.

How could someone so aware of a woman's feelings ever have been so obtuse?

To *conceal*. To *hide*. To disguise the shadow behind his eyes.

"The roses are fine," Vivien said. "I'll settle for the roses."

"You are, as I said, very just. And far too kind."

Now he didn't move away. Yet in another second he must do so. Then, of course, she would never see him again. He would take care she didn't, sparing her the nasty event.

He said, "Look, Vivien, can you allow me five minutes more of your time?"

It was almost precisely what Lewis had said to her on the phone.

Cautious now, Vivien said, "I have a taxi coming any minute."

"Just until it arrives, then. I really don't expect you to invite me in. We can talk out here."

It seemed to Vivien that Connor, like Lewis, wanted to tell her the truth that lay beneath Connor's actions. Did she want to know? Would she be a fool not to accept the chance of finding out? Some mystery, crouching and sinister, hung, both across the flat Addie had so insensitively inhabited, and on the man who, with such unusual humbleness, now offered himself up for her judgment or her censure.

"I need to put the flowers in water," Vivien said. "Why don't you come in?"

He glanced at her bags in the hall, but made no comment. The flat by now was shadowy, until Vivien switched on some side lights.

She knew she wouldn't be leaving until Connor had told her whatever it was he meant to say.

In the kitchen, he stood against one of the despised white walls, watching Vivien as she put his flowers into a vase.

She had never felt, she thought, so self-conscious doing anything. When one of the roses dropped onto the floor, Connor, like an Elizabethan courtier, picked it up and gave it back to her.

Oddly, their hands did not touch. They hadn't ever touched, even by accident, even outside, when first he offered her the flowers.

It seemed, she thought, that he was trying *not* to make physical contact with her. But was she doing the same with him?

All this time, ever since coming into the flat, they had said little to each other, just a trivial word or two.

Their double silence lay in darkening swaths across the kitchen.

When Vivien went back into the octagonal room, he walked behind her.

There was something both disturbing and exciting about this that Vivien refused to acknowledge.

When she had put down the vase, the spray of roses vivid as fire, she saw, too, the opened bottle of Merlot, still almost full, which she had carelessly forgotten.

Connor sat down only when she suggested he do so.

These rooms had been his. He knew them, but was uneasy here. So much was now evident. Why? And why had he sold the apartment to Addie? Gone away and left behind the "collectible" statue of Patrick Aspen Sinclair?

"Do you drink wine?" Vivien asked.

"Sometimes."

"May I offer you a glass of this?"

How formal she sounded—how formal and constrained both of them were now. It had been easier to communicate in rage.

They sat facing each other across Addie's Persian carpet, drinking wine in the lamplight, as the sky beyond the French doors faded and the garden changed from bronze to ebony.

"I like the wine, Vivien— You don't mind my calling you by your first name?"

"Just not *Viv,* Mr. Sinclair."

"No. *Vivien,* always. Try Connor, would you?"

Vivien smiled. She spoke his name obediently, and felt a flush, seeming as vivid as the roses, flare in her cheeks. She ignored it. She said, primly, "Then, what was it you wanted to say to me…Connor?"

"I think Lewis told you about my ancestor, Patrick,

the guy the statue was modeled on? Am I right? You won't be breaking Lewis's confidences, he's a gossip and I know it. I concentrate on his good qualities.''

"He did say something."

"Did he tell you what happened with the sculptor, Nevins?"

"Yes."

"He told you about Emily, and—" Connor paused. He drained his glass of wine, then began to turn the empty vessel in his hand. "Patrick shot her and himself. And left Nevins alive. An interesting move. Not what Othello meant to do."

"I really do know the play."

"Of course you do. So do I. I've acted in it—oh, not Othello himself. A black actor took that part. I had the pleasure of acting the lying villain Iago. It's strange, isn't it, that Nevins had the Othello quote cut in the statue's base. Ironic. He died in 1906 in Paris, from alcohol and laudanum. A waste, like Patrick and Emily."

Another long silence came.

Vivien thought, *The story is horrible, and sad, but how can it be only this that haunts him?*

"Look, Vivien, I can't go into details. Something— Something bad happened to me when I lived here. Something bad, so bad—to me, and to someone else— I got out and sold the flat to Adelaide. I thought that her flawlessly unimaginative and stomping life would exorcise the place. Maybe it has. And maybe not. But I was dreading coming back here. And the statue…I don't know if objects carry a stigma, but for my money that one does. The moment I got the interest from the movie people I knew it was too good a chance to pass up. And a real bonus to get rid of the thing while I was at it. I *inherited* that statue, Vivien. About all I did inherit. But that's yet another story.''

"Why did you come here at all, if you dreaded to? Wouldn't Lewis—"

"Yes, of course. But the dreams started again. I just thought, I have to do this, face it, finish with it, now and forever. I even armed myself with dear batty Cinnamon. I thought she would certainly quash any lingering darkness here. And then, you opened the door.''

Vivien blinked.

Connor looked down into the empty glass. "A girl in a cloud of hair, like a Waterhouse nymph in a bathrobe.''

What could Vivien say to that? Waterhouse was the pre-Raphaelite painter famous for his depictions of water nymphs and mermaids, so Connor was flattering her. Also he was telling her so much—yet telling her, really, nothing....

"I'm sorry I upset you," she said quietly.

"I had no right to be upset by anything as graceful, lovely or wonderful as you, Vivien. But that was the trouble, I'm afraid. The unforgivable bloody trouble.''

Vivien got up. She carried the bottle to him and refilled his glass. He sat there looking at it.

"It's all right, Connor. Thank you for explaining. It doesn't matter. I promise—" again she smiled "—I really won't sue.''

She didn't expect it—but then she hadn't been able to expect anything he had done tonight. He stood up in front of her, tall and symmetrically strong, a burning barrier between her and the light. Against the lamp, she couldn't see his face, but she felt his hands come weightlessly to rest on her upper arms.

Though weightless, the heat of his touch carried a

charge of the fiercest electricity. She was relieved she had put down the wine bottle, or she might have dropped it. She was glad they hadn't touched before.

After all, she *could* see him. He was the only thing she could see in the room....

Vivien gazed upward into his face, which hovered over hers, so close now, she felt his warm breath on her lips.

Then he straightened abruptly away from her.

"No," he said. The coldness in his voice she had heard before.

Vivien recoiled.

"Wait—" he said. He had let her go. He spoke softly. "I'm sorry, yet once more. You don't want this. Not from me."

But she thought, Oh, Connor, I do. I *do*....

An appalling alien noise exploded through the room. It was the doorbell.

"Your taxi," he said.

"Yes..."

"Shall I— I'll tell him to wait a minute."

Vivien said lamely, "It's all right. I'll do it."

She walked out of the room and down the hall, and opened the front door. The man outside presented an unfriendly face, apparently annoyed she hadn't heard him sounding the car horn on the street, so he had had to walk a few feet to the house. He seemed very scruffy and had black sunglasses of incongruous fashionableness.

"I'm sorry," she said. So many apologies tonight. "I won't be needing your cab."

"Is that right?" He appeared actually menacing.

It seemed prudent to add, "My friend just arrived."

As if to assist, from the eight-sided room came the quiet *clink* of glassware.

She felt the glare through the shades. "Well, thanks a bunch, lady. You people— Next time call and cancel, all right?"

She gave him a couple of pounds, guilty to have misled him. Ungraciously he pocketed the coins and went off.

Vivien hesitated in the hall. What was she doing? Did she, after all, mean to stay in this place—the place where something so "bad" had happened?

Yes.

Connor was standing now by the French windows, looking out into the black garden. The second glass of wine, undrunk, sat on a table.

Again, time stopped.

Then he turned and looked at her. Turned and looked *through* her.

With a courtesy that scalded her now more than his abrasiveness had before, Connor Sinclair said, "You've been fantastic, Vivien. Thank you for so generously letting me off. I won't forget it. Take care of yourself. I hope everything goes well for you, always."

He walked past her. He walked out into the hall. She heard the front door open. Close. He was gone.

Sternly she held herself motionless, seeing before her the gaping abyss of her empty life, void of him, the life where he had wished her well for always.

Chapter 5

Exhaustion, physical and mental, sent Vivien to sleep almost the moment she lay down in bed. She hadn't thought it could.

Somewhere, though, in the dark of night and slumber, she dreamed she heard a series of soft noises, passing up and down the apartment, now in the eight-sided room, now along a corridor—footsteps, a faint *thud*, like a cat jumping from a windowsill....

Even in her dream, Vivien took charge of herself. *Don't be stupid.* There's nothing there. All places make sounds, especially after a hot day when the night air is cooler. This time I'm *not* going out to see.

She woke near dawn and recalled the dream. She thought with great clarity, If I'm going to stay on, I need to pull myself together. Statues don't move—it was rain or soil subsiding. As for the rose in the conservatory, Addie hasn't looked after the frame, just as she's left the garden to riot. There's probably some tiny hole and something got in, some little animal (curious image of a mouse carrying a rose...). All my problems here, *all* of them, are to do with an overactive imagination.

The alarm clock woke her at seven-thirty.

She didn't feel refreshed by her long sleep, but leaden. Even the shower didn't help. Deciding on strong leaf tea in preference to coffee, she traipsed along to the kitchen with—despite her resolve—a slight feeling of apprehension.

But nothing was wrong. And out in the conservatory the rose had withered away.

She drank the whole pot, staring at nothing, tasting nothing.

She thought, *Be glad he turned out to be a decent guy, Vivien. He tried to behave well. That's got to be better, even if—*

But, she thought, he had wanted to kiss her. He *meant* to kiss her—the very air of the room had been alight with his wanting that. Or was it only *her* wanting it that she had felt?

The last rejection, three years ago, had been far more simple. Her lover had used her—no other term was possible—once only, and discarded her after like a broken pencil. Her bewildered, tactful attempt to discover what she had done to offend him had met with, "Oh, come on, Vivien. Can't we have a bit of fun without it turning into grand opera?"

She couldn't imagine Connor Sinclair, even at his worst, behaving in such a way. She had sensed about him last night a quality more appealing even than his awareness, or his charm—a kind of loyalty. Yes, he could lash out with words, but he was ultimately honorable.

Then again, what did she know about him?

Next to nothing. And now, she never would.

Too sluggish for work yet, Vivien decided to clean the flat properly. This was something else Addie never bothered with. She periodically hired girls to clean and then sacked them, or had them walk out in disgust at Addie's manner.

Housework, though, could take your mind off other things.

Vivien located a few dust cloths and took the deluxe Hoover from its cupboard. Then she walked into the eight-sided room.

''What—'' Vivien stalled.

She stared. The fine hairs rose on the back of her neck, and something icy trickled down her spine—

She had left the remainder of the wine in its bottle, uncorked. By it on the table, Connor had placed his undrunk second glass, and she her undrunk half glass.

Vivien knew this, had no doubts.

The bottle was empty and lay on its side on the carpet. Both glasses were empty also.

But this wasn't the worst. Oh, no.

Every single long-stemmed rose had been removed from the vase, the heads cut off, and stalks and petals scattered over the carpet and the wooden floor beyond.

Last night she hadn't drawn the drapes at the French windows, and now the garden lay outside, ripe and sun-lit—*innocent*.

Vivien backed out of the room. Outside, she walked quite briskly down the hall to the telephone. And so passed the dining room on the right.

It was a somber room, done in maroon, and not huge in size. Even so, Addie kept in there, along with an

oak table and chairs, her only bookcase. None of these
things had yet been packed or sheeted over.

Vivien saw the book at once, lying where it hadn't
been yesterday, facedown on the table.

It had obviously been pulled out of the case—or had
itself sprung across the room.

Vivien, feeling as though she had stopped breathing
and never would breathe again, walked to the table and
turned the book right side up.

She knew which page it would be open at.

How convenient for it—whatever *it* was—that Addie, who seldom read anything longer than five hundred words, kept the regulation show-off classics.
There in the bookcase, a set of Jane Austen in leather
and gilt, a purple-backed Milton and Shelley, and four
volumes of Shakespeare in white cloth: Comedies, His-
tories, Sonnets—and Tragedies.

It was the Tragedies on the table, naturally.

Unable to resist, Vivien found herself reading the
words on the page.

Oth: ...A fine woman! a fair woman! a sweet
woman!
Iago: Nay, you must forget that.
Oth: Ay, let her rot, and perish, and be damned
to-night; For she shall not live; no, my heart is
turned to stone; I strike it, and it hurts my hand...

Vivien snapped the book shut. Somehow then she
dropped it. Maybe not surprisingly—her hands weren't
quite steady.

It landed back on the table, open again. This time at
the title page. An old photograph had been reproduced
as a frontispiece. Vivien stared at it. A woman in a

long pale robe, tightly belted at her narrow waist, her very dark hair unbound and springing, her large eyes gazing… The credit read: ''The actress Emily Sinclair, in one of her most famous roles: Ophelia.''

Someone had written on the title page—slapdash, in bold yet feminine handwriting: *To C with love from K. I bet you wish you could meet this gorgeous great-gran of yours! If you do, I guess I'd better leave!*

K, then, was someone in Connor's life, or had been. For C was definitely Connor Sinclair, since this was the picture of his great-great-grandmother, Emily—the faithless wife Patrick Sinclair had shot.

Connor's book, then. Left behind. Like the statue. Like K?

Unwillingly, so unwillingly, Vivien's eyes strayed back to the photograph. In her head she could hear a voice telling her, facing up to what Vivien herself didn't want to face. For Emily Sinclair very, very closely resembled Vivien Gray.

No one else had called the flat after Lewis Blake had done so the previous evening. Vivien, as she pressed the required 1471 to see if his number had been registered, noted her hands were trembling. But the first hurdle was quickly passed. Lewis hadn't thought to withhold his number.

Vivien stabbed at the buttons again.

After eight rings, a girl's voice, very young, announced, ''Hi, this is Scavengers. Can I help?''

Vivien asked for Lewis.

''Sorry, he's out. Do you want to leave a message?''

Vivien faltered. All this while, standing here, she kept looking over her shoulder at the quiet sun-and-shadow hall.

"No. It's all right, thank you."

What a liar she was. It was far from all right.

Anyway, what would she have said to Lewis? *Listen, I know you're a gossip, your friend and business associate Connor told me so. So tell me what you wanted to before. Now I really need to know.*

Something made a sound in the eight-sided room.

Vivien jumped.

After a moment, she pushed herself forward. Reaching the room, she stood in the doorway, staring around wide-eyed. But nothing seemed altered. The wine bottle and roses were still lying on the floor.

No, after all, she wouldn't stay here. Whatever was going on was unbelievable, and deeply threatening. Vivien felt she had had enough.

Her bags were still mostly packed. She shoved back in whatever she had taken out last night. She had to fight with the folding easel. *It* didn't want to go.

Thinking of Addie still, however, Vivien made herself do certain things. She replaced the Shakespeare in the bookcase. She cleared up the roses and the bottle, washed the glasses and dried them and put them away in the drinks cabinet of the octagonal room.

Everything she did was punctuated by turning constantly, to look over one shoulder or the other. Nothing happened. It was *lulling* her.

Outside the windows the summer had opened its generous wings. Birds sang in the private garden and from the public park; traffic murmured. All this informed Vivien she was being silly, had made a mistake.

She couldn't call last night's cab firm. Going on how the driver had reacted, they would refuse to send anyone. Two she found in the phone book said they had no cars to spare.

So, after she had checked every bolt and lock, Vivien let herself out of Addie's flat and trudged with bags and easel towards the nearest tube station. Rather ironically, as she was leaving the square, she thought she actually saw the sunglassed driver from Cwick Cabs shoot past her in an unmarked car. If the recognition was mutual, he paid her no attention—she was now beneath his notice.

The tube was crowded and subject to delays. Altogether it took almost two hours to get back to her flat off the West Camden Road.

Her phone was ringing as she staggered in. She had a wild idea Lewis had found her number in the directory and called her back.

"Yes— Hello…"

"Good morning, and wow! You sound *so* together and collected," said Ellie. "Whatever are you at, Vivien Gray?"

"Oh, Ellie—"

"Hey." Concern sharpened the sparkling tones. "Take it slowly. You've really been on my mind. Did I sense something? What's going down there?"

Vivien seated herself on the floor, her back to the wall, and told Ellie everything, over the blessed miracle of the transatlantic line.

Vivien had eaten lunch and drunk most of a two-liter bottle of water. She sat in the afternoon light, looking out of the window of her hot little front room, away through the traffic fumes, over roofs and between church steeples, to the fashionable end of Camden that lay opposite to her own.

Talking to an Ellie 8:00 a.m. fresh on a New York morning had calmed Vivien and cheered her. But Ellie invariably had this effect. Working as she did in quite a high-powered bookshop in downtown Manhattan, Ellie's philosophy was deceptively straightforward. On her office wall was pinned a large black square with large pink lettering that read *Carpe diem*—its unflinching advice slightly offset by the cartoon of someone struggling with a fish, and the yellow print beneath which said, *Seize the carp*.

But Elliot Leiber *did* seize the day, every day. She had a gift for it.

"Listen, Vivien," she had said over the phone. "First of all, what happened back there—I bet it has some ordinary explanation. Things like that—ghosts— maybe they do exist, but they're never going to hurt you. That's for books and movies. So even if there is a ghost, it just likes a drop of booze, gets high and spills the roses. Hey, it's spent all its time in the backyard—what do you expect? House-trained?"

"It bit the flowers' heads off, Ellie."

"How d'you know? Maybe they just broke when they hit the floor. It didn't break the vase, did it? Or the glasses and bottle? As for the photo of Emily— you're pretty het up, girl. Maybe the likeness is less strong? Though, if you're right, that could help explain why this guy turned into a monster when he saw you. You must have scared him half to death. Which brings me to *this guy*."

Vivien said, "Well, there's not much I can do now."

"Oh, you English. Say, Vivien, take off the crinoline. From what you told me the man is drooling over you. Okay, he didn't have the cheek to just kiss you, but honey, that means he has the guts to realize he acted like a louse before. So he rode off into the sunset.

But you've got the number of his outfit now. Why don't you call him?''

"I *can't,* Ellie.''

"Chicken.''

"Ellie, he is in some awful trouble—''

"Then, give him some help, why don't you. Yes, it's a risk. He may turn on some more of his freeze-out repartee. But you have to take the risk now and then, because if you never jump those high fences, for all the times you jump them and land in the garbage, you are going to miss that one special time you land on the feather bed. And just think who might be sharing that feather bed with you!''

"I just don't think—''

"Sure. You don't. Call him.''

"What do I say?''

"Oh my lord— Say, 'Hi, Connor, are you free for a coffee, a drink, a kiss?' ''

"He will say no. To all three.''

"Right, it stinks. But what have you lost? Your dignity? Suppose he says *yes?*''

Vivien diverted the conversation after that. Ellie let her. They talked about other subjects for a laughing, dollar-eating half hour before Ellie had to hang up and go to work.

Sitting in her own front room, Vivien knew she wasn't going to call Connor Sinclair. She didn't have the courage.

On the other hand, she *was* going to call Lewis.

It was true, the…ghost hadn't hurt her. If it was Patrick Aspen Sinclair…trapped in a marble statue…

Even Addie, surely, would have noticed things like the roses, the wine. Presumably such things never *had* happened when she was there. She had exorcised the place, just as Connor had said.

But Vivien was different. Even if she wasn't Emily's twin, she *was* over-aware, and carried her own baggage of sorrow, frustration, rage. And Connor also had come back, driven by this second secret he hadn't disclosed.

What had gone on in that apartment? What had happened bad enough to change him from a man so easily to be desired, to be *loved,* into a block of ice and poison?

The voice on the phone was known, but it wasn't exactly a joyous reunion.

"This is Cinnamon Boyle-Martin at Scavengers. How can I help?"

"I'd like to speak to Lewis Blake, please."

"Who is *that?* Wait—I know. It's Ms. *Whoever,* isn't it? Hi, Ms. Whoever. What do you want Lew for?"

"I'll tell him when I speak to him," said Vivien, trying to find the balance between politeness and authority.

Cinnamon of course was immune to both.

"Lew is very busy. Maybe you can bring yourself to give me the teeniest itty-bitty bit of an idea."

"Thank you. But that will only waste your time. Lew is the one I'd like to speak to."

"What if I say you can't?" Cinnamon sounded now like a bullying child.

"I would think Lewis might wonder why you were blocking a perfectly legitimate call."

"Or not. You do know Lewis is happily married, *don't* you, Ms. Whoever?"

Anger scorched through Vivien's veins. She tried to stay calm. "I beg your pardon?"

"Beg away. Just thought you ought to know before you got in over your head. I suppose I could push the errand boy your way—bit young for you, but beggars can't be—"

Vivien put the receiver down. The nasty little—

Stay cool. Try again later. Cinnamon isn't always going to be there. There was that girl who answered last time. Or even Lewis might answer. She hadn't tried to locate his home number, it hadn't seemed appropriate.

Anyway, Ellie, so much for your notion of calling *Connor*. I can just imagine how Cinnamon would deal with that.

Vivien tried Scavengers again at 4:00 p.m. Cinnamon answered brightly—gleefully?

Vivien broke the connection without speaking.

She wondered why she and Cinnamon had taken such an instant dislike to each other—aside from Cinnamon's general rudeness. Karma?

Vivien thrust all this from her mind, at least for now. She hadn't bothered to unpack anything but the essentials. She must try to work.

At six o'clock she broke for some tea, and drank it, nerving herself now to ring Addie at the number near Perpignan. As she stretched out her hand, the phone rang.

Was it Addie, by some strange coincidence? Bracing herself, Vivien lifted the receiver.

"Is that Vivien Gray?"

"Connor…"

"It *is* Vivien Gray. Do you know you are part of quite a sisterhood of Grays in the London directory?

Luckily Adelaide spelled your name for me, and only two of you spell Gray with an *A*. The other lady accused me of trying to sell her double glazing.''

Vivien sat down slowly. She held the receiver as if it were something very fragile, and priceless.

''Are you still there, Vivien? Have I called at a bad time?''

He was so straightforward. Joking—playful again. It was just as if he were a friend, one of long-standing, known and welcome.

''Yes, I'm still here. No, it isn't a bad time.''

He sighed.

She wondered, astounded, if he, like she, had been holding a breath.

''Look, Vivien. I have to ask a favor of you.''

''Yes?''

''I obviously realize you've left Adelaide's flat—I saw you'd packed to go last night. The trouble is, Lewis or I, and the team, need to get in to shift Patrick out. I could get some spare keys off Adelaide possibly, but knowing her, that might take a while. I'd rather have everything wrapped up as soon as I can. Could I ask you to let me borrow the keys she gave you? I'll let you have them back the minute we're through.''

''Yes,'' said Vivien softly, ''that's all right. When— When do you want to collect them?''

''Tonight? It'll be me. I hope that's okay?''

A kind of fiery-cold heat enveloped Vivien.

''Why not,'' she said. ''That's fine.''

''Thanks, Vivien. I appreciate this.''

After she put the phone down, Vivien said to herself, He'll come to the door and take the keys and go. Tomorrow he'll return them. Maybe, that time, not even him. Someone else.

But still, for a few moments, he would, tonight, be there.

Don't love him, she thought. Gray, you are not to fall in love with Connor Sinclair.

Her own thoughts answered with stony calm: *You loved him before you even met him. You loved him the moment you saw the statue.*

She had showered again, and put on a linen skirt and loose green top. She looked at herself in the ornate mirror. Yes, you look nice, yes, just casual enough, as if you hadn't changed just because he was coming here. And all this for two minutes on the doorstep.

By seven, Vivien had become almost unbearably nervous.

The doorbell went.

She felt her heart contract and expand as if it meant to explode.

"Hello, Vivien."

The instant she saw him, any ordinary nervousness was washed away by a tide, like that of the most buoyant and warmest sea. All thought drained from her head. Elated, frightened, she gazed up at him and heard herself say, reasonably, as if she were still entirely sane, "Hello."

A white shirt now, and not jeans but narrow dark trousers, with, surprisingly, tough-looking boots that seemed as if they could withstand a trek over some rocky Welsh mountain. The odd combination was somehow exactly right.

And, as before, he came armed with a gift. It was a bottle of Merlot, and she could tell from one glance at it, as he held it out to her, that it had cost rather more than her own.

"Really, there wasn't any need—"

"It's that sort of evening, Vivien. An evening for red wine."

Her hall was so narrow and brief that she didn't make the mistake of standing aside to let him by, but walked ahead into her kitchen.

"Here are the keys."

"Great. I'll let you have them back by next Monday at the latest. Meanwhile, perhaps you have a corkscrew for this bottle? It's at the perfect temperature, just needs to take a breath or two."

It's not alone in that, she thought, remembering to inhale.

Vivien opened a drawer and handed him the corkscrew. She took two wineglasses, unmatched—she had none that *did* match—one green, one blue, rinsed and dried them.

The wine stood on the windowsill, glowing against the deepening gilt of the sky.

"How are you?" he said, smilingly formal.

"Very well. And you?"

"Ravenously hungry and longing to walk somewhere. I've been stuck up a ladder, or crouched over nearly double all afternoon, removing unbelievably old and crumbling plasterwork. Lewis, who was up the other ladder, sends you his best, by the way."

He handed her the green glass, black with red wine.

It was perfect, the wine. But she didn't really taste the sips she took.

"This is wonderful. Thank you."

"'*A votre santé, mademoiselle.*'"

He had told her he was hungry, and wanted to walk. He wouldn't be staying long. Already he had pocketed Addie's keys.

"There *is* a third thing I *would* like," he added, "apart from dinner and exercise. I would truly value your company during both. I know it's short notice, but is there any chance?"

Confident; arrogant, just slightly. How many women would have said no to such an invitation from him, however short the notice? She should refuse. She was already in far too deep.

"I'd like to."

His smile broadened. It became a grin, startling as it undid the handsome sculpted face and made it irresistibly human.

While she went to get a handbag, Connor took his glass of wine through into her front room, with a relaxed "May I?"

When Vivien rejoined him, he was studying her two paintings up on the wall.

"Are these yours?"

"Oh. Yes."

"They're extremely good. Better than that."

"Thank you. They finished up how I wanted them to come out. That often doesn't happen."

"Delicate," he said, "yet strong. Mysterious. An unusual combination." He looked at her steadily.

His eyes made it plain that he didn't refer only to her painting style as he added, "I think I shouldn't be amazed at that."

Chapter 6

Having asked her if she minded walking, which she didn't, they duly walked through the lively, sun-setting city streets for twenty minutes, to a small restaurant he apparently knew.

By the time they were seated and choosing their food, Vivien found he and she were talking to each other as if they had known each other much longer and, perhaps, done this several times before. He seemed to know what she liked, for example, when he recommended to her from the list of starters an avocado dish she was already deciding on.

The restaurant was pleasantly lit and not hot, and only about half-full. As the sun went and evening settled in the open windows, a waiter came to light the rosy candles on the tables.

Connor told her then some of his history. Of an acting career he had mostly now jettisoned in favor of the work of Scavengers. A little about his gambling father, who had destroyed any joint family capital and then walked out on Connor's mother. Connor spoke of this briefly. He added no flavors either of anger or bitterness. Despite the controlled editing, Vivien's heart ached for him and the child he had been.

In turn Vivien displayed something of her rather uneventful if precarious life—her "unworldliness"—secondary school to art school, to a series of makeshift jobs, then the breakthrough into book-jackets and occasional exhibitions at modest venues. She told him, too, quickly, of her disapproving parents—her gruff father and chilly mother. She seldom saw them now, and spoke to them less often. Of Ellie Leiber, Vivien spoke at much more length, with warmth and a nostalgia Connor readily seemed to acknowledge.

"You can't choose your family, but you can make a new one with your friends," he said.

Neither of them spoke of former lovers.

She had little enough to say on that score. But with Connor, she sensed a shadow—darker by far than his fecklessly gambling father—that hung across Connor's emotional past.

Was that shadow, then, the mysterious K? Surely not. Her note to Connor in the volume of Shakespeare tragedies had been contrastingly humorous and light. K had sounded—*OK*. So, where was she now?

But that was silly, too. People part, not always in horrible ways.

When Connor and Vivien didn't select a dessert, the waiter brought them a dish of fresh fruit, nuts and cheese, and two tiny liqueurs, in vessels like metal thimbles. "On the house, Mr. Sinclair. With Milo's compliments."

Later Milo, the restaurant's owner, appeared with the

coffee, to exchange a few words with Connor, and to bow to Vivien, as if they had all traveled back in time and geography to the Italy of the 1700s.

"The restaurant got a credit on a film we worked for," Connor remarked later on. "Milo said it increased business, and never stops thanking me. It wasn't anything, but he's one of the good guys."

After the meal, they walked again, more slowly, through still darkening evening streets beginning to blush with neon and street-lighting.

"Light pollution," said Connor scathingly.

"I wish just sometimes I could see the stars," Vivien agreed.

"There are places tucked away in London where you can. For example, there's a public garden not ten minutes from here round the side of St George's Church. The lamps along the paths are low-key. If the sky's clear, which it is, the stars are to be seen."

They walked to the park.

Vivien still did not know if this was a "date." Surely it was—yet she could not be sure. And she remained uneasy, even beneath her enjoyment of this time spent with Connor. It was a truly weird combination; never ever before had she felt, also, so strangely comfortable in the company of any man.

Be careful! said her mind. *Yes, Mother.*

The church stood up, dimly lit and pale among its pillars, and the garden opened beyond, behind wrought-iron gates. A few people roamed the paths or sat on benches, singly or in pairs. There was no noise, no disturbance. A peaceful spot, cool with summer night and scented by the foliage of tall trees.

A path wound up a slope. Connor took her hand and

led her, telling her where tree roots, barely to be seen, broke the paving.

The clasp of his hand electrified her. She could hardly bear it, but worse would be the moment when he let her go....

Up among the trees, they stood now on a little hill. Above, the vast sky opened like the dome within some great cathedral, indigo velvet, sewn with a thousand stars.

They stood gazing upwards.

As if he had forgotten to, Connor had not relinquished Vivien's hand.

Neither of them spoke.

She thought, childishly, foolishly, Let this moment go on and on....

"Vivien..."

How dreamlike—yet familiar—the touch of his hands, firmly, gently, turning her towards him. After the heaven of stars, where else could her eyes travel but to his face?

For one second only, the hint of reticence, of a question in his gaze. Gone. Presumably, she had answered it.

He leaned towards her, and the rough silk mane of his hair fell over her cheeks, her neck and shoulders. It closed them in a night-dark tent. Then his left hand curved to support the back of her neck, and through her own hair she felt the heat of it on her skin. She saw, to the last instant, his eyes watching her, intent, certain of her now, and kingly, cruel with the impetus of desire.

His mouth was on hers. Her lips parted. His tongue, cool yet burning, tasting of wine and fruit, of night and leaves—of *him*—the essential maleness and power of him...

Vivien felt herself spinning off into the sky itself. Only the irresistible anchoring hand on her neck, the vital protecting arm encircling her, held her safe in a vortex where she rushed, all gravity disposed of.

Her hands slid on his back. Beneath the smoothness of his shirt, smooth muscles, strong enough to control all this, to hold her through the dashing whirlwind of need.

Crushed together, flying through space and constellations, she wanted nothing else.

One kiss ended, resumed, became another. When the second kiss ended, he lifted his head again and looked at her. In his face she saw, by that bright starlight, her own deep hunger mirrored. Never in her life had she wanted any man as she wanted this one. No, not even that one time in the past. She raised herself on tiptoe, drawing herself upwards against him, until every muscle of his chest beneath the shirt pressed into her, and she felt his body against her breasts as if both of them were naked. His response was immediate. His mouth returned to hers. The third kiss lasted far longer.

When again he drew back, however, quietly and in gradual stages, he let her go.

His eyes were blacker now than any night.

"Vivien," he said. That was all.

"Connor," she answered.

They stood looking at each other, connected by some pulsing chain of invisible yet nearly tactile force.

"What now?" he said. He smiled. "In fact, I'm sorry, Vivien, I have to meet Lewis in about an hour, back at the plaster ladders."

These words made no sense to Vivien at all. She nodded mutely.

"There's a private premier tomorrow—an art house–type film Scavengers worked on. Quite a decent film, apparently, if it can find the right distributor. Historical—French and English, with supernatural elements. Would that appeal to you?"

"I—"

"Because if it would, I've got the regulation complimentary tickets. Could be interesting—these private film events sometimes are. And sometimes the movies end up winning at Cannes."

Vivien's heart bounded along as if already en route to the show.

"Yes, I'd really like to see the film."

"Some of the rest of the team are going. Lewis and Angela. His wife. I mention this to reassure you you'll be protected from my lust."

"That's a relief," she said.

"Yes, isn't it, Vivien Gray? But once we're out of the theater, I don't promise anything. Perhaps if you run away the moment we're out the door, I might not catch you. But yes, I think I *would* still catch you."

"And I would always," she murmured, "run very slowly."

He put his hands, lightly now, on her shoulders. He bent to kiss her with a closed, decorous, yet possessive kiss. "I'll find you a taxi."

In the dream, she lay on the bed of rose-colored satin. There were drapes of thinnest gauze that floated round her, drifting in some unseen breeze.

Material and breeze, too, played on her naked body, arousing her in a remote and curious way.

Soon, he would be with her.

His hands would travel her body, forming her—*inventing* her—like the hands of a sculptor working upon her human clay.

She would be anything he wished.

There was no choice. None.

Vivien heard a footstep. She opened her eyes once more. The light shone dimly amber from secret candles or lamps. Through the light, a shadow came. A white shadow.

"No—"

Her body was stone, would not move...or barely.

As she rolled her head in fear, Vivien saw, cast dark as night on the floating curtains and the wall, the shadow-shape of two beings embracing. He—and she.

It seemed already he took her—already she consented.

But maybe it was not love he brought, but retribution—and for a crime of which she was innocent.

I am *not* Emily—

A hand brushed her ribs, her stomach. A fluttering deliciousness...

How dim the light. She could not see anymore, not the shadows, nor whether her lover was formed of flesh—or marble.

She heard his voice.

It was not Connor's voice. And again, she thought what she could not say—*I am not Emily.*

"A fine woman..." said the voice "...a fair woman... a sweet woman..."

Vivien knew she must wake up. And woke.

It was ninety degrees in London. It felt like two hundred.

Connor arrived to collect her in a taxi that evening

at six o'clock. He stood there a moment, looking at her. "You're beautiful," he said, and leaning forward, kissed her lightly on the cheek.

She had chosen her one really "good" dress, a sleeveless, scoop-necked glide of pale gray silk, ending just on the knee, that described her figure closely without clinging to it. Her shoes were pale green, high-heeled sandals she had bought in New York, at Ellie's insistence: "When shall I wear *these?*" "When you are being Vivien," Ellie had enigmatically replied. Vivien also wore the long drop earrings of clear, lime-green glass, found in the market at Camden Lock.

Gradually she realized Connor, too, was wearing a gray silk shirt—of a gray so dark it was almost black. His clothes tonight looked tailored, though remained immaculately casual.

In the taxi they talked decorously about the film that was going to be shown.

"*Age of Aries*—it's set in the Napoleonic period, when France was at war with two-thirds of the world. Other sections run parallel in England. The link is a werewolf theme. Lewis and I glimpsed the actor once in full fur—quite impressive even by day, and even though he was having to eat his lunch through a straw to save his prosthetic snout."

The theater, a private one, lay among the net of roads behind Wardour Street, and the taxi pulled up short at the entry to the cobbled roadway.

An imposing man in full dress-uniform of the Napoleonic era welcomed them in through the door, saluting Connor, bending to Vivien's hand.

Laughing, they went up a narrow stair and into the hospitality suite.

Vivien, startled, stopped in the doorway.

The long room lay under a carpet of scarlet petals, and for a second an image of broken roses chilled her. Then she heard Connor say, "Geranium petals. That would be, I imagine, because the Empress Joséphine introduced geraniums to France…"

Vivien looked at him. "You're very clever."

"I am now." Connor pointed at a suitably curlicued notice on the wall, from which he had read the information about geraniums.

All around were similar snippets of knowledge, and prints dating from the early 1800s, depicting sieges, battles and naval engagements, full of fatly puffing, creamed-potato clouds of cannon smoke.

A glittering chandelier blazed overhead, adding to the heat, while on a central table rose a champagne fountain of crystal glasses waiting to be filled by streams of wine.

"It says, the shape of the champagne glass is modeled on one of Marie Antoinette's flawless breasts," said another voice.

Lewis stood there, beaming, in velvet trousers and a white ruffled shirt, somewhat incongruous with his eyebrow ring and shaven crown.

"We just don't know which one," added a redhaired woman at Lewis's side. She was thin and elegant, and wore a white cotton suit. "Hi, I'm Angie. You must be Vivien." Vivien greeted her. Lewis's wife held out a manicured hand.

Something about Angela made Vivien slightly uneasy. Vivien wasn't sure quite what. Perhaps her harshness with lawns, as reported by Lewis?

As the conversation went on, Angela seemed self-assured and friendly, and yet it was almost as if she had honed her social skills as part of some needful defence—even *attack.* Her eyes met everyone's openly, but otherwise they often scanned the room, as if looking for someone. Perhaps she was.

They took wine from a tray, one of several borne about by young women in the semitransparent or décolleté fashions of 1800s Paris and London.

Vivien noticed that Angie thirstily gulped her wine, then reached out at once for another glass.

"I can't drink red," she said to Vivien. "It gives me headaches. But then, white is so much cooler on a night like this."

"It's murder in London," said Lewis. "Ange reckons it's up to a hundred."

A man in a loose Indian shirt and with an eager, nervous look had engaged Connor in talk. A second man, who had on a joke tuxedo whose back was covered in yellow polka dots, kept soothing the first man and handing him glasses of ginger beer.

"That's the bods who made the film. J.D.'s ulcer is clearly playing up, hence the ginger. The hoped-for distributor hasn't turned up yet," croaked Lewis to Vivien in a stage whisper.

"Hush, Lewis," hissed Angela sharply. "He'll hear you."

"Sorry, ma'am." Lewis smiled at Angela. "My missus," he added to Vivien. "She keeps a strict eye on my manners. One of the reasons I love her so."

"Oh, I see, Lewis," said Angie, "*that's* why you love me." For an instant something waspish hung on the air. Then Angela smoothed it with a "Oh good, that stern man who's just swept in with his assistant— The hoped-for distributor has arrived!"

There was a flurry after this, a kind of dance where

everyone kept changing partners—Vivien lost Connor in the crowd, while waiters were arranging champagne bottles. A man dressed as an officer in the army of George IV presently sliced off the corks with a sword.

Exclamations were loud as the corks soared, narrowly missing the chandelier, and a river of bubbling silvery wine flowed delicately down into every breast-shaped glass.

"My, aren't we color-coordinated."

Vivien turned to find Cinnamon at her side with two glasses of champagne.

Vivien looked at her flatly.

Undeterred, of course, Cinnamon announced, "One of these is for Conn. Where is he? Oh, with the distributor... I see he's lost *you,* then. If he wants to, Conn's good at losing women."

Vivien, taken aback, stared at Cinnamon.

"Oops," said Cinnamon, then added, "This second glass is mine by the way. I didn't get it for you. Hope you don't mind."

"I don't mind at all."

"You don't know much about Connor, do you," Cinnamon asked coyly, around her champagne glass. "The initial *K* doesn't mean anything?"

Vivien felt something—her heart? the floor of her stomach?—drop through her body.

Quietly she said, "Presumably it does to *you.*"

"*Me?* Not a chance. Did I say something?"

Vivien thought, I am not going to play this game with you, Cinnamon. Vivien had met Cinnamon's type before. Troublemakers, ready with anything to throw you off balance. Cinnamon fancied Connor and was jealous of Vivien.

Yes, Vivien knew about a K. Funny, humorous K. Who surely no longer had any part in Connor's life?

Cinnamon's feral eyes were brightening, lifting.

Ah, Connor had come back....

Someone she had known through a hundred lifetimes touched Vivien's arm. With a deep, wounding, bewildered joy, she thought, I would know his touch, the sensation of his hands on me—anywhere—among a million others.

Connor gave a glass of champagne to Vivien, having already collected one for himself. "Here's to *Age of Aries*. Oh, Cinnamon, *two* drinks? That's rather greedy, isn't it?"

"One of them's for Ange," invented Cinnamon, shaking earrings that put the chandelier to shame. "We all know, she'll need as much as we can pour down her before we can even wheel her into the movie."

"Cinnamon, use your mouth to drink with."

"*Ooh*, don't be so *cruel* to me, Conn-conn—"

Connor turned his back on her. He led Vivien calmly away through the crowd: "There's someone I want you to meet."

The room behind the bar was also crowded, but gave on a balcony, open to a shimmering red-gold evening packed by roofs and fire escapes. No one else was out there, having given up on the notion of getting any air—there seemed very little.

Connor stood Vivien quietly before him.

"Who is it you want me to meet, Connor?"

"Me."

"Oh. I thought we'd met."

"Did you."

His mouth brushed hers, softly, quickly, and any

doubt, however fleeting, perished. She shivered the length of her body in the boiling sunset.

"How do you do, Vivien Gray. I'm sorry," he said, "for that business in there. Scavengers is a kind of family. And families fight."

"It doesn't matter."

A fanfare volleyed across the hospitality suite.

"Our summons. I hope you'll like the film."

She thought, Even if I hate the film, I'll still love every moment.

Chapter 7

"Luckily we're safe now. If we meet any werewolves, we can force these silver bullets down their throats."

"But, Connor, they're made of chocolate."

"*Really?* Better eat them, then, Vivien, do you think?"

"Both?"

They set the two bullets, an example of which had been offered to every person entering the movie theater, side by side on the table.

"Silver foil over candy coating," said Connor. "They look almost real." He gazed up and away into nothingness for a moment. She saw it happen, the shadow rising behind his eyes. "Counterfeit. Funny how something can be a lie and still seem true." Then he pushed the shadow back inside himself. "Would you like some brandy with your coffee?"

Vivien shook her head.

"I will. I need it, after that scene with J.D."

The film, which had been two hours long and rather marvelous, had proved a success with the hoped-for distributor, and J.D. and tuxedoed Ronald Whiting, the film's makers, had broken out more champagne. J.D. had gone round to everyone who had worked in any capacity on the film, wringing their hands over and over. Reaching Connor, J.D. had gone overboard in his praises: "We couldn't have done it without him!"

"We only supplied and organized the expected stuff. For which they paid handsomely, despite a low budget," Connor had protested later.

"Oh, come on, Conn, don't sell us short," said Lewis. "Who ever heard of making a film set during the Napoleonic wars and not showing a single battle? Okay, it was rendered on the personal level, a family saga with a werewolf in the closet—but how we dressed those sets made the thing work."

"You've forgotten a few actors, Lewis. And a director and producer. And the design team."

"Yes, yes, okay—"

"Not to mention camera work that deserves an Oscar."

"Sure, but—"

Cinnamon had interrupted this discussion, which took place on the baking pavement of a now-nocturnal ten-thirty London, milling with rambling crowds. "I'm *hungry.*"

"Let's go eat," said Angela.

"Where are we going?" demanded Cinnamon.

"Don't know where *you're* going, Cinn," said Lewis. "To hell on a bicycle?"

"I mean *dinner,* Lew."

"Wherever you like."

"Oh, then—"

"No," said Lewis firmly. "I mean Angela and I are eating at Goya's. And you are not fit to be seen there in that Kleenex of a dress you're wearing. Vivien, though, and just possibly Connor, if he can agree with me for once, would be welcome."

Cinnamon's face set in a mulish rage. So, after all, she *could* be wound up.

Connor said, "Thanks, Lewis, Angela. Vivien and I have a table booked elsewhere."

Viven shook hands with Lewis, who kissed her on both cheeks. "Watch out for Connor—isn't it full moon tonight? If that long hair of his gets longer, *run!*"

Angela kissed Connor, hugged him with surprising warmth, and shook hands with Vivien without either hug or kiss.

"Terrific to meet you, Vivien." Then, turning to her husband, she said, like a schoolmarm, "Now, we can't leave poor little Cinnamon all on her own. Her dress is all right." And Lewis was saying something very odd that sounded like, "Hey, Ange, being a bit cattish, aren't you?" Perhaps he meant catty....

It all faded behind them as Vivien and Connor ran for the taxi he had hailed.

In the cab, they talked on about the movie. Anecdotes he now told her about the production, particularly one that involved a runaway cannon chasing a herd of cows, ended in laughter.

This second restaurant to which he brought her was quite large, like a luminous cavern lit by pearly spotlights. It stayed open until 2:00 a.m. Mozart and Beethoven sang through speakers.

All through the meal they talked, laughed.

Then, quite suddenly, the meal was over, the plates

gone, the glasses dry, the coffeepot emptied. She thought, with an abrupt jolt, as if seeing the cliff's edge before her, *What now?* They were the very words he had said to her in the park behind the church.

For would he leave her now? Was there some new appointment he must keep? And after tonight, anyway—what?

"Vivien, maybe I should take you home."

"What time is it?"

He looked at his watch. "Nearly a quarter to one."

"And you haven't become a werewolf. How disappointing."

"And your clothes didn't fall off at midnight," he said, "like Cinderella's. Even more disappointing. At least, to me, and most of the men in here."

They stared at each other.

He said, softly, "I want to go back with you, Vivien. I want to be invited into your fascinating little flat, hung with mirrors and paintings. Not for coffee or a drink. I want to take you to bed, Vivien, my Vivien, and make love to you." His eyes were seas of darkness. She swam there, and to help her swim, he held both her hands. "Is that too soon?" he said. "Or am I assuming too much? Tell me. Either."

"Not too soon," she whispered. "Not asking too much. I want all that too."

"*Alors, ma belle,*" he said. He stood up. "*Allez-vous à moi.*"

Now, my lovely one, come you to me....

Her mind translating, the respectful formal French of *vous* not lost on her, Vivien rose in a kind of trance. He had already settled the bill. But she didn't afterwards quite know how they walked from the restaurant. Yet there they were on the pavement, pressed side to

side, his arm about her, and from the London night
came a taxi, ordered by angels, it seemed, just for them.

The taxi was traveling easily, the night's heavier
traffic finished, when Connor's mobile phone sounded.

He took the slender wafer from his jacket, scowling
at it.

"I turned this off for the movie." He didn't attempt
to answer the call. "Wait, I loaned it to Lewis afterwards. *He* left it on—" The twanging call, which had
stopped, began again. "Vivien, sorry. I'd better see
what this is."

Vivien sat mutely, lost in him.

How could anything as ordinary as a phone call matter?

"Hi, Lewis. What the hell's up? No. No, she isn't.
You'd better ask *her*. Okay." A long gap. "Right. Yes,
you're right, I'm the one with the keys. Fine. I'll let
you know— Not tonight, then." Connor broke the connection. "Vivien, we need to make a detour."

"What is it?" she asked, as Connor leaned back
from redirecting the irked taxi driver, who now spun
the cab squealingly around on the empty road. "May
I know?"

"I think you'd *better* know. Lewis had some business of his own after dinner, it seems. En route he
drove past Adelaide's flat."

Vivien sat bolt upright. "What is it?"

"There are lights on, apparently."

"Oh no."

"You didn't leave any lamps switched on, did
you?"

"No. *No,* I'm sure I didn't—"

"He asked if you were living there, because he said

he had the impression, from a couple of things you said tonight, that you were back in Camden. Look, Vivien, it's probably nothing. Maybe there's some automatic master switch she forgot to tell you about.''

''I'm sure there isn't. Addie's— She'd never bother to install anything like that. And I'd have seen it happen when I was there.''

''Look. I'm going to stop off for the keys at the place I rent when I'm in London. It's a bare, uncomfortable hole, which is why I haven't asked you back there—good enough for working and sleeping, and that's all. But for now I suggest I drop you off there. While I deal with this.''

''You think someone has broken into Addie's flat.''

''No, I just think we need to be sure.''

''If they have, it's my fault. I should have stayed— that was the whole idea. Oh God, I didn't even get round to calling her. I have to come with you.''

Connor looked at her assessingly. She thought he would say no, and she would have to argue.

Instead, after a moment, he nodded. ''All right.''

It was after two by the time they reached Coronet Square. A pall of London silence and dark hung everywhere, only the fake Victorian street lamps offering their milky glow. In the park, disturbed by the taxi's engine, a bird woke and shrilled harshly.

The driver spoke. ''Are you going to be long? I *have* got a home to go to, mate.''

Connor handed him a couple of notes. ''I'd appreciate it if you'd wait.''

Taking the notes, the driver folded his arms resignedly.

''Vivien, maybe stay in the cab.''

"No. I feel responsible. I'm coming with you."

"Okay. But I go first."

At the end of the tree-garnished terrace, where no lights otherwise showed, Addie's flat blared out like a lighted Christmas tree.

"If it's a thief, he's charmingly indiscreet," said Connor.

He put a key into the lock. The door swung back to display the fully illuminated hall.

There was no sound. No sense of movement. In the glare of light, nothing else seemed unusual or disturbed.

They advanced slowly, Connor keeping Vivien behind him. The octagonal room ahead was also lit, and the dining room to the left—but the cloakroom and cupboard doors, too, had been opened and their lights turned on.

They edged forward, at first cautious, and entered the main room, where every lamp, plus the overhead bulbs, blazed.

After they had checked there, finding nothing, they moved silently on to the other areas of the apartment.

Everything was the same. Rooms, hallways, bathrooms and cupboards opened and fully lit. And nothing, aside from that, seemed different.

Reaching the kitchen at last, after a painstaking search, they halted in perplexity.

"Nothing's been touched—has it?"

"I don't think so, Connor. Maybe I wouldn't know...little things—but nothing feels different. Only this sense someone was here. I've checked the clothes she left in her wardrobes—they don't look as if they've been touched. But then, I don't know what they were like to start with. All the dust sheets seem to be in place. What about the boxes?''

"They look fine. And the crates." Connor leaned back on a counter in the blindingly white world of the kitchen. "They did open the fridge, but you say it was empty."

"I think they opened the fridge like the cupboards— so the light would come on."

"Yeah. I think you're right, Vivien. Listen, I'm going out to check the statue."

Vivien's heart plummeted like a stone. She had been trying so hard *not* to think of the statue, all this while.

"Could that be what they were after?"

"Possibly. Although going over the garden walls might have been more simple. No one's tried to force the French doors. And look, the conservatory's locked up, and that padlock takes some shifting."

Vivien said nothing.

Connor said, "The obvious solution is they had keys. But there's only this one set we know of. And Adelaide's own, which she'll have with her in France. And no, I don't think she's suddenly come back. I know her schedule. France, then Barcelona. She wouldn't pass that up."

"Connor—"

"What is it?"

Faltering, instead she murmured, "Let's check the statue."

"Not us. This time you stay in here. Leave all the lights on. I've got the flashlight, too. Just in case. Frankly, this looks to me more some sort of imbecilic joke."

"*Joke.*"

He undid the awkward padlock of the conservatory door.

Vivien watched him go out. She thought of the rose, now crumbled and invisible, and the other roses, decapitated in the octagonal room, and the wine drunk. She wanted to follow him along the path, but common sense told her he needed to concentrate out there, not be looking out for her.

She poised on the brink of the garden, between dark and light.

The pleasure of desire and anticipation had drained from her, leaving her cold and trembling.

Connor had vanished into darkness.

And what did the darkness hold? Only something so bizarre as a jokey burglar? Or something far worse....

The garden was so quiet, all she could hear now was her heart. London seemed to have gone away.

And Connor didn't come back. And didn't.

Vivien took two steps forward, her movements about to tilt into a run.

A man's figure came from the tangled lilacs. For a second it was only white—then the flashlight beam speared ahead of him. Connor.

"Hey, Vivien, it's okay. Darling, you're shaking. Come on. We'll go back inside."

"Is it there?"

"The statue? Oh, Patrick's just fine. Still a bit skewed on the plinth, but no worse than before. I didn't know you cared about him so much—" He was half laughing, holding her to him, kissing her hair. "Should I be jealous?" he said. And then a kind of iron stillness seemed to fill him. She felt it through his clothes, his skin. "No," he said softly, "I'm not the jealous type, am I."

"Connor?" She raised her head to tell him everything that had already happened here—sinister, uncanny events that must have some rational explanation. But in that instant, she saw his expression. "What is it?"

"Nothing. It's nothing."

But his face seemed itself carved and soulless. His eyes black gems, impenetrable—without life.

"Connor," she said again. *"Connor."*

She felt him take a breath.

The terrible, beautiful mask his face had become slowly grew human again. The eyes, alive once more, stared harshly into hers.

His voice rang cold, searing her with ice. "But that I am forbid, I could a tale unfold, whose lightest word would harrow up thy soul, freeze thy young blood—" Suddenly his head tipped back. Connor bellowed with laughter. Astounded she gazed at him—until he looked down at her again, his face the face she knew. "Sorry, Vivien. And yes, I have acted the ghost of Hamlet's dad. Direct quote."

"I know the quote. You'd have gone on to tell me the tale would knot up my hair like quills on the fretful porpentine."

"Yes, my lovely girl, how could I ever think you wouldn't know every play I've ever acted in, let alone hammed up."

With relief, she was now laughing a little, too, but also shivering. She pressed into the warmth of his body, and his arms held her close. While somewhere, unheeded, the inner voice warned on and on that the dark was not separate from him. It lived *within* him.

What did any of that matter?

His mouth sought hers. He had put the flashlight

down on the ground, where its light splashed up at them. Light blazed everywhere, but darkness was *here* in the circle of his arms, and she loved this darkness.

She had lived, she confusedly thought, for these kisses, waiting and waiting for them, and for this pressure of their two bodies one on the other—like the relief from hunger or thirst.

Arousal had fooled her. Rather than leave her, it had only lain in wait.

His tongue moved in her mouth. Her tongue encircled, played with his, a duel of delight. Pure energy coursed down her spine. She was filled with an electric current, as if her blood altered to lightning.

The brick wall of the house pushed roughly into her back. So what.

Connor's mouth had moved from hers, traveled to her neck, melting her flesh—his hands slid over her breasts, and liquid shudders rushed through her. Through both their clothing his own hunger for her, swollen hard against her, signaled its intention impressively. Her legs were weak.

Nothing mattered—it was true—nothing but this.

"Vivien." He spoke hoarsely into her skin. "Listen to me. This flat— Will you mind if—"

"If...?"

"Do we have to wait? I heard that idiot's taxi drive off a minute ago. There's a bed here—the bed you slept in, yes? But not if you don't want to..."

His fingers, skillful, glorious, woke buds of starry sweetness on her breasts. Her belly was molten. Her whole body thrummed like the struck strings of guitar.

"Yes," she said. "Here. Anywhere."

Anywhere...against this wall...a tree...on the paving in the utter dark...

She didn't care, so long as they possessed each other now. Nothing was real but this.

He paused to lock the conservatory door, but all the while he gripped her against him, kissing her deeply even as he coaxed the key to operate the lock. Then, without apparent effort, he swung her up off the floor and into his arms. He held her in the air, kissing her body through the dress, and her arms and the tops of her breasts that the dress left bare.

They kept every light on. Or forgot every light. In the bedroom, the bed, stripped of everything but its mattress, received their bodies.

Here he peeled the dress from her. Vivien fought the urge to rip the shirt off his back. Together they undid the buttons. He pulled it off and threw it away.

Vivien filled her hands with his upper body, his back, so hard and smoothly made, the evenly tanned skin, the lean athlete's muscles. High in the dark hair that fanned across his chest, her fingers found a narrow ridging scar, but in those moments, it was only one with his intoxicating flesh. His pants and shorts had been added to the heap of clothes slung on the carpet. They lay across Vivien's undergarments…possessively.

Now the central hardness of his body, let free in its arrogant power, became Vivien's plaything, for a while subservient to her stroking fingers, the teasing of her tongue and lips. He lay back, holding her to him, his hands tangling and working in her cascading hair, groaning as she toyed with and savored the promise of his dominance over her.

Ripples of pleasure, that she could clearly feel, pulsed through the flat, hard belly under her hands. His long, sculptured body had tensed to an immeasurable tautness. He was rigid now as any marble, with desire—but each sound of pleasure he gave, every tiny spasm that crossed through his bowstring tension, scored its resonant echo over and over, deep within Vivien's core. With every caress she offered him now, her own trembling, dizzying need increased. Finally, having enslaved him, she herself was helpless, weak and moaning with her longing. Then he drew her away, folded her body closely down again upon his own, her thighs now lying over his, her feet on his ankles, her breasts on his chest, her face on his face. He kissed her with a total and wonderful invasion, sparing no infinitesimal area of her lips or mouth. Immobilized, blended into his body, Vivien lay there, his subject now, *his*.

When he had had his fill, for the moment, of this, he turned her, as if she were light herself as a piece of silk. He pinned her beneath him, lying down on and over her, heavy, remorselessly in charge, then lifted away again, letting her see all she wanted of him, and of the peak of desire to which she had brought him.

This man—breathless she ran her hands around his hips, upward to his ribs—against the light, his face was partly shadowed—a leopard's face with eclipse-dark eyes, and the fine pelt of his hair sketched over his body, and falling like wings of dense black fire from his head, across his back... A black wave of this hair came gliding forward as he dipped his hands, his mouth, to her breasts, fluttering them, scorching them, bringing her such piercing tremors and starts of sensation, she felt she must turn inside out.

She arched upward, catching his hair, his neck. He held her back, shook his head, accepting only her sur-

render, forcing her to endure once more the exquisite
torture of his tongue and lips. She could not have said
which of them breathed the fastest or more desperately.

The leopard raised his head. Again he leaned above
her, his eyes narrowed and blazing.

"Connor—"

"Now, Vivien?"

She thought she could not speak again—

"I should make you wait," he said. "After the struggle I've had to keep myself on leash since I met you."

But his breathing was still as ragged and rapid as
her own. Vivien, confident suddenly in her own pow-
ers, stretched herself for him, like a cat. She raised her
arms to display for him her breasts, swollen and themselves erect from his kisses. She offered her body like
a feast for his starvation.

"Make me wait, then, Connor. If you can."

"Oh, I can make you wait, my love. You and I, I
think, we both know how to do that."

Through the golden delirium, a shadow seemed to
scud across the light—she let it go, had no time for it.
Instead she idled her hand on him, on that carven belly,
that arrogant maleness that was both her slave and her
master. Connor laughed deep in his throat. He leaned
down to her body, and his smolder of hair poured
across her stomach like a curtain.

Within the secrecy of her thighs now, points of irresistible and kissing flame. Primal music flowered inside her. She flung out her arms and gripped the sides
of the bed to keep herself afloat on this leaping sea of
ecstasy.

He lifted away only twice more. The first time,
through dazzled, swimming eyes, Vivien watched as
he flaunted himself, adeptly dressing himself for her

protection—she had never before seen a man perform this necessary act as such an elegant and provocative type of theater.

Then he lay back flat on her, his face against her thighs, going on with the scarcely endurable intimacy of his kisses—while his arms slid up her body, the fingers fastening again, with a madness of tickling sweetness, circling on her breasts.

From far off, Vivien felt herself begin to dissolve—but he had judged her reactions to a hairsbreadth.

There came a surge, a heat of connection and longed-for impact. He caught her to him, his eyes now pitiless and black, finding her core, but this time neither with mouth or fingers, his body at last sheathed within her.

He had filled her, the force and strength of him, an anchor in the tempest.

Together, one creature, they thrust and strove, blinded and calling to each other under the crash of the approaching tidal wave.

Only Connor now could hold her through the cataclysm. Frenzied, her hands slid down his back, tightening on his buttocks, as she crushed herself against and against the shield of his body.

The wave broke. She felt the steel of his control shatter at her singing cries. As all final barriers gave way, in the tumbling agony of joy, she heard his voice join with hers—wordless, a sound like pain—and held him—to protect, to love, to cherish and adore, even if the sky should fall, till death, and beyond.

The room still murmured—inaudibly but unmistakably—with the aftershocks of fulfilled sexual love.

Under her skin, Vivien's body sparkled.

She found she was not afraid that he would now change towards her—not afraid either of shadows or statues or anything at all.

They lay side by side, looking at each other, their hands lightly clasped.

They said nothing. Nothing needed to be said.

After a while, he raised himself on his elbow, leaned over her and kissed her, chastely and intently, almost thoughtfully.

"What shall we do now?" he said.

"Climb Everest?"

"Why not, my sorceress. But why anything so ordinary?"

"True, it's very banal. Perhaps swim the Atlantic."

"Without backup, right? No support vessels."

"Absolutely none."

"Vivien," he said, "you are the most beautiful woman I have ever known. Everything about you, Vivien. I think you are *the* Vivien, Merlin's downfall, the woman who shut him in the crystal cliff, or whatever it was." He lay back. "Thank you for this. Thank you for letting this happen—here. I believe we just performed the perfect exorcism."

She laughed. She didn't care as to the exorcism of *what*.

"Where are you going?" he said.

"Thirsty. Water, and some coffee?"

"Yes. Adelaide's coffee is quite good. She stores it like a squirrel. But we can replace it for her tomorrow."

Tomorrow, Vivien thought. There will be a tomorrow for us.

Naked, they walked together back to the kitchen. There, in the bright white light, they drank bottled water and constructed a wonderful pot of Addie's best roast Havana coffee. They took it back to bed, along with some sheets. But though the bed was made up, they next made the mistake of lying down on it. And soon the wonderful coffee set to cold gravy in the pot.

Chapter 8

Vivien's decision to move back into Addie's flat was dictated mostly by her sense of honor. But, she had to admit, she had taken on board Connor's remark about exorcism. It seemed to her their lovemaking had indeed cleansed and lightened the rooms. In the sunny morning, as they made fresh coffee from Addie's rifled store, Vivien half wondered if her anxieties, or her hang-ups from the past, had even caused some kind of poltergeist activity.

There was no trace of the rose in the conservatory. She began to ask herself if she had imagined it. Imagined the other episode... Falling in love, she had heard, was like the onset of a dangerous fever. Even the photo of Emily...

"I wish you wouldn't stay here, Vivien."

"I'll be fine. I'm leaving soon after you do—and then I won't be back until about four. And this man I know, just a casual acquaintance, has promised to join me at six-thirty for iced tea in the garden.''

"The man you know also said he ought to get the locks changed here.''

She hadn't told him anything about the previous incidents, or her own tentative conclusions. Perhaps even now, she didn't quite trust him enough— No, it wasn't that. She didn't want to appear silly, or fey.

"You're worrying about Adelaide's reaction,'' he said. "Don't. I'll deal with her.''

"Connor, it's just I feel so *guilty*—''

"So you should, you lascivious and greedy doxy.''

Which ended the discussion in the way discussions between them, right now, seemed generally to end.

They tore apart from each other at 11:00 a.m. Connor left in a taxi, already late for an appointment. Vivien, after tidying the flat cursorily, left it an hour later, without a backward glance. She hadn't even remembered to glance out into the garden, let alone to enter it.

On the underground, slightly overdressed in last night's silk dress, she thought of Connor. Of his body and his mouth, his hands on her, her hands on him, the rhythm as he moved within her.

Nothing ghostly would get by her now. She was centered in the flesh, no longer a magnet for the supernatural or the merely creepy. She was alive again— alive as she hadn't been for three years.

It was at ten minutes to three that the doorbell sounded in Vivien's flat.

By then her bags, which she hadn't properly unpacked, were fully *re*packed, easel refolded, all standing ready in the hall. Now in her jeans and T-shirt, she was accumulating, in a sturdy plastic carrier, a selection of food and drink.

She opened the door and was surprised to find Lewis Blake smiling on her threshold. His eyes swerved knowingly over the bags.

"Like a lift, Vivien? Back to Adelaide's—yes?"

Had Connor told Lewis about her return to Addie's?

"Did Connor ask you to? That's kind of you—but it's really okay, Lewis."

"Well, he sort of suggested it. You know Connor. If he wants something, then 'I hear and obey, great chief!' is always best. But really, it's fine, Vivien."

Vivien wasn't displeased. Getting cabs in her area was often awkward, and she hadn't wanted another trip on the tube with all this baggage.

"If you're sure."

"Sure I'm sure."

"How's Angela?" Vivien asked, as, twenty minutes later, Lewis carried her bags downstairs to his vehicle, a ferocious-looking Jeep of some sort.

"Ange? Oh, she's off doing her accountancy."

"She's an accountant?"

"Well, yes. Couldn't you tell?"

"Not really."

"Scavengers has a lot to be grateful to her for. She got Connor's books straight, and they were a mess. I guess she felt she owed him that. But clever lady, my woman."

Vivien no longer felt envy at Lewis's praise of his wife. Oddly, now that she didn't, she thought she detected a slight mockery in his tone—but Lewis was easygoing, it was only his way. Though why Angie owed Connor anything was a mystery.

Once the bags were loaded, Lewis helped Vivien spring up into the Jeep.

They drove off along West Camden Road.

Lewis was Connor's friend—presumably part of that "chosen" family Connor had mentioned. Vivien had liked Lewis from the first. She liked him now...only—

There was something she couldn't put her finger on today. Something slightly brash, and strangely also too hesitant in his manner. Despite the chivalrous lift. Nor did he chat as they drove. But some people preferred silence when they were at the wheel, especially in the heart of London.

Vivien recollected that call he had made to her at Addie's: *"I didn't know whether to tell you or not..."* and then, *"I'd better spill the beans."* She thought how he had also muttered, *"Two of a kind,"* enraging her by lumping her in with Connor.

How wise Lewis had been.

But what had he been going to say?

That question hadn't ever been answered. Now, did it matter less—or much, much more?

They trundled now fast, now sluggishly, by Kensington Gardens, absorbed an orange afternoon glow, and a Hyde Park green as if newly painted. There were detours to add to the congestion. The Jeep swung easily into and out of them, and down side streets, until, emerging to pass the statue of Eros, they crawled back into south-flowing traffic. Despite the herds of vehicles, only buses—or perhaps tanks—seemed fit to take on the Jeep; it was a mighty beast indeed.

Vivien had tried to enjoy the overground ride. But why was Lewis so edgy?

She scolded herself. Why start worrying now?

Oh, she was probably Connor–starved. After all, she

had been five hours without him. Or perhaps Eros, since she had just passed by, had trickily fired one more invisible arrow of love into her breast.

Despite everything, when they reached Coronet Square, Vivien felt an unexpectedly sharp apprehension rise in her. She had thought she was through with all that.

As they went round to the door, Lewis's own jollity seemed repaired.

"Gather it wasn't a burglar or vandal, then, last night?" he said, as she undid the front door with the keys Connor had left in her keeping.

This was the first time Lewis had referred to the incident which he himself had reported.

"No break-in. Just weird."

"Yes, I guess it would be pretty weird."

"How much did Connor tell you?"

"Not much. But I was out last night. Went straight in to Scavengers this morning, and passed Connor heading out again. We hardly spoke— What's up?"

"I can't get the door to open."

"Let me try," said Lewis.

He took the key and jammed it back in the lock. As he did this he pushed at the door with his shoulder. It gave. "Heat," said Lewis, "makes the paint stick."

Vivien realized she hadn't been breathing again— why not? Had she thought *something* had got in, blocked the door against her?

The hallway looked normal: lights off, shafts of sun, the eight-sided room ahead, dining room to the left. No cupboard was open; nothing lay on a table or the floor.

Lewis went by, carrying the bags.

Don't be silly, Vivien. Yes, doors stick in the heat. Sometimes. Just calm down.

Lewis stood in the octagonal space as Vivien opened the French windows for some chance of air.

Green and graceful in its lush July neglect, the garden looked only appealing.

It was getting on for five. Just one and a half hours until Connor arrived.

This morning, this place had · seemed innocuous, cleansed and ordinary. But now, the atmosphere had subtly changed. There even appeared to be a scuff mark on one wall—had it always been there?

Stop being a fool.

"Thanks, Lewis. That was really helpful. Would you like some tea?"

"I'd rather have a beer, Vivvy."

Vivien didn't let him see her aversion to the abrupt, unwieldy abbreviation of her name.

"Oh yes. I've got some for Connor. They won't be very cold."

"I like 'em hot, Viv. Cold beer—that's a U.S. taste."

Vivien took the bag of groceries along the hall to the kitchen. She hadn't liked the nicknames—never did. Nor the slight superiority in his voice at the comment on "U.S. taste." U.S. taste, Vivien thought, was often first-rate. And who wanted tepid beer, anyway, unless it was genuine real ale, or scrumpy.

As she undid the beer bottle she glanced into the conservatory. All was peaceful.

And down the path, hidden, Patrick Aspen Sinclair would be standing, handsome as a god. Like Eros—just a statue.

Lewis ambled into the kitchen, which suddenly seemed, like that famous Western town, not big enough for both of them.

He took the beer from her, gulped.

Vivien put the kettle on for herself.

"Yucko—do you drink *that?*"

"Mint tea? Oh yes. Or there's lemon and ginger, apple—"

"No more! Please don't tell me. You're worse than Ange. At least she sticks to Ty-phoo."

"I like Ty-phoo as well."

Vivien put the tea bag into the mug and stood studying the kettle, which, of course, through being watched, would take twice as long to boil. Sympathetic magic did exist, everyone knew.

She was realizing that Lewis, though she had partly wanted to detain him to keep her company here, was making her very uncomfortable.

When he touched her bare arm, she nearly jumped across the stove.

"Whoa, lady! Hey, you're nervy today."

"Sorry. I just—"

"Nervy, but never less than attractive."

"Thank you."

"Yes, I'm impressed, Vivvy. You impress me. Conn, too? Well that's okay. I tell you what, forget tea, come and have a drink. There's a great pub just—"

Something cold filled Vivien's solar plexus.

"No, thank you."

"Yes, go on. Loosen up a bit." His hands came unwanted and unplanned for, to the back of her neck. "You're like a rock, here, lady. Is that what Connor does to you? Tightens up your neck like this?" He began to knead her shoulders.

Revulsion shot through her. She moved away from him. "Lewis, I think—"

"What? You don't want to play? But you do. You like me, I'm likable."

"Yes, and you're also married. I've met your wife."

"Angie doesn't mind. She's used to me and my girls."

"I'm not your girl."

"Too hooked on the great god Connor? I tell you, he ain't such a bargain. All right, tell you what—even though you've been flirting and leading me on, I'll let you off. I'll settle for one kiss. How's that?"

Vivien, appalled, asked herself how she hadn't seen this coming.

"I won't kiss you. You'd better leave, Lewis."

"Ah, she's all angry now. Look, babe, that's really all. One kiss. You won't miss it—"

In a horrible parody of Connor in the garden last night, Lewis was backing her against the wall.

Vivien spoke quietly, intensely. "Move away. I mean it. *Move away.*" She thought of the kettle, boiling close by.

Lewis hesitated, as if mind-reading the threat. He loomed over her. "Viv, I reckon, whatever else, you should know. Yeah, Connor is pretty, but he is bad news. I should have said all this before, insisted—but you're going to hear me out now. He hasn't told you what went on here. The woman he lived with in this flat, an actress. Ever hear of Kate Mortimer? Big on TV quite a while. Ever see a scar on his chest?"

Panic slammed through Vivien's body. Somehow she didn't externally respond.

"Well," said Lewis, "put it this way, *he* got the scar, and poor old Kate— Well, Kate just vanished

from our lives. Didn't know that, did you. Didn't know
the police were very interested for a while in His Lord-
ship Connor Sinclair?''

Vivien stared at Lewis. She couldn't see him through
a mist—

The kettle was boiling. Steam filled the kitchen.

Someone spoke from the doorway.

"Get away from her, Lewis."

Lewis lumbered round. ''Ho! Connor. Connor saves
the day. Again. Just been telling her about Katie.''

''I heard you. The front door's that way.''

Lewis lurched back to Vivien again, his face all concern. It seemed he was the true actor. ''Vivien, I tell
you—watch out for yourself.''

Connor spun Lewis around as if he were a doll. He
slapped Lewis hard across the face, a contemptuous
backhanded blow. ''Get out.''

Even more repulsive than the harassment and the
violence was Lewis crumpling there, teary-eyed and
cringing. ''Sorry, Conn. Sorry. Bit of lunchtime booz-
ing... Never suits me—''

''Get the hell out.''

''Maybe I shouldn't drive—''

Connor said nothing. Lewis slunk across the room.
Only then did Connor follow him out.

Distantly, in a while, Vivien heard the front door
slam.

She leaned on the counter. She felt sick to her stomach. After a minute, she turned out the kettle.

When Connor walked back in, she raised her eyes
and said, almost wildly, ''How did you—''

''Get in? Nothing mind-blowing. There was another
set of keys all the time.'' His face, in its tan, was still
very pale. He threw the second bunch up in the air,

caught them with a jangle. "Someone, it seems, requested an extra set from Adelaide. They've been in the office all the time, cleverly filed in an unmarked drawer. Only, I didn't know till this afternoon."

"Is Lewis all right?"

"Don't tell me you're concerned?"

"He just made an idiot of himself, that's all."

"*Did* he? I thought it was a bit more serious than that."

"I'm trying to be fair. Why are you so angry?"

"Why do you think?"

"I don't mean with Lewis. I mean angry with *me*."

"Again. Why do you think?"

Vivien straightened. "I don't know," she said coldly. "Perhaps you should tell me. Or is that one more thing you'd prefer to keep to yourself?"

As soon as the words were out she could have bitten off her tongue. Why had she said such a thing to him?

The inner voice scrabbled in her brain, hissing: *Because he keeps secrets from you. Because you know, in your innermost heart, you can't trust him, however much you may wish you could.*

Vivien tried to steady her breathing. "I'm sorry. I shouldn't have said that."

"But you did."

"Connor, I didn't know Lewis was going to behave like that...not any of it—"

"No. Anyone else can always tell he will, but little Vivien, so naive, misses all the clues."

"*Connor!* You don't think I encouraged him?"

"Anyone's guess what you did. He plays the field, but he doesn't usually force himself on someone who's unwilling. After all, you called up and asked him for a lift, apparently."

Vivien said, "I didn't. He told me *you'd* suggested that—"

"I hadn't even told him you were going anywhere."

"Then, he must simply have found me in the phone book—I'd said I lived in Camden. He called round and guessed—" Vivien's eyes widened "—yes, he *did*, he *guessed* when he saw the bags—" Connor looked at her. She remembered this look. "Connor," she said, trying to keep a pleading note out of her voice, "why on earth would I be interested in Lewis?"

"I have no idea."

"Stop it."

"I didn't start it. I turned up here early to surprise you. Well, we were all surprised."

Silence filled the kitchen, where the remnants of the steam still hung, wet as tears along the surfaces.

"I suppose," he said, "I have to tell you about Kate."

He didn't now look at her, but through the conservatory glass at the garden. On the paths the shadows of birds rushed over, and were gone. So swiftly things could pass—could love fly away so quickly?

"If you don't want to talk about it, Connor…"

"No, I don't. But it seems, after he's put so much poison about, I have to. My God, I've wondered in the past— It's been him. He can't keep his mouth shut. Painting me in the worst possible light—"

"He said she—vanished."

"In a way she did."

"I don't understand."

"She's dead. She died."

Vivien felt the kitchen, and the world, drop away. She hung in space, void and without words.

"Yes, Vivien. She died, and she died *here*. And it

was because of me. Is that enough for you? No? It's all I'll give you.''

He turned. He cast the spare keys down on a counter. ''I suggest if you stay here tonight, you lock up carefully. No one else will be trying to get in. You're safe. Just don't answer the door. Because it might just be Lewis, and then you might make another mistake.''

Chapter 9

After all, it was obvious, wasn't it? Bury her head in the sand as much as she liked—and she *had* liked, hadn't she? Connor Sinclair was not the lover of Vivien's dreams. Maybe only of a woman's nightmares.

He had admitted it. Arrogant, because for some unknown reason, the law hadn't been able to pin anything on him.

Kate Mortimer was an actress Vivien had indeed seen once or twice in a TV drama. A good actress, with shiny blond hair and a delicate, serious face— almost a childish look, but a woman's intense slate-blue eyes.

Kate—*K*.

To C with love from K.

Emily had had an affair with the sculptor, Nevins. With whom had humorous, lighthearted Kate "betrayed" Connor? It wasn't noble, but who knew how it had happened—maybe Connor, moody, sarcastic, difficult, had driven her to seek solace elsewhere.

And Connor, like Patrick, had found out.

As Patrick had killed Emily, Connor had killed Kate. *K* for Kate. *K* for killed.

"Something bad happened to me when I lived here...and to someone else..."

Yes, Connor, that would be quite bad, wouldn't it. To find your lover preferred another man, and then to murder her.

How had he escaped arrest? Presumably there hadn't been enough evidence—it was impossible, without more of the facts, to decide. And why had Vivien never heard of this case? Oh, she didn't bother with newspapers, or news items of this sort. Unworldly Vivien.

Certainly Kate must have tried to defend herself. Somehow she had cut him, there across the upper-right pectoral, with a serrated knife whose purpose was probably to slice bread or fruit....

And so, whatever else she could delay or conceal from herself, Vivien had seen—and felt—that ridged scar, where the jagged knife had gone in, where the subsequent stitches had held the wound together as it healed.

But was it believable? Connor, so handsome, so self-assured, an amusing and kind companion, a wonderful and generous lover—?

Yes. It was believable.

Vivien saw before her his face, as she had first seen it. When he was in that mood, he was cold, cruel, indifferent—dangerous.

Perhaps insane.

She wouldn't cry. There had been enough of that in her past.

She wandered about the apartment for a formless while, picking things up and replacing them distractedly. When she unpacked one of her bags, looking for the extra bottle of water she had shoved in there, she noticed the absence of a shirt she had packed. It was one of the pet shirts she worked in—the black one. She had worn it when she was here that very first morning—

An absurd new panic seized her. She began to throw her belongings out of both bags, searching—terrified by the loss of this piece of cotton.

But it was the loss of Connor, she knew, that she was trying to understand—to refute.

In the end, the shirt still unfound, Vivien sat down on the floor of the eight-sided room. The French windows remained wide open on the garden, where the hot coppery shadows of sunfall were beginning. In here, darkness gathered prematurely in knots of plasterwork above.

Birds called. There seemed, as before, very little other sound. Only the unfamiliar creaking of Addie's walls and floors, like the timbers of an anchored ship.

Vivien put her head in her hands.

You'll get over this.

She knew she wouldn't. She was no good at "getting over" things. The very awareness and intensity that fueled her art worked havoc with her emotions.

And she loved him. She always would love him, even though, now, she must teach herself to despise and fear him.

She tried to visualize him killing Kate Mortimer. But it was an image of shadows. She couldn't make him out— Not Connor. Never him.

And if he *were* this madman, it was as if she still

wished she could protect Connor from the very thing he had become—protect him from *himself*.

Perhaps her judgment was wrong.

No. Why else had he engineered the argument with her, walked out and left her? Once he had seen she must know, or that she could soon work it out, he had admitted it to her—and then he hadn't dared remain.

The *Fatal Man*. In some movies, and in books, so very attractive. But heaven help the real-life woman who trusted such a creature.

Kate had done so.

Kate was dead.

Outside, in the hall, the telephone rang. On and on. How many times had it done that? About twenty.

Wearily, at last, Vivien got up and went to answer. She knew it wouldn't be him.

Nor was it. When she lifted the receiver, no one spoke. There was no breathing—no sound at all.

Vivien cut the connection drearily and dialed 1471—but the caller had withheld his or her number.

This was all crazy.

She must get out now and stay out.

She walked back into the octagonal room, to the mess of her scattered clothes. She was so sick of packing, partly unpacking, repacking and lugging them about.

Away down the garden, a flock of birds rose clattering, as if frightened, from the lilacs.

From that spot too, around the corner of the path where the statue was, and hidden from her, came a single metallic *clank*.

Vivien froze.

She hung there, waiting for other noises—for the birds to come back. Neither happened.

It was nothing.

Face it, Vivien, she thought. You're always wrong, aren't you. Dead men don't return to haunt you. It's the live ones you love who turn out to be demons.

She walked straight out of the French doors and down the path, quickly, her fists clenched.

Warmth, and fast-ebbing day, caused her to relax. The mosaic shade of foliage dappled the path. She could smell the roses, the leaves of the lilac trees, the sooty electric backdrop of London. The unseen sun was nearly down. Shadows... Anything could lurk in those bushes, but nothing—*listen, Vivien*—nothing did.

She turned the corner.

The statue stood there, melancholy and glimmering white. Unreadable.

Of course it hadn't moved. Only that one foot still with its toes slightly off the plinth. Otherwise it was unchanged.

But she hated the statue—beautiful Patrick Aspen Sinclair, who shot his wife because his heart was stone. And then shot himself.

That, at least, Connor had failed to do. No suicide for *him*. She thought this bitterly, but tears tore from her eyes. She must learn to hate Connor. When she tried it, her heart—not stone at all—broke.

She stood there on the path below the statue, forcing herself not to cry, and indoors she heard the phone begin to ring again. Somehow the idea of Cinnamon, also jealous and maybe off her head, flashed through Vivien's brain—

Enough of all this! Vivien would pack and run. None of it was her concern, not even Addie's wretched flat.

Stingy Addie, with all her money, who wouldn't pay anyone to look after the property and was "holding out" for a better offer on the place...

As Vivien marched in again through the windows, something caught the fading light.

It must have been ejected from her bag, unnoticed until now. It—they—lay there, shining up at her—a group of eyes....

She bent over them, staring back.

Buttons. All the buttons off her black shirt, the shirt she hadn't been able to find.

The phone stopped ringing again, abruptly and with a sort of hiccup. No bird sang now in the garden. It was in that moment that Vivien heard, loud and clear, and unmistakably *real*, footsteps—pacing to and fro in the empty flat over her head.

Alone in the middle of the room, Vivien stood with her head tilted up, staring at the ceiling, blank between its cornices of plaster adornments, listening, listening.

What was up there?

Every flat in this building was supposed to be vacant. And next door the same—one of Addie's reasons for wanting a flat-sitter.

The footsteps paced slowly, slowly, and with a faint dragging undertone... They didn't sound quite...human.

Ridiculous. Of course they were human. Someone had got in and was illegally squatting in the apartment above—

How had they got in? There had been no signs of a break-in—did they too have keys? For someone at Scavengers had got hold of extra keys to Addie's flat, and used them—cutting the heads from roses, cutting buttons off a shirt....

Vivien shook herself. She crossed to the French doors and shut them quietly, next locking them and shooting home the bolts. So far as she knew, there were no other windows or doors undone in the flat, but she must check.

Whoever was up there, and it *was*—they *were*—human—might also be desperate, and accordingly dangerous.

The sun had gone. The garden beyond the doors plunged all at once into a brownish afterglow that glared like bronze on the edges of things but gave no real light.

Vivien stepped back from the doors abruptly.

Something had changed out there—not the coming of dusk— What was it?

With no warning, down past the windows something hurtled—huge and black and shapeless.

Vivien choked off her own scream. She stood in the grip of shock, staring out into the half-light, straining to see.

Oh God. The thing was rising up, billowing, bouncing against the glass.

Vivien felt a disbelieving wave of relief—false relief—as she realized suddenly the *thing* which had landed just outside was a cluster of balloons. All in the darkest colors, almost black in twilight, they wobbled there, drifting to the windows, bouncing off, turning now, impelled by their own volatility, like a strange alien entity, bobbling off along the garden path into the trees.

Above her, there in the upstairs flat, Vivien heard the weirdest laugh. It was cracked and unctuously *evil*—the perfect product of some 1930s horror movie starring Boris Karloff. Laughable in most situations, here it, like the balloons, was a harbinger of fear. The intention to unnerve—in conjunction with previous events, to *terrify*—was apparent. Which surely indicated madness in the perpetrator.

Vivien swallowed. She wasn't safe here, never had been.

Who was it that menaced her? She thought of Lewis—pushy, sulky and humiliated. Was he violent, too? What might he have done if Connor hadn't shown up when he did? Vivien recalled her own thought of defending herself with the boiling kettle—it demonstrated how alarmed she had been in those moments.

But then, Cinnamon kept coming back into Vivien's mind. Cinnamon fancied Connor, disliked Vivien. Was Cinnamon capable of using those spare keys to enter the flat and vandalize it just enough to make Vivien uncomfortable—roses, buttons, lights, balloons…and the laugh somehow carried that same childish and unstable taint.

After the laugh, silence lay heavy now in the apartment.

Vivien kept glancing up. But the ceiling couldn't tell her anything. She couldn't see through plaster, joists or floorboards.

They, whoever they were, were playing games now, making her wait for the next installment of fear.

Damn this flat. She was out of here.

Vivien grabbed her handbag. She would have to leave the rest. Retreat was the only sensible plan.

She moved quietly, crept out through the door, down the first hall, leaving the lights off though darkness was coming thick and fast. She thought it was the dark that

made her awkward with the front door. Then it seemed
to her that it was more than that.

The door would not open. Would *not*—

Vivien dispensed with quietness. She pulled and
wrenched. Nothing would give. It had stuck again? No.
Lewis had freed it up, and Connor had had no trouble
coming in—they hadn't even heard him—or leaving.
Something had happened to the door since its last clo-
sure.

On impulse, Vivien put the key into the lock. Or
tried to. The key would not go in.

The keyhole had in some way been blocked up.

She could smell now just the faintest whiff of ace-
tone—some resin or glue.

True fear caught at Vivien and sank in its claws.
Whoever was doing this, sane or mad, man or woman,
they meant business.

Holding herself in a firm mental grasp, Vivien went
over to the phone. She picked up the receiver. She felt
little astonishment, only a dull, deadly pang, when
there was no dialing tone. She tried depressing the cra-
dle a couple of times. Ritual only. She knew that, as
in the best horror movies, the line had been cut. And—
just like those helpless heroines of old—she had no
mobile phone.

In desperation, Vivien turned then to switch on the
lights in the hall. Only, she didn't, because the switches
clicked and no light appeared.

Ah, yes. What else? Phone out. Lights out. Trapped
by immovable door.

Slowly, softly, Vivien put down her bag. She took
off her shoes. Barefoot, she walked back into the octagonal room.

No sound.

Then, the sound.

The voice called, muffled and gentle, almost whee-dling, down through the ceiling. "Are you there, girlie? Are you *there?* How do you like it *now?* Is it *nice?* Is it *fun?* Are you *there?*"

And the voice, though distorted and still melodra-matically actorish—*hamming*—was a man's.

Chapter 10

He had told her—either a slip or a boast. It was his fault Kate Mortimer died: *"...because of me."*

Connor.

And he had been the one to bring her the extra keys, and he had been the one to shut the front door last. Maybe he had shut it in a much more permanent way than was usual....

Vivien stared at her thoughts.

It isn't Connor.

But how can you be sure, Gray? He likes sleeping with you, fine. But now he's told you the truth. Now you're his enemy.

It isn't Connor. It isn't.

You were like this before. Wouldn't believe the other guy dumped you till he rubbed your face in it.

Above the ceiling, a new sound. A scraping and scratching.

It was like squirrels or birds in the roof—but there was no roof above, only the other flat.

This was the noise she had heard here before, that second night, after her first dream of the statue, just before the single rose appeared in the conservatory.

Scratching, like stone fingers.

Impelled by some instinct beyond mere flight, she stood in the eight-sided room, staring up.

It was now so dark, really only the French doors showed, two tree-interrupted oblongs of dim dusk. But her eyes were now dark-adjusted. From the windows, the vaguest light reflected up onto the ceiling.

So she saw it.

The ceiling was moving.

Up among the ornate plasterwork, a section was unhinging and slipping down—a slab of plaster fruits and flowers unfolding, dangling—while a slot of blackness opened behind, a void, as if into some other appalling dimension.

As Vivien stared, *something* came crawling through.

It was pale, shimmering—like a snake. A *rope.*

In dreams, sometimes you can't move. Awake, sometimes you can.

Vivien broke for the French doors, the keys still clutched in her hand. Somehow she shot back the bolts, too. Then she was outside, on the path, among dusk and shadows, where ghostly street lamps sent down the most insubstantial glow.

Vivien slammed the doors shut again, closing the flat. She locked them, her hands jumping from the judder of her heart. All the glass was bulletproof, Addie had said. The *thing,* too, would now have some difficulty breaking out.

She ran down the path, loose pebbles and flints stinging her bare soles. The garden walls were ten feet high, but she had climbed walls and trees as a kid—in jeans it shouldn't be so difficult, particularly given the alternative—

But what *was* the alternative? Vivien didn't know. What she clung to now was her blind faith that none of this was to do with Connor. No matter how the evidence looked.

He might be many things, perhaps, under great emotional duress, even a killer—but not like this. He wasn't mean of spirit.

Something stirred in a shrub, reaching out for her. No— No, only the stranded balloons.

She flung herself round the lilacs, tripping, stumbling on a root.

Before her now, amid massed darkness and against the aperture of the faintly lit London sky, Patrick Aspen Sinclair waited, in his shell of whitest marble. As if for an agreed appointment.

Vivien stopped.

Her instinct, now primitive and raw, warned her of some other element.

Behind her, back down the path, someone was thumping and rattling at the French doors. She heard what sounded like a chair crashing into presumably ungiving glass.

That threat was still escapable. But there…*here* was something else. Some kind of wall—unseen, unfelt, unreal, yet entirely present—barred her way.

"Let me by, Patrick Aspen," Vivien murmured. "You've got enough guilt to deal with. And *I'm not Emily.*"

The breathtaking face—*Connor's* face—stared down at her, cold-eyed, indifferent yet harsh.

Another crash sounded—more liquid, louder—as if, after all, progress was being made on smashing the glass.

To wait was stupid. She ran forward, straight by the statue and through some psychic barrier beyond her ability to understand, aiming for the leap and scramble upwards.

And sheer blackness erupted from the leaves in front of her, burst, flowed and rushed down.

Not balloons. It was hot and solid, animate, growling like a feral dog. It had her, seized her, and she smelled the alcohol on its breath.

Vivien fought. She scratched with her nails, with the keys, and jabbed upward with her knee at her male assailant's thighs and the vulnerable areas directly above and between them. But he was agile; he twisted, and twisted her and twisted her hair into a knot of shrieking pain.

Vivien screamed at the full pitch of her lungs.

"Shut up, you silly cow. Or I'll give you something to shout about." The cliché was horribly effective.

A man with a gruff London accent. A smell of stale tobacco smoke on his clothes. Not Connor. *Not* Connor. Something fell from him, out of a pocket, landed on the dimness of the path at her feet, and broke.

"Look now, you rotten little piece of muck. I haven't got *your* dosh. Cost me over fifty quid, they did. You owe me for that."

Jet-black sunglasses, in three pieces.

Vivien stopped struggling. She knew who this was. They had met before. The cabdriver, the one from Cwick Cabs whom she had turned away that night when Connor was there, gave Vivien's hair another vicious tug. She asked herself dazedly if a lost fare was

sufficient grounds for this much assault and battery—
and decided it wasn't.

"Well, darling," he said. "Like it better now, do
you? I tell you, you've been a very bad girl, Adelaide."

"I'm not Adelaide," she said. The clearness of her
own voice was strange to her.

"No? Don't give me that," he said. "I'm gonna
have to teach you a bit of a lesson—"

Footsteps—lightly pounding, like the pads of some
enormous cat—evolved from nowhere.

She thought the second man must have got himself
out of the flat, shattering the French doors despite their
bulletproofness. One more lie, one more meanness of
Addie's. Now it would cost more than money....

With deathly rationality, Vivien thought, *They're going to hurt me, whatever I say or do. For something I
haven't done anyway—they think I'm Addie. Not
much chance, then. I'll make sure I hurt them back as
much as I can*—

Then came a cascade of noises, like some huge engine driven right up and over the garden wall. That
was where the other one—the second assailant—came
from then, where she had planned to escape.

The Cwick Cabs man, trying to keep a firm hold on
her, was also turning round. Something, like a ton of
bricks, slammed into them both.

Her attacker was slung right over, letting her go as
he fell. He smashed down by his broken shades on the
path. A leopard was on his back, the great paw rose—
Not a leopard. A man.

The thug gave a disapproving grunt as he was
dragged over and clubbed in the midsection. Still stag-
gering, Vivien leaned against the trunk of a tree. They
were fighting now—the two men—into and out of

shadows, roots, one noisy—her first attacker—and the other entirely silent.

It made no sense to her. The second man who had scaled the wall was tall and muscular and had very short black hair. That was all she could make out. Now was the time to get away. Something held her there.

From the depths of the dark, half a white face startlingly rose, as softly brilliant as a polished coin. A cloudy moon had topped the trees, the wall, and by its light Vivien saw Connor Sinclair, his hair tied back and clubbed like the mane of a fighting Roman gladiator, drive his fist home against the cabman's jaw.

Then, the other two came round the corner of the path.

She didn't know them. Both were big. One rubbed his arm ruefully, resentfully, perhaps having bruised it, either climbing down the ceiling rope or when destroying the French doors. He carried a chair leg off one of Addie's chairs. The other toted an unsheathed Buck knife. In the slender moonlight, its short, meaty blade shone with sharpening—and *use?*

Connor had stood up. He was positioned directly beneath the statue. At any other time, the irony of the likeness between them would have melted her heart. Now it was somehow hideous. The statue was stone. *It* couldn't be harmed. Connor, even now, didn't glance at Vivien. She could see him evaluating the men, the chair leg, the lethal glistening knife. His hands were empty, and his cheek bled.

"All right," said the knife man. "It's stopped being a laugh now."

Oddly, the other one with the bit of chair *did* laugh at this. And Vivien realized that the absurd horror-film cackle she had heard through the ceiling must be natural to him.

The knife man concluded, weightily as a judge, "None of yuse'll do what you're told, will ya? So we'll have to make ya."

Connor shrugged. "You're welcome to try."

Vivien's eyes darted here, there. What could she do to assist—to protect him? She could see his danger. Only that. These two with their weapons, and the other one Connor had felled, who was even now surging up again. Yes, Connor could inflict some damage, but it was three to one. No, three against *two*. The only trouble was, *she* had never been trained to fight.

She hadn't expected it, what they did. Perhaps she should have done. Wild dogs fought in a pack—

Just as it happened, Connor nodded at her, a brusque careless nod. She knew it was his signal to her to run away.

Then the men from the house bounded right past her, pushing her aside. She tried to snatch at them. The knife man cut back at her, a high blow and only with his elbow, but it caught her shoulder and spun her. As she toppled into the left-hand bank of roses, she saw the pack land on Connor—two at the front of him, and one grappling at his arms. She screamed his name as she ripped herself from the talons of the roses, tearing her skin, tearing out her hair, fighting back to him. She heard the first thick blow crack down, saw the flash of the knife.

They had their priorities fixed now. Connor first.

He had given her the chance to get away. Perhaps at the cost of his life. She would never take it.

In that instant, her hands raised, unarmed, she started forward, and a shadow slanted across her. It had nothing to do with trees or cloud, or the figures struggling below the wall. It was the shadow of a tall man swiveling and pivoting, high in the air—

Vivien lifted her head.

The statue of Patrick Aspen reeled on its plinth. Its arms swung upward, stiff and jointless, like those of some mechanical doll or robot, its head veered on its neck. The foot that had skewed kicked stiffly free of the base.

The four fighters had dropped apart. They stood, gaping up at the statue, even the now red-knifed man, even Connor who sagged between them.

Time stopped. One moment stuck for an hour in stasis. Then another moment began—

The statue of Patrick Aspen Sinclair plunged headlong from the plinth. It dropped like a weightless thing of white paper. But where it struck their bodies, and the path below, it detonated into ten million fragments, flinders, splinters, shards, into dust clouds like steam and cannon smoke, into a noise like the end of the world.

Vivien crouched, hearing the noise, which would never be over.

But the noise *was* over. There was no noise at all. A kind of blank. And then she heard the gradual spattering of a thin hail—the final debris falling, settling.

The world had not ended. Only been adjusted.

Connor was now the only man standing. The other three were down, immobilized, two apparently struck by chunks of marble, and unconscious. Connor and Vivien were unique in that, beyond the injuries they had already received, nothing from the falling statue, impossibly, miraculously, had hit either of them. Not a scratch. Not even any grit in the eye.

She heard Connor's voice from far off, and marveled she could ever have mistaken any other voice for his, ever.... He was talking into his mobile, asking coolly for the police. She ceased to listen to the words, listening only to his voice. And then she looked down at the path, and saw that something had rolled there, to her feet.

It was the head of the statue. Also impossibly, it, too, had mostly survived the impact. It lay there on the ground, one cheek blunted a little, staring up at her with such composed yet bitter sadness. Even when Connor took her in his arms, she stared on into its face, until her own tears blinded her.

Chapter 11

The hammock swung gently.

Vivien lay back on the cushions, looking up through half-closed eyes at a sky of deep August blue.

Somewhere there was the distant noise of a harvester in the fields, over the walls of the garden. From the old orchard, bees buzzed back and forth, and she could smell flowers…. No roses. Not here. She was glad of that. It might take her some while, she thought, to like their perfume again.

Her mind turned back, flipping over its pages like a well-thumbed book. She let it. It was no good always running away from the past.

In the most bewildered way, Vivien hadn't wanted the necessary police to arrive at Addie's flat that July night. Eventually she saw she was irrationally trying to protect Connor from having to deal with them. Because, if they had previously suspected him of murder (she would have sworn, suspected him wrongly), surely this must be for him a grisly ordeal.

But Connor was only straightforward with the police, and they with him. It seemed they, too, must have concluded all former suspicions were unfounded.

When the turmoil of cars, uniforms, flaring lights, rounding up and questions were over, Connor and Vivien, on police advice, sought the casualty department of the nearest hospital. It was Thursday night, and "custom," as an orderly put it, slight; they didn't have to wait too long. Their injuries were minor. Even the knife slash along Connor's upper arm, though colorful, needed only two stitches. The doctor seemed as much concerned at Vivien's rosebush scratches. Filled with tetanus boosters, they left the hospital around 1:00 a.m.

A *non*-Cwick cab took them to Vivien's flat.

On edge, and high with adrenaline, they sat most of the night in her little front room, eating toast and drinking tea. Near sunrise they went to bed, crammed close together on the narrow mattress, not making love but burrowing into each other, despite the heat, like animals in winter.

When Vivien woke at 3:00 p.m. the following afternoon, she lay a long while, looking at Connor's sleeping face. Returning with mugs of coffee, she stroked his hair and kissed his mouth. One, then two coffee-matching black eyes unclosed, and two strong tanned arms—one bandaged—took hold of her.

"An unreasonable argument, an attack by villains, a ride in a police car to an A and E department, plus a night with absolutely no sex. Wow, Vivien. Don't ever say I don't know how to show you a good time."

"The only trouble is, however can we surpass such

a wonderful date? Nothing could possibly equal
it...could it?''

"Let's see..."

"Oh, you're so bruised, Connor—''

"Then, kiss it better.''

Surely by then there were scarcely any restraints on
them. They had talked it all through. Almost all. Vivien
thought that finally she knew the majority of the facts,
everything that was of an ordinary human origin. Most
important, she didn't now believe that Connor had murdered Kate Mortimer. Though she had yet to hear Connor's version of events, the profile of psychopath didn't
fit him. The evidence was against it now.

Even so, the plot *was* quite unnerving. A group of
unscrupulous developers had been buying up part of
Coronet Square, and Adelaide Preece, by refusing to
shift and holding out for a better deal, had got in the
way of their scheme.

The would-be purchasers had then conceived the
idea of frightening Addie, an old and traditional
method among their kind. But Addie was far too un-
aware to notice or reflect on any unusual pressure. And
by the time the developers put their backup plan of
coercion into effect, Addie was in France, and Vivien
had been installed instead.

Armed with duplicate keys, three hired thugs let
themselves into the flat above, which was already sold
and empty. Cutting down through joists and ceiling,
removing and replacing a piece from the plasterwork
with a hinged facsimile, they had soon gained a way
into the lower apartment. Connor had suggested Adelaide was so unobservant, this "building work" might
well have gone on when she was off the premises.

The ceiling entry was an ingenious route. It enabled any of the men, whenever they wanted, to enter the lower flat by a rope, later pulled up with help from a companion above. Generally their excursions went undetected—except for the penultimate time, when one of them had evidently kicked the wall in transit, leaving a scuff mark.

The gang would arrive in the flat quietly, normally at night. Their mandate, as the police confirmed, was to stay within certain boundaries, stealing the occasional garment—unnoticed at first by Vivien, since the stolen clothes were Addie's own—removing food from the fridge and wine from the larder racks, also unnoted.

It seemed, too, that in avoiding Addie so scrupulously, they had never *seen* her and so did not grasp that Vivien, when she moved in, was someone else. But when Vivien—Addie, as they thought her—had visitors, of whom one way and another there had been quite a few, the villains cautiously lay low.

They had presently, noting the absence now of a car, put the card of an invented cab company under the phone for her. People sometimes forgot they had accumulated such items, and the appearance of the card wasn't meant to alarm. They hoped she would use it, and so end up in a car with two of them. No doubt threats would then have been offered, though again, probably not going too far. But when the driver arrived to take Vivien (Adelaide) off for this jaunt, Connor had been in the flat. Dismissed, the "taxi driver" had had to go.

The decapitated roses were also their work. And they had kindly finished the wine from bottle and glasses.

"But you frustrated them constantly, Vivien," Connor had said. "You didn't notice so many of the would-be worrying clues they were leaving for you. Not because you're a blockhead like Adelaide, but because the territory wasn't your own. So then, they needed to rev it all up.''

Vivien said, ''Was the business of switching on all the lights part of that?''

''No. *That* wasn't. I'm afraid it was Cinnamon. She's been—how shall I put this?—*seeing* Lewis. When she saw he'd developed much more interest in you—as well as going off to dinner with his wife, Angela, and then to meet one of the wine waitresses from the premier—Cinnamon, who is scared of Angela actually, decided to try a little freak-out of her own on you. She used the spare keys she'd previously got from Addie for Scavengers use—and then, being Cinnamon, forgot to tell me about. She confessed all this to me the next afternoon. That was why I came over directly to Adelaide's flat, to explain about the lights. And there you were with Lewis, exactly as Cinnamon had sniveled you would be.''

''You believed *her?*''

''No. I just— It was being there again. I was okay there with you, my darling. But that next day, the kitchen with all that steam…''

''So why did you come back later, just in time to save me so dramatically?''

''I'm an actor, remember. No, I'd regained my sanity. After which I'd called you. At Adelaide's, at Camden. I couldn't get any answer, and then, calling Adelaide's one last time, the line went. No fault. No excuse. I knew it had been cut.''

''And you were right.''

That last night, offended by Vivien's (Adelaide's) lack of response to terrorization, the versatile villains had opted to step up the campaign. They saw to the phone and the lights. The crowning touch had been the resin gum applied to the front door and keyhole.

"I got to the door and saw the resin—they hadn't made a neat job of it. I didn't waste any more time. The way in over the back gardens is comparatively easy. Remember, I'd lived there. Then I heard your scream. You have wonderful lungs, Vivien, fortunately. I never sprinted so fast in my life."

The villains had gone too far, further than they had been told to go. They had panicked. And so the only option left, out there in the wild garden, was to beat Connor up and "soften" Vivien to a state where neither she, nor Connor, would seek police help.

"They wanted the tenant—you, they thought—out, and the flat free. Otherwise they wouldn't get paid. Being brainless, they never thought any of it through."

During the following days, extra information filtered through from a helpful police superintendent. Vivien, it seemed, was not the only victim of this particular gang. The police thought it unlikely either she or Connor would need to be involved any further.

Almost every question was being answered. But not quite all.

Certain things stayed stubbornly unsolved.

Who had left the first rose in the conservatory—and how? No one, amid all the plethora of wrongdoing, would admit to that. As for the opened book thrown down on the table, the villains—who anyway stridently denied touching anything that might be valuable, such as an expensively bound book—seemed unlikely to have knowledge of the text or its aptness.

Pieces of the puzzle remained undone.

Pieces of both puzzles—the supernatural, if so it was, and the past.

Four days after the events at Addie's, Connor went back and rescued Vivien's stuff for her. By then there was an unobtrusive police presence in Coronet Square, and Connor had called Addie, "rampaging through Barcelona, trampling the Gaudis." He had told her, it seemed, in answer to her complaints, that she was lucky Vivien wasn't going to sue.

That night, too, he told Vivien he was through with Scavengers. "Lousy friends like Lewis betray their friends. It isn't just lousy lovers that do it. He can deal with the movie company as well, the ones who want the statue of poor old shattered Patrick. I hope they make him sweat."

It seemed there was a chance of a film role for Connor. It was to be shot in Italy. "I'd like it. Providing it won't get in the way of us."

He had left acting alone two years ago, for a reason, Connor said. He would tell her. But not here, not in London.

At the thought of confronting the last piece of the real enigma, something made Vivien draw back, half-afraid.

But then he started to tell her about his house in Gloucester. "It's where I live when I'm out of London." A small, four-square stone building, with two acres of garden, a stream and apple orchard, situated among fields, and about one and a half miles outside Fairford. He added very seriously, "The church at Fairford has some of the oldest authentic fifteenth-century glass in England. The first window concerns the temptation of Eve. It involves apples—"

Lunch had been sumptuous. Connor had cooked it. After the strawberries and cream, he vanished into the house to make coffee, and Vivien lay back in the hammock, slowly swinging, watching distant blue sky and green gnarled apple boughs heavy with red fruit.

This was a dream house. And she was safe, safe with her lover, who loved her....

The light *clink* of coffee mugs brought her back.

"You were asleep. You look beautiful when you sleep. But then you wake up and you're even more beautiful. Clever Vivien." He kissed her. "Your mouth is beautiful. And this...and this...and these..."

But then he drew away. It was almost as if someone invisible had pushed him. He sat down on the wooden seat by the tray of coffee, staring at her. Silent.

Vivien's heart knocked against her breast.

"What is it?"

"I think, if you don't mind— I think I'd better tell you now. I mean, about Kate."

Vivien sat up—difficult in the swaying hammock. She said nothing. The strawberries seemed to turn to coils of iron in her stomach. What would he say? Until now—nothing. What had he *done?* She had almost been able to forget.

"I'm sorry. It's the wrong time, probably. Would there ever be a good one? But I need to do this. I need you to know. Oh, Vivien, I loved Kate, but she's gone. I don't want her in the garden here with us, or in the bed with us. I have to put her to rest."

Vivien found air, from somewhere.

"Go on."

"Kate and I—we met four years ago. What I have to say is that she was wonderful. That's all I want to say directly about Kate.

"Right after we got together, there was a lot of luck,

suddenly a lot of work, and quite a bit of money. I—
We hadn't expected it. I bought the flat in London—
Adelaide's flat now—because it was pretty central, and
opulent in a way neither of us had ever known. We
should have been happy. We were. Then things
changed.

"The first thing was the statue. Suddenly a solicitor
landed me with it, due to some arrangement my de-
serting wastrel skunk of a father made. Perhaps he
meant well. I just think he'd never found a buyer. But
Kate and I liked the statue. To start with. We used to
sit in the garden in the evening, reading or learning
lines. Kate used to speak to Patrick. Yeah. I remember
that.

"But then she started to talk *about* him a lot. She
knew the whole thing, plenty of people do—Nevins,
Emily, all that. She kept saying, 'Wouldn't it make a
fantastic period drama, Connor, you could play Patrick,
I could play Emily.' I used to say, 'Just be careful who
you're going to cast as Nevins.' She even found a
book—Shakespeare—with a picture of Emily in it.

"That July, I got the lead role in *The Crucible*—*the*
role—John Proctor. It was quite an important production, in Leeds. Kate wanted Abigail. She auditioned for
it, thought she'd done well. Then they decided she was
too old for the part. She was only twenty-six. On a
stage that wouldn't have mattered—but they'd made
up their minds. We talked it over. Kate was terrific
about it. She said I must go ahead. She'd come down
at weekends. We'd make a holiday of it. And she'd be
there for the first night."

Connor paused. His face had no expression.

"A girl called Alex took the part of Abigail Wil-
liams. She *was* young enough, apparently, about sev-

enteen, eighteen. But also she was an astonishingly good actress. She wasn't better than Kate—and certainly not so polished or skilled. Alex didn't know enough yet, but she had a kind of quality...a letting go. She'd come out on stage, even in rehearsal, in jeans, with her hair tied back in an elastic band—and she was...gone. Abigail was there instead. Alex had some special gift not all of us get.

"Vivien, I liked this girl, and I admired her ability. She was easy to work with, and ready to learn. And yes, she was attractive. But there was nothing else between us, except what's in the play. I need you to believe that, Vivien. Kate never did."

Vivien sat, still as he. She felt cold under the sun. She said nothing, nor did he prompt her.

"Maybe if I'd been on my own, I might have been interested. But I wasn't. And it was Kate I was in love with. Oh, I really was. I'd go crazy every Friday night, knowing she'd be there on Saturday. I used to hate saying goodbye on Monday morning. I kept saying to her, 'Come and stay for longer.' At first she said she couldn't. Then she wouldn't. Then, when she did come, it was different. She'd started to try to trap me—that's how she described it afterwards. To catch me out. I didn't notice how she kept on and on about Patrick and Emily and Nevins. Kate thought Alex and I were having sex. We weren't.

"Perhaps I praised Alex too much. I don't know. I've tried to know. I think for Kate it was being alone in London. No work. No me. In the beginning we'd speak on the telephone every night. Until the calls got weird. That was when she'd decided I was cheating on her, and she was trying to *trap* me. And I was too much of a klutz to realize what was going on. So I'd try to coax her into a better mood, and she'd start lamming into me down the phone—how I didn't care about her, wanted it all ways. Insane stuff. I'd get angry myself. Didn't figure it out. I had a lot on my mind with the play. Didn't think. I was a bloody fool.

"Then it was first night. Actors can be superstitious. Even if I hadn't been— I got a card from Kate, which I'd half expected, even though I was supposed to meet her off the train that day. I opened it—it was a plain postcard, and she'd written slantways across it. I still remember exactly. It said: *Shan't be there, sweetie. Because you don't need me. You've got your glorious Alex. Just like your rotten father had his gambling, and rotten Emily had her Nevins. So enjoy your rotten selves.*

"I called the flat. No one answered. I couldn't let everyone else down. So I thought. I got through that damned play somehow. About 2:00 a.m. I took a train down to London."

Connor stood up. He turned from Vivien and looked out across the orchard to the fields in wavering sunlight. All Vivien wanted was to hold him, shield him from the edge of this awful memory—but she found she could not move.

"When I walked in through the door of the flat, Kate was sitting there in the room with eight sides we'd both liked so much. She hadn't showered or washed her hair—but she'd chopped it short, unevenly. She looked up and grinned at me. 'What kept you?' she said. 'Couldn't drag yourself off her?'

"Then it all came out. All she thought I'd done. I tried so hard to explain it away. You think that if you're not lying, you're going to be believed.

"She wasn't even shouting or being particularly

spiteful, the way she'd got over the phone. She just brushed everything I said aside. Then she said, 'Let's have a cup of tea.' I let her go into the kitchen—I was trying to get myself together. Then I realized she'd been gone a long time.

"When I went into the kitchen, it was full of steam. It was like that time with you, when Lewis— Just like that. She was standing there over the teapot, crying, while the water boiled away. I put my arms round her and she threw me off. She made me stand across the room, and she refilled the kettle. I thought she'd scald herself—somehow she didn't. Then we just stood there, the kettle boiled, and she made the tea.

"She said to me 'I made this with love.' I drank the cup down. It was bitter—I didn't think. She stood looking at me, and then she said, 'My love for you comes in a little bottle marked Sleeping Pills. That's what I mixed in the tea. I reckon you've just swallowed about six.'

"I didn't believe her. Then the kitchen went round and I found myself flat on the floor. I blacked out before she used the knife on me. She could have finished me. I don't know what stopped her. It didn't stop her from—"

Connor's voice ended. It was like a theater, one actor alone on the stage. Vivien saw this. She saw she was the single audience. She thought, No, it isn't that.

Then his voice, steady and perfect with its training, resumed. "She swallowed the rest of the pills. By the time I came round, it was too late. The ambulance guys kept telling me that. Kate left a suicide note. Somehow I can't recall what that one said."

Chapter 12

When the doorbell went, Vivien crossed her tiny flat, neither quickly nor slowly, and opened the door. If she had had any feeling left in her, she might have been surprised to see Angela Blake, not the postman, standing there in a smart linen dress.

"Can I come in? Yes, I can. Thank you so much, Vivien." She slid straight by, passing Vivien with the slickness of a thin fish. In the front room Angela halted, waiting for Vivien to join her.

"What do you want?"

"To know why you left Connor up in Gloucester."

Vivien said, "That's none of your business."

"Yes, it is. But anyway, I've guessed. He told you about Kate, the whole disgusting saga two years ago. And I assume, from your prissy flight back to Camden, you didn't believe him. You thought he drove Kate to what she did by his unfaithfulness, lies and cruelty."

Vivien felt something give way inside her. She

hadn't let it do so until now. All through the journey back, all through these three days, the phone unplugged, her bed unslept in, she had been steel.

Even now, rationally, she said, "I didn't want to believe that. But he is an *actor*. And…it was a perfect performance."

Angela scowled at her with icy blue eyes. She looked abruptly familiar, as though Vivien had seen her many times in the past. Why confide in her, though?

Vivien heard herself say, softly, "Let's face it, Angela, anyone could say what he said to me. How can I ever know if it's true?"

"Couldn't you just have trusted him—after he told you so much?" Angela seemed angry. Well, she was Connor's friend apparently.

"I trusted someone before. No, it wasn't anything like this. But I know me, I get taken in—"

"For heaven's sake!" Angela, annoyed, was impressive. Hot, then cold once more. She said, "Sit down. I've heard you. Now you'll listen to me."

"Why should I?"

"Because Kate Mortimer was my sister, may the lord forgive my parents. I can prove it. Oh yes, *I* know you, too. I've brought the proper documents with me." She clapped the slim-line bag at her side. "I have them here, and my marriage lines, to show my maiden name of Mortimer. Oh, and something from a private detective Kate hired to investigate Connor. The man couldn't find anything against him. Made no difference to Kate."

"Her…sister?"

"That is what I said. I wish I hadn't been. She was an insecure and untrustworthy kid, who grew into an unbalanced and manipulative woman. And jealousy?

Kate *invented* it. She was jealous of everyone. Of me. Of our brother. And worst of all, of every man she ever had. And she used to get back at us. Connor? She *adored* Connor, couldn't wait to get him. Then she got him. Then she started being jealous of him, following her usual timetable. He could never see it then. If he sees it now, he'll never say. He is *loyal,* Connor. Infuriatingly so. Even to Lewis for so long. And to Cinnamon, that idiotic little tramp—''

Astounded, Vivien stared.

''Kate resented every good acting role that Connor landed. That may sound odd, but it's completely true. When he went to Leeds, she said one thing to him and something else to everyone else she knew. She spent hours whining to me about the part she'd been cheated of, and how he'd left her alone with nothing. What she was really saying was, *I want what he has.* It was her only creed. Then she fed herself the idea he was two-timing her. *Connor.* I said he's loyal. And he loved her. That's the worst part. Loved her to bits.''

''Then—''

''Then finally she managed to drive herself completely off her own head. Connor was cheating, had shamed her. And all he'd done, Vivien, was love her, and be too blind not to see what she really was. In the end she was mad enough with pills and drink to do what she did. To both of them. But I try to think it was some mangled remaining shred of decency that made her miss with that knife.''

''You say—''

''I say Connor is blameless. I can give you a list of people who know all the facts. Who knew *Kate*—years before he did, which is more to the point. But maybe the word of a sister will do. God knows, it's partly why

I put up with Lewis. And why he slings it all up at me when he has his little flings. 'Going to go mad like sis?' he says to me. 'Feeling a bit *Katish* today?'

"I—" said Vivien.

"*You*. You should be ashamed. You left him. But here you are, look at this." And Angela put down on Vivien's lap the documents she had spoken of, all laid out in a folder with insulting neatness.

Vivien didn't look at them. She whispered something.

"What? If you want to know why I came here, it's because I don't enjoy lies. And I care about Connor. He's been hurt enough."

"Actually," Vivien answered, "I just asked if he was still in Gloucester."

"London. Here's the number. Go and call him. Pray that he answers or I may kill you myself."

Vivien went to the phone. She prayed Connor would answer. He did.

Connor's rented London flat was as dire as he had described. There was nothing to look at there but each other, nothing to do there but make love. It was heaven on earth.

Astride her lover, Vivien gazed down into his agonized face.

His bare chest rose and fell with his racer's breathing, skin like matt satin over muscles of bronze. Through the smoke of dark hair, the wicked scar, forgotten. She would erase his pain. Where another woman had harmed him, Vivien would make him whole.

"Wait—" he gasped.

"*No.*"

"Darling, if you don't...I can't promise..."

Vivien smiled, shook her head.

Dominant and determined, she moved on him, drawing him in and in, holding him, taking away his reason.

"You're mine," she said.

His body arched, giving in to her desire and to his own. His hands gripped her. The torrent of his streaming hair, the golden body—bringing him to the summit of delight tipped Vivien also away among the stars.

They fell together back to the world. It wasn't, after all, such a bad place to be.

"Vivien, I brought a book with me from Fairford. I want you to see it."

Into her hands he gave an old, green-cloth-covered volume. She read the faded gilt of the title: *No Way But This: The Shakespearean Tragedy of Emily Rose and Patrick Aspen Sinclair.*

"Connor, I'm not sure I want to read this."

"Just one piece. I've marked the place."

Vivien opened the book slowly. She glanced at the publishing date, which was 1912. Then she turned to where the bookmark had been inserted.

"This is the last letter he wrote—"

"Before he shot himself. I know."

"Then, why—"

"You told me about the rose in the conservatory, and the quote from *Othello*. And the dreams. You told me about the photograph... My God, as if I needed to be told. You— You look so like her, like Emily. The moment you opened the door of the flat that morning... And Kate— She'd written that foul, joking, meaning-it *threat* on the book—how if I met Emily, Kate would be out of it. And Vivien, she *was*. And if you never knew why I behaved the way I did, well, there it is.''

"Yes. Connor—''

"An explanation for the supernatural? I've never been that much into psychic stuff—but, *Vivien*. The way the statue moved—fell—three men disabled, you and me without a scratch. Please—read Patrick's last letter.''

She read.

"O, Emily, my Rose. My Life.
I killed my own self in those moments that I ended your existence. To follow you is nothing. But yet, I dreamed last night I lay unsleeping on my couch, and your ghost came to me, white, like a girl of stone. I knew you had come to summon me away to death and punishment, but I was not afraid. For on the wall, before ever you touched me, sweet, I saw our two shadows, yours and mine, locked in one holy kiss. In this I read a distant forgiveness, and a love reborn.

I have damned myself. But God is all merciful, unlike his creation. Centuries I must suffer, and gladly will, but when I have served my time in Hell, I believe that I may find you once more. Our lips will meet again in Paradise.''

Vivien raised her head. "It was what I dreamed— the other way round. What does it mean?''

Connor said slowly, "I don't know. Maybe what he says—forgiveness, redress… Maybe love doesn't make him angry anymore. Maybe we set him free.''

"I hope so. Forgive me, then, for leaving you when you told me.''

"Ah, Vivien. But you never left."

"That's true."

They sat leaning together.

"There is," he said at last, "one further thing you should do. Call your friend Ellie."

"I already have."

"Call her back. Ask her over for a wedding."

"Whose?"

"If I said ours, would that be too soon?"

Vivien looked into his face, his eyes. Further.

"Only if you'd prefer me to ask *you.*"

"Ask me."

She knelt down, smiling and naked before him, on one knee.

"Mr. Connor Sinclair, will you do me the great honor of becoming my lawfully wedded husband?"

He drew her up again into his arms. "I accept, Vivien Gray. Now, seal it with a kiss."

Outside the windows, the moon rose on London, white as marble.

* * * * *

Dear Reader,

Love and fear are two of the great archetypal themes.
Nearly everyone uses them, from Shakespeare to
Walt Disney. They're the main ingredients of some
of the oldest stories on earth.

They create, too, a perfect balance—fear stops the heart,
but love makes the world go round.

Having an opportunity to write a novella where love
and fear were the major driving forces was to me both
a challenge and a fascination. Though I often deal in
both commodities, this concentrated canvas gave me
a different freedom. And where fear was the salt and
pepper, love certainly became, for me in this work, almost
a character in its own right—so much so that I couldn't
resist a reference to Eros, the Greek god whose arrows
pierce the hearts of humans and cause them to fall in love.

Love dominates these pages, now playful, now tender, now
erotic, a thing of desire—yet, too, a source of deepest pain.

This mysterious magic that can possess us, rule us, make
us mad—or more sane than we've ever been—what is it?
Scientists can explain it away in whatever biological or
pheromonal terms they wish. For though we're perhaps
preprogrammed to sexual desire—where does *love* come
from? It's the triumph of the human race, as well as its
stumbling block. And I think we, as people, should be
boastfully proud of this wonderful gift we have, which
brings with it so much delight and, even in heartbreak,
so much knowledge of ourselves and those around us.
Perhaps it really *is* true. Love makes the world—that
is, the world of the senses and the spirit—go round.
So…let's keep ourselves moving!

THE DEVIL SHE KNEW

Evelyn Vaughn

I got help from some great critiquers—
Deb, Mo, Kayli and the Writers of the Storm—
and I am grateful for every bit of it.
But this one's gotta go to Leslie and Paige.

Part 1

Marcy wrapped a towel around herself, crossed from her bathroom to her bedroom, opened her walk-in closet—

—and nearly fell into a roiling tunnel of otherworldly flame.

Smoke billowed into her bedroom, darker than midnight, as if the tongues of bright orange fire were casting sooty black shadows. The stench of heat and something else, something unidentifiable, seared her nose and her lungs and stung her widening eyes. And the sound of it, like a hiss, like a scream…

Like a whole lot of screams.

Marcy slammed the door.

For a long, stunned moment she stared at it, uncomprehending. Then she ran, still towel-clad and barefoot, for her apartment's kitchen. She kept a fire extinguisher there because she'd read she should. Should she use it now or call 911 first? Necessities clashed for order. She had to get her cat, Snowball, out, and to warn the rest of the building, and to—

It was the laugh that stopped her.

Deep and malevolent, it splashed out of the bedroom doorway and eddied around her like something physical, something sticky, something downright dangerous. Marcy hesitated.

A *laugh?*

Stuttering reason battled with a different instinct. A more primal understanding clawed upward through her panic.

Somehow, that fire wasn't fire.

The closet's crystal doorknob hadn't been hot under her hand. She wasn't burned, although she and the peach-colored bath sheet she'd wrapped around herself, after her shower, now felt unnaturally dry.

Yes, she'd seen flames—what she thought were flames—but she hadn't actually seen her neatly hung clothes or her built-in dresser burning. In fact, the fire had seemed to swirl, like water spinning down a drain, like a...

Portal. The word came unbidden, crazy. Like a *portal* of some kind.

And *fires don't laugh.* Not even happy ones.

Marcy's sense of reality balked. If it really was a fire, every second counted! Extinguisher, 911, cat, neighbors.

But if it wasn't...

Oh no.

A second helping of guilt now iced her fear, except that she wasn't sure which outcome she dreaded more. Would it be worse if her apartment really was on fire, or if something strange and otherworldly, something that really couldn't be happening, was...well... happening?

Especially if it was her fault?

Either way, insane or not, she had to be sure. She took a deep breath and turned reluctantly back toward the bedroom. *After* grabbing her little white fire extinguisher from under the sink.

She made herself approach the closet, tentatively reached out her free hand...

And touched the old-fashioned, crystal doorknob.

No heat. No stench of smoke. Nothing.

She turned the knob and, very carefully, cracked the door. Everything in her walk-in closet looked normal. She drew it wider, relief washing through her—

Poof! In a sudden burst, flames and a heavy, inky smoke roiled out toward her. It *was* a kind of tunnel, swirling counterclockwise far deeper into her closet than any five-by-eight dimensions should allow. Marcy now recognized the hissing, screaming noise as actual hissing and screaming. *Inhuman* hissing and screaming. A sulfuric stench mingled with the smoke that tore at her throat. The word *brimstone* came to mind. And over it all, through it all, rolled that deep, dark, unhappy chuckle—and a sudden thought, as clear as if it had been spoken.

At last...

Marcy dropped the fire extinguisher on her foot, too scared to even cry out. Then she slammed the closet door again. Even if nothing else made sense, *that* sure did! She backed out of the bedroom, limping. She bumped into the doorjamb and bit back a scream. She kept going, backward, all the way into the living room. She was completely dry now, despite having just gotten out of the shower, and very possibly insane as well, but...

But this sure didn't seem to be something the fire department could help her with.

Either she was imagining it all, or there was a...

Think it.

There really was a portal to Hell in her walk-in closet.

But why? How? When...?

Slowly Marcy turned to her glass-topped coffee table. On it sat the remains of the white candle she'd used last night after getting home from a disappointing ten-year class reunion to face a dismal twenty-eighth birthday. Trails of semitranslucent wax had hardened in middrip down the side of the brass candlestick, like stopped time. Remnants of charred paper still curled in the china saucer beside it, waiting for her to bury both the ashes and candle stub like a good mage was supposed to. A trade-size paperback book, *Magic for Beginners,* still sat under the table—all of it a mocking reminder of Marcy's first spell attempt ever. She'd been reading about magic for months now, and it wasn't supposed to work like whatever was in the closet. This spell in particular should have been simple, innocent, harmless. A meditation, practically. A where-have-I-been-and-where-am-I-going spell.

Clearly something had backfired, and now she was in well over her head. Maybe over anybody's head. But with flames behind her closet door, Marcy couldn't waste time reviewing her meager collection of store-bought books on modern witchcraft. She certainly couldn't do nothing. She needed help.

So she did what any other single, urban-dwelling

woman would do. She telephoned the maintenance man.

Tomas Martinez was a scary guy, true.

But this, at the moment, seemed scarier.

Tomas was having a good time frightening little old ladies when his cell phone beeped.

"Me, I'm not so much into the old traditions," he was admitting from his perch atop an aluminum ladder. He deliberately rolled the *r* in *traditions,* though he normally had no accent, for effect. He was hanging garlands of red, yellow and brown silk leaves for Mrs. Roberts's party tomorrow. Something about her insistence on providing a "more godly alternative" to the supposedly satanic celebration of Halloween had brought out the devil in him.

Not hard. The devil in him was never far from the surface, especially when he found himself annoyed by someone else's self-imposed fragility.

"What sort of traditions?" asked his white-haired tenant, keeping her distance.

"It's for my grandparents' sake we still do the *Día de los Muertes*." He unhooked the phone from his belt clip as he spoke. "Day of the Dead. We picnic in the cemetery, we eat skeleton candy, we commune with relatives who have passed on to the next world." He shrugged. "The usual, eh?"

Though Mrs. Roberts's mouth opened, nothing escaped.

Tomas winked as he asked into the phone, "What's up?"

"Mr. Martinez?" Speaking of self-imposed fragility! The use of his surname, the waver in the voice—it had to be Marcy Bridges from the third floor. She was extremely polite, that one, despite her apparent terror of him. He wasn't sure which annoyed him more.

"Last time I looked, that was me." Tomas used his free hand to drape more fake foliage on hooks he'd installed above the living-room drapes. "What can I do for you, Ms. Bridges?"

"I shouldn't have called," she said quickly, which annoyed him further. Any good rabbit should know that running was practically an invitation to be chased.

"Ah, but you did." Leaving an end of garland dangling, Tomas jumped effortlessly from the ladder so that he could better concentrate on her meek little Midwestern voice. "Might as well tell me why."

Whatever she said next came out so rushed and breathy that he couldn't understand, so he frowned and asked, "Pardon?"

She said, more slowly, "There's something... something *bad*...in my closet. I'm sorry. I didn't know who else to call...."

Some days he wished this building had more male tenants. He sighed and bent to retrieve another strand of autumnal garland from Mrs. Roberts's bin. "Is it a spider?"

"Um..." Marcy's voice wavered again. "Nooo. Not a spider."

"A mouse?" He noticed that Mrs. Roberts looked even more concerned about mice than she had about him communing with the dead, and he grinned at her.

Marcy Bridges wasn't answering. Not a good sign. Maybe he should be worried about her closet after all. "Something larger?"

"Arhwuhh..." Was she covering her mouth? Then she simply whispered, "Please hurry."

The "please," timid but clearly desperate, worried him.

"I'm on my way." Tomas dropped silk leaves back into their bin. "Do not worry. I will handle it." *Whatever it was.*

These apartments were his responsibility. He'd put time, sweat, even blood into them. He would accept no other outcome.

After jogging downstairs for a mousetrap and a baseball bat, Tomas took the old, rumbling ironwork elevator to the third floor. When he knocked on 3B's door, he startled a scream from inside.

Something was definitely wrong. Marcy Bridges might not be the most courageous woman he'd ever met—whenever she was forced to request his help, she seemed worried he might murder her in cold blood rather than fix her plumbing. Probably something to do with his long hair. The tattoo circling his left wrist. The fondness for black leather. The unvanilla heritage.

But a *scream?* That sounded as if she might be up against more than figments of her fearful imagination.

Tomas banged on the door harder. "Ms. Bridges? Hey, you okay?"

Locks rattled. In a moment, Marcy flung the door open.

Tomas stared, grip tightening uselessly on the baseball bat.

She was wearing a towel. *Just* a towel. He'd never really thought of Marcy Bridges as a looker before this moment. She had light brown hair and a medium build, nothing flashy or sexy about her...except maybe her mouth. Her wide, inviting mouth usually seemed out of place on so timid a woman. Or so he'd thought. That had annoyed him, too, the waste of such a mouth.

Now, what with all that soft, pale, *naked* skin, her mouth did not look out of place at all.

Her wide green eyes, darting back to the apartment behind her, did.

"What's wrong?" he demanded.

"I can't find Snowball." Her voice shook. "We've got to find Snowball!"

Snowball was her little white cat. Tomas knew that, because he had never once crossed her threshold without some plea, in person or in writing, for him not to let her furry feline demon escape. Go figure, that she'd be the one to lose the cat, except...

Well, she did say that whatever had frightened her was bigger than a mouse. "Is the cat in the closet?" he asked.

Marcy plastered a hand to her mouth and moaned.

Normally, the man kind of, well, concerned her. Tomas Martinez dressed like a biker. He wore his long, dark hair in a braid down his back. His golden eyes, like a tiger's, always managed to look simultaneously bored and predatory, neither of which Marcy enjoyed.

But she had worse fears to contend with. The closet. Her culpability. And now, worst of all, her cat.

Not Snowball. Not in that strange fire.

"I haven't seen her since I got out of the shower," she explained, limping hurriedly back to the bedroom with Tomas stalking after her. The cat was her roommate, her friend, the closest thing she had to a child. *Where was she?* "We played shower tag—she likes to balance on the ledge of the tub and pat at me through the curtain—but then I came in here..."

The bedroom looked normal.

Her step slowed, hopeful despite her previous fake-out. She even reached out and smoothed a wrinkled corner of her bedcovers. Maybe she'd imagined it. Maybe...

"Hey, lady." Tomas caught Marcy's arm with a large, warm hand, forcing her to either fully stop or try to drag him forward with her sheer strength. Not having an abundance of sheer strength, she faced him. He looked as solid as ever, somewhat annoyed, competent...and dangerous. For the first time ever, she felt relieved that he looked dangerous.

Fire with fire, and all that.

He said, "Not that I mind, but—have you noticed you're wearing nothing but a towel?"

Oh. Was she?

Marcy clutched the edges of the bath sheet closer together, then saw that the maintenance man's golden gaze, though still predatory, looked increasingly less bored or annoyed. Awareness oozed down her spine, and not from cold. Was he...?

"My cat may be in Hell and *you're scoping me out*?"

"In Hell?" repeated Tomas Martinez blankly. He did not deny the scoping. In fact, he blatantly continued to scope.

Marcy pointed dramatically at the closet door, and her towel began to slip. She caught it, then pointed again. "There's something in my closet and, well..." Only one way to say it. "I think it's some kind of portal to a hell dimension."

It took Tomas a long time to look away from her perilous towel, toward the closet. Then he squinted back at her, even more darkly intrigued. "Have you maybe been drinking, or have I?"

"Neither!"

He shrugged with a little sideways nod of his head, then went calmly to the closet door—and opened it.

Marcy closed her eyes.

"Here, kitty kitty kitty," he said, sounding more like he wanted to capture and eat the kitty than like he wanted to give it yum-yum treats and chin rubs.

Marcy winced her eyes back open.

Clothes filled her closet, hanging neatly from rods lining both sides. A long, six-drawer dresser stood against the inside wall under the shorter items. Her shoes sat in ordered pairs on top of that.

Not a bit of it burned with the fires of eternal damnation.

Good! Except... "That's not right," she said.

"Not right?" Tomas drew the door wider, to show her. "Ms. Bridges, if this is Hell, then Mr. Clean must be Satan. Not that people haven't had their suspicions..."

Normally, Marcy would have been more startled by the maintenance man's wicked smile. His sense of humor made him seem a little less dangerous...and in some ways, a little more. Now, she had no time to be startled. She limped a step closer. "No. I mean, this isn't how it was before."

Tomas shrugged and turned back to the closet. "Kitty? Hey, cat. *Gata.* Get your fuzzy butt out here."

Marcy moved up behind him, then leaned slowly around. *Please don't let Snowball be in there. Please let it all be some kind of delusion.* Her bare shoulder brushed his arm—and the air seemed to lurch around them. A gout of flame spiraled into existence in the center of the closet. It flared outward into a fiery ring, deepening in the center—

"*¡Madre de dios!*" Tomas yanked Marcy against his

side and spun as if to protect her as the widening ring became a tunnel. His hands were hard, and his broad shoulders blocked the flame. He pushed them both away from the closet, but his voice cracked. *"What the hell is that?"*

Marcy couldn't answer. She was numbly watching a flock of darting, black-winged things spill out of the portal in her closet, amidst the smoke, and wheel around her bedroom. One of them caught in her curtains, thrashing about. Another knocked a picture off the wall. They left black, smoky streaks across the walls and ceiling.

Again, she heard the throb of laughter, deep and malevolent and inescapable.

Give up, it seemed to say. *Send this fool away and give up yourself, give up your reality, give it all…*

To me.

Despondency washed over her, drew her down, pulled her under….

Tomas startled Marcy by spitting out a curse and catching her under the arms. His thumbs dug into her flesh, very near her breasts, holding her up. Marcy blinked, realizing that she'd been sinking and was halfway to the floor, hanging from his hold.

Embarrassed and disoriented, she tried to regain her bare feet while the maintenance man kicked the closet door shut. He didn't make it easier by dragging her out of the bedroom and shouldering that door closed, too.

Then he let her crumple to the cold linoleum, opening his grip only once she was safely down. She didn't mind, what with him pressing his back against the bedroom door as if to stop anything from getting out. He seemed even larger from her vantage on the floor. His eyes looked wild in more ways than one.

"What was that?" he demanded again.

"You heard it, too?" *Please have heard it, too.*

"Heard? What, heard? Did you *see* that thing? What *is* it?"

"I don't know!" Which was true—she hadn't had a lot more time to grasp this than he had. So why did she feel as if she was lying? "I left Snowball in the bathroom, and I opened my closet and…it happened."

"Why this morning?" But he didn't seem to expect an answer; he was wondering out loud. "Why here?"

I think it's because I did a spell. She had to tell him. She always did the right thing, and there Tomas Martinez stood like some dark street warrior between her and danger; of course she had to tell him. She parted her lips, drew a bracing breath…

And she couldn't force the words out.

"I—" she tried, looking up at him from the linoleum, but her throat closed. What she knew about magic was New Age theory, maybe the emotional attributes of certain colors, scents, crystals. Nothing she'd read had led her to believe she could summon anything so dramatic as whatever was swirling around in her closet. Snowball was gone. Her foot hurt. Now she'd drawn Tomas Martinez into danger. And something possibly evil and definitely otherworldly seemed to be speaking in her head.

Could this really be her fault?

"I—" she tried again, then sighed in defeat. She couldn't look up at this man and confess something this big. Not yet. "Maybe this is because it's my birthday?"

Tomas stared down through his tiger eyes. "Happy birthday."

"Thank you," whispered Marcy.

''Maybe it's not real,'' he said decisively, sharply, wonderfully. If only he was right! ''Stay here.''

He ducked back into the bedroom without her—to go one-on-one with hell.

The room looked normal as Tomas shut the door between it and the soft-skinned, towel-clad woman in the kitchen. Her wide eyes no longer annoyed him. *He* was freaked, and he'd probably had a lot more exposure to occult stuff like this than some Anglo chick had. Enough to know that what they'd seen in the closet had to be an illusion, anyhow. Didn't it?

Magic just didn't work that…dramatically.

He took his time glancing around Marcy Bridges's neat bedroom—reconnoitering, he told himself, not stalling. She'd apparently made her bed even before showering. The yellow bedspread and pillow covers matched the flowered drapes on the window, drapes with nothing struggling in them. Several obnoxiously cute stuffed animals sat evenly on her shelves, but those were the only creatures, or pseudocreatures, he saw.

Nothing dark and erratic wheeled around the room. Nothing sooty or black stained the walls.

''Not real,'' he muttered, speaking the words out loud for extra emphasis, or maybe extra power…but not so loud that Marcy might come in yet.

Not until he went *mano-a-mano* with that closet, just in case.

Tomas hadn't lied to old lady Roberts about his family's *Día de los Muertes* celebrations. Hispanic traditions had their share of mysticism. His grandmother had considered herself a *bruja*, a witch, complete with charms, spells, even the occasional curse.

He'd just accepted that as the way things were—except for her insistence that he was somehow sensitive. No guy in his right mind aspired to be *sensitive,* after all. Tough, sure. *Macho.*

Not sensitive.

So he'd been around his *abuela*'s superstitions and charms enough to know that what even a *bruja* considered magic wasn't likely to show as much attitude as what he'd seen in Marcy's closet. Therefore, there was nothing in her closet at all.

But something sure was making them think there was.

Considering it, Tomas sniffed the air. No weird, psychotropic fumes.

He picked up the fire extinguisher lying on the floor beside the closet, just in case. He tested the doorknob and then the door with his hand, like firemen taught third-graders, right along with drop-and-roll. He sniffed again, this time for smoke. *Nada.*

He opened the door—and relaxed. Nothing in her closet but closet stuff…including, he saw on closer inspection, a surprisingly slinky red dress with the tag still hanging off it. Never worn, but at least she owned it. He raised his eyebrows, increasingly intrigued by Marcy Bridges.

Just in case, though, he went through the ritual of protection his *abuela* had taught him and his siblings right along with table manners. He crossed himself three times, murmured a quick *Ave Maria,* then extended his hand and drew an invisible cross over the entrance to the closet.

Tomas hadn't been to church for years, but it was amazing what a man retained.

''You are nothing here,'' he said to the closet. ''Be gone.''

The barest hiss warned him. Flame flashed out. He threw himself backward, clear of the closet, and landed into a somersault, still clutching the fire extinguisher. Rolling onto his knees, catching his balance with one hand, he aimed the hose at the closet—and panted.

Nothing. Rather, nothing unusual. Just clothes.

So which part was real?

''Are you all right?'' called Marcy through the door.

No. He wouldn't be all right until he knew what the hell was going on. ''Stay out there,'' he called, regaining his feet. He didn't want to be distracted by all that smooth, clean skin just yet. No damn closet was going to get the best of him.

''You are not real,'' he challenged—and shot a spray of foam into the middle of the nice clean closet.

The foam sizzled and evaporated, as if it had hit something unbearably hot, before ever reaching the clothes.

Tomas took a quick step back, crossing himself from instinct instead of ritual. ''I said, you *are not real.*''

Something laughed. *She's mine,* it warned...except it didn't actually say anything. Even as he recognized the words, Tomas knew he hadn't heard them. Not with his ears.

But they were in his head, echoing as if they'd been screamed.

As he stared, a burst of flame appeared in the middle of the nice neat closet. It expanded into a ring, then a tube, then a tunnel, swirling harder, faster, like last time....

But then it lunged at him.

He threw the fire extinguisher at it—and the canister vanished down the tunnel of smoke and flame as if inhaled. He ducked behind the closet door, shutting it before the heat could do more damage, biting back a cry as a final tongue of flame licked out across his left hand.

He drew the burn to his mouth, then thought to look down at his hand. Yes, that was a burn all right. No matter what he wanted to believe, this was painfully real.

He actually spun, startled, when the bedroom door opened and Marcy peeked in from the kitchen. "Oh," she said softly, miserably.

Looking around again, Tomas now saw the damage to the room that his need for normalcy had blinded him to moments before. Superimposed across the neat-as-a-pin bedroom, charred streaks marked the ceiling and walls. Rips tattered the yellow curtains. The longer he looked, the more quickly normalcy faded to this new reality. A sulfuric stench seared his throat and lungs, almost as sharply as his burned hand, and several red-black, otherworldly, lizard-looking things lurked in the corners and on one of Marcy's bedposts.

Salamanders?

In *Chicago?*

"You're hurt." Marcy started into the bedroom but Tomas quickly intercepted her, shouldering her back out to the kitchen.

"This is crazy." He shut the door behind him with a second kick. He wished his *abuela* was there, fully there, so he could tell her he was finally taking her magic seriously…and maybe get some help! "Something crazy is happening."

"You're *hurt*." Marcy hitched up her slipping towel, opened the freezer and retrieved a bag of frozen peas to press onto his burned hand. "It *hurt* you."

"Damn thing's real after all," he admitted, barely noticing the hand.

Marcy, he noticed. She lifted one foot and stood on the toes of the other, drawing from a cabinet what had to be the biggest first-aid kit he'd ever seen outside of an ambulance. Reality may have pulled a fast one on him in her bedroom…but it was also shifting right here in the kitchen.

And no burn could keep him from appreciating those long, bare legs, or this woman's fingers on his.

"We should get out of here," he murmured.

Gentle, healing fingers, attached to long, bare arms…and softly rounded, pale shoulders…and the slope and swell of breasts, barely hidden beneath pink terry cloth…

The way Marcy peeked at the damage under the bag of peas, wincing at what was barely worse than a sunburn, reaffirmed her sheer niceness. So did her surprisingly firm "I won't leave my cat."

Now that she was spraying a cooling burn treatment onto his hand, then blowing on it, *nice* was surprisingly attractive. Lifting her clear green gaze toward his, fingers on his wrist, she didn't seem as scared of him, either. Had he thought her annoying before?

She smelled really good. And clean. And naked.

They stood very close, together against whatever lurked on the other side of those last two doors. Together in the danger. Together in this new, freakish reality. Together in understanding as he leaned closer, human warmth to human warmth, breath to breath…

"MROWRM!"

With a cry of delight, Marcy Bridges spun away from Tomas.

Marcy recognized that cry from over her head. It was Snowball's "Mommy!" cry, the one she used when she climbed a tree and couldn't get down, or when Marcy got home from a long weekend away, or when someone she disliked disturbed their home. The cat, clearly upset, drew it out into two syllables. *"MRO-WUM!"*

"Snowball!" Turning toward the call was an instinct even more deeply ingrained than whatever had compelled her to gaze up into Tomas Martinez's tiger eyes and...

And nothing. Of course nothing. The important thing was that Snowball was all right, crouched on top of the refrigerator, green eyes wide and accusing, white fur puffed spikily along her spine. Marcy raised a hand to her and Snowball completed the ritual by delicately sniffing, making sure Marcy was no imitation.

"MROWR!" the cat then wailed in displeasure, opening her mouth wide, showing most of her sharp little teeth.

"Oh, poor baby." Marcy reached over her head to catch Snowball and draw the cat's silky, warm body to her towel-wrapped breasts. "Were you up there the whole time? I was so scared!"

The towel began to slip. Marcy caught it up again. Snowball helped. Marcy didn't believe in declawing.

"Mommy was so scared for her baby," she murmured, kissing the sleek top of Snowball's head before the cat burrowed into the crook of her elbow, the way she might at the vet's. Marcy felt so relieved, she didn't even care if Tomas heard her talking baby talk, or referring to herself in the third person. "She was so scared."

"Mommy should be scared," Tomas reminded her, finally stepping away from the bedroom doorway. Either he figured nothing was coming after them from there—or he figured something was. "Mommy has a gate to Hell in her closet!"

Marcy felt somehow more sane hearing that he, too, thought it was a gate to Hell. Naming something gives one power over it, right? That's what her magic books said....

Then she remembered she couldn't necessarily trust her magic books. "That's what it looked like to me, too, but I wasn't sure... I mean, how *could* it be?"

Tomas said, "I can't fix hell."

No, she didn't imagine he could, no matter how complete his toolbox. She shouldn't have called him here, gotten him involved, gotten him injured.

And yet she was so glad he was here. As relieved as she felt to have an armful of Snowball again—to be gently rubbing behind the cat's ear, to feel Snowball's purring attempt to comfort them both—Marcy was just as relieved not to be alone in her kitchen, her apartment, her dilemma. Even if she was a horrible person for involving Tomas, even if she'd somehow damned herself—

—further—

—she was so very glad to have him here that she could have wept with relief.

If she was lucky, she could weep on his shoulder. It really was some shoulder.

Even better was when, with a single nod, he took charge.

"Come on," he said decisively, striding toward the front door.

She followed willingly, putting more weight on her hurt foot. "Where to?"

"My place."

In other circumstances, Marcy would have balked. She didn't know this man very well, and what she knew about him worried her. What made his apartment so safe?

But of course, that would be the *absence of portals to Hell*.

He was the one who stopped in her living room. "Wait."

That was less of a relief. She wanted to believe he was *good* at being in charge. "What is it?"

"You're only wearing a towel." His gaze slid down her in an extra, lingering reminder. "Me, I have no complaints. The other tenants...no need to worsen suspicions they might already have, if you know what I mean."

Marcy stared at him while Snowball burrowed deeper between her elbow and her towel, purring more frantically. Snowball wanted to leave, too. "I don't know what you mean."

"Reputations?" He said it like a teacher trying to walk a student through what should be an easy question. "Suspicions about what people might be up to...?"

"Oh! You mean them thinking you're a thug?"

Tomas scowled. His tiger eyes narrowed, and his lips thinned. Marcy's stomach flip-flopped. As long as he was on her side, she supposed she shouldn't mind the murderous look, but if he ever changed sides—or got hungry—she was in trouble.

He said, "People think I'm a *thug?*"

"Isn't that what you meant?"

"I meant *your* reputation, Miss Too-Quiet-and-Keeps-to-Herself."

Marcy stared. Snowball, in her arms, purred and burrowed.

"Miss Must-Be-Up-to-Something," Tomas prompted. "Miss Never-Brings-People-Home."

"You've been spying on me?" The only thing more unsettling than that thought was the momentary, politically incorrect trickle of delight that accompanied it. He was interested? Too bad he was a voyeur. "How could you spy on me?"

"I don't spy on you. Mr. Gilbert across the hall spies on you, and so does Mrs. Roberts downstairs, so you should probably wear something other than a towel before leaving with me." Tomas scowled. "Who is it thinks I'm a thug?"

"Uh...nobody?" She wouldn't even mention Ms. Hurt, from the second floor, even if Ms. Hurt was awfully obnoxious by the mailboxes. Not unless Tomas tortured her for names. "Anyway, I can't put on anything else."

"Why not?"

Dramatically, she turned, stretched out her cat-free arm and drew big, invisible loops in the direction of her bedroom door. "Hello? Gate to damnation in my closet?"

"Don't you keep any clothes...?" Apparently he remembered the dresser in the walk-in. "Who the hell keeps all their clothes in one closet?"

"It was an idea in an article from *Living* magazine," Marcy protested. "To clear one's bedroom and make it more airy."

Tomas squinted at her, clearly not up on the different home-and-living magazines.

"The one Martha Stewart puts out," Marcy clarified.

"Like Mr. Clean," he muttered.

Marcy said, "You can't blame this on—"

But she fell silent as Tomas Martinez began to undress, right there in her living room. *Wow.*

He shrugged off his black leather vest, careful of his hurt hand, then started tugging his T-shirt out of his jeans. Marcy stood completely still—except the slow sinking of every cell in her body, melting down into hot-sugar-goo somewhere below her stomach.

Somewhere. Right.

He pulled the shirt up and he had such abs. Such ribs. A chest that could grace a beefcake calendar. Shoulders. Upper arms with working-man muscles, and all of him a warm, toasty brown, like the most beautiful tan…. She felt meltier and meltier….

The spell of his beauty only released its hold on her when the collar of his T-shirt caught momentarily around his head, like some kind of nun's habit. Tomas Martinez might be sexy as hell, so to speak, but *Sister* Tomas….

In that momentary reprieve, Marcy managed to form words. "What are you doing?"

"My shirt should be long enough," he explained, holding it out to her. Some of his hair had pulled out of its braid to sweep across his cheekbone and tickle at his neck. That and his bare chest more than made up for that momentary nun image. "Put it on."

Now he was giving her the shirt off his back?

"I can't." Marcy felt unable to move for more reasons than her precarious towel, the purring cat she held, for even more than the melty feeling. He looked so…bronzed. Half-naked. He had some kind of thorny pattern tattooed around his wrist. And he smelled of something rich and earthy and just a little spicy.

Thinking suddenly seemed difficult.

Dangerous.

"Here," he sighed, taking the cat to give her the shirt.

Marcy extended a hand in warning—Snowball hated strangers!—but her cat had already twisted into action. Snowball growled, and squirmed, and hissed and dug her claws into Tomas's beautiful, bare arm.

Tomas narrowed his eyes in big-cat warning and hissed right back.

Snowball put her ears back but sat coiled and still, purring sulkily to comfort herself.

Marcy studied the Spanish words on the shirt, trying not to look as if she were inhaling Tomas's scent off of it. "What's that say?"

"Maybe you should put it on inside out." He looked a little embarrassed.

So she turned away from him and did so, breathing deeply. Only once she'd smoothed the shirt down all the way to her midthighs did she undo the tuck of towel underneath, letting peach terry cloth fall to her feet.

Funny…she felt even more naked wearing just the shirt. But he was right. They shouldn't stay in here any longer than necessary. Not until they knew what to do.

By the time she turned back to him to reclaim Snowball, something had changed. The energies in the room had changed—and Tomas looked more dangerous than ever.

"Take the book, too," he growled, with a nod toward the coffee table. In her panic over her cat's absence, she hadn't gotten around to clearing it. Apparently he'd just noticed *Magic for Beginners.*

Oh.

Marcy wasn't sure whether the weight of foreboding was because she'd been a fool to keep her spell from him...or because his immediate assumption mirrored her own worst fears.

Whatever was happening might well be her fault for playing with magic.

That scared her even more than the voice, the sort-of voice that curled through her head as she and the maintenance man left her apartment.

There is no place you can run, it seemed to warn. *I am everywhere.*

And you are mine.

Part 2

So Little Miss Good Girl was a witch wanna-be. That was the only assumption Tomas could make from the paperback, since *Magic for Beginners* wasn't exactly the kind of dusty, handwritten tome he'd sometimes seen at his *abuela*'s.

Great.

The part that annoyed him the most was that, clearly, she wasn't even any good at it. If she were a highly skilled magic user, at least he could admire her competence. But the idea that she may have been sitting in her neat living room foolishly summoning God-knew-what, for heaven knew what purposes...

It was almost enough to distract him from her wide, worried mouth.

Nowhere near enough to distract him from her legs.

In his shirt, and nothing else, she looked as if she'd just gotten out of bed. After sex. With him. He should be so lucky, her having legs like that...

Witch, he warned himself. But his *abuela* had been a witch.

Summoner of portals to Hell, he reminded himself, which went further toward keeping his distance.

"Should we warn Mr. Gilbert?" asked Marcy, shifting from foot to foot while they waited for the lumbering, old-fashioned elevator. He'd given her back the demon cat as quickly as possible, and she was cuddling it to her chest. Now she looked past him, at the other doors on her floor. Her leaning hitched the shirt up sinfully higher. "Or the Kendalls?"

"Warn them about what?"

"Whatever's in my closet! If the fire spreads..."

"It's not really a fire."

When she stared at his gauze-wrapped hand, he clarified. "We can pretend otherwise all we want, but you and I both know it's something magic. And it's after you, not them."

Still eyeing his hurt hand, she raised her eyebrows and looked stubborn. Sometimes he got the feeling she had more guts than she let on. But the feeling was usually fleeting.

"I got in the way," he said.

"But we should tell them something. If they were to get hurt because of me..."

Fine. Since the elevator was so slow, Tomas went to each of the doors and knocked. Nobody home at one place. Nobody home at the other. Thank heaven for Saturdays. The third apartment was vacant—good. He dug some *Fumigating: Please Keep Out* signs from his toolbox and hung them on the doors. Done.

Marcy watched him with something close to awe. He didn't know why, but that unsettled him. She didn't expect him to be the good guy here, did she? He'd fix what he had to fix, sure...

But he had his own reasons. His own responsibilities.

With a rumble, the old-fashioned elevator finally made an appearance and sat there, waiting for them to pull open its grillwork doors.

"In case of fire," murmured Marcy. He thought maybe she memorized those kinds of safety tips for fun. But looking at the elevator's close, closetlike interior, he kind of had to agree.

"Stairs," they said, deciding together. But when she lingered, forehead furrowed, as if the elevator might gobble up some innocents once left unattended, he reached in and switched it off. One more sign from his toolbox to hang on the inside door—Out of Order— and they were in business.

Only once they reached his first-floor apartment—a far messier place than hers—did Tomas confront his meekest tenant about her attempts at magic.

"What did you summon?" he demanded, pacing back from his bedroom with another T-shirt.

She said, "Do you have a pet?"

He stared at her, flat-out confused. If she'd summoned that thing in the closet as a pet, she was sure as hell breaking her lease!

She said, "If you have a pet, I should put Snowball in the bathroom so there won't be trouble."

Trouble? As opposed to *her* place?

"I don't have a pet," Tomas said through gritted teeth, so she reluctantly put down the cat, front paws first. The cat immediately hunkered low, wide green eyes surveying this new locale, then stretched out its neck and delicately sniffed an empty beer bottle on the floor. Then it glared at Tomas.

Pulling on the new shirt, Tomas refused to feel guilty about the mess. He hadn't planned on having guests. Compared to the magical mess Ms. Bridges had made, a little casual clutter hardly mattered...though his *abuela* would have disapproved of both kinds of messiness. Cleanliness being next to godliness and all.

Tomas didn't figure he'd been next to godliness for some time, either way. "You summoned something out of that book, right?"

"You keep saying that." She looked embarrassed. "I did a spell, but I didn't summon anything."

Right. It was just a coincidence that she was doing magic right before a portal to Hell appeared in her closet. "What kind of spell?"

"A direction spell, I guess you'd call it. I wanted some insight about my life—where I've been, where I'm going. My ten-year high-school reunion was last night," she added, and at first he thought it was another nonsequitur. "It was so strange, seeing how far so many of my classmates have come since I knew them last. Some had these great careers, and most of them were married. Some people have died already! A few seemed stuck in the past, and I really didn't want to become one of them. It got me thinking...so since I've been reading about magic for a while now, I decided to try the spell."

Frowning, Tomas took the book from her. "Which—?"

The page was marked with a pink Post-it note. Hardly eye-of-newt, toe-of-frog stuff. The glossy cover showed three pretty, young women of different ethnic origins, smiling as if to imply that even beginner magic users could find happiness and good looks if they would only shell out $14.95 for the book.

The whole mass-market presentation weirded him out. He imagined Marcy trying to decide whether to pick up a new Russell Crowe DVD or a book of spell craft. This was definitely not his grandmother's magic.

But he'd known that when he'd seen the portal.

He opened the book to the flagged page. Bold letters in a jazzy font pronounced:

Lifting the Fog—A Spell for Clarification.

"*This* is the spell you did?" he demanded.

Marcy nodded, looking embarrassed but stubborn. "I did it exactly like it says."

Tomas began reading. He was no expert, but that didn't mean he couldn't make some educated guesses. Who knew? Maybe if his *abuela* really was a *bruja*—instead of just being spooky and eccentric—magic was in his blood, too. Maybe he had a knack for understanding this kind of thing.

One page later, he had to discard that theory. "I don't understand any of this."

Marcy, who'd sunk onto a corner of his sofa to pet her evil white cat, seemed relieved to have a reason to look at him directly instead of sneaking embarrassed peeks. "What's there not to understand? Light the candles, say the rhyme, burn the paper. Then you wait for a sign."

Her eyes seemed especially large and vulnerable when she added, "Maybe whatever's in the closet is my sign."

He turned a page and saw a heading for a new spell—Magic to Foster Optimism. After that came Drawing Love into Your Life and so on. He turned back to the one-page Spell for Clarification. "This is all of it?"

Marcy stretched upward a bit, to peek at the book. Her cat, seeming annoyed, leaped soundlessly from her lap and slipped under the sofa in protest. "Yes."

"This is the spell you did."

Now her gaze turned wary, as if his stupidity worried her. "Uh-huh."

"How could this summon anything? It has you ask for protection, then to see more clearly, and that's about it. It's got to say *for the good of all* at least three times!"

"Uh-huh."

"This isn't magic. This is like an episode of *Oprah*!"

Marcy cocked her head, increasingly suspicious. "And you'd know the difference?"

It occurred to Tomas that, as suspicious as he'd been a few minutes ago, she might be twice that suspicious if she learned his particular background. "My mother watches *Oprah*," he hedged.

"And the magic part?"

Tomas swore, which made her lean back into the sofa cushions. Marcy Bridges was scared of him already, right? It might be better for everybody if he kept it that way. "Never mind about the magic part. You stay here—feel free to get some clothes out of the bureau. Stay out of trouble. I'll be back when I'm finished."

"Finished what? Where are you going?" Maybe she wasn't as timid as he'd thought, at that.

Grabbing his leather jacket off the hook by the door, Tomas said, "I'm going to do whatever it takes to fix this."

* * *

Marcy frowned at the closed door where Tomas had vanished. Well, wasn't *he* confident?

Then she frowned at herself. Wasn't his confidence a good thing?

Didn't she *want* someone to solve this? Just as she'd wanted someone—something—to tell her where she was going in her life. Life was easier when you got your information and protection and validation from outside sources.

So why did she feel so dissatisfied?

No matter—she did. There must be something *she* should do, *especially* if she was at fault in the first place because of her spell.

Tomas doesn't think your spell did this. That, more than anything else, brought her the first true relief she'd felt since finding Snowball.

But Tomas might not know everything. Right?

And if he did…Marcy had to wonder where he'd learned it.

Tomas had ducked his head into his helmet, straddled his Harley and ridden almost a mile before the spires down the block showed him where he'd instinctively headed.

The realization surprised him so much that he swerved into the closest parking lot and throttled down, lowering his booted feet to the pavement. Okay, so he was flying blind, here. It was one thing to let Marcy think he knew what he was doing with this portal-to-Hell business. It was another to actually know.

But this?

His *abuela* had been the magic user, not him. And she wasn't particularly good at listening anymore. So he'd automatically headed in the only direction where, instinctively, he'd thought he might find help.

Our Lady of Serenity. The nearest Catholic church.

Tomas swore. He'd been raised Catholic; gone through first communion and even confirmation. But after he left his parents' home, he also left behind the habit of regularly going to mass, much less confession. He'd thought he left behind the whole complex belief system, too.... Well, most of it.

And here he sat, running to a priest at the first sign of trouble.

Except this wasn't your average trouble. This wasn't a parking ticket, or a night in jail, or even getting a girl pregnant—and he would take that last one pretty damn seriously. This was some kind of otherworldly portal with fire and brimstone! This was a deep, disembodied voice that could only be demonic.

If this didn't merit holy intervention, then he didn't know what did.

Still...church? No.

Throttling up, he turned a tight circle and headed in the opposite direction, into the older suburbs, until he reached his grandparents' house. It had once been a perfectly good house, sometime after World War II. Nowadays it had an air of age and shabbiness that no amount of his repairs or fresh paint could completely stave off.

But the place was paid for. Unlike a certain apartment building he could name.

His grandfather, shoulders stooped and dark eyes bright, was standing inside the front door waiting by the time Tomas made it up the walk. "It's not Monday yet. We're not ready for Monday."

Monday, November 1, would be the *Día de los*

Muertes. The family really would be visiting the cemetery with traditional food and candles. He hadn't lied about that.

"I know, Poppi." Tomas bent to kiss the old man on his leathery cheek. "It's Saturday. I just need to talk to Nani about something."

Poppi raised his eyebrows. "What's that?"

"I know," insisted Tomas, ducking into the living room where—as expected—his white-haired *abuela* sat in her rocking chair in front of a Spanish soap opera. "But I wasn't sure where else to go."

Lie. He could've gone to Our Lady of Serenity, or any number of Catholic churches between here and there.

"*Hola*, Nani," he greeted, kissing her and kneeling beside her chair as he had his whole life. "How are you doing today?"

Nani didn't even look at him. She just smiled and rocked—just as she had for the last three years.

Poppi, coming in behind him, asked, "What's so important you need to bother your *abuela?*"

Tomas ignored that—his grandmother hardly looked bothered. "Nani, it's Tomas. Mano's oldest boy. I don't know if you can hear me, but I need to ask you something."

She smiled and rocked.

Tomas took her frail brown hand, its wedding ring wrapped in tape to stay on. "Nani, were you really a *bruja?* Did you really do magic?"

Poppi swore in Spanish and sank into his worn recliner. At least he was finally interested.

"I need to know because one of the tenants in my building has got a problem, Nani. A magic problem. I think it's a *diablero*."

For a moment he thought she hadn't heard any of it at all. Then, still rocking and smiling, Nani lifted her right hand to her forehead. Then her heart. Then her left shoulder.

She was making the sign of the cross.

"*Sí,*" said Tomas. "A *diablero*. And I need to know what to do."

Nani finished her benediction against evil and dropped her hand to her lap again, still rocking. Still smiling.

"She just told you what to do," said Poppi softly.

Tomas looked at him, confused.

"Pray," said his grandfather.

"But there has to be something else. This isn't—I don't think this is a religious kind of magic."

"Tomasito." Poppi shook his head, not even thrown by the idea of *diableros* and magic. "She *was* a *bruja*. Her power came from the Virgin Mary. That is the only kind of magic she could have given you, even before."

And from what Tomas could remember of his grandmother's magic, that was true. There had been charms, yes, and advice about when to light candles or when to turn around three times with your eyes closed. But it always went along with praying and saying the rosary.

He let his head fall forward in something that felt half like defeat and half like hope.

Our Lady of Serenity, it was.

Okay, so *this* was weird.

Marcy paused in the midst of digging through Tomas Martinez's drawers for a reality check. She had some kind of magic portal in her closet, and she thought going through a man's clothing was weird? Comparatively speaking, this was Disney World.

"Might as well check out Fantasyland," she murmured through the doorway toward Snowball, who'd come out from under the sofa only after Tomas left. The cat now sat on a small stack of newspaper, licking her flank as if to clean off the man's touch.

Some kind of heavy, spicy scent hung in the air of his bedroom, the scent she'd been savoring off his shirt. Aftershave, cologne, soap—or just him? The heavy brown drapes were closed, throwing the whole room into shadow, but when she'd switched on the overhead light, she saw the room was dominated by a large, unmade bed.

So here was where he slept.

Alone?

It was none of her business, of course. But when Marcy thought of her twin bed upstairs, and all her quiet nights alone, the contrast seemed to beg making. Tomas Martinez radiated sexuality—maybe that was the undercurrent of scent in here—and facing his bed only emphasized that. Especially facing his bed, wearing just an oversize T-shirt.

His oversize T-shirt.

She turned back to the chest of drawers. "Clothes."

His clothes were almost as fascinating as his bed— loosely folded shirts, fleece pants…and briefs. Pulling on his cotton underwear, which was a little baggier than hers and had a flap in front, felt unnervingly intimate. But the soft drawstring shorts, cinched tight at her waist, helped her achieve some measure of independence. If she had to, she could now leave the apartment without risking arrest for indecent exposure if a wind blew up.

This was October, after all. And the Windy City.

Thus armed with clothing, she went back into his living room. Snowball silently followed her. He had heavy oak furniture; even the table in the corner with a computer on it was thick and manly. The cushions were dark brown, also somehow masculine. She felt as if she were standing in the middle of a lion's den.

But it still had to be safer than her own apartment.

Her apartment. She really should be doing something herself, not counting only on him. But what? He seemed so competent, so capable. What could she do that wouldn't just get in his way?

Without even thinking about it, she began to pick up clutter. The place wasn't a terrible mess—not bad enough to make her uncomfortable touching things. But the man could use a small wastebasket in the living room. She threw three empty beer bottles into the kitchen trash, stacked papers and magazines on the thick oak coffee table, and fluffed his sofa pillows. Then she went back to the kitchen, drawn by the dirty dishes in the sink, and began to run hot water. She'd added soap and was sponging out a bowl, when she realized what she was doing.

Not just cleaning—which, while unasked, wasn't necessarily a bad thing, since he was helping her with *her* mess.

She was avoiding the real question.

She should be doing something herself. But *what?*

Her dishwashing took on a jerky, nervous edge. Briefly, she considered going back up to her apartment alone. But that just seemed stupid, especially if Tomas was coming back with a better solution. She didn't want to be one of those stupid women in a horror movie, going down into a dark basement to check out a noise when a killer was on the loose. She considered going to the library to do some research, but really...how likely was a standard public library to have anything that dealt with this situation?

Besides, she'd left her purse upstairs.

Stumped, draining the now-empty sink, she turned in a slow circle...and noticed his computer. It was running with a soft hum, a geometric screensaver playing across the monitor.

No. That was his computer, his private property. What if she got into it and found that he was into cybersex or had downloaded all kinds of pornography? She shouldn't be touching his things.

But she had to do something.

She looked at Snowball again, where the cat sat silent vigil. "I'm wearing his underwear," she pointed out.

Snowball didn't disagree.

With a deep breath for courage, Marcy sat down at Tomas's computer and moved the mouse. A standard opening screen came up, and she was relieved to see that he used the same Internet connection as she did. She could log on to do some research under her own name, and his secrets could stay secret.

That *was* what she wanted, wasn't it?

"One thing at a time," she said to Snowball, and logged on to the Internet.

The local library might have limited resources about magic and portals to Hell, but really, you could find *anything* on the Internet.

By the time Tomas got back and Marcy heard his key in the lock, she'd forgotten to worry about having appropriated his computer. She barely managed to look up.

Then she saw him, standing in the open doorway as if he didn't even mean to come in, and she managed looking up just fine. It felt good to have someone to share all this with. "Wait until you hear some of the stuff I've turned up online. It's pretty chaotic, and I can't vouch for the legitimacy of most of it, but—"

"I'm going upstairs," Tomas said in that dark, vaguely accented voice of his. "Stay here."

And he shut the door.

Marcy blinked after him. Why wouldn't she stay there? And why was he going upstairs? Why was it safe for him but not her?

Then again, she'd just found a site called Sacrifices and Sorcery, posted by someone claiming to be a "wizard." There was plenty she could do in the safety of Tomas's den.

She stayed there.

Marcy's apartment looked completely normal. Almost stereotypically normal—no touch of ethnicity, not even Celtic or Norse or whatever; no touch of any kind of social rebellion. It was so neat and normal, it could be a model apartment which Tomas could probably use to rent other apartments to other Middle Americans.

This made it something of an anticlimax for Father Gregory.

The middle-aged priest looked into Marcy's very normal walk-in closet with solemnity. "You wouldn't be playing some kind of Halloween prank on me, would you, Tony?"

"Tomas," Tomas corrected. Our Lady of Serenity was not his parents' church, only the closest. He and

Father Gregory had only just met. "And no, Father. This is no prank. I swear to you…"

Funny, how even after years, he took an oath to a priest so seriously that he had to swallow first.

"Earlier this morning there was flame in there," Tomas said. "And things flew out of it, leaving stains on the wall. And I heard a voice."

Father Gregory looked concerned. "Was the voice telling you to do something, Tomas?"

"No, it was talking about Marcy. Ms. Bridges."

"The woman who rents this apartment."

"Yes."

"Does she know that you come in here when she's gone?"

Tomas rolled his eyes heavenward, as if that would help him deal with Heaven's spokesman. But he couldn't really blame the priest. He'd been just as doubtful when he'd first answered Marcy's call, and he *believed* in magic.

Of a sort.

Father Gregory had already told Tomas that he was no exorcist, and that he questioned whether exorcism was anything more than old-world superstition. But he was the only priest available on short notice.

"Yes, she knows I am here. She was here earlier as well. She heard the voice, too."

Father Gregory considered that. "Would you be willing to attend some counseling sessions, Tomas?"

Frustrated, Tomas stepped closer to the closet and, tentatively, reached a hand out. Nothing. Wary, he reached for a pair of heels sitting on the chest of drawers. Nothing kept him from taking them.

He turned back to the priest. "I'm sorry to have

wasted your time, Father. Could you at least—would you please bless the closet? Just in case?''

Father Gregory nodded. ''I see no reason not to. If you would make room…''

Tomas stepped out of the closet so that Father Gregory could stand just inside the doorway. The priest straightened his shoulders, raised his chin and made the sign of the cross in the air. ''In the name of the Father, the Son—''

No! The protest in Tomas's head did not sound worried. It didn't sound like anything, technically. But it echoed with fury all the same. ''Um…Father?''

''—and the Holy Spirit. May this…closet…be sanctified by God's grace. May this place be illuminated by the grace of God.''

There was a strange popping sound. Tomas reached for the priest. ''Father!''

''May this place—'' Father Gregory stumbled to silence as Tomas forcibly yanked him backward. ''Really!''

Tomas looked quickly around them. A salamander sat on one of Marcy's bedposts. Something black fluttered across the ceiling. And from the seemingly normal closet, he could now scent a hint of brimstone. ''Do you see anything unusual, Father? Like, about the bed? Anything at all?''

The priest glanced right past the salamander and the bat, finishing with a quick, ''Amen.'' Then he said, ''About that counseling, Tomas.''

Something from the closet chuckled darkly, and from the priest's expression he hadn't heard it. That, Tomas realized, put Father Gregory in even more danger than he and Marcy had faced.

''Let's talk about it in the hall,'' he said quickly.

* * *

Marcy stared at the computer screen in disbelief. What the so-called wizard had written about curses on the Sacrifices and Sorcery Web site rang horribly, twistedly true. But it couldn't be…could it?

Could somebody have cursed her that way? *Why?*

She suddenly felt a lot more vulnerable here, alone in Tomas's apartment, than she liked. She needed to go upstairs and get him. Maybe he'd have an opinion on her theory.

Though how he knew so much, she still wasn't quite sure. Nor was she sure she wanted to know.

"Stay here, pooky," she said to Snowball, who was currently sitting on top of Tomas's refrigerator where it was warm and she had a good view. "I won't even go inside the apartment—I'll just knock on the door. That should be safe enough, shouldn't it?"

Snowball stared, unblinking, from her regal height.

Marcy left Tomas's place. Head filled with the disassociation of a long time online, and the arcane information she'd found there, she automatically stepped into the open elevator. Just as she did every day.

Only as the grilled doors slid shut did she remember that Tomas had turned the elevator off. On the third floor.

She lunged for the doors—

And everything around her turned to flame.

Part 3

The flame surrounded her. Bright and alive, it wrapped her in its writhing, sizzling embrace. Marcy shut her eyes to scream.

Surprise that she wasn't hurt silenced her.

She *felt* the fire, definitely. Her whole body felt hot. Heat scraped across her skin like claws. But she wasn't actually on fire.

She squinted her eyes open—and found herself staring into a shifting pattern of flame and smoke that formed some kind of sharp, planed face. The edges flickered and flared, so that sometimes it had sharp ears, sometimes horns, sometimes spiky hair, but the face stayed recognizable.

It really was somebody. Some*thing*. The fire was its own being.

Sooty eyes with an underglow of red, like cinders, held her gaze. Sharp sparks of teeth, almost too bright to bear, twisted into something resembling a leering smile. Its heat writhed up her legs, down her arms, sharp as a blade.

But some kind of intelligence was holding back, not burning her.

Not yet.

She wasn't in Hell, she realized. Not exactly. She *was* still in the elevator.

But she was in the elevator in the towering, all-encompassing embrace of some kind of demon!

You aren't afraid of me? Its semblance of a mouth moved with its challenge, but that was for show. Like a poor dubbing, the undulations of the living flame didn't match its words. Instead of hearing with her ears—her miraculously uninjured ears—Marcy was hearing its hiss in her head.

"Of course I'm afraid," she said, and almost gagged from the heat of its presence drying her mouth. She tried to pull back, but it held her, powerless. "What do you want?"

What else would I want?

"My soul?"

Its black-cinder eyes flared with more red heat. Amusement? Or...

Eventually, it sizzled.

Now it *was* starting to burn her...sort of. Heat shuddered deeper into her breasts, her stomach, her abdomen. Tongues of flame licked at her bare legs, her bare arms, her neck. She tried to shift position, tried to readjust to its intensity, but it held her fast, closer, hotter.

Tongues of flame singed into her ear—and the creature's sordid meaning sank in.

"No!" She wasn't just beginning to panic—she passed panic and was making headway on hysteria. "Oh no no no. And no means no. Absolutely not!"

She shut her eyes to its leering, shifting face and its heat-mottled gaze, but it glowed red through her eyelids. She tried again to struggle free. But how did one escape something that couldn't even exist?

Could she be imagining *this?*

She clung desperately to the hope of mere insanity. "I've been studying witchcraft!" she gasped, but it made a weak warning. "Witches don't believe in the devil."

THE devil? it asked.

She had to peek again, at the sardonic note in the creature's nonexistent voice, and winced from the brightness of its amused grimace.

You're no witch, taunted the creature. *Magic takes personal power. The one who summoned me, who promised you to me as sacrifice so long ago—his despair gave him power. You've not even that. As for devils...*

Its laugh shuddered through her, as if the floor itself was moving. *You do believe in evil, do you not? Then...*

The last came out a roar, its wavering mouth stretching as wide as a portal itself: *Believe in ME!*

Marcy cringed away—or tried. "No!"

You will believe readily enough tonight, my little mate. You will believe for eternity!

"I won't!" But she sensed the helplessness of her words even as they whimpered from her lips. She *wasn't* a witch. She *didn't* have personal power, and really never had. Even as she futilely spread her hands, as if to claw the creature, her fingers met nothing but flame...a flame that was singing her painfully now, fully capable of destroying her in one blast. It held her, licking around her, possessive, licentious—eternal.

Tears that squeezed from her eyes sizzled and evaporated from her cheeks.

Give up yourself. Give up your reality. Give it all...

This was really happening to her, and she was helpless to stop it!

"At least tell me who did this," she begged, defeated. "When? Why?"

Again the laugh shuddered through her, around her, and she was so very hot, and she couldn't breathe the searing air around her.

No, the creature taunted.

Then, as if from a distance, Marcy heard some kind of clanging noise. She thought she felt something besides flame on her face. Air? Coolness? Then hands closed on her shoulders—real hands, human hands—and dragged her backward.

Out of the elevator, onto the third floor.

And into Tomas Martinez's competent arms.

"You could come for individual counseling," Father Gregory had been saying moments before. "Or you could join one of our groups."

Tomas, unsettled by how the priest hadn't been able to see anything unusual in Marcy's apartment, was barely listening. Were he and Marcy Bridges crazy? The burned red slash on his hand said differently, priest or no priest.

Maybe Father Gregory was just too godly to recognize something that evil...which also said interesting things about Tomas and Marcy.

"It might do you some good to share your challenges with others," the priest continued over the rumble of the arriving elevator.

Arriving?

Hadn't Tomas turned it off and put an out-of-order sign on it? He wondered what meddling tenant had been messing with a broken elevator...or one that was supposedly broken.

Then a cage of pure flame rose to the third floor—and someone stood in the center of it, weirdly untouched.

Marcy!

Tomas didn't stop to think. He tore open the door, iron grillwork burning his palms, and reached into the flame. His hands closed on Marcy's shoulders and he yanked her clear, backing quickly away.

Only as her arms closed desperately around him did he realize that he wasn't injured. The grillwork had been hot, but not injurious. And Marcy—

He pushed her back from him, oddly reluctant to do so, but needing to see. She wasn't burned either. Not at all. Her pale skin had a feverish flush of pink about it, but her brown hair and wide, winsome lips seemed untouched. How was that possible?

Were they really imagining...?

But Father Gregory, Tomas now saw, was staring, horrified, at the flaming elevator. No...he was staring at the creature that the flames created. Fire. Horns. Darkness.

"In the name of the Father, the Son and the Holy Spirit," the priest said, hoarse, "I command thee to be gone!"

Two coal-like eyes in the midst of the flaming form seemed to spark with unearthly emotion.

"In the name of the Lord and all the saints," insisted Father Gregory, extending the crucifix that hung around his neck, "I command thee, be gone!"

And in a puff of smoke—it was.

Just like that.

Marcy, with a mew that wrung Tomas's heart, ducked her head back into his chest. He not only let her, he closed his arms around her, tight. Possessive.

What the hell was that?

And why did Marcy feel so good?

"Thank you, Father," he said belatedly.

The priest did not say *you're welcome*. He was too busy clutching his crucifix and staring at the empty elevator. "Good God."

That's what Tomas hoped, anyway.

"You weren't making it up," said Father Gregory, bending to lean into the iron cage, looking more closely for signs of fire damage. "This is really happening."

With a little snuffle, Marcy turned her head so that her cheek, instead of her nose, was smooshed against Tomas's chest. When Tomas tucked his chin to better see her, she looked confused. Then her eyes widened. "No!"

Tomas looked back—but not in time to stop a spiral of flame, from the center of the elevator, surrounding the priest....

And vanishing with him.

"No!" screamed Marcy again, but it sure wasn't making a lot of difference.

All but paralyzed, she watched Tomas launch himself into a full-body dive for the priest. Flames swallowed the clergyman too quickly, with an audible pop, leaving nothing to tackle. Tomas landed hands first, somersaulting with his momentum, and crashed into the barred, back wall of the elevator. Then, pushing himself up into a sprawled sit, he swore.

Darkly.

It was Spanish, but Marcy got the gist. She also saw that he was in the elevator. "Get out!"

He lifted his furious tiger eyes, half-lost under long strands of dark hair, to meet her gaze.

"Tomas, get out! What if it comes back?" She reached for him—but from a safe distance, several feet back from the cursed contraption. She wanted to step forward, to pull him out. She wanted to be a person of action, like him.

After her ordeal with the demon, she couldn't seem to make her feet move.

"Please," she whispered, hot tears finally welling out of her eyes and down her cheeks without evaporating.

Tomas glared at her a moment longer, then levered himself up. He didn't leave the elevator. "Hand me my toolbox," he said, his voice deep with threat.

Marcy didn't think the threat was meant for her, but when she spotted the big red box sitting beside her apartment's door, she picked it up—with both hands, and without being able to straighten herself again—and waddled it over to the elevator.

Closer, anyway. Then she kneeled and pushed it the rest of the way with both hands. "Please get out."

Tomas reached into the box and pulled out a screwdriver, then did something with the number panel on the elevator. Then he exchanged the screwdriver for a hammer—

And he beat the crap out of the thing. Curses flew from his lips with every blow, to match the bits of wire and fuse that flew out of the box.

Marcy watched him, half afraid, half envious. After destroying the workings, he pulled out a rope and threaded it through both the interior and exterior grille of the elevator so that nobody could step into the box without having to dodge ropes, and the elevator itself would have to work very hard to pull loose.

Unless the ropes burned....

As Tomas finally stepped out of the box, and leaped with catlike grace up onto the crossbar that ran four feet high beside the shaft, Marcy's fear eased...and her envy turned into something more like yearning.

She didn't just want to be able to do that, she thought, watching the flex of Tomas's legs and butt under his black pants, watching the easy shift of his chunky leather boots as he kept balance. *She wanted that.*

Of course, anything would be better than a demon, right?

Tomas jammed a crowbar into the pulley system of the elevator, momentarily finishing his destruction, and looked back down at her, panting. "Son of a bitch," he said. He had more of an accent when he swore.

Marcy stepped silently back, and Tomas jumped noiselessly back to the floor in front of her and immediately began to pace.

Maybe anything *would* be better than a demon. But this wasn't just anything. Or anyone.

Tomas paced like a caged animal, with long strides and sudden turns, finally stopping to face Marcy head-on. "It ate my priest."

She still hadn't fully made peace with the idea that the mysterious maintenance man had brought a priest here in the first place. But she nodded.

Tomas kicked the elevator. "It ate my f—" Then he looked down, fisted his hand, shook his head as if chiding himself. "My freaking priest," he finished.

Marcy swallowed. Hard. "I think I know what it's after."

"Whatever it is," said Tomas, spinning back into more pacing, "it's not getting it."

"Good. Because it wants me."

He pivoted back to her, eyebrows lifting. "You?"

"That's what it said. Thought. Whatever. It called me its bride."

Tomas's glare didn't waver. "Why you?"

What—was she such a loss that not even demonic creatures of the underworld could want her? "I'm not sure, but I think…someone seems to have cursed me. Someone desperate."

Tomas leaned closer, eyes narrowing dangerously, and hissed his question. "Because you did what?"

"I don't know!" All she knew was, she liked this man better when he was holding her so tight that, for a moment, it had felt as if nothing could hurt her. Not even Hell. Now she was backing away from the sheer force of him. "I'm just—I'm trying to tell you what it told me. I read something on the Internet about a curse—how a person can curse someone else as his or her sacrifice in order to gain some kind of demonic favor."

Tomas stared.

"And I came to tell you," she added quickly, taking another step back.

He took another step forward and gestured widely behind him, without looking that way. "In the *elevator?*"

Another step back. "I wasn't thinking. It was a mistake."

"You *think?*"

She bumped into her apartment door. "I'm sorry."

Instead of stalking her farther, Tomas seemed to draw himself back. He shoved a splayed hand past his forehead, pushing some of the long, loose hair out of his face, and sighed. Tension seemed to ease out of him as he sighed, and his next question sounded almost…normal. "What else did the demon say?"

"It said that I didn't summon it." *That I have no personal power.* She didn't want to admit that, though. He probably thought it was obvious. "It said whoever did the summoning had power from his desperation, that whoever it was had promised me to it long ago. And it said…tonight…"

She suddenly felt dizzy with the memory of it, of the creature's sordid laughter, of the way its hot tongues had slithered across her. To her relief, Tomas stepped forward and took her arm, the promise in his burning gaze sending a completely different kind of dizziness through her.

"We will figure this out," he said.

"It's not like there's a help line," she said.

"We know a lot more now," he insisted, and kissed her on top of the head. Marcy went very, very still. Was that a big-brotherly kind of kiss on the head? Or could it possibly have meant more?

Surely not. She had no personal power….

"If this really is a curse," said Tomas, "then whoever cursed you should be able to uncurse you. Right?"

"I have no idea." And why was it he did?

"It makes sense," he insisted. "As much as any of this does. So now you just have to think of who you know that might have wanted to make a deal with the devil. Someone you knew long ago. Someone who wouldn't mind sacrificing you for his own gain."

"I don't like thinking any such person even exists!"

"Me," said Tomas, "I don't like thinking that our demon friend there exists. But it has my priest, so maybe it's time to join the program."

He sounded vaguely annoyed, and he hadn't kissed her again. On the other hand, he was still holding her arm. She would take that. "I honestly can't remember knowing a single person who could have been involved in...in the dark arts. When I first started reading about Wicca last summer, the idea of *any* magic was completely new to me."

"Some people hide their involvement," Tomas said—again knowing more than seemed usual. How did he know this much?

Marcy felt a chill when she realized that, of all the people she knew, *he* was the only one who'd shown any knowledge of the dark side of magic. Would *he* mind sacrificing her?

She'd been living in this building, the one Tomas worked at, for three years now.

How long ago had the demon meant by long ago?

"I really don't know anyone who matches that description," she lied very carefully, feeling far less safer in Tomas Martinez's company. To her relief—and maybe a flush of foolish disappointment—when she shrugged her shoulders with discomfort, Tomas stepped easily back from her. No meant no. He smiled a half smile, as if in silent apology for being so forward.

Damn it, she'd liked the forward part. It was the familiarity-with-the-dark-arts part that worried her.

"What I still don't understand," he said, as if her ego weren't bruised enough, "is why you? Not that you aren't attractive."

Attractive enough for a demon, anyway? But that

was something. "Maybe whoever cursed me just thought I was...convenient."

"No, that doesn't make sense." And yet Tomas seemed almost fluent with the idea. "If you're trying to land a big business deal, you don't take your client to a fast-food joint. Marcy, something about you makes you prime rib to a demon looking for sacrifices. But what..."

Then he froze, eyes widening. "No!"

She felt increasingly wary. "No what?"

"You're not!"

"Not...?" But she couldn't pretend not to know what he meant. So much for keeping her own secrets. "Okay, fine. So I'm a virgin."

That was the part of the curse she'd read about that she hadn't wanted to divulge.

"Wouldn't Mr. Gilbert and Mrs. Roberts be surprised! They swore that your politeness and quiet ways meant you were hiding a wild side—may be even a killer!"

"It's not that big a deal," insisted Marcy, uncomfortable. "More women abstain from sex than movies and TV would have you believe."

"Well, sure," he agreed, though his gleaming eyes still indicated that it was a big deal. "I was raised Catholic, remember? My unmarried sisters are virgins."

She widened her eyes, questioning that.

He narrowed his. "They'd better be. But of course, not all Catholics are *good* Catholics. Depending—" he grinned "—on how you define good."

"My choices had nothing to do with religion," Marcy insisted. "I just felt like waiting until I was ready. I didn't want to sleep around."

"Around?" His grin widened.

She folded her arms.

"To sleep around, you need multiple partners. If you sleep here, and here, and here—" he pointed at random spots on the floor, making a circular pattern "—then you've slept around. You haven't even slept."

"Well, maybe I would have if I'd known about this."

He spread his arms. "Easy fix."

"What?"

And since she still was standing framed by the jamb of her apartment, and he was still right in front of her, he planted a hand on either side of her and she was effectively trapped. "I said," he murmured, leaning closer. Close enough that his breath warmed her cheek in a completely pleasant way. Close enough that his lips brushed hers as he whispered, "Easy. Fix."

Then he kissed her.

Tomas was teasing her, of course. She made it too easy. Who would have guessed prudish Marcy Bridges really was *prudish* Marcy Bridges?

Besides, he kind of liked the harmless image of himself as a sexual predator.

But then he trapped her against the door, and he pressed his lips to hers...and things got far less harmless. Her innocence suddenly became something bigger than a silly word—*virgin*—or even a reason for demons to be stalking her. Her innocence suddenly became something tenuous, and precious, and completely...her.

Her lips seemed to tremble under his.

He drew back quickly, ready to apologize—then saw the yearning in Marcy's wide eyes. Why *was* it she'd never felt ready?

He leaned back in, using his bent arms to lever his face to her level, holding her gaze with his.

She didn't look away.

He nuzzled toward her ear, exhaling hot breath onto her neck, and kissed a tender, sweet spot on the side of her throat. She shuddered, but it seemed to be a good shudder. So he drew his mouth to hers again, inordinately pleased when she turned her head to meet him halfway, parting her lips for his.

Now he kissed her in earnest. Her innocence. Her sweetness. Her tentative hunger. He relaxed his arms until he was leaning, full body, against her, sandwiching her against the door.

Marcy shifted, languorous, beneath the weight of him. Her bare foot slid slightly up his jeans, then down, exploring the hardness of his leg. He murmured encouragement between one kiss and another, glad to have her use him for her education, more than happy to move on to advanced courses sooner than he'd ever expected.

Damn. No wonder the demon wanted her. He could sell his soul for someone like her, himself.

Then someone cleared his throat behind Tomas— and when he looked over his shoulder, he wondered if he'd damned himself after all. He was staring at three people: an older man whose wide mouth resembled Marcy's at its most prudish; an older woman whose willowy shape looked like Marcy's surely would in thirty years; and a younger woman about his age who, well, looked like Marcy. Just older with more makeup and a more sophisticated hairstyle and wardrobe.

Tomas stared at them, still dazed from the kiss, as uncertain about their reality as he'd been about the demon's.

Then Marcy, half-hidden behind him, said, "Hi, Daddy. Mom. Sharona."

They were real.

"Let me guess," said Sharona. "Tomas the maintenance guy?"

Straightening so that he wasn't pressed so lewdly against the family's younger daughter—but moving slowly so that he wouldn't look too guilty—Tomas glanced from her to Marcy and back. Had Marcy described him to her sister?

Marcy looked embarrassed. Interesting.

"Hey," he said. "Sharona, right?"

Actually, he'd never heard of the woman, but information was information. He went with the idea and offered a hand to her father. "Mr. Bridges. Mrs. Bridges."

Okay, so he sounded as if he belonged on a sixties sitcom and should be wearing a letterman sweater. It still bought time.

"Pleased to meet you," said Mrs. Bridges, forgiving him for making out with their daughter more quickly than her husband seemed to. She had a firm grip when she shook his hand. "Excuse my appearance. The elevator doesn't seem to be working."

Mr. Bridges looked at the elevator, with its web of rope and the wedged crowbar, and his expression didn't soften. "You do maintenance work for a living?"

"No," said Tomas. "I also manage the building."

"You do?" asked Marcy, addressing him for the first time since the kiss. She was blushing. It was adorable.

He shrugged. He'd never said he *didn't.*

"So you're coming to lunch with us, right?" asked Sharona. "For Marcy's birthday?"

Mrs. Bridges said, "Marcy, honey, you aren't wearing that, are you?"

That meant Tomas's inside-out T-shirt and his drawstring shorts, which looked great on her, leaving her legs long and bare. Between the demon, and losing the priest, and kissing her, Tomas hadn't had the full opportunity to admire her legs in those shorts.

Now seemed a bad time.

Marcy looked at the apartment door behind her, and Tomas suspected he knew what she was thinking. She didn't want to go into that apartment. The demon might be behind any door. "Um...yes?"

"You at least need shoes," insisted her mother. "What restaurant will let you in without shoes?"

Tomas said, "I'll get them."

"No!" protested Marcy.

"Really. Just tell me where they are."

"I'll go with you."

Tomas glanced at her parents, who looked understandably dubious at this interchange. They could probably use some privacy anyway. "Fine. C'mon."

When he unlocked her door with his passkey, he didn't miss Mr. Bridges's disapproval. Both Tomas and Marcy held their breath—but nothing greeted them through the doorway except an overly neat living room...and a whiff of brimstone.

"What's that smell?" asked Mrs. Bridges.

Marcy said, "Fumigation." Then she darted in, Tomas following and closing the door behind them.

"Your *family?*" he demanded.

"I forgot they were coming! It's been an unusual morning." Which was true, what with portals to Hell, curses...

Tomas noticed a pink flush spreading across Marcy's

cheeks, intrigued. Had the kissing been that life changing, too?

Even he'd been shaken by it.

Maybe Marcy saw something in his eyes. "I'm not
sleeping with you just to screw over the demon. So to
speak."

Had he actually asked her? "I thought you said you
weren't saving it for any particular reason?"

"Except to wait until I'm ready, and I've got to tell
you, this whole day has not made me ready. Even *before* my parents showed up."

"Look, I'm not suggesting anything." But as soon
as he said that, Tomas found himself considering suggesting things after all. A lot of things. "We don't have
to grab a quickie while your family's waiting in the
hallway. But let's not forget, you seem to be on some
kind of deadline. Even if I weren't fairly good at this—
which, by the way, I am—I'd have to be a better first
time than that…that *thing*."

Something chuckled, deep and sadistic, from the
bedroom and in their heads.

Tomas said, "Please tell me your shoes aren't in the
closet."

Marcy would never, ever have imagined Tomas
Martinez riding beside her in the cramped back seat of
her parents' minivan, on their way to her birthday
lunch. He looked completely out of place, from his
coiled size to his black clothing to the spiky tattoo that
circled his dark wrist. From the way Sharona kept turning to glance at them from the middle seat, and the
way Dad kept catching her gaze in the rearview mirror,
the family was taken aback as well.

Then again, maybe it was the whispering that was catching their attention.

"I am just saying," hissed Tomas into Marcy's ear, tickling, "your sister seems to be the kind of woman who notices people."

He paused to grin forward at Sharona. Sharona grinned back.

Marcy wished she were the kind of woman who noticed people, but clearly she wasn't. "So?"

"So maybe she'll remember the person who cursed you, even if you don't."

"You don't think she would have *mentioned it?*"

Tomas narrowed his eyes at her sarcasm. But a man could only look so dangerous when strapped into the corner of a van's back seat with a shoulder belt. "I meant, she might know if anyone around you was into black magic."

Mom called back, "We were thinking of going to that Indian place you like so much, Marcy. Is that all right with you?"

"I love that place," agreed Marcy—then considered how her day had been going. Demons in her apartment. Demons in the elevator. Innocent priests vanishing into a puff of smoke. She could tell, when she met Tomas's gaze, that he was equally wary. "So much, that I've overdone it. Let's not go there."

"How about the new steak house?" suggested Sharona, as eager to spend their father's money as ever.

Marcy had wanted to try that one since it opened, so...not the steak house. "Let's go to that old Chinese restaurant," she suggested quickly. "The one in the strip mall."

Mom said, "You're sure? I thought you had some trouble with them."

Exactly. They'd made extra charges on her credit card. She glanced guiltily toward Tomas. "I'd really like to try them again."

Tomas said, "The place by the laundry? They aren't so good. Their hot-and-sour soup is—*yes,*" he finished, about-facing as he finally caught on. "I would like to go there, too."

If they had to endanger a restaurant, why not one with lousy soup?

Sharona glanced over her shoulder again, suspicious, but Dad said, "You're the birthday girl, Marcy."

Tomas leaned in close again. "Sharona seems like the kind of person who picks up on things. What could it hurt to ask her?"

Other than not wanting her big sister to think she was crazy? Or doomed? "We went to different colleges," Marcy protested. "She wouldn't remember anyone beyond…"

Her stomach sank, and not from motion sickness.

"High school," she whispered.

Tomas ducked his head even closer to hers. "What?"

Dad said over the traffic noise, "So, Marcy, I ran into Joe Pierson's son on the golf course the other day. Remember him?" *Subtle.*

"High school," she repeated softly, ignoring her father. "This may not have anything to do with my birthday. It might have something to do with last night's high-school reunion."

Tomas looked annoyed, as if she should have told him sooner. "Did anyone there seem…?"

"Magic?" she finished for him. "No. That, even *I* would have noticed." Even if she wasn't Sharona.

Dad, in the driver's seat, said, "Good fellow, Biff Pierson."

Tomas widened amused eyes and mouthed, *Biff?*

Marcy ignored them both.

The Chinese restaurant looked just as it always had—red and gold decorations, a mixture of booths and tables, a large aquarium by the door. There was only one exception.

What looked like a salamander lurking in the corner.

Marcy realized that what looked like dirt on the wall behind it was actually a sooty tail track. Nobody else, other than Tomas, seemed to notice the creature. So far, it was part of their reality, but hadn't intruded on anyone else's. Yet.

Father Gregory's fate pretty much showed it could.

So the salamander made her decidedly nervous for such a small mythical creature.

As if to distract her from one disaster with another, Tomas said, "So, Sharona, what kind of guys did Marcy date in high school?"

Sharona looked up from her Chinese astrology place mat with a snort. "You think Marcy dated in high school?"

Tomas raised his eyebrows, intrigued.

"I did so date," protested Marcy. "Not so very, very often as you did, of course, but…"

Sharona stuck out her tongue. Something about being together brought out the child in them. Then she turned haughtily to Tomas. "When she did go out, it was usually with the leftovers. You know—the guys she felt sorry for because nobody else was dating them."

What a mean thing to say—about those boys, not Marcy. "That's not true!"

"Chess club," Sharona continued, warming to her topic. "Computer geeks. The one time she dated a guy on the baseball team, he was the shy one who was always on the bench."

"Any gamers, maybe?" asked Tomas. "You know…Dungeons and Dragons types? Or maybe Goths?"

Marcy said, "There's nothing wrong with people who play Dungeons and Dragons. And no," she insisted when both Sharona and Tomas looked expectant, "I didn't date any gamers…they never had the time anyway. I was just friends with a lot of them."

Sharona took a long sip of green tea. "Really, Tomas, you're about the most interesting person she ever dated."

Marcy picked up her little cup of tea, trying not to spill it. *Please don't tell them we aren't dating,* she thought, not even sure why it seemed so important. *Please don't tell them that.*

Blessedly, Tomas let Sharona's assumption slide. "But a lot of guys had to be interested in her, even if she didn't date them," he pushed. "Even the strange ones."

Sharona said, "That's so nice that you think that!"

Marcy put down her tea untouched, deciding she didn't want to risk a bathroom run. Not knowing what might just lurk behind the stall doors. "It's nice that he thinks I attract weirdos?"

"It's nice," clarified her sister, "that he's able to see how attractive you are, period. It's kind of subtle, Marce. A lot of guys aren't perceptive enough to really see you."

Now Marcy blushed. She blushed even harder when she realized Tomas was studying her, intrigued.

His smile, this time, was more quiet than usual. "It's amazing, what some people can look past."

Against her will, she glanced toward the salamander smoldering in the far corner of the wall. But when she looked back at Tomas, his gaze hadn't moved off her.

Something deep inside her shivered in a very pleasant way. This probably was not good. He wasn't really interested; he was only playing a role. Then there was that dangerous air he wore and his surprising grasp of black magic—something that she, having only studied the "harm none" practice of Wicca, preferred not to tamper with.

But good golly, he was sexy. When his gaze slid off her at the approach of their blond waitress, the sensation was not unlike that of a towel sliding sensuously from her body.

Casting desperately about for more reasons not to risk her heart, here, Marcy thought, On top of everything else, he's just a building manager. But damn it, he was a really *good* building manager! Competent. Consistent. Clearly ready in any emergency. That had to count more than the prestige of other jobs held by men she'd dated.

Except Tomas wasn't dating her.

Thank goodness the soup was here.

If someone had told Tomas that he'd be joining Marcy Bridges's birthday lunch with her caricature of a Middle American family in a mediocre Chinese restaurant...that might have seemed like a good definition of Hell.

Therefore, it surprised him tremendously to realize,

halfway through the egg rolls, that he was enjoying himself. Marcy's father was stiff enough to use as a display in a store, and her mother had a Junior League edge that still made him nervous, but both parents clearly loved their daughters. Sharona had a wicked sense of humor that made him wonder where Marcy had hidden hers. And Marcy herself...

Well, Sharona was right. When you looked close, she really did have a subtle but distinct attractiveness to her. It was nowhere near as obvious as her great legs or her sexy mouth. It had more to do with how she held herself, how she quietly defended everyone, from a slow waitress to the D&D-playing nerds from high school that she hadn't even dated. It had more to do with how she looked at the world.

It wasn't that Marcy didn't notice people, he saw now. She simply didn't notice their worse qualities.

With that kind of vulnerability, he thought, she was lucky not to have been sacrificed to a more mundane evil long ago. Thank God for women who played it safe.

"So, Tomas," said Mr. Bridges, well into the entrée. Marcy's father didn't much like Tomas, but he wasn't getting in Tomas's face about it, so it wasn't a problem. "How did you get into doing...maintenance?"

"Yes," said Marcy quickly, coming to his defense just as she did to everyone else's. "You're so good at it."

Had he once thought she was meek, simply because she didn't confront people to stand up for herself? She sure stood up for everyone else! Funny, how Mr. Bridges's opinion of him became increasingly important, the more clearly Tomas saw the man's younger daughter.

"I was having trouble hiring anybody who was competent and would agree to be on call," he said. "So when emergencies came up, half the time I fixed them myself. I finally decided to take some lessons at the hardware store and stop placing want ads."

He sensed Marcy staring at him. It was Mrs. Bridges who asked, "So you've got administrative responsibilities, too?"

"I manage the building," clarified Tomas. This was the second time he'd said it, and Marcy still looked surprised.

"So how was the class reunion, Marcy?" asked Sharona brightly, to cut the awkward moment. "Were you depressed, or did you feel validated?"

"Did you see a lot of your old friends, dear?" asked Mrs. Bridges.

Interesting, how Marcy avoided the question about the friends. "It *was* kind of depressing," she admitted. "Especially the people who *weren't* there. Do you realize, seven people from my graduating class have died? Traffic accidents, cancer—and fires! What are the chances that three separate women in the same class would…?"

Tomas had put the pieces together before Marcy's words petered off. Was it possible Marcy was number *four* on someone's list? *"Madre de Dios,"* he said.

The rest of the Bridges family looked from him to Marcy, blissfully oblivious to their connecting of dangerous dots.

"Fires, you say?" prompted Marcy's father after a moment of awkwardness. "That's a bad way to go."

Marcy took a strangled breath, and Tomas found her hand under the tablecloth and squeezed it. Nobody was going to hurt her. *Nobody.*

"Liz Carpenter," she said, squaring her shoulders as she returned the squeeze on Tomas's hand. "And Judith Barstow. And Cassie Adams. Do you remember any of them, Sharona?"

Sharona made a face. "Not really, thank God. Wasn't Cassie a cheerleader?"

"I don't remember," said Marcy. "I wish I did—"

"Happy birthday to you," sang a group of voices from across the restaurant, then, and their waitress approached with a cluster of other staff, carrying a birthday cake, serenading Marcy.

"Oh, Dad," protested Sharona, when Marcy only stared in dismay. "You didn't!"

"It's her birthday," insisted Mrs. Bridges.

"So you put her through hell?" her sister demanded.

Tomas leaned closer to Marcy. "And here I thought we left Hell back in the elevator."

Marcy's smile came out crooked...but at least she made the attempt.

Someday, he thought, she would have to start standing up for herself. But the better he got to know Marcy, the more he could see it wouldn't be over a birthday cake with her parents.

She was too afraid of hurting other people.

He just hoped that didn't apply to people who deserved hurting.

Marcy didn't want to say goodbye to her family. She hadn't felt this kind of separation anxiety since summer camp. But now she had a far better reason to cling to normalcy.

As her parents and Sharona drove away in their wonderfully normal minivan, they unknowingly left Marcy to a world of demons, curses, possible fiery deaths...and definitely fiery maintenance men.

Managers, she corrected herself, still having trouble readjusting to that particular bit of reality.

"Let me guess," said Tomas beside her as the van rounded a corner and vanished. "Your yearbooks are in the closet, right?"

"They're in the living-room bookshelf," she corrected him. "But going anywhere near that apartment is too dangerous now. We should...just..."

There was no reason to finish her suggestion, since Tomas had paused by his own door and opened it, but was now stalking toward the stairs. "You stay down here. Don't open any doors on your own."

"Wait!" she called.

"No," he called back, vanishing up the first flight.

She stared after him, annoyed and impressed and envious. What would it feel like to have an impulse and just *follow* it, right then, and damn the consequences? No comparison of pros and cons. No deep worries about worst-case scenarios. Just pure, fearless action.

What could it possibly feel like?

"I hope," she murmured to herself, "that it doesn't feel like eternal damnation."

Then, hesitating a moment longer, she turned and went into his apartment, wondering only briefly how he'd deduced that the demon seemed only able to get at them from doorways.

She would try to hunt down her magical stalker first. Then she would worry about Tomas Martinez's fount of occult knowledge.

By the time he brought in the yearbooks, blessedly whole if a tad sooty, Marcy was on his computer, pe-

rusing the Web site one of her classmates had created
for the reunion. They'd already posted quite a few dig-
ital pictures.

"I got them," announced Tomas, dropping the
books on his coffee table.

Marcy said, "Good for you," without looking up.
She was busy scrolling past pictures, after all. She
didn't want to miss a clue.

"No, really." Sarcasm gave Tomas a thick accent.
"It was my pleasure."

She clicked ahead to yet another picture, using the
computer's mouse. "I get that."

Then he was standing right beside her, his hip near
her shoulder, and she couldn't have ignored him if she
wanted to. She wasn't sure why she would want to.
But she felt a tightness in her neck, in her shoulders;
a strain in her forehead. It made her short-tempered.

"What does that mean?" asked Tomas as she looked
reluctantly up at him. He seemed dark and glowering
all over again, as well as sooty. She could only imagine
what had happened in the apartment. "You get what?"

Actually, she wasn't sure she *could* imagine. Had he
been fighting with the demon, or conferring in other
ways?

That's stupid, she thought, and looked back at the
computer screen. "I get that it was your pleasure," she
said. "Why else would you go barging into an apartment that's already proved dangerous? You like taking
chances."

Tomas said, "Ha." Then he strode back to the coffee table and sank into an easy crouch beside it.

Marcy turned in the computer chair. "Ha?"

He sorted the yearbooks in quick, strong movements.

"What you consider taking chances is what other people consider normalcy."

Oh. She should have realized he wouldn't let *that* topic drop so quickly. "You think sleeping around is the only measure of normalcy?"

He made a *tsk-tsk* noise, and drew an invisible circle around him with his index finger, a reminder of his definition of sleeping around. "I have only slept here," he said, pointing in one direction. "And here." He pointed in another, then considered it. "Maybe here, depending on your definition. But it is not a round. A triangle, maybe. Maybe a quadrangle."

"That doesn't make either of us more normal than the other," she insisted. "I'm not about to be black-mailed into having sex. We've got to find out who it was who cursed me. That's the only way."

The catlike ease with which Tomas rose from his crouch made her throat hurt. "I was teasing before, Marcy. But what if we don't find out in time? Death before dishonor?"

To be honest, the word *dishonor* didn't sound any-where near as bad as it should. Not when she'd gotten such a great demonstration of the power in this man's thighs. "Talk to me again at eleven-thirty," she said, forcing herself to turn back to the computer.

Tomas grinned and, just like that, the tightness in Marcy eased. "It's a date."

"*If* we don't find the bastard who cursed me," she reminded him.

"What, you have other plans?"

She grinned at the computer screen, scrolling past pictures. Was Tomas Martinez *flirting* with her? He might be right. She wasn't exactly an expert on taking chances. It had been so much easier to stay home with

Snowball, where she was comfortable and could judge her companion's contentment by the purring, that she'd gotten out of the habit of socializing with humans.

On that topic…

"Snowball," she said, pushing her chair back on its castors.

Tomas raised his eyebrows.

"I forgot to leave a faucet dripping for her," Marcy explained, heading for the bathroom. "She likes to have fresh water. Here, kitty kitty kitty."

She turned on the faucet in the bathroom sink, then turned it down to a bare trickle. It wasn't the best way to save water, but it kept her cat's kidneys in good working order. "Here, puss puss."

But Snowball didn't come running.

Frowning, Marcy stepped to the doorway into the hall. *Something was wrong.* "Kitty?"

"Maybe she's hiding under the bed." Tomas turned another page in the yearbook he was skimming and grinned at something he saw there. Probably a picture of her with braces.

"She doesn't—" But who knew, maybe Snowball had adopted new habits since demons took up residence in her closet. She went into the bedroom and kneeled on the carpet. "Snowball?"

No cat. She burned her knees on the carpet, spinning to then look under the bureau, under the dresser. "Snowball!"

"You can't find her?" Tomas stood in the doorway. Maybe he'd heard something in her voice. Her relief not to be alone mingled with her fear that something in his apartment had hurt her cat. Had he left some unscreened window open? Put out poison for bugs or mice? Was there some dangerous cranny or nook where a curious cat could trap herself, or hurt herself...or worse?

"She's got to be here," Marcy insisted, voice uneven. "She's got to."

Tomas gave her a hand up, steadying her, comforting her. "Where did you see her last?"

"She was on top of the refrigerator."

He guided her into the kitchen—but no Snowball watched them from the top of either cabinets or appliance. Marcy hoisted herself onto a counter to look behind the unit, but Snowball wasn't there, either.

"Nobody would have been here since we left, would they?" she asked, and swallowed hard. "Nobody who might have gotten something out of the dryer, or the oven, or—"

She stared at the refrigerator door—and this time she refused to dwell in inaction. She yanked it open.

And whimpered.

Part 4

Tomas responded instantly, wrapping his arms around Marcy and spinning her away from the gout of flame that spat out of his Frigidaire.

He couldn't protect her so easily from the feline wail that warbled out, along with a malicious chuckling, from the depths behind the flames.

"No!" screamed Marcy, struggling in his arms. "Snowball!"

"Leave her." He pressed his cheek against hers both to make himself heard over the demonic noise and to somehow steady her. "Leave her, Marcy!"

"I can't!"

"You've got to!"

Another cat cry wailed into the kitchen—and he kicked the door shut. With a soft sigh, the refrigerator sealed.

Marcy twisted free of his embrace, not the least bit timid now. "No! Not my cat!"

She reached for the refrigerator. He grabbed to stop her—and she bodychecked him out of the way. If he'd expected it, maybe it wouldn't have worked; the woman was no linebacker. But since she took him by surprise, she had a chance to pull open the door almost ten inches before he shut it again.

Both of them glimpsed the milk, condiments and bag of bread in the appliance's lit interior before the door resealed.

This time when Marcy opened the thing, Tomas let her. Again, it was just the interior of a refrigerator.

"No," she repeated, pushing food aside without any care of whether it spilled or not. "No. It can't have Snowball."

"Marcy—"

She fixed him with a glare that actually made him step quickly back. "Why didn't you let me get her?"

"Because that's what the thing wanted! *You're* what it wanted. If you'd gone in after your damn cat, it could have closed up behind you permanently."

"I don't care!" And she started to push around some to-go boxes.

He grabbed her by both arms and drew her back, again kicking the door shut. "Of course you care!"

"But she's my..." To his horror, her eyes swam with tears. He didn't necessarily get that she could feel this much love for a cat. But there was no doubt that she did; that the quiet Marcy Bridges was capable of almost unimaginable love and loyalty.

He drew her to his chest—and felt lucky to have that chance. "Of course she is. And as long as the portal stays open, maybe we can get both her and the priest back. But Marcy, listen to me. If you're right, and the one thing it wants is you..."

She searched his gaze, as if starving for his logic. "Then when it has me, the game's over?"

He nodded, and she tucked her head under his chin, and he rested his cheek on her hair. It felt good. It felt right. It felt like something he'd rather die than lose the chance of. "Except that it's more than a game, *querida*."

"How do you know that?"

Her words caught him by surprise and, despite the surprisingly intense pleasure of simply holding her, he drew slightly back. "What?"

She dropped her gaze, momentarily looking like the old Marcy Bridges. Then, perhaps because the stakes were so high, she raised her eyes and faced him dead on again. "I've been reading about Wicca and magic for months, Tomas, and this seems completely foreign to me. But you speak its language. You seem to understand how it thinks, how it works. You're the one who says that if we find the person who cursed me, we can stop this. But how is it you know so much in the first place?"

He found himself surprisingly reluctant to confess. As if her opinion of him mattered more than he'd ever guessed it could.

Maybe it did. But her opinion of all of him, the real him, meant more. So he told her. "It runs in my family."

She swallowed hard, and her next question came out as a croak. *"Demons?"*

"No! Magic. My *abuela*—my grandmother—was a *bruja*. That's like a witch," he explained, studying her, hunting for any clue that this was too much for her. "She believed very strongly in protecting against demons and devils. I was never sure if any of it was real or not, but I was still around it, and I guess…"

He shrugged.

She waited.

He said, "I guess some of it rubbed off."

Marcy nodded.

He waited there in front of her, in the kitchen. There were few people outside of his own culture that he'd told about his *bruja abuela*—and all she did was nod?

Then she stepped closer to him, rose up on her toes—and kissed him. Soft. Light. But not at all timid.

The sensation swam through him like lemonade on a fiery day. He recognized it, despite never having felt quite this kind of easy understanding before. *Madre de Dios.*

He was falling in love with Marcy Bridges!

"Thank you for being here," she whispered, her heels sinking back to the linoleum.

He could have simply said she was welcome. He could have made another joke about inoculating her against sacrifice by taking care of that little virginity problem. But her virginity *wasn't* a problem and, to be honest, he understood exactly why she wasn't going to be blackmailed into doing anything against her will.

He respected the hell out of her for it.

So he said, "Let's go look at all those pictures again."

Maybe a half hour later, they found their man.

It happened when, after having little luck examining yearbooks and class-reunion pictures, Marcy thought to find more information about her classmates who'd died. While Tomas looked up every possible picture of them in the old books, she did more Internet searches, confirming that all three women had been killed in suspicious fires.

"How suspicious," asked Tomas from the sofa, "is suspicious?"

"Their bodies seem to have burned more than anything else around them. I found a Web site that's using one of the deaths as proof of spontaneous human combustion."

"Okay," he agreed. "That's suspi— Hold it."

She turned to look at him. He looked good, leaning over the coffee table, his elbow braced across his knees. She felt guilty for admiring the long, supple line of his body when a priest and Snowball were both gone, possibly—

But no. She couldn't allow herself to accept the possibility that they might be as dead as Liz Carpenter, Judith Barstow and Cassie Adams, much less that tonight *she*...

No.

She would not become the bride of the fiery *thing* that had stalked her since this morning, especially not if that meant the person who'd done this to her in the first place would get some kind of demonic referral points. She would sleep with Tomas before she let that happen....

She realized that the idea of sleeping with Tomas Martinez wasn't at all unpleasant. She would prefer to take her time, of course, to get to know him better, to have a better reason than some kind of demonic deadline.

A reason like love?

She looked quickly away from the lean, swarthy man thumbing through her old yearbooks. True, he'd come to her rescue more than once. And he seemed to get along with her family. And his kiss gave her hope that sappy movies and romance novels got some things right after all. But there was a good chance he felt little attraction to her, kisses aside—circumstances had all but dared him into those. He might just be doing this as a thorough apartment manager, or because the abduction of his priest made things personal.

On the other hand, he'd complimented her at lunch. And the kisses *could* be more than a dare.

Was it possible that falling in love could feel this easy?

If anything about this day could be called easy.

Then Tomas said, "Here! Marcy, look at this!"

She went gladly to his side, and not just because he might have a solution to all this. She went gladly because sinking onto his sofa, the slope of cushions sliding her hip against his, felt surprisingly right.

Surprisingly safe.

He showed her a glossy black-and-white rendition of early nineties varsity cheerleaders forming a pyramid, Cassie Adams second from the top.

"She was a cheerleader," said Marcy. "Why's that matter?"

Tomas moved his index finger, which had been indicating Cassie, to note a small form standing in the background of the picture, watching. "Who's that?"

Just like that, she knew. Her common sense struggled against such certainty—they needed more proof before they went around accusing people of anything, much less black magic. And yet—it felt right.

"That's Rick Everitt," she said, remembering how the former varsity baseball player had sought her out last night. How he hadn't seemed to have changed much since high school. How his puppyish attentions made her feel uncomfortable.

But it hadn't been a help-me-he's-dangerous uncomfortable. It had been more of a how-can-I-go-find-real-friends-without-hurting-this-guy's-feelings uncomfortable. He'd seemed more like a victim waiting to happen than a practitioner of the demonic arts!

"What makes you think—?"

But Tomas had already turned to another page. It was the Spanish club, and Liz Carpenter, as club president, stood proudly on one end.

One row of students behind her stood Ricky Everitt, looking at her instead of the camera.

Marcy had a hard time drawing her next breath. Even before Tomas showed her the third picture he'd found—Judith Barstow dancing in the hallway and Ricky Everitt watching from the partial cover of a locker door—she knew it was him.

"I dated him once," she said, or tried to. Her voice sounded odd in her ears. "He was so...formal. I couldn't relax around him."

"Maybe you couldn't relax around him because on some level you knew he was a nutcase?" challenged Tomas.

"But he wasn't! He was a baseball player and a B student. Shy. Quiet. Never into trouble."

"Isn't that what neighbors say about serial killers?"

"And about shy, quiet people who are never in trouble."

Tomas said, "I think we need to talk to someone a bit more observant."

"Ricky Everitt?" repeated Sharona's voice over the speakerphone. "Was he the one who ate ketchup right out of the packet for lunch all the time?"

"That was Rodney Pruitt," said Marcy. "Ricky was on the baseball team."

She met Tomas's gaze through a long moment of Sharona making "Hmm" noises. Then her sister said,

"Yes! I remember now. You dated this guy once, right? And I told you not to let him take you by any cemeteries."

Tomas raised his eyebrows, his expression somewhere between curiosity and accusation.

Marcy said, "You did not!"

"I did so! Or I wanted to. The guy was creepy."

Tomas spread his hands and mouthed, *Creepy how?*

"Creepy how?"

"He liked dissecting things in biology class. He loved old languages so much, they created a fourth-year, self-study Greek class just for him. He drew goats' heads on his notebooks. You know...creepy!"

Marcy stared at the speakerphone, appalled. *"And you let me go out with him?"*

"With a warning about cemeteries," Sharona reminded her. "You never wanted to hear anything bad about anybody. That's why I never told you how mad he was afterward."

"Mad? About what?"

There was a long silence on the phone. Then Sharona asked, "Why do you want to know?"

Marcy thought fast. "Someone slipped a note under my windshield wiper at the reunion last night," she lied. "Some kind of love note...but I couldn't really read it. Just a few words. It's creepy."

It wasn't a great story, but it didn't suck, either.

"So Tomas is trying to figure out who to beat up?"

Marcy's family certainly had been quick to believe the whole dating-Tomas story, hadn't they?

As well as to believe that Tomas beat people up. He did give that impression.

"You said Ricky was mad? At *me*?"

"Uh-huh."

"I went out with him!"

"Yeah," agreed Sharona. "But you didn't kiss him good-night."

"He didn't *try* to kiss me good-night," Marcy said while Tomas prepared to go beat up Richard Everitt.

In this case, that meant looking up the man's number and street address in the phone book. Interesting, that a man who would take out revenge for his own frustrations on innocent women would be trusting enough to keep his number listed.

"So, do you think he would live uptown, downtown or about ten miles from here?" Tomas asked, comparing Richard Everitts.

"Ten miles from here. He mentioned last night that he was living in his parents' old house."

Tomas circled the listing, then tore the page out of the book and stuffed it in his pocket. It wasn't as if he didn't get a new phone book what seemed like every month.

"I remember that at the time, I almost hoped he *would* kiss me good-night," Marcy continued, following him to the coatrack by the front door. "It seemed like it was part of some mysterious series of requirements for a proper date, you know? But I thought the guy was supposed to initiate it, and he just said good-night, so I said good-night, and that was that. Afterward, he didn't talk to me in school anymore…which was kind of a relief, since it wasn't that great a date. But you'd think if he— Where are you going?"

Tomas was shrugging into his leather jacket. He gave her a *Duh* look.

She said, "Let me get my purse."

"No."

"No?"

"You're staying here where it's safe." And he turned to leave.

Marcy caught him by the waistband of his jeans and yanked him back. It was more the surprise that stopped him than her strength. *"Excuse me?"*

"I'll take care of this."

"I don't *think* so!"

Great. *Now* she grew a backbone? "I already told you my *abuela* knows all about protecting against these kinds of people."

"So maybe we should ask your *abuela*."

Admitting that felt almost as embarrassing as her knowing he'd called in a priest. "I tried. She doesn't remember."

"Then I'm the closest thing to a magic user that you have, aren't I?"

Tomas barked out a laugh, reached behind him and tugged her hand free from his pants. Not something he would normally be doing, but these were extreme circumstances. "You call that spell you did last night *magic?*"

"Besides," Marcy said, looking dangerous herself, "Rick isn't the one who wants me. He's trying to sacrifice me, remember? It's the demon who wants me."

Tomas had grasped the doorknob, but now he hesitated, closing his eyes. Damn.

"It's my apartment," she insisted. "It's my responsibility."

She was right.

So he turned around in defeat. "You'll need to change into pants, and wear a jacket. We're taking my motorcycle."

Rick Everitt lived on a quiet old suburban street with tall shade trees and walk-up mailboxes on the front

doors. It didn't look like the kind of place where someone would summon demons.

Then again, if he'd started this ball rolling in high
school, it was probably where he'd begun his career,
alone in his bedroom. Why not continue?

When Tomas thought about what else the boy
might've been doing in his bedroom, concerning Marcy
Bridges, he figured beating a retraction out of him
would be a pleasure. He parked the bike against the
opposite curb, dropped the kickstand and killed the engine.

Then he had to unwind Marcy's arms from around
his waist. Speaking of pleasures...

"Now will you wait here?" he pleaded. "There
aren't even any doors out here. You know that thing
only seems to appear when doors are opened."

"Actually, no," she said, clambering off the bike
and ducking her head out of his spare helmet. "I don't
know that. That's your theory. And this is my problem."

Tomas hung both helmets on the handlebars before
facing her, trying to look his most dangerous. And he
really could be dangerous. She was about to see that.
"You are *not* going after this guy alone."

Something odd caught in Marcy's gaze at that.
Something almost...sad? But all she said was "I didn't
say I could do this alone. I said I'm coming with you."

He guessed that was as good as he would get.

She wished she *could* handle this alone.

As they took the front walk to the screened front
door and rang the bell, Marcy felt increasingly useless.
Tomas had been doing pretty much everything so far.
He'd found the priest. He'd talked to his grandmother.
He'd fought the demon more than once. He'd protected

her, and he'd endangered himself, and he'd tolerated her family pretty well instead of telling them that he'd never had any interest in her. He'd also come up with almost every really good idea of magical common sense—or maybe uncommon sense—that they'd used.

And she, who'd spent the last half year of her life reading about magic in the desperate hopes of finding some kernels of personal power, had done little more than computer research. Now that they knew just about everything they had to know, and the moment of confrontation was at hand, she still needed Tomas to finish this.

But at least she could be here for it.

Then, when Rick answered the door, she wondered if maybe she could take him after all.

Rick Everitt was as skinny as he'd been in high school, but while teenage boys towering to their full height had reason for that awkward, lanky look, a man of almost thirty just seemed...frail. He wore his hair the way he had in high school, too, short on the sides and long on the top, and even had on jeans and a Go Lumberjacks! T-shirt.

He was wearing his class ring from high school, too. Last night, Marcy had assumed that was because of the reunion.

"May I help you?" he asked, his gaze focusing worriedly on Tomas—until he noticed Marcy beside him. "Wait, I know you. Marcy from high school, right? Marcy...Bridges?"

He grinned, delighted to see her, and Marcy's stomach sank. What if they were wrong? *What if Tomas beat up the wrong guy?*

"Hi, Ricky," she said, shouldering herself between the poor, lost guy and her taut maintenance man. "I mean, Rick."

"I still go by Ricky," he assured her. Well...that kind of went with the T-shirt, didn't it?

"This is going to sound odd," she warned him, "but some strange things have happened since the reunion last night, and I was wondering if you knew anybody in our class who might have—"

Her shoulder hit the doorjamb as Tomas pushed by her and into the foyer, grabbing the collar of Rick's shirt. "What the hell did you sic on her, you son of a bitch?"

Rick's eyes widened. "What?"

Marcy scrambled in after them, hoping nobody called the police. This would be very hard to explain to authorities. "Tomas, wait!"

Tomas kept going, Ricky scrambling backward before *his* personal power. "You were frustrated about her not kissing you after your little date, right? When you didn't have the *cojones* to make the first move. God knows how many women you blamed for your own pitiful desperation, but this one isn't going to feed your pet evil, got it?"

They stopped only when Ricky thudded against the back wall. "I don't know what you're talking about!"

His voice came out strangled. That was probably because of Tomas's hold on his collar strangling him.

Marcy grabbed Tomas's wrist and pulled. With both hands. No reaction, not even when she put her whole weight into it.

Wow, he was strong.

"We need to make sure it's really him," she insisted.

"It's really him," Tomas growled.

"I'm not going to let you hurt an innocent," she warned him.

The look Tomas sent her was almost mocking. He

was the big, tough Latino, after all, with his tattoo and his long braid, and she was just Marcy. "How exactly do you plan on—ow!"

She'd just stomped, hard, on his booted instep. While he bent over from that, she jabbed her elbow at his nose. With a guttural grunt, he spun away from her, hands to his face.

She stared, stunned that she'd even remembered those moves from an old college self-defense class. She'd never once tried them. She'd never thought she would have the, well, *cojones*.

It felt kind of good.

Ricky Everitt made a whimpering noise—and bolted through a side door, to safety. And probably to call the cops.

Tomas was still slightly hunched, both hands to his nose, but he was facing her again. "Bud de hell buz dad?"

That seemed to mean, *What the hell was that?* The question would match the fury blazing from his tiger eyes.

"What if it wasn't him?" she demanded. "How could it be? Did you see him? He was just a..."

"A bimp?"

"I wouldn't have put it that way, but yes."

"Bud udder kind of person bould deed to combensade by subbonding debons?"

"What other kind of person would need to compensate by summoning demons?"

Tomas, gingerly testing his nose with his fingers, just glared at her.

"Wait a minute! I've been studying some magic, too—"

He rolled his eyes.

"I have so. And maybe it wasn't to compensate for anything. Maybe it was because it…it called to me."

Something tickled at her awareness, subtle but significant.

"Maybe because it felt right," she continued.

It was a smell.

"Maybe because—" Then she paused, and sniffed. *Oh no.*

Tomas frowned at her and managed to ask, "Whad?" with only a little congestion.

"Do you smell that?"

"Marcy, I don'd sbell eddy—" He tried again, more slowly. "Anything."

She turned and looked at the door Ricky Everitt had escaped through. Oh no. She'd been wrong.

"Brimstone."

Tomas forgot about Marcy clocking him in the face and tried the door. Locked.

Well, he damn well knew doors. This one was wood, at least forty years old and poorly set in its frame.

It took him one solid kick on the jamb to crash through.

He took longer to grasp what he saw on the other side.

The room had once been a sunken living room/den with dark paneling, probably the height of fashion when the house was built, complete with a wet bar for entertaining. Ricky had kept the avocado shag carpet, the panels, the wet bar. He'd kept the glass case of small trophies and ribbons, the display rack of old baseball bats.

But he'd painted a circle on the shaggy floor with weird, occult symbols along its border, like something out of a B-level horror movie. He'd turned the wet bar into some kind of altar, complete with skull and candles and a huge, heavy-looking book. And he'd hung grotesque banners on each of the dark walls, strange pictures painted in Tomas-didn't-want-to-know-what.

All except the wall behind the altar. That one was decorated with a spread of photographs of teenage girls, including many of the ones Tomas had been looking at in Marcy's yearbooks. Several pictures looked more modern—probably from the class reunion.

The son of a bitch!

"I know what you're thinking," said Ricky Everitt, circling warily behind the bar. "You're wondering why I—"

But Tomas vaulted across his Formica altar and slammed the bastard into his wishing wall before the man could even finish.

Ricky made a terrified, squeaking noise.

"You think I care?" demanded Tomas, using his full weight to keep this self-styled Satanist pinned against the paneling, breathing into his face. He was careful to enunciate past his hurt nose. "You think I give a damn what miserable part of your little loser life made you think you had the right to hurt innocent women?"

"But they *weren't* innocent," protested Ricky, trying to duck. He didn't stand a chance of movement. "That's why we had to keep going. We—"

Tomas dug his fingers into the wimp's scrawny shoulder, shaking him again so the back of his head thumped against the paneling. He narrowed his eyes, lowered his voice to an even more dangerous growl and let an edge of his parents' accent roll through the words. "Why are you still talking?"

Ricky pressed his lips tightly together—and Marcy, behind Tomas, said, "I want to know."

Tomas rolled his eyes, unable to contain a sigh. But

at least she'd stopped fighting him to protect this waste of breath. "What I want to know," he said, "is how soon Ricky here can call his pet monster off."

Ricky said, "I can't."

Tomas shook him again. "Wrong. Answer."

Marcy asked, "What do you mean, you had to keep going?"

Ricky slid his fearful gaze to Tomas, who reluctantly nodded. "Make it fast."

"Daiesthai only needed one virgin, just one, as payment, so it seemed weird that I had to provide a whole list of names and pictures and hair clippings—"

Both Tomas and Marcy repeated, *"Hair clippings?"*

"Or lollipop sticks or chewed gum or used Kleenex—anything with their DNA on it. I never thought it would get as far as any of the others, like Marcy, but who knew Jenny Black was such a slut?"

Tomas blinked at him. "Jenny Black?"

"She died at a party in our junior year." To judge from Marcy's hushed voice, she knew exactly who he meant. "The rumor was she was doing drugs and caught herself on fire...."

"Four? You killed *four* women?" Not, Tomas realized, that they could ever prove it in court.

He decided to worry about that once they solved Marcy's problem—at no matter what cost to Ricky.

"Then it turned out we had to wait over two years before Daiesthai could try again," continued Ricky, voice uneven. "There's always a catch, isn't there? That, and the fresh DNA sample, and the stupid chanting..."

As if he was griping about a bad lease contract on a car!

Marcy said, "And after two years?"

"Liz was away at Columbia, and I guess she wasn't

a virgin anymore, either. Then Judy. Hell, by the time we got to Cassie, she'd been married and divorced!''

"So you killed them," said Tomas.

"No! Daiesthai killed them! I just, sort of…pointed them out."

"But why?" demanded Marcy. "What do *you* get out of all this?"

Ricky actually smiled. Tomas was close enough to tear the man's nose off with his teeth, and of a mood to do it, and the bastard smiled a wishful, faraway smile like someone contemplating an old love. "Whatever I want," he said, savoring the words. "*Anything.* Wealth. Power. Women. Can you imagine? I couldn't believe it when I managed to translate the incantation, doing my research paper on ancient languages. I mean, who wouldn't risk a few lives in order to have *whatever they want?*"

Tomas looked at Marcy. "I'm going to kill him now."

Ricky said, "Not if you want your cat back."

Crap. Tomas saw the change in Marcy at the very possibility of it. "Snowball?" she echoed. "Where?"

Ricky said, "Or the priest." Like a footnote.

"Don't do it," warned Tomas, knowing the futility of it even as he spoke. Hell, in her place, wouldn't he do the same?

"Where?" she demanded. "Tell me how to get them back."

Tomas let go of Ricky's left shoulder to span his throat with one hand. "And tell her the price."

He'd never killed anyone before, though he'd come close in a few fights. His own certainty that he could do it now both unnerved and satisfied him.

"Through that door," said Ricky.

Tomas looked quickly from Ricky to Marcy, back

and forth. One magic user unfazed at costing people their lives, another who could barely drum up the willpower to do a harmless spell for her own benefit. He knew who he'd bet on in a contest. "Marcy—"

"I know what a door means." But damned if she wasn't walking slowly toward it. "It's still not Snowball's fault, or Father Gregory's, that this happened to them."

"It's not your fault either, *querida*."

"Maybe not, but they didn't even have a choice." She stood in front of the narrow door. "At least I have a choice. That's worth something, isn't it? And I choose to risk this."

Ricky tried to take advantage of Tomas's distraction to wriggle loose, so Tomas turned back to him—and squeezed. "If anything happens to her, you won't live long enough to get anything you want."

"I will if I get my wish before I'm dead." Ricky was wheezing as his air got cut off, but still he managed to slant his gaze toward the book open on the altar, past Tomas's elbow, and to cry out a hoarse "Ελατε σε με!"

Tomas stared at him. "What?"

Marcy reached out with one hand and opened the door, loosing a blast of searing heat.

Part 5

It may have been the most stupid thing she'd ever done. Marcy knew that. She wasn't just risking her own life but the priest's, and her cat's.

And Tomas's. *Oh, God. Tomas's.*

But it was also her bravest moment.

Heat hit her like a shock wave, blasting across the room. Behind the door and yet not, amidst the roiling chaos of some kind of parallel Hell dimension, reared the demon. The one who'd trapped Marcy in the elevator. Who'd licked its flames up and down her body. Who'd forced defeating thoughts into her mind, against her will.

But here it didn't stay behind the door.

Smoking and malformed, it shambled into the room—and bravest moment or not, she took three quick steps back. The creature swelled, larger and larger until the flickering horns of flame on its head seared the ceiling and the orange, black and scarlet breadth of its shoulders crowded the room's crown moldings. From behind it, lizardlike salamanders slithered through the portal and across the walls, their tails leaving sooty streaks behind them. A fluttering of skittery, batlike creatures whirled out and around the room like some crazed circus of evil.

Behind her, Marcy heard Ricky call, "Here she—"

But his words strangled into silence. *Tomas.*

Turns out Sharona was right about his more violent abilities.

Here in Ricky's strange temple, the creature seemed to finally find its voice. Its gravelly words boomed not only in Marcy's head, with splitting volume, but around her. It shook the glass in Ricky's display case and fluttered the banners on the panel wall. *Thank you,* it growled in Ricky's direction.

Then it turned to loom up and over Marcy, an inferno of sadistic pleasure, of desire, of greed—

And she swung at it with the baseball bat she'd taken from Ricky's display rack while nobody was looking.

She put every bit of strength into the blow. Every bit of upset she'd felt since she opened her closet this morning. Every bit of anger at the unfairness. Every bit of fury that whatever she'd been discovering all day with Tomas Martinez might not have a chance to become something wonderful. It felt great. Freeing. Cathartic.

Until the bat impacted the creature—and the shock of it ricocheted up Marcy's arms and shoulders. *Pain!*

Behind her, she thought she heard Ricky saying something like "No, no, no." Maybe Tomas hadn't killed him after all.

The demon creature made an odd, choking sound that Marcy realized was laughter. It arched even farther up and over her, staring down with flickering, red-on-black coal eyes, and the shadow where its mouth should be stretched wide.

Cute, it boomed.

It thought she was cute? As in, amusing?

Damn condescending spawn of Hell! She swung again, and this time the impact almost dislocated her shoulder, but she swung again anyway, ready to go down fighting if she went down at all.

The bat burst into flames in her hands, catching on its rounded end and quickly flaring up its length like a too-dry match.

Marcy dropped it before the fire reached her hands, and the room around her shook with the demon's next words.

Very cute.

Like a puppy. Like a kitten. Like something without any power at all, something that it could play with, or crush, however it wished.

Marcy took another step back, seriously rethinking her bravest moment. The demon swelled forward, stretching, reaching for her.

The ''No, no, no'' behind her got closer—and Tomas and Ricky, grappling with each other, stumbled into the searing space between her and the creature.

''No!'' wailed Ricky. But he was no match for the way Tomas strong-armed him toward the door Marcy had opened. Tomas had never looked so vicious, so dangerous, so competent.

God, but she could really love him.

Then Tomas pushed Ricky through the door. The demon sizzled, *Good enough.*

And with a sudden rush of hot air, the door slammed shut, leaving complete normalcy behind it.

Normalcy, and no Tomas.

Marcy stared, panting, for barely a moment. Then she lunged forward, wrenched open the door and nearly tripped over the toilet in a small, perfectly normal half-bath.

No. No! She wasn't going to lose him.

Desperate, she ran to the wet bar and looked at Ricky's grimoire. At the top of the page, in big letters, it said:

δαιμουαζ

Not Latin, that was for sure. Greek, maybe? Either way, she couldn't read it...except that the first letter looked like a D. Could it be the name Ricky had given the demon? What was it...

Daiesthai.

It didn't do her a lot of good; she couldn't read the short sentence that came after it, and she couldn't remember clearly enough to repeat it. It had sounded like "El" something, but what? *What?*

To her horror, she felt tears burning her scorched eyes. She shouldn't have been so hesitant to learn magic, shouldn't have been so afraid to disturb the universe. Now it might be too late. Now all she had left was her own meager power....

But this time she couldn't allow herself the luxury of that kind of thinking. Meager power? What the hell made her so meager? So she couldn't speak Greek, or Latin, or whatever it was.

She ran back to the door, to the half bath, and shut it. Then she drew herself up, took a deep breath, and with every bit of power in her shouted, *"Daiesthai,* open!"

And she opened the door.

And a furnace of heat surged out at her. Hell, again.

Marcy thought back to the spell she'd done last night, to all the reading she'd done for months. She could do this. She *had* to do this.

She spread her hands, spread her arms as if to embrace everything she'd been given. Every bit of life. Every bit of hope. Her family. Her years with Snowball. Her day with Tomas—

And she ad-libbed.

"I call upon the Goodness of the Universe," she called out. "I draw your power to me and around me, for the good of all and according to the free will of all. Protect me and mine amidst this darkness. Let me see more clearly, to give more back into this world. By all the gifts I have been given, let it be so!"

And she stepped through, into the portal.

Like that, she was falling, tumbling, through the darkest of darkness, being thrown about the chaos and confusion and heat and misery. Screams of the damned echoed around her. Hisses and slithers and slices of despair cut across her, but she clung to her gratitude like a lifeline. To her gratitude—and one thing more.

Love.

When she looked deep inside herself, where her strength had always been, dormant, waiting for her to access it, she sensed a light. A connection. It was love, and not just for her beloved cat. Love drew her soul to another, out there in the chaos. It drew her to Tomas Martinez.

She reached out and said, "Be there." At least, she thought she did. In this great, roiling void, she heard nothing.

But her spread arms, which had stayed open like

wings, wrapped around a hard, solid body that she recognized by more than its rich, spicy, earthy scent. She recognized Tomas on more levels than she'd ever suspected she could access. She held him, tight, trying not to give in to the fear that now, so close to having everything she'd hesitated to dream of, she was afraid she might lose it.

She would not lose it. Not to Ricky and his pet demon.

Even if there were psychos like Ricky Everitt in the world, there were heroes like Tomas. Even if there was a Hell dimension paralleling her own reality—and who knew how many other kinds of dimensions beyond that—her reality paralleled them right back.

She wasn't falling through chaos. She refused to be.

She was standing in a suburban half bath.

"Home," she shouted, summoning the last of her flagging strength. Again, she couldn't hear her own voice, so she tried again, louder.

"Home!"

This time she heard it. She also heard the outraged cry of "MROWRM!"

Marcy forced her eyes open—and her gaze met the golden tiger eyes of Tomas Martinez, his own gaze peering through the messy fall of long, dark hair to caress her face with amazement. She'd done it.

She'd done it?

She realized she was wedged fairly tightly against the doorjamb, because the half bath was unnaturally crowded, what with a dazed Father Gregory standing, unhurt, behind Tomas—and something warm and wriggly trapped between Tomas and her.

Was it…?

She looked down, and saw her cat's sooty face peering back up from Tomas's arms, clearly annoyed with the way her day had gone.

That's when she began to cry.

Tomas kissed her hot, sensitive cheeks, and reached past her to open the door back into Ricky's temple.

Cool air flowed into the close, cramped room like a blessing.

All Tomas wanted to do was to get Marcy—and Snowball—back to their apartment. She'd stopped crying almost immediately, but they'd been through enough for one day. Maybe enough for one or more lifetimes.

On the bright side, she'd proved damn resilient.

When Father Gregory said he would call some of his colleagues over, Tomas was just as glad to leave the priest behind to deal with the spiritual cleanup. He had more important things on his mind.

Only the first being how to get a ticked-off cat home on a motorcycle.

By unspoken agreement—they'd hardly spoken since their dazed exodus from the half bath—Tomas and Marcy, carrying Snowball, headed up the stairs to her apartment. Both were, not surprisingly, in mild shock.

He used his passkey to unlock her door. "Stand back."

"It's all right," she said with quiet certainty.

Sure enough, the door to 3B swung open into a perfectly normal, neat apartment. Snowball launched herself from Marcy's arms and streaked toward the bedroom, hitting the door hard enough to jar it open.

Tomas moved to go after the cat, but Marcy stayed

him with a soft hand on his arm. "The portal's closed."

"How can you be so sure?" He shut the door behind them, then quickly opened it. Hallway. He shut it again.

"I feel it," she said. "It's kind of like one of those sounds you hardly notice until it stops, like the refrigerator hum or traffic outside on the street. I think some part of me was vaguely aware of this…this *threat* for a long, long time." She laughed, uneven. "But it's not the sort of thing you'd guess in Twenty Questions."

"Not even Two-Thousand Questions!" He looked at her now, really looked at her for the first time since they'd escaped Hell together.

Correction—since she'd led him from Hell. He hadn't asked her what the experience had been like for her. But for him, there'd been pain. There'd been fire. He wasn't sure by what luck, other than all his mother's and grandmother's prayers, he'd survived, much less found Snowball and Father Gregory. But every moment of it had been agony.

And then Marcy had been there, and when she'd wrapped him in her arms the pain not only stopped, it…reversed. Her goodness had protected and healed him.

It was the purest magic he'd ever known.

Had he really not thought of her as good-looking before today? Their adventures had left her silky brown hair in a mess, tousled by wind and hellfire, pressed down by a helmet, and framing the prettiest, soot-smeared elfin face and that wide, sensuous mouth of hers. Her long, long legs in his drawstring sweats had a grace to them. Her curves under his T-shirt, while subtle, were equally graceful. And her green eyes held magic.

Marcy Bridges might just be the most beautiful woman he'd ever met. So, which had changed, him or her?

Or both?

"Maybe it was that sound, that threat that kept you from taking a lot of chances," he suggested. It made sense.

So much for him judging timid people without the full story.

Marcy laughed a funny, self-deprecating laugh. "It might not be the right explanation, but I sure like it."

Tomas found himself grinning back. It wasn't just shell shock, was it?

Marcy cocked her head, squinting at him. "What are you thinking?"

"I'm thinking you've probably had enough men coming after you tonight."

She nodded solemnly. "Especially bad boys, huh?"

Was she teasing him? But considering the tattoo on his wrist and the black leather and the long hair, he didn't guess he could deny the impression now. "Would it help if you knew I owned the building?"

Marcy said, "It makes absolutely no difference that you own the building." But she said it in a good way, so he kissed her. She kissed him right back. Her purity flowed over him, through him, healing him in even more ways than before.

Cool. *Like a blessing.*

When he straightened, to check her reaction, Marcy leaned into him, her arms wrapping his waist, her cheek resting on his shoulder. He encircled her, too, and rested his cheek on her hair.

He could get used to this.

He already was.

"What I don't understand," she murmured after a long moment, "is why the demon didn't even try to get me. When we were in...wherever."

"Hell." Tomas doubted it was *the* Hell—the one he'd learned about in catechism—but it had been a similar flavor all the same.

"I was protecting myself." Marcy tipped her face up toward his, which meant he had to hold his own head up but, on the bright side, meant he got to see her proud smile. "With magic."

"With magic," he agreed.

"But it's as if Daies—"

Tomas kissed her, quickly, then drew back to explain, "Let's not say its name, all the same. Something I learned from my *abuela*."

She nodded. "It's as if it didn't even want me anymore."

Tomas blinked down at her. "This is a *bad* thing?"

"No!" She laughed, free and happy and maybe, just maybe, his. Given time and a little risk-taking. "I'm just curious."

Tomas considered it—and grinned at the most likely conclusion. "Did the demon really say it wanted to make you its *bride*?"

"Yes! It said..." But she stopped herself, eyes widening. "No, you're right! It said I would become its *mate*."

"I think," said Tomas, trying not to laugh, "that Ricky Everitt was a virgin."

Marcy didn't look as if she was fighting a laugh...but she didn't look particularly saddened by Ricky's fate, either. If the man had been going to sacrifice anybody, it was only right he should sacrifice himself.

"Now I'm the only one who'll decide where I'm going," she said, thoughtful. "But you know...I still don't think there's anything wrong with waiting for the right lover."

Then she smiled a slow, remarkably devilish smile.

* * * * *

*Look out for Evelyn's next title,
coming out in late 2004
from our upcoming Bombshell line!*

Dear Reader,

Being invited to work on the *When Darkness Falls* anthology was a joy for me. I've admired Silhouette's forays into the dark side of romance since before the short-lived Shadows line, and appearing with such great authors as these is quite an honor! And yet coming up with a story that was short enough for this venue, and something new for me and yet something grounded in enough classic mythology to counter the humor I wanted to toss in, was quite the challenge.

Then, at a fantasy-writing convention, I picked up a button that read "Open a dark portal to a dimension of incalculable evil first thing in the morning, and nothing worse will happen to you for the rest of the day."

I thought: that depends on what comes *through* the portal.

Thus "The Devil She Knew" was born. By creating a hero and heroine who already knew each other, and keeping their story down to one day, I stayed within the limits of the novella. Although I've written Wiccans before, I'd never explored a character so uncertain about her personal power that she's afraid to use her own magic. And as for classic...what can be more classic than a sacrificial demon-bride story?

Whether I nailed the humor, and yet managed to keep it scary, is up to you to decide. But isn't that what Halloween is all about? A little fun. A little fear. A little magic...

Happy Halloween.

Vaughn

The author of
The Gingerbread Man
returns with a chilling tale
of romantic suspense

USA TODAY bestselling author

MAGGIE SHAYNE

*It was called a haven for runaway teens. In truth, their
time there was a nightmare—one that ended in fiery
violence sixteen years ago. Or so its survivors believed…*

THICKER
THAN WATER

"A moving mix of high suspense and romance, this
haunting Halloween thriller will propel readers to
bolt their doors at night."
—*Publishers Weekly* on *The Gingerbread Man*

*Available the first week of November,
wherever paperbacks are sold!*

MIRA®

Three full-length novels from
#1 *New York Times* bestselling author

NORA ROBERTS

S U S P I C I O U S

This collection of Nora Roberts's finest
tales of dark passion and sexy intrigue
will have you riveted from the first page!

Includes *PARTNERS, THE ART OF DECEPTION*
and *NIGHT MOVES*, all of which have been
out of print for over a decade.

Available in November 2003, wherever books are sold.

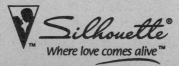

Silhouette®
Where love comes alive™

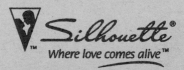

LUNA

Coming January 2004...

LUNA will offer stories about powerful, gifted and magical women living in fantastical worlds. These wonderful worlds and spirited characters are created by fantasy fiction's top authors, as well as new, fresh voices.

LUNA is...

...the imprint dedicated to women and fantasy fiction

...sweeping stories that focus on strong female characters

...adventurous plots complemented by satisfying, romantic story lines

...bridging fantasy and romance

Available at your favorite bookseller, Winter 2004.

LBPA03